GULLIVER'S
TRAVELS

Jonathan Swift
1667-1745

GULLIVER'S TRAVELS

JONATHAN SWIFT

With an introduction by
PETER QUENNELL

HERON BOOKS · LONDON

JONATHAN SWIFT

JONATHAN SWIFT was born in Dublin on November
30th 1667, the posthumous son of Jonathan Swift of
whom little is known except that he—the son of the
Reverend Thomas Swift, a clergyman who had suffered
in the cause of Charles I.—had settled in Ireland where
he had married Abigail Erick from Leicester. His untimely
death left his wife almost destitute.

Jonathan Swift junior was taken to England by his
nurse, reared at Whitehaven, and brought back to Ireland
at the age of four, to be put under the care of his uncle
Godwin Swift who sent him to school at Kilkenny. At
fourteen Jonathan entered Trinity College, Dublin as a pen-
sioner. His University career was most undistinguished and
he only just succeeded in obtaining a degree by ' special
grace ' in 1685. He remained on at Trinity College until
1688, and after a short stay with his mother at Leicester
obtained (in 1689) a post as Secretary to Sir William
Temple, a retired diplomatist and man of some literary
distinction, at Moor Park near Farnham. With two inter-
ruptions (1690-91 and 1694-95 when he went to Ireland
to take Holy Orders, and for about fifteen months held
the living of Kilroot near Belfast) he remained at Moor
Park until 1699, gradually establishing himself in a position
of trust as Temple's right-hand man.

His position gave him the opportunity of doing a
prodigious amount of reading (and thus to remedy the
deficiencies of his college education), of meeting a number
of distinguished people (including William III) and of
gaining insight into politics and public affairs. At Moor
Park also he first met Esther Johnson—said to have been
an illegitimate daughter of Sir William Temple—who was
to play such a large part in his life. She became the
' Stella ' of Swift's *Journal*. At the time of their first
meeting in 1689 Esther was a girl of eight and her relationship to Swift that of pupil to teacher.

Swift's early literary activity consisted of verse-writing,
and of those early efforts three long examples (now form-

ing part of his collected *Poetical Works*) survive. During 1697-99 he wrote *A Tale of a Tub*, his most famous satire apart from *Gulliver's Travels*, and two shorter pieces, the *Battle of the Books* and the *Mechanical Operation of the Spirit*. The three works were published together in 1704.

Sir William Temple died in 1699 leaving Swift a small legacy and the profit that might accrue from publishing his *Memoirs*. In the autumn of the same year Swift was appointed domestic chaplain to the Earl of Berkeley, one of the Lords Justice of Ireland, from whom in due course he obtained the livings of some parishes centred on Laracor, a small village near Dublin, as well as a prebend at St. Patrick's Cathedral. He went to reside, first at Dublin Castle, and later at the Vicarage of Laracor, where for some years he led the ordinary life of a country parson. He made frequent visits to Dublin where he took the degree of Doctor of Divinity and soon became a notable figure.

In 1701 Esther Johnson (' Stella '), now in her twentieth year and her companion Rebecca Dingley came to live near Laracor, and from then on the relations between Swift and ' Stella ' took on the character of a tender and intimate friendship, which character they were to maintain ever afterwards. Swift was strongly averse to matrimony, and though he was able to adduce the most convincing rational grounds for his aversion there can be no doubt that it was deeply rooted in his psychological make-up. He suffered from many inhibitions, phobias and obsessional habits, to which were added recurrent attacks of deafness, vertigo and nausea—specific symptoms associated with an affliction now known as Menière's Disease.

Between 1701 and 1704 Swift also paid several visits to Leicester and London where he became the friend of Addison, Pope and Steele. His ' London Period ' proper began in 1707 when he was sent to England on an official Church mission. He did not accomplish his mission, nor did he obtain the advancement in his own ecclesiastic career which he had been seeking. However, he made many friends and established his reputation as a brilliant wit and as the author of *A Tale of a Tub*. While in London he wrote a number of pamphlets on Church questions and some poems on London life which were published in the *Tatler*. He returned to Ireland in 1709, but was sent out again to London in the autumn of 1710. During this second stay he became involved in political controversy on the highest level and played an important part in the shaping of the affairs of the State.

Having been on the side of the Whigs, he went over to the Tories and attacked the Whigs in the *Examiner* (a Tory periodical founded by Viscount Bolingbroke) and in a series of pamphlets e.g.: *The Conduct of the Allies* (1711) and *The Public Spirit of the Whigs* of which the former stands out as perhaps the most forceful piece of political pamphleteering of all times. Its effect on public opinion contributed in a large measure to bringing about the Peace of Utrecht (1713) which ended England's participation in the War of the Spanish Succession.

But again Swift did not succeed in obtaining the ecclesiastic advancement (to a Deanery or Bishopric in England) which his eminence as a churchman and his services to the Government had richly deserved him. However, some recognition was given to him when in 1713, on the instigation of Lord Oxford he was made Dean of St. Patrick's, Dublin. The following year Queen Anne died and the Whigs took office. For Swift this meant the end of his political influence in London, the end also of his hopes and ambitions. England was his spiritual and intellectual home; Ireland, where henceforth he was to live, was to him an exile.

While in England Swift had written a series of letters, mostly in journal form, to Esther Johnson. They cover the period from September 1710 to June 1713 and have become famous as the *Journal to Stella*. But while in England Swift also formed a relationship with another young woman, Esther Vanhomrigh (' Vanessa ') to whom he addressed many letters and the poem *Cadenus and Vanessa*. ' Vanessa ' fell passionately in love with him and followed him to Ireland. For several years ' Stella ' and ' Vanessa ' lived in or near Dublin, each in ignorance of the other's existence, and each bound to Swift by ties which were stronger than those of ordinary friendship but less strong—at least on Swift's part—than those of love. It is probable that Swift secretly married ' Stella ', but he never lived with her. 'Vanessa' died in 1723; 'Stella' was to survive her by about five years.

As Dean of St. Patrick's, Swift lived a retired life surrounded by a small circle of friends. He devoted much energy to Irish affairs and in the course of years attained extraordinary popularity. His *Drapier's Letters* (1724) by which he prevented the introduction of ' Wood's Halfpence ' into Ireland made him a national hero. To the Irish people he was henceforth ' The Dean'.

In 1726 he went to England to arrange for the publication of *Gulliver's Travels*, which he had begun some five years earlier. It was the only work of his for which he received payment (£200). Its success was immediate. In 1727 he went once more to England, staying as in his previous visit with Pope. The following year ' Stella ' died.

For a number of years Swift's life continued unchanged. He wrote much verse and many pamphlets on Church questions and Irish affairs; he kept up his correspondence with friends in England; he made visits to country houses. Gradually however, with the increasing severity of his physical illness, his temper changed; he became irritable and misanthropic and increasingly prone to morbid brooding, alternating with fits of rage. He became haunted by the fear of losing his mind—which indeed was to be his fate, though not before his physical ailment had robbed him of most of his faculties.

He died in October 19th 1745. He was buried in the Cathedral of St. Patrick where the monument over his tomb bears an epitaph in his own words.

H. d. R.

CONTENTS

INTRODUCTION

THE prejudice and petulance of some critics proves often far more valuable than the plodding integrity of others. Johnson and Ruskin belong to the privileged class. Ruskin, indeed, contradicted himself in his critical works so frequently and boldly that he was obliged to elaborate a theory of what he called ' polygonal truth ', according to which (just as Mont Blanc was ' set between opposite fan-shaped strata') two contradictory propositions might enclose and buttress up a central intermediate verity. Thus it was possible to despise the Renaissance, and attack it as a period of ' concealed national infidelity, and of domestic corruption,' and yet admire the astonishing genius of Tintoretto and Veronese. Less scrupulous than the great Victorian critic, Johnson gave thunderous expression to his preferences and dislikes how and when it pleased him; but, thanks to the strength of his intellect and the wealth of his imagination, his pronouncements, even though we may violently disagree, are almost always memorable. He denigrated the Metaphysical Poets; and his condemnation is so stimulating and so well-phrased that it helps us love them better. Of *Gulliver's Travels* he made a criticism that would at first sight appear both malicious and unjustified. But by putting the reader's mind to work, and encouraging us to produce an opinion of our own to oppose to Johnson's heresy, he performs a more important service than half a dozen pious commentators.

His remark was hasty and ill-considered: like many of Johnson's remarks, it was also somewhat ill-tempered. He denied the *Travels* much original value, observing in his large and majestic way that ' when once you have thought of big men and little men, it is easy to do all the rest.' Here, as elsewhere, he was talking for effect; and the effect on the modern reader's mind is immediately to start him arguing. What Johnson said was relatively true—true so far as it went—no more true, however, than

11

if he had asserted that, to become the creator of *Don Quixote*, a writer had only to imagine a fat squire and a lean knight! In each book, the simplicity of the basic conception was the foundation of its greatness; and an ability to grasp such simple yet irresistible ideas is denied to all but a very few of the most gifted and independent artists. As for the rest being easy enough—what an enormous gap exists between brilliant conception and masterly execution! How much must depend upon imaginative detail! And Johnson himself, harried by Boswell, 'at last, of his own accord, allowed very great merit to the inventory of articles found in the pocket of " the Man Mountain ".'

Johnson, in short, by sheer blustering perversity has sent us back to Swift; and a return to Swift is always enjoyable, since one of the oldest of human desires is the longing to be told a story, and as a story-teller Swift is unsurpassed; for in his approach to the art of fiction he combines the richness of adult intelligence with the clarity and directness of a child's mind. He was writing, moreover, at an unusually happy period in the history of English prose style. Having outgrown its Elizabethan extravagances, and not yet assumed that ' inflated Rotundity and tumified Latinity of Diction ' which it was to acquire under Johnson's spell during the later eighteenth century, our prose language had attained to a point where the sublime and the matter-of-fact, lofty flights of eloquence and passages of sober scientific exposition, seemed equally within its compass. Such a style was particularly well-suited to Swift's fantastic narrative; for half the fascination of *Gulliver's Travels* lies in that air of sober realism with which the author introduces his hero, establishes his background and leads Gulliver across the seven seas, from the territories of the real to the realms of the imaginary. Lemuel Gulliver is a prosaic person, as businesslike in his methods and as limited in his opinions as the protagonist of *Robinson Crusoe*. Son of a poor country gentleman with ' a small Estate in *Nottinghamshire*,' he passes three industrious years at Cambridge and then begins to study medicine, 'Navigation and other Parts of the Mathematicks,' which enables him at length to go to sea as ship's surgeon in a vessel named 'The Swallow.' All this—together with the circumstances of his first shipwreck, caused by 'a violent Storm to the North-West of *Van Diemen's* Land' —is conveyed to us in a clear, concise, uncoloured and unemphatic fashion. And proportionately sharp is the surprise we feel when Gulliver, having struggled ashore and fallen asleep on the grass, 'which was very short and soft,' opens his eyes to discover that he can by no means rise again:

'... As I happened to lie on my Back, I found my Arms and Legs were strongly fastened on each Side to the Ground; and my Hair, which was long and thick, tied down in the same Manner. I likewise felt several slender Ligatures across my Body, from my Armpits to my Thighs. I could only look upwards; the Sun began to grow hot, and the Light offended my Eyes. I heard a confused Noise about me, but in the Posture I lay, could see nothing except the Sky. In a little time I felt something alive moving on my left Leg, which advancing gently forward over my Breast, came almost up to my Chin; when bending my Eyes downwards as much as I could, I perceived it to be a human Creature not six inches high, with a Bow and Arrow in his Hands, and a quiver at his Back. In the meantime, I felt at least Forty more of the same Kind (as I conjectured) following the first. I was in the utmost Astonishment, and roared so loud, that they all ran back in a fright ... However, they soon returned; and one of them, who ventured so far as to get a full Sight of my Face, lifting up his Hands and Eyes by way of Admiration, cryed out in a shrill, but distinct Voice, *Hekinah Degul* ... '

We have already arrived in Lilliput; but—so adroit is the transition—we do apprehend that we have thereby lost touch with the world of ordinary men and women.

Lilliput, we soon discover, is a scale-model of European life, worked out down to the very last inch (if we allow a very few miscalculations) with the most painstaking exactitude. It resounds, not to the horns of elf-land, but to the buzz and excitement of familiar human passions.

Of the four sections of the book, *Lilliput* is the most poetic: *Brobdingnag* the strangest and most grotesque: *Laputa* the least successful, though the account of the flying island contains brilliant and prophetic fancies: while *A Voyage to the Country of the Houyhnhnms* is incomparably the most savage. *Gulliver's Travels* was written between 1720 and 1725, and published anonymously, like all Swift's works, during October 1726. The author was then in Ireland, but he returned to England the following year and enjoyed the immediate popular success with which his book had been rewarded, eventually retiring to Dublin for the last time in October 1727. Soon afterwards died Esther Johnson, the devoted friend for whom his deep, though ambiguous, affection is reflected in the pages of the celebrated *Journal to Stella*, and for whom he had invented the mysterious 'little language.' From that moment, until his own death on October 19th 1745, Swift's existence can best be described as a slow descent towards the underworld. His maladies increased: the knowledge that he might one day go mad grew more and more appalling. His delightful *Verses on the Death of Dr. Swift* were written in 1731; but by 1738 his health and sanity, long precarious, had definitely broken down; and *Gulliver's Travels* was the last major work of its ageing, splenetic and bitterly disillusioned author. No masterpiece has a darker and angrier tone; yet it is a curious and illuminating fact that, apart from its effect upon adult readers, this collection of envenomed fables has always charmed the nursery.

In common with its juvenile admirers, posterity has decided that the satirical basis of the story, though by no reckoning unimportant, is certainly less important than

several other aspects. True, Gulliver's account of Lilliputian court-life is thickly strewn with concealed references
to the current state of English politics; while his picture
of the fierce contention between the Big-Endian party
and their equally bigoted opponents is a miniature representation of the strife of Catholics and Protestants.
Yet, had the key been entirely lost, *Gulliver's Travels* would
remain one of the most absorbing volumes in any modern
literature, both by virtue of its poetic qualities—the sheer
delight of the narrative, the wonderful thoroughness and
ingenuity with which Swift builds up and consolidates
an imaginary universe—and as a resounding commination
directed at mankind in general. Here, expressed to the
full, are at once the creative and the destructive sides of
Swift's tormented character. That he had a strain of
almost feminine tenderness is revealed by the journal that
he kept for Esther Johnson; and that he had moods of
ferocious misanthropy, during which his fellow men appeared to him as grovelling and malevolent insects or
filthy and libidinous Yahoos, is sufficiently demonstrated
by *Gulliver's Travels* and by many of his less decorous
and more notorious verses. Previous satirists had been
inclined to concentrate on specific types or characters, or
on vices—pride, avarice and lust—to which men and
women of the period seemed particularly subject. Swift's
indignation is universal, and his target is Man himself,
Man who builds only to destroy, and loves only to betray
and pollute, who before Swift's birth had invented gunpowder and after his death was to stumble delightedly
upon the secret of the Atom Bomb.

Hence the fable of the Houyhnhnms, that lordly and
magnanimous equine race, who use their strength tem-
perately and exercise their virtues mildly:
' I confess, it was whispered to me, (Gulliver writes) that
I was bound in Duty as a Subject of *England*, to have given
in a Memorial to a Secretary of State, at my first coming
over; because, whatever Lands are discovered by a
Subject, belong to the Crown. But I doubt, whether our

Conquests in the Countries I treat of, would be as easy as those of *Ferdinando Cortez* over the naked *Americans*. The *Lilliputians* I think, are hardly worth the Charge of a Fleet and Army to reduce them; and I question whether it might be prudent or safe to attempt the *Brobdingnagians*: Or, whether an *English* army would be much at their Ease with the Flying Island over their Heads. The *Houyhnhnms*, indeed, appear not to be so well prepared for War, a Science to which they are perfect Strangers, and especially, against missive Weapons. However, supposing myself to be a Minister of State, I could never give my Advice for invading them. Their Prudence, Unanimity, Unacquaintedness with Fear, and their Love of their Country would amply supply all defects in the military Art. Imagine twenty Thousand of them breaking into the Midst of an *European* army, confounding the Ranks, overturning the Carriages, battering the Warriors Faces into Mummy, by terrible Yerks from their hinder Hoofs. . . But instead of Proposals for conquering that magnanimous Nation, I rather wish they were in a Capacity or Disposition to send a sufficient Number of their Inhabitants for civilizing *Europe*; by teaching us the first Principles of Honour, Justice, Truth, Temperance, publick Spirit, Fortitude, Chastity, Friendship, Benevolence, and Fidelity. The *Names* of all which virtues are still retained among us in most Languages, and are to be met with in modern as well as ancient Authors; which I am able to assert from my own small reading.'

No book could have a gloomier close, or contain implications more alarming and more saddening. How is it then that *Gulliver's Travels* may still be read with continuous enjoyment? To solve this problem, we must look to the nature of art which, constantly at work on the raw material of experience, produces harmony from cacophony, order from disorder, and makes it possible still to love a world that rarely ceases to offend us. Swift believed that he hated the world; and, as he grew older, his sense of frustration increased till at length it overwhelmed him.

But, had he hated life, and despised mankind as vehemently and unreservedly as he now and then pretended, we can be sure from what we know of the creative processes, that he would not have been an artist; for it is the struggle in the artist's mind of two conflicting sentiments—one encouraging hope, while the other prompts despair: one urging him towards acceptance, the other towards rejection—that sets up the fruitful confusion in which a work of art is usually engendered. Real gaiety and a tremendous zest for living co-exist in *Gulliver's Travels* with a strain of darkly ingrained pessimism; and this pessimism (we may come to consider) is very largely counter-balanced by the existence of the book itself. Mankind's gift for lucid self-appraisal and unsparing self-indictment is among our strangest and most precious assets. So long as human beings can think clearly and write forcefully and beautifully, we need not cease to expect that at some period, no doubt in the very far future, they may yet show that they have discovered how to conduct their lives with decency.

PETER QUENNELL

GULLIVER'S TRAVELS

NOTE BY JOHN HAYWARD

'The chief end I propose to myself in all my labours is to vex the world rather than divert it.' So Swift wrote from Dublin in the autumn of 1725 when he was finishing the most celebrated of all his works. *Gulliver's Travels*, as the book is commonly called, was published in two volumes a year later, on October 28, and as Dr Johnson remarks 'was read by the high and the low, the learned and illiterate. Criticism was for a while lost in wonder.' What was to have vexed the world diverted it then and has continued to do so ever since.

According to Swift's habit, the publication was arranged mysteriously, and it is believed that Pope or Ford delivered the manuscript to Motte, the publisher, by the odd expedient of dropping it at his door from the window of a hackney coach. It was, however, generally known that Swift was the author.

The text, particularly of the third and fourth parts, of Motte's early editions—there were six of them between 1726 and 1735 —is unsatisfactory in several respects. Owing to Motte's timidity, words and whole passages in the MS. were altered or omitted without the author's knowledge. Fortunately, Swift indicated these alterations and omissions to his friend Charles Ford of Woodpark, who corrected them in his own interleaved large-paper copy of the first edition. This volume, now in the Forster collection, is of the highest textual importance. Although Motte had received a list of verbal and typographical corrections from Ford in January 1726/7 and incorporated nearly all of them in his fourth octavo edition [1727], it was not until Swift's Irish publisher, George Faulkner, published *Gulliver's Travels* as the third volume of the first collected edition of Swift's works in 1735 that all the words and passages noted by Ford in his own copy were restored. It is now known that Swift, though originally antagonistic to Faulkner's proposal, eventually submitted to it and was persuaded to look over the sheets of the first four volumes [v. Swift to Ford, Oct. 9, 1733].

While it is true that the text of the first edition has a sentimental interest as the original version given to the world, it is obvious that Faulkner's revision follows more closely Swift's MS. The principle hitherto adopted by editors of *Gulliver's Travels* has been to reprint Motte's edition incorporating Ford's corrections. I have preferred to reprint Faulkner's text. The result, I venture to believe, is a more exact and reliable text than any that has been published in the last two hundred years.

J. H.

TRAVELS

into Several Remote
Nations of the
World

★

In Four Parts,
viz.

I. A Voyage to Lilliput.

II. A Voyage to Brobdingnag.

III. A Voyage to Laputa, Balnibarbi,
Luggnagg, Glubbdubdrib,
and Japan.

IV. A Voyage to the Country of the
Houyhnhnms.

★

By Lemuel Gulliver, first
a Surgeon, and then a
Captain of several
Ships.

A LETTER

from Capt. Gulliver, to his
Cousin Sympson

I HOPE *you will be ready to own publickly, whenever you shall be called to it, that by your great and frequent Urgency you prevailed on me to publish a very loose and uncorrect Account of my Travels; with Direction to hire some young Gentlemen of either University to put them in Order, and correct the Style, as my Cousin* Dampier *did by my Advice, in his Book called,* A Voyage round the World. *But I do not remember I gave you Power to consent, that any thing should be omitted, and much less that any thing should be inserted: Therefore, as to the latter, I do here renounce every thing of that Kind; particularly a Paragraph about her Majesty the late Queen* Anne, *of most pious and glorious Memory; although I did reverence and esteem her more than any of human Species. But you, or your Interpolator, ought to have considered, that as it was not my Inclination, so was it not decent to praise any Animal of our Composition before my Master* Houyhnhnm: *And besides, the Fact was altogether false; for to my Knowledge, being in* England *during some Part of her Majesty's Reign, she did govern by a chief Minister; nay, even by two successively; the first whereof was the Lord of* Godolphin, *and the second the Lord of* Oxford; *so that you have made me* say the thing that was not. *Likewise, in the Account of the Academy of Projectors, and several Passages of my Discourse to my Master* Houyhnhnm, *you have either omitted some material Circumstances, or minced or changed them in such a Manner, that I do hardly know mine own Work. When I formerly hinted to you something of this in a Letter, you were pleased to answer, that you were afraid of giving Offence; that People in Power were very watchful over the Press; and apt not only to interpret, but to punish every thing which looked like an* Inuendo *(as I think you called it.) But pray, how could that which I spoke so many Years ago, and at above five Thousand Leagues distance, in another Reign, be applyed to any of the* Yahoos, *who now are said to govern the Herd; especially, at a time when I little thought on or feared the*

Unhappiness of living under them. Have not I the most Reason to complain, when I see these very Yahoos *carried by* Houyhnhnms *in a Vehicle, as if these were Brutes, and those the rational Creatures? And, indeed, to avoid so monstrous and detestable a Sight, was one principal Motive of my Retirement hither.*

THUS much I thought proper to tell you in Relation to your self, and to the Trust I reposed in you.

I DO in the next Place complain of my own great Want of Judgment, in being prevailed upon by the Intreaties and false Reasonings of you and some others, very much against mine own Opinion, to · suffer my Travels to be published. Pray bring to your Mind how often I desired you to consider, when you insisted on the Motive of publick Good; *that the* Yahoos *were a Species of Animals utterly incapable of Amendment by Precepts or Examples: And so it hath proved; for instead of seeing a full Stop put to all Abuses and Corruptions, at least in this little Island, as I had Reason to expect: Behold, after above six Months Warning, I cannot learn that my Book hath produced one single Effect according to mine Intentions: I desired you would let me know by a Letter, when Party and Faction were extinguished; Judges learned and upright; Pleaders honest and modest, with some Tincture of common Sense; and* Smithfield *blazing with Pyramids of Law-Books; the young Nobility's Education entirely changed; the Physicians banished; the Female* Yahoos *abounding in Virtue, Honour, Truth and good Sense; Courts and Levees of great Ministers thoroughly weeded and swept; Wit, Merit and Learning rewarded; all Disgracers of the Press in Prose and Verse, condemned to eat nothing but their own Cotten, and quench their Thirst with their own Ink. These, and a Thousand other Reformations, I firmly counted upon by your Encouragement; as indeed they were plainly deducible from the Precepts delivered in my Book. And, it must be owned that seven Months were a sufficient Time to correct every Vice and Folly to which* Yahoos *are subject; if their Natures had been capable of the least Disposition to Virtue or Wisdom: Yet so far have you been from answering mine Expectation in any of your Letters; that on the contrary, you are loading our Carrier every Week with Libels, and Keys, and Reflections, and Memoirs, and Second Parts; wherein I see myself accused of reflecting upon great States-*

Folk; of degrading human Nature, (for so they have still the Confidence to stile it) and of abusing the Female Sex. I find likewise, that the Writers of those Bundles are not agreed among themselves; for some of them will not allow me to be Author of mine own Travels; and others make me Author of Books to which I am wholly a Stranger.

I FIND likewise, that your Printer hath been so careless as to confound the Times, and mistake the Dates of my several Voyages and Returns; neither assigning the true Year, or the true Month, or Day of the Month: And I hear the original Manuscript is all destroyed, since the Publication of my Book. Neither have I any Copy left; however, I have sent you some Corrections, which you may insert, if ever there should be a second Edition: And yet I cannot stand to them, but shall leave that Matter to my judicious and candid Readers, to adjust it as they please.

I HEAR some of our Sea-Yahoos find Fault with my Sea-Language, as not proper in many Parts, nor now in Use. I cannot help it. In my first Voyages, while I was young, I was instructed by the oldest Mariners, and learned to speak as they did. But I have since found that the Sea-Yahoos are apt, like the Land ones, to become new fangled in their Words; which the latter change every Year; insomuch, as I remember upon each Return to mine own Country, their old Dialect was so altered, that I could hardly understand the new. And I observe, when any Yahoo comes from London out of Curiosity to visit me at mine own House, we neither of us are able to deliver our Conceptions in a Manner intelligible to the other.

IF the Censure of Yahoos could any Way affect me, I should have great Reason to complain, that some of them are so bold as to think my Book of Travels a meer Fiction out of mine own Brain; and have gone so far as to drop Hints, that the Houyhnhnms, and Yahoos have no more Existence than the Inhabitants of Utopia.

INDEED I must confess, that as to the People of Lilliput, Brobdingrag, (for so the Word should have been spelt, and not erroneously Brobdingnag) and Laputa; I have never yet heard of any Yahoo so presumptuous as to dispute their Being, or the Facts I have related concerning them; because the Truth immediately strikes every Reader with Conviction. And, is there less *Probability* in my *Account* of the Houyhnhnms *or* Yahoos, *when it is manifest as to the latter, there are so many Thousands even in this City, who only differ from their Brother Brutes in* Houyhnhnmland, *because they use a Sort of a* Jabber, *and do not go naked. I wrote for their Amendment, and not their Approbation. The united Praise of the whole Race would be of less Consequence to me, than the neighing of those two degenerate* Houyhnhnms *I keep in my Stable; because, from these, degenerate as they are, I still improve in some Virtues, without any Mixture of Vice.*

DO these miserable Animals presume to think that I am so far degenerated as to defend my Veracity; Yahoo *as I am, it is well known through all* Houyhnhnmland, *that by the Instructions and Example of my illustrious Master, I was able in the Compass of two Years (although I confess with the utmost Difficulty) to remove that infernal Habit of Lying, Shuffling, Deceiving, and Equivocating, so deeply rooted in the very Souls of all my Species; especially the* Europeans.

I HAVE other Complaints to make upon this vexatious Occasion; but I forbear troubling myself or you any further. I must freely confess, that since my last Return, some Corruptions of my Yahoo *Nature have revived in me by conversing with a few of your Species, and particularly those of mine own Family, by an unavoidable Necessity; else I should never have attempted so absurd a Project as that of reforming the* Yahoo *Race in this Kingdom; but, I have now done with all such visionary Schemes for ever.*

April 2, 1727.

THE PUBLISHER TO
THE READER

THE AUTHOR *of these Travels, Mr.* Lemuel Gulliver, *is my antient and intimate Friend; there is likewise some Relation between us by the Mother's Side. About three Years ago Mr.* Gulliver *growing weary of the Concourse of curious People coming to him at his House in* Redriff, *made a small Purchase of Land, with a convenient House, near* Newark, *in* Nottinghamshire, *his native Country; where he now lives retired, yet in good Esteem among his Neighbours.*

ALTHOUGH *Mr.* Gulliver *were born in* Nottinghamshire, *where his Father dwelt, yet I have heard him say, his Family came from* Oxfordshire; *to confirm which, I have observed in the Church-Yard at* Banbury, *in that County, several Tombs and Monuments of the* Gullivers.

BEFORE *he quitted* Redriff, *he left the Custody of the following Papers in my Hands, with the Liberty to dispose of them as I should think fit. I have carefully perused them three Times; The Style is very plain and simple; and the only Fault I find is, that the Author, after the Manner of Travellers, is a little too circumstantial. There is an Air of Truth apparent through the whole; and indeed the Author was so distinguished for his Veracity, that it became a Sort of Proverb among his Neighbours at* Redriff, *when any one affirmed a Thing, to say, it was as true as if Mr.* Gulliver *had spoke it.*

BY *the Advice of several worthy Persons, to whom, with the Author's Permission, I communicated these Papers, I now venture to send them into the World; hoping they may be, at least for some time, a better Entertainment to our young Noblemen, than the common Scribbles of Politicks and Party.*

THIS *Volume would have been at least twice as large, if I had not made bold to strike out innumerable Passages relating to the Winds and Tides, as well as to the Variations and Bearings in the several Voyages; together with the minute Descriptions of the Management of the Ship in Storms, in the Style of Sailors: Likewise the Account of the Longitudes and Latitudes; wherein I have Reason to apprehend that Mr.* Gulliver *may be a little* dissatisfied: But I was resolved to fit the Work as much as possible to the general Capacity of Readers. However, if my own Ignorance in Sea-Affairs shall have led me to commit some Mistakes, I alone am answerable for them: And if any Traveller hath a Curiosity to see the whole Work at large, as it came from the Hand of the Author, I will be ready to gratify him.

As for any further Particulars relating to the Author, the Reader will receive Satisfaction from the first Pages of the Book.

RICHARD SYMPSON

PART ONE

A VOYAGE TO LILLIPUT

Hogs I.

P. Mintaon

I. Good Fortune

I. Nassow

SUNDA

SUMATRA

Sillabar

Straits of Sunda

Blefuscu

Lilliput

Mendendo

Discovered A.D. 1699

Dimens
Land

CHAPTER ONE

THE AUTHOR GIVETH SOME ACCOUNT OF HIMSELF AND
FAMILY; HIS FIRST INDUCEMENTS TO TRAVEL. HE IS SHIP-
WRECKED, AND SWIMS FOR HIS LIFE; GETS SAFE ON SHOAR
IN THE COUNTRY OF LILLIPUT; IS MADE A PRISONER, AND
CARRIED UP THE COUNTRY.

My Father had a small Estate in *Nottinghamshire*; I
was the Third of five Sons. He sent me to *Emanuel-College* in *Cambridge*, at Fourteen Years old, where I
resided three Years, and applied my self close to my
Studies: But the Charge of maintaining me (although
I had a very scanty Allowance) being too great for a
narrow Fortune; I was bound Apprentice to Mr. *James
Bates*, an eminent Surgeon in *London*, with whom I continued four Years; and my Father now and then sending
me small Sums of Money, I laid them out in learning
Navigation, and other Parts of the Mathematicks, useful to
those who intend to travel, as I always believed it would be
some time or other my Fortune to do. When I left Mr. *Bates*,
I went down to my Father; where, by the Assistance of him
and my Uncle *John*, and some other Relations, I got Forty
Pounds, and a Promise of Thirty Pounds a Year to maintain me at *Leyden*: There I studied Physick two Years and
seven Months, knowing it would be useful in long Voyages.

Soon after my Return from *Leyden*, I was recommended
by my good Master Mr. *Bates*, to be Surgeon to the
Swallow, Captain *Abraham Pannell* Commander; with
whom I continued three Years and a half, making a Voyage
or two into the *Levant* and some other Parts. When I came
back, I resolved to settle in *London*, to which Mr. *Bates*,
my Master, encouraged me; and by him I was recommended to several Patients. I took Part of a small House
in the *Old Jury*; and being advised to alter my Condition,
I married Mrs. *Mary Burton*, second Daughter to Mr.
Edmond Burton, Hosier, in *Newgate-street*, with whom I
received four Hundred Pounds for a Portion.

But, my good Master *Bates* dying in two Years after,

and I having few Friends, my Business began to fail; for
my Conscience would not suffer me to imitate the bad Practice of too many among my Brethren. Having therefore
consulted with my Wife, and some of my Acquaintance, I
determined to go again to Sea. I was Surgeon successively
in two Ships, and made several Voyages, for six Years, to
the *East* and *West-Indies*; by which I got some Addition
to my Fortune. My Hours of Leisure I spent in reading
the best Authors, ancient and modern; being always provided with a good Number of Books; and when I was
ashore, in observing the Manners and Dispositions of the
People, as well as learning their Language; wherein I had
a great Facility by the Strength of my Memory.

The last of these Voyages not proving very fortunate, I
grew weary of the Sea, and intended to stay at home with
my Wife and Family. I removed from the *Old Jury* to
Fetter Lane, and from thence to *Wapping*, hoping to get Business among the Sailors; but it would not turn to account.
After three Years Expectation that things would mend,
I accepted an advantageous Offer from Captain *William
Prichard*, Master of the *Antelope*, who was making a Voyage to the *South-Sea*. We set sail from *Bristol*, *May* 4th,
1699, and our Voyage at first was very prosperous.

It would not be proper for some Reasons, to trouble the
Reader with the Particulars of our Adventures in those
Seas: Let it suffice to inform him, that in our Passage from
thence to the *East-Indies*, we were driven by a violent
Storm to the North-west of *Van Diemen's* Land. By an
Observation, we found ourselves in the Latitude of 30
Degrees 2 Minutes South. Twelve of our Crew were dead
by immoderate Labour, and ill Food; the rest were in a
very weak Condition. On the fifth of *November*, which was
the beginning of Summer in those Parts, the Weather being
very hazy, the Seamen spyed a Rock, within half a Cable's
length of the Ship; but the Wind was so strong, that we
were driven directly upon it, and immediately split. Six
of the Crew, of whom I was one, having let down the
Boat into the Sea, made a Shift to get clear of the Ship, and
the Rock. We rowed by my Computation, about three

Learning navigation

Leagues, till we were able to work no longer, being already spent with Labour while we were in the Ship. We therefore trusted ourselves to the Mercy of the Waves; and in about half an Hour the Boat was overset by a sudden Flurry from the North. What became of my Companions in the Boat, as well as of those who escaped on the Rock, or were left in the Vessel, I cannot tell; but conclude they were all lost. For my own Part, I swam as Fortune directed me, and was pushed forward by Wind and Tide. I often let my Legs drop, and could feel no Bottom; But when I was almost gone, and able to struggle no longer, I found myself within my Depth; and by this Time the Storm was much abated. The Declivity was so small, that I walked near a Mile before I got to the Shore, which I conjectured was about Eight o'Clock in the Evening. I then advanced forward near half a Mile, but could not discover any Sign of Houses or Inhabitants; at least I was in so weak a Condition, that I did not observe them. I was extremely tired, and with that, and the Heat of the Weather, and about half a Pint of Brandy that I drank as I left the Ship, I found my self much inclined to sleep. I lay down on the Grass, which was very short and soft; where I slept sounder than ever I remember to have done in my Life, and as I reckoned, above Nine Hours; for when I awaked, it was just Day-light. I attempted to rise, but was not able to stir: For as I happened to lie on my Back, I found my Arms and Legs were strongly fastened on each Side to the Ground; and my Hair, which was long and thick, tied down in the same Manner. I likewise felt several slender Ligatures across my Body, from my Armpits to my Thighs. I could only look upwards; the Sun began to grow hot, and the Light offended my Eyes. I heard a confused Noise about me, but in the Posture I lay, could see nothing except the Sky. In a little time I felt something alive moving on my left Leg, which advancing gently forward over my Breast, came almost up to my Chin; when bending my Eyes downwards as much as I could, I perceived it to be a human Creature not six Inches high, with a Bow and Arrow in his Hands, and a Quiver at his Back. In the mean time, I felt at least Forty more of the same Kind (as I conjectured) following the first. I was in the utmost Astonishment, and roared so loud, that they all ran back in a Fright; and some of them, as I was afterwards told, were hurt with the Falls they got by leaping from my Sides upon the Ground. However, they soon returned; and one of them, who ventured so far as to get a full Sight of my Face, lifting up his Hands and Eyes by way of Admiration, cryed out in a shrill, but distinct Voice, *Hekinah Degul*: The others repeated the same Words several times, but I then knew not what they meant. I lay all this while, as the Reader may believe, in great Uneasiness; At length, struggling to get loose, I had the Fortune to break the Strings, and wrench out the Pegs that fastened my left Arm to the Ground; for, by lifting it up to my Face, I discovered the Methods they had taken to bind me; and, at the same time, with a violent Pull, which gave me excessive Pain, I a little loosened the Strings that tied down my Hair on the left Side; so that I was just able to turn my Head about two Inches. But the Creatures ran off a second time, before I could seize them; whereupon there was a great Shout in a very shrill Accent; and after it ceased, I heard one of them cry aloud, *Tolgo Phonac*; when in an Instant I felt above an Hundred Arrows discharged on my left Hand, which pricked me like so many Needles; and besides, they shot another Flight into the Air, as we do Bombs in *Europe*; whereof many, I suppose, fell on my Body, (though I felt them not) and some on my Face, which I immediately covered with my left Hand. When this Shower of Arrows was over, I fell a groaning with Grief and Pain; and then striving again to get loose, they discharged another Volly larger than the first; and some of them attempted with Spears to stick me in the Sides; but, by good Luck, I had on me a Buff Jerkin, which they could not pierce. I thought it the most prudent Method to lie still; and my Design was to continue so till Night, when my left Hand being already loose, I could easily free myself: And as for the Inhabitants, I had Reason to believe I might be a Match

for the greatest Armies they could bring against me, if
they were all of the same Size with him that I saw. But
Fortune disposed otherwise of me. When the People
observed I was quiet, they discharged no more Arrows:
But by the Noise increasing, I knew their Numbers were
greater; and about four Yards from me, over-against
my right Ear, I heard a Knocking for above an Hour,
like People at work; when turning my Head that Way,
as well as the Pegs and Strings would permit me, I saw
a Stage erected about a Foot and a half from the Ground,
capable of holding four of the Inhabitants, with two or
three Ladders to mount it: From whence one of them,
who seemed to be a Person of Quality, made me a long
Speech, whereof I understood not one Syllable. But
I should have mentioned, that before the principal Person
began his Oration, he cryed out three times *Langro Dehul
san*: (these Words and the former were afterwards repeated
and explained to me.) Whereupon immediately about
fifty of the Inhabitants came, and cut the Strings that
fastened the left side of my Head, which gave me the
Liberty of turning it to the right, and of observing the
Person and Gesture of him who was to speak. He appeared
to be of a middle Age, and taller than any of the other
three who attended him; whereoı one was a Page, who
held up his Train, and seemed to be somewhat longer
than my middle Finger; the other two stood one on each
side to support him. He acted every part of an Orator;
and I could observe many Periods of Threatnings, and
others of Promises, Pity and Kindness. I answered in a
few Words, but in the most submissive Manner, lifting up
my left Hand and both my eyes to the Sun, as calling him
for a Witness; and being almost famished with Hunger,
having not eaten a Morsel for some Hours before I left
the Ship, I found the Demands of Nature so strong
upon me, that I could not forbear shewing my Impatience
(perhaps against the strict Rules of Decency) by putting
my Finger frequently on my Mouth, to signify that I
wanted Food. The *Hurgo* (for so they call a great Lord,
as I afterwards learnt) understood me very well: He

descended from the Stage, and commanded that several
Ladders should be applied to my Sides, on which above
an hundred of the Inhabitants mounted, and walked towards my Mouth, laden with Baskets full of Meat, which
had been provided and sent thither by the King's Orders
upon the first Intelligence he received of me. I observed
there was the Flesh of several Animals, but could not distinguish them by the Taste. There were Shoulders, Legs,
and Loins shaped like those of Mutton, and very well
dressed, but smaller than the Wings of a Lark. I eat them
by two or three at a Mouthful; and took three Loaves at a
time, about the bigness of Musket Bullets. They supplyed
me as fast as they could, shewing a thousand Marks of
Wonder and Astonishment at my Bulk and Appetite. I
then made another Sign that I wanted Drink. They found
by my eating that a small Quantity would not suffice me;
and being a most ingenious People, they slung up with great
Dexterity one of their largest Hogsheads; then rolled it
towards my Hand, and beat out the Top; I drank it off
at a Draught, which I might well do, for it hardly held
half a Pint, and tasted like a small Wine of *Burgundy*, but
much more delicious. They brought me a second Hogshead,
which I drank in the same Manner, and made
Signs for more, but they had none to give me. When I
had performed these Wonders, they shouted for Joy, and
danced upon my Breast, repeating several times as they
did at first, *Hekinah Degul*. They made me a Sign that
I should throw down the two Hogsheads, but first warned
the People below to stand out of the Way, crying aloud,
Borach Mivola; and when they saw the Vessels in the Air,
there was an universal Shout of *Hekinah Degul*. I confess
I was often tempted, while they were passing backwards
and forwards on my Body, to seize Forty or Fifty of the
first that came in my Reach, and dash them against the
Ground. But the Remembrance of what I had felt,
which probably might not be the worst they could do;
and the Promise of Honour I made them, for so I interpreted my submissive Behaviour, soon drove out those
Imaginations. Besides, I now considered my self as bound

by the Laws of Hospitality to a People who had treated
me with so much Expence and Magnificence. However, in my Thoughts I could not sufficiently wonder at
the Intrepidity of these diminutive Mortals, who durst
venture to mount and walk on my Body, while one of my
Hands was at Liberty, without trembling at the very Sight
of so prodigious a Creature as I must appear to them.
After some time, when they observed that I made no more
Demands for Meat, there appeared before me a Person
of high Rank from his Imperial Majesty. His Excellency
having mounted on the Small of my Right Leg, advanced
forwards up to my Face, with about a Dozen of his Retinue;
And producing his Credentials under the Signet Royal,
which he applied close to my Eyes, spoke about ten
Minutes, without any Signs of Anger, but with a kind of
determinate Resolution; often pointing forwards, which,
as I afterwards found, was towards the Capital City,
about half a Mile distant, whither it was agreed by his
Majesty in Council that I must be conveyed. I answered
in few Words, but to no Purpose, and made a Sign with
my Hand that was loose, putting it to the other, (but over
his Excellency's Head, for Fear of hurting him or his
Train) and then to my own Head and Body, to signify that
I desired my Liberty. It appeared that he understood
me well enough; for he shook his Head by way of Disapprobation, and held his Hand in a Posture to shew that
I must be carried as a Prisoner. However, he made
other Signs to let me understand that I should have Meat
and Drink enough, and very good Treatment. Whereupon
I once more thought of attempting to break my Bonds;
but again, when I felt the Smart of their Arrows upon my
Face and Hands, which were all in Blisters, and many of
the Darts still sticking in them; and observing likewise
that the Number of my Enemies encreased; I gave
Tokens to let them know that they might do with me
what they pleased. Upon this, the *Hurgo* and his Train
withdrew, with much Civility and chearful Countenances.
Soon after I heard a general Shout, with frequent Repe-
titions of the Words, *Peplom Selan*, and I felt great Numbers

of the People on my Left Side relaxing the Cords to such a Degree, that I was able to turn upon my Right, and to ease my self with making Water; which I very plentifully did, to the great Astonishment of the People, who conjecturing by my Motions what I was going to do, immediately opened to the right and left on that Side, to avoid the Torrent which fell with such Noise and Violence from me. But before this, they had dawbed my Face and both my Hands with a sort of Ointment very pleasant to the Smell, which in a few Minutes removed all the Smart of their Arrows. These Circumstances, added to the Refreshment I had received by their Victuals and Drink, which were very nourishing, disposed me to sleep. I slept about eight Hours as I was afterwards assured; and it was no Wonder; for the Physicians, by the Emperor's Order, had mingled a sleeping Potion in the Hogsheads of Wine.

It seems that upon the first Moment I was discovered sleeping on the Ground after my Landing, the Emperor had early Notice of it by an Express; and determined in Council that I should be tyed in the Manner I have related, (which was done in the Night while I slept) that Plenty of Meat and Drink should be sent me, and a Machine prepared to carry me to the Capital City.

This Resolution perhaps may appear very bold and dangerous, and I am confident would not be imitated by any Prince in *Europe* on the like Occasion; however, in my Opinion it was extremely Prudent as well as Generous. For supposing these People had endeavoured to kill me with their Spears and Arrows while I was asleep; I should certainly have awaked with the first Sense of Smart, which might so far have rouzed my Rage and Strength, as to enable me to break the Strings wherewith I was tyed; after which, as they were not able to make Resistance, so they could expect no Mercy.

These People are most excellent Mathematicians, and arrived to a great Perfection in Mechanicks by the Countenance and Encouragement of the Emperor, who is a renowned Patron of Learning. This Prince hath several Machines fixed on Wheels, for the Carriage of Trees and

other great Weights. He often buildeth his largest Men
of War, whereof some are Nine Foot long, in the Woods
where the Timber grows, and has them carried on these
Engines three or four Hundred Yards to the Sea. Five
Hundred Carpenters and Engineers were immediately
set at work to prepare the greatest Engine they had.
It was a Frame of Wood raised three Inches from the
Ground, about seven Foot long and four wide, moving
upon twenty two Wheels. The Shout I heard, was upon
the Arrival of this Engine, which, it seems, set out in four
Hours after my Landing. It was brought parallel to me
as I lay. But the principal Difficulty was to raise and place
me in this Vehicle. Eighty Poles, each of one Foot high,
were erected for this Purpose, and very strong Cords of the
bigness of Pack thread were fastened by Hooks to many
Bandages, which the Workmen had girt round my Neck,
my Hands, my Body, and my Legs. Nine Hundred of
the strongest Men were employed to draw up these Cords
by many Pullies fastned on the Poles; and thus in less
than three Hours, I was raised and slung into the Engine,
and there tyed fast. All this I was told; for while the
whole Operation was performing, I lay in a profound
Sleep, by the Force of that soporiferous Medicine infused
into my Liquor. Fifteen hundred of the Emperor's largest
Horses, each about four Inches and a half high, were
employed to draw me towards the Metropolis, which, as
I said, was half a Mile distant.

About four Hours after we began our Journey, I awaked
by a very ridiculous Accident; for the Carriage being
stopt a while to adjust something that was out of Order,
two or three of the young Natives had the Curiosity to see
how I looked when I was asleep; they climbed up into
the Engine, and advancing very softly to my Face, one of
them, an Officer in the Guards, put the sharp End of his
Half-Pike a good way up into my left Nostril, which tickled
my Nose like a Straw, and made me sneeze violently: Whereupon they stole off unperceived; and it was three Weeks
before I knew the Cause of my awaking so suddenly. We
made a long March the remaining Part of the Day, and

rested at Night with Five Hundred Guards on each Side of me, half with Torches, and half with Bows and Arrows, ready to shoot me if I should offer to stir. The next Morning at Sunrise we continued our March, and arrived within two Hundred Yards of the City-Gates about Noon. The Emperor, and all his Court, came out to meet us; but his great Officers would by no Means suffer his Majesty to endanger his Person by mounting on my Body.

At the Place where the Carriage stopt, there stood an ancient Temple, esteemed to be the largest in the whole Kingdom; which having been polluted some Years before by an unnatural Murder, was, according to the Zeal of those People, looked upon as Prophane, and therefore had been applied to common Uses, and all the Ornaments and Furniture carried away. In this Edifice it was determined I should lodge. The great Gate fronting to the North was about four Foot high, and almost two Foot wide, through which I could easily creep. On each Side of the Gate was a small Window not above six Inches from the Ground: Into that on the Left Side, the King's Smiths conveyed fourscore and eleven Chains, like those that hang to a Lady's Watch in *Europe*, and almost as large, which were locked to my Left Leg with six and thirty Padlocks. Over against this Temple, on the other Side of the great Highway, at twenty Foot Distance, there was a Turret at least five Foot high. Here the Emperor ascended with many principal Lords of his Court, to have an Opportunity of viewing me, as I was told, for I could not see them. It was reckoned that above an hundred thousand Inhabitants came out of the Town upon the same Errand; and in spight of my Guards, I believe there could not be fewer than ten thousand, at several Times, who mounted upon my Body by the Help of Ladders. But a Proclamation was soon issued to forbid it, upon Pain of Death. When the Workmen found it was impossible for me to break loose, they cut all the Strings that bound me; whereupon I rose up with as melancholy a Disposition as ever I had in my Life. But the Noise and Astonishment of the People at seeing me rise and walk, are not to be expressed. The Chains that held my left Leg were about two Yards long, and gave me not only the Liberty of walking backwards and forwards in a Semicircle; but being fixed within four Inches of the Gate, allowed me to creep in, and lie at my full Length in the Temple.

CHAPTER TWO

THE EMPEROR OF LILLIPUT, ATTENDED BY SEVERAL OF THE NOBILITY, COMES TO SEE THE AUTHOR IN HIS CONFINEMENT. THE EMPEROR'S PERSON AND HABIT DESCRIBED. LEARNED MEN APPOINTED TO TEACH THE AUTHOR THEIR LANGUAGE. HE GAINS FAVOUR BY HIS MILD DISPOSITION. HIS POCKETS ARE SEARCHED, AND HIS SWORD AND PISTOLS TAKEN FROM HIM.

WHEN I found myself on my Feet, I looked about me, and must confess I never beheld a more entertaining Prospect. The Country round appeared like a continued Garden; and the inclosed Fields, which were generally Forty Foot square, resembled so many Beds of Flowers. These Fields were intermingled with Woods of half a Stang, and the tallest Trees, as I could judge, appeared to be seven Foot high. I viewed the Town on my left Hand, which looked like the painted Scene of a City in a Theatre.

I had been for some Hours extremely pressed by the Necessities of Nature; which was no Wonder, it being almost two Days since I had last disburthened myself. I was under great Difficulties between Urgency and Shame. The best Expedient I could think on, was to creep into my House, which I accordingly did; and shutting the Gate after me, I went as far as the Length of my Chain would suffer; and discharged my Body of that uneasy Load. But this was the only Time I was ever guilty of so uncleanly an Action; for which I cannot but hope the candid Reader will give some Allowance, after he hath maturely and impartially considered my Case, and the Distress I was in. From this Time my constant Practice was, as soon as I rose, to perform that Business in open Air, at the full Extent of my

Chain; and due Care was taken every Morning before
Company came, that the offensive Matter should be carried
off in Wheel-barrows, by two Servants appointed for that
Purpose. I would not have dwelt so long upon a Circumstance, that perhaps at first Sight may appear not very
momentous; if I had not thought it necessary to justify
my Character in Point of Cleanliness to the World; which
I am told, some of my Maligners have been pleased, upon
this and other Occasions, to call in Question.

When this Adventure was at an End, I came back out
of my House, having Occasion for fresh Air. The Emperor
was already descended from the Tower, and advancing on
Horseback towards me, which had like to have cost him
dear; for the Beast, although very well trained, yet wholly
unused to such a Sight, which appeared as if a Mountain
moved before him, reared up on his hinder Feet: But that
Prince, who is an excellent Horseman, kept his Seat, until
his Attendants ran in, and held the Bridle, while his Majesty had Time to dismount. When he alighted, he surveyed
me round with great Admiration, but kept beyond the
Length of my Chains. He ordered his Cooks and Butlers,
who were already prepared, to give me Victuals and Drink,
which they pushed forward in a sort of Vehicles upon
Wheels until I could reach them. I took these Vehicles, and
soon emptied them all; twenty of them were filled with
Meat, and ten with Liquor; each of the former afforded
me two or three good Mouthfuls, and I emptied the
Liquor of ten Vessels, which was contained in earthen Vials
into one Vehicle, drinking it off at a Draught; and so I
did with the rest. The Empress, and young Princes of the
Blood, of both Sexes, attended by many Ladies, sate at
some Distance in their Chairs; but upon the Accident that
happened to the Emperor's Horse, they alighted, and came
near his Person; which I am now going to describe. He is
taller by almost the Breadth of my Nail, than any of his
Court; which alone is enough to strike an Awe into the
Beholders. His Features are strong and masculine, with
an *Austrian* Lip, and arched Nose, his Complexion olive, his
Countenance erect, his Body and Limbs well proportioned,

all his Motions graceful, and his Deportment majestick.
He was then past his Prime, being twenty-eight Years and
three Quarters old, of which he had reigned about seven,
in great Felicity, and generally victorious. For the better
Convenience of beholding him, I lay on my Side, so that
my Face was parallel to his, and he stood but three Yards
off: However, I have had him since many Times in my
Hand, and therefore cannot be deceived in the Description. His Dress was very plain and simple, the Fashion of
it between the *Asiatick* and the *European*; but he had on his
Head a light Helmet of Gold, adorned with Jewels, and
a Plume on the Crest. He held his Sword drawn in his
Hand, to defend himself, if I should happen to break loose;
it was almost three Inches long, the Hilt and Scabbard were
Gold enriched with Diamonds. His Voice was shrill, but
very clear and articulate, and I could distinctly hear it
when I stood up. The Ladies and Courtiers were all
most magnificently clad, so that the Spot they stood upon
seemed to resemble a Petticoat spread on the Ground, em-
broidered with Figures of Gold and Silver. His Imperial
Majesty spoke often to me, and I returned Answers, but
neither of us could understand a Syllable. There were several of his Priests and Lawyers present (as I conjectured
by their Habits) who were commanded to address themselves to me, and I spoke to them in as many Languages
as I had the least Smattering of, which were *High* and *Low
Dutch, Latin, French, Spanish, Italian*, and *Lingua Franca*; but
all to no purpose. After about two Hours the Court retired,
and I was left with a strong Guard, to prevent the Impertinence, and probably the Malice of the Rabble, who were
very impatient to croud about me as near as they durst;
and some of them had the Impudence to shoot their
Arrows at me as I sate on the Ground by the Door of
my House; whereof one very narrowly missed my left Eye.
But the Colonel ordered six of the Ringleaders to be seized,
and thought no Punishment so proper as to deliver them
bound into my Hands, which some of his Soldiers accordingly did, pushing them forwards with the But-ends of their
Pikes into my Reach: I took them all in my right Hand,

put five of them into my Coat-pocket; and as to the sixth, I made a Countenance as if I would eat him alive. The poor Man squalled terribly, and the Colonel and his Officers were in much Pain, especially when they saw me take out my Penknife: But I soon put them out of Fear; for, looking mildly, and immediately cutting the Strings he was bound with, I set him gently on the Ground, and away he ran. I treated the rest in the same Manner, taking them one by one out of my Pocket; and I obscrved, both the Soldiers and People were highly obliged at this Mark of my Clemency, which was represented very much to my Advantage at Court.

Towards Night I got with some Difficulty into my House, where I lay on the Ground, and continued to do so about a Fortnight; during which time the Emperor gave Orders to have a Bed prepared for me. Six Hundred Beds of the common Measure were brought in Carriages, and worked up in my House; an Hundred and Fifty of their Beds sown together made up the Breadth and Length, and these were four double, which however kept me but very indifferently from the Hardness of the Floor, that was of smooth Stone. By the same Computation they provided me with Sheets, Blankets, and Coverlets, tolerable enough for one who had been so long enured to Hardships as I.

As the News of my Arrival spread through the kingdom, it brought prodigious Numbers of rich, idle, and curious People to see me; so that the Villages were almost emptied, and great Neglect of Tillage and Houshold Affairs must have ensued, if his Imperial Majesty had not provided by several Proclamations and Orders of State against this Inconveniency. He directed that those, who had already beheld me, should return home, and not presume to come within fifty Yards of my House, without Licence from Court; whereby the Secretaries of State got considerable Fees.

In the mean time, the Emperor held frequent Councils to debate what Course should be taken with me; and I was afterwards assured by a particular Friend, a Person of great Quality, and who was as much in the *Secret* as any; that the Court was under many Difficulties concerning me. They apprehended my breaking loose; that my Diet would be very expensive, and might cause a Famine. Sometimes they determined to starve me, or at least to shoot me in the Face and Hands with poisoned Arrows, which would soon dispatch me: But again they considered, that the Stench of so large a Carcase might produce a Plague in the Metropolis, and probably spread through the whole Kingdom. In the midst of these Consultations, several Officers of the Army went to the Door of the great Council Chamber; and two of them being admitted, gave an Account of my Behaviour to the six Criminals abovementioned; which made so favourable an Impression in the Breast of his Majesty, and the whole Board, in my Behalf, that an Imperial Commission was issued out, obliging all the Villages nine hundred Yards round the City, to deliver in every Morning six Beeves, forty Sheep, and other Victuals for my Sustenance; together with a proportionable Quantity of Bread and Wine, and other Liquors: For the due Payment of which his Majesty gave Assignments upon his Treasury. For this Prince lives chiefly upon his own Demesnes; seldom, except upon great Occasions raising any Subsidies upon his Subjects, who are bound to attend him in his Wars at their own Expence. An Establishment was also made of Six Hundred Persons to be my Domesticks, who had Board-Wages allowed for their Maintenance, and Tents built for them very conveniently on each side of my Door. It was likewise ordered, that three hundred Taylors should make me a Suit of Cloaths after the Fashion of the Country: That, six of his Majesty's greatest Scholars should be employed to instruct me in their Language: And, lastly, that the Emperor's Horses, and those of the Nobility, and Troops of Guards, should be exercised in my Sight, to accustom themselves to me. All these Orders were duly put in Execution; and in about three Weeks I made a great Progress in Learning their Language; during which Time, the Emperor frequently honoured me with his Visits, and was pleased to assist my Masters in teaching me.

We began already to converse together in some Sort; and the first Words I learnt, were to express my Desire, that he would please to give me my Liberty; which I every Day repeated on my Knees. His Answer, as I could apprehend, was, that this must be a Work of Time, not to be thought on without the Advice of his Council; and that first I must *Lumos Kelmin pesso desmar lon Emposo*; that is, *Swear a Peace with him and his Kingdom.* However, that I should be used with all Kindness; and he advised me to acquire by my Patience and discreet Behaviour, the good Opinion of himself and his Subjects. He desired I would not take it ill, if he gave Orders to certain proper Officers to search me; for probably I might carry about me several Weapons, which must needs be dangerous Things, if they answered the Bulk of so prodigious a Person. I said, his Majesty should be satisfied, for I was ready to strip my self, and turn up my Pockets before him. This I delivered, part in Words, and part in Signs. He replied, that by the Laws of the Kingdom, I must be searched by two of his Officers: That he knew this could not be done without my Consent and Assistance; that he had so good an Opinion of my Generosity and Justice, as to trust their Persons in my Hands: That whatever they took from me should be returned when I left the Country, or paid for at the Rate which I would set upon them. I took up the two Officers in my Hands, put them first into my Coat-Pockets, and then into every other Pocket about me, except my two Fobs, and another secret Pocket which I had no Mind should be searched, wherein I had some little Necessaries of no Consequence to any but my self. In one of my Fobs there was a Silver Watch, and in the other a small Quantity of Gold in a Purse. These Gentlemen, having Pen, Ink, and Paper about them, made an exact Inventory of every thing they saw; and when they had done, desired I would set them down, that they might deliver it to the Emperor. This Inventory I afterwards translated into *English*, and is Word for Word as follows.

Imprimis, In the right Coat-Pocket of the *Great Man Mountain* (for so I interpret the Words *Quinbus Flestrin*) after

the strictest Search, we found only one great Piece of coarse
Cloth, large enough to be a Foot-Cloth for your Majesty's chief Room of State. In the left Pocket, we saw a
huge Silver Chest, with a Cover of the same Metal, which
we, the Searchers, were not able to lift. We desired it
should be opened; and one of us stepping into it, found
himself up to the mid Leg in a sort of Dust, some part
whereof flying up to our Faces, set us both a sneezing for
several Times together. In his right Waistcoat-Pocket, we
found a prodigious Bundle of white thin Substances, folded
one over another, about the Bigness of three Men, tied
with a strong Cable, and marked with black Figures; which
we humbly conceive to be Writings; every Letter almost
half as large as the Palm of our Hands. In the left there
was a sort of Engine, from the Back of which were extended
twenty long Poles, resembling the Pallisado's before your
Majesty's Court; wherewith we conjecture the *Man Mountain* combs his Head; for we did not always trouble him
with Questions, because we found it a great Difficulty to
make him understand us. In the large Pocket on the right
Side of his middle Cover, (so I translate the Word *Ranfu-Lo*,
by which they meant my Breeches) we saw a hollow Pillar
of Iron, about the Length of a Man, fastened to a strong
Piece of Timber, larger than the Pillar; and upon one
side of the Pillar were huge Pieces of Iron sticking out,
cut into strange Figures; which we know not what to make
of. In the left Pocket, another Engine of the same kind.
In the smaller Pocket on the right Side, were several round
flat Pieces of white and red Metal, of different Bulk: Some
of the white, which seemed to be Silver, were so large and
heavy, that my Comrade and I could hardly lift them. In
the left Pocket were two black Pillars irregularly shaped:
we could not, without Difficulty, reach the Top of them
as we stood at the Bottom of his Pocket: One of them was
covered, and seemed all of a Piece; but at the upper End
of the other, there appeared a white round Substance, about
twice the bigness of our Heads. Within each of these was
inclosed a prodigious Plate of Steel; which, by our Orders,
we obliged him to shew us, because we apprehended they

might be dangerous Engines. He took them out of their Cases, and told us, that in his own Country his Practice was to shave his Beard with one of these, and to cut his Meat with the other. There were two Pockets which we could not enter: These he called his Fobs; they were two large Slits cut into the Top of his middle Cover, but squeezed close by the Pressure of his Belly. Out of the right Fob hung a great Silver Chain, with a wonderful kind of Engine at the Bottom. We directed him to draw out whatever was at the End of that Chain; which appeared to be a Globe, half Silver, and half of some transparent Metal: For on the transparent Side we saw certain strange Figures circularly drawn, and thought we could touch them, until we found our Fingers stopped with that lucid Substance. He put this Engine to our Ears, which made an incessant Noise like that of a Water-Mill. And we conjecture it is either some unknown Animal, or the God that he worships: But we are more inclined to the latter Opinion, because he assured us (if we understood him right, for he expressed himself very imperfectly) that he seldom did any Thing without consulting it. He called it his Oracle, and said it pointed out the Time for every Action of his Life. From the left Fob he took out a Net almost large enough for a Fisherman, but contrived to open and shut like a Purse, and served him for the same Use: We found therein several massy Pieces of yellow Metal, which if they be of real Gold, must be of immense Value.

Having thus, in Obedience to your Majesty's Commands, diligently searched all his Pockets; we observed a Girdle about his Waist made of the Hyde of some prodigious Animal; from which, on the left Side, hung a Sword of the Length of five Men; and on the right, a Bag or Pouch divided into two Cells; each Cell capable of holding three of your Majesty's Subjects. In one of these Cells were several Globes or Balls of a most ponderous Metal, about the Bigness of our Heads, and required a strong Hand to lift them: The other Cell contained a Heap of certain black Grains, but of no great Bulk or Weight, for we could hold about fifty of them in the Palms of our Hands.

This is an exact Inventory of what we found about the Body of the *Man Mountain*; who used us with great Civility, and due Respect to your Majesty's Commission. Signed and Sealed on the fourth Day of the eighty ninth Moon of your Majesty's auspicious Reign.

Clefren Frelock, Marsi Frelock.

When this Inventory was read over to the Emperor, he directed me to deliver up the several Particulars. He first called for my Scymiter, which I took out, Scabbard and all. In the mean time he ordered three thousand of his choicest Troops, who then attended him, to surround me at a Distance, with their Bows and Arrows just ready to discharge: But I did not observe it; for my Eyes were wholly fixed upon his Majesty. He then desired me to draw my Scymiter, which, although it had got some Rust by the Sea-Water, was in most Parts exceeding bright. I did so, and immediately all the Troops gave a Shout between Terror and Surprize; for the Sun shone clear, and the Reflexion dazzled their Eyes, as I waved the Scymiter to and fro in my Hand. His Majesty, who is a most magnanimous Prince, was less daunted than I could expect; he ordered me to return it into the Scabbard, and cast it on the Ground as gently as I could, about six Foot from the End of my Chain. The next Thing he demanded was one of the hollow Iron Pillars, by which he meant my Pocket-Pistols. I drew it out, and at his Desire, as well as I could, expressed to him the Use of it, and charging it only with Powder, which by the Closeness of my Pouch, happened to escape wetting in the Sea, (an Inconvenience that all prudent Mariners take special Care to provide against) I first cautioned the Emperor not to be afraid; and then I let it off in the Air. The Astonishment here was much greater than at the Sight of my Scymiter. Hundreds fell down as if they had been struck dead; and even the Emperor, although he stood his Ground, could not recover himself in some time. I delivered up both my Pistols in the same Manner as I had done my Scymiter, and then my Pouch of Powder and Bullets; begging him that the

former might be kept from Fire; for it would kindle with
the smallest Spark, and blow up his Imperial Palace into
the Air. I likewise delivered up my Watch, which the
Emperor was very curious to see; and commanded two of
his tallest Yeomen of the Guards to bear it on a Pole upon
their Shoulders, as Dray-men in *England* do a Barrel of
Ale. He was amazed at the continual Noise it made, and
the Motion of the Minute-hand, which he could easily discern; for their Sight is much more acute than ours: He
asked the Opinions of his learned Men about him, which
were various and remote, as the Reader may well imagine
without my repeating; although indeed I could not very
perfectly understand them. I then gave up my Silver and
Copper Money, my Purse with nine large Pieces of Gold,
and some smaller ones; my Knife and Razor, my Comb
and Silver Snuff-Box, my Handkerchief and Journal Book.
My Scymiter, Pistols, and Pouch, were conveyed in Carriages to his Majesty's Stores; but the rest of my Goods
were returned me.

I had, as I before observed, one private Pocket which
escaped their Search, wherein there was a Pair of Spectacles
(which I sometimes use for the Weakness of my Eyes)
a Pocket Perspective, and several other little Conveniences;
which being of no Consequence to the Emperor, I did not
think my self bound in Honour to discover; and I apprehended they might be lost or spoiled if I ventured them out
of my Possession.

CHAPTER THREE

THE AUTHOR DIVERTS THE EMPEROR AND HIS NOBILITY OF
BOTH SEXES, IN A VERY UNCOMMON MANNER. THE DIVERSIONS
OF THE COURT OF LILLIPUT DESCRIBED. THE AUTHOR HATH
HIS LIBERTY GRANTED HIM UPON CERTAIN CONDITIONS.

MY Gentleness and good Behaviour had gained so far
on the Emperor and his Court, and indeed upon the
Army and People in general, that I began to conceive
Hopes of getting my Liberty in a short Time. I took all

possible Methods to cultivate this favourable Disposition. The Natives came by Degrees to be less apprehensive of any Danger from me. I would sometimes lie down, and let five or six of them dance on my Hand. And at last the Boys and Girls would venture to come and play at Hide and Seek in my Hair. I had now made a good Progress in understanding and speaking their Language. The Emperor had a mind one Day to entertain me with several of the Country Shows; wherein they exceed all Nations I have known, both for Dexterity and Magnificence. I was diverted with none so much as that of the Rope-Dancers, performed upon a slender white Thread, extended about two Foot, and twelve Inches from the Ground. Upon which, I shall desire Liberty, with the Reader's Patience, to enlarge a little.

This Diversion is only practised by those Persons, who are Candidates for great Employments, and high Favour, at Court. They are trained in this Art from their Youth, and are not always of noble Birth, or liberal Education. When a great Office is vacant, either by Death or Disgrace, (which often happens) five or six of those Candidates petition the Emperor to entertain his Majesty and the Court with a Dance on the Rope; and whoever jumps the highest without falling, succeeds in the Office. Very often the chief Ministers themselves are commanded to shew their Skill, and to convince the Emperor that they have not lost their Faculty. *Flimnap*, the Treasurer, is allowed to cut a Caper on the strait Rope, at least an Inch higher than any other Lord in the whole Empire. I have seen him do the Summerset several times together, upon a Trencher fixed on the Rope, which is no thicker than a common Packthread in *England*. My Friend *Reldresal*, principal Secretary for private Affairs, is, in my Opinion, if I am not partial, the second after the Treasurer; the rest of the great Officers are much upon a Par.

These Diversions are often attended with fatal Accidents, whereof great Numbers are on Record. I my self have seen two or three Candidates break a Limb. But the Danger is much greater, when the Ministers themselves are commanded to shew their Dexterity: For, by contending to excel themselves and their Fellows, they strain so far, that there is hardly one of them who hath not received a Fall; and some of them two or three. I was assured, that a Year or two before my Arrival, *Flimnap* would have infallibly broke his Neck, if one of the *King's Cushions*, that accidentally lay on the Ground, had not weakened the Force of his Fall.

There is likewise another Diversion, which is only shewn before the Emperor and Empress, and first Minister, upon particular Occasions. The Emperor lays on a Table three fine silken Threads of six Inches long. One is Blue, the other Red, and the third Green. These Threads are proposed as Prizes, for those Persons whom the Emperor hath a mind to distinguish by a peculiar Mark of his Favour. The Ceremony is performed in his Majesty's great Chamber of State; where the Candidates are to undergo a Tryal of Dexterity very different from the former; and such as I have not observed the least Resemblance of in any other Country of the old or the new World. The Emperor holds a Stick in his Hands, both Ends parallel to the Horizon, while the Candidates advancing one by one, sometimes leap over the Stick, sometimes creep under it backwards and forwards several times, according as the Stick is advanced or depressed. Sometimes the Emperor holds one End of the Stick, and his first Minister the other; sometimes the Minister has it entirely to himself. Whoever performs his Part with most Agility, and holds out the longest in *leaping* and *creeping*, is rewarded with the Blue-coloured Silk; the Red is given to the next, and the Green to the third, which they all wear girt twice round about the Middle; and you see few great Persons about this Court, who are not adorned with one of these Girdles.

The Horses of the Army, and those of the Royal Stables, having been daily led before me, were no longer shy, but would come up to my very Feet, without starting. The Riders would leap them over my Hand as I held it on the Ground; and one of the Emperor's Huntsmen, upon a large Courser, took my Foot, Shoe and all; which was in-

deed a prodigious Leap. I had the good Fortune to divert
the Emperor one Day, after a very extraordinary Manner.
I desired he would order several Sticks of two Foot high,
and the Thickness of an ordinary Cane, to be brought
me; whereupon his Majesty commanded the Master of
his Woods to give Directions accordingly; and the next
Morning six Wood-men arrived with as many Carriages,
drawn by eight Horses to each. I took nine of these Sticks,
and fixing them firmly in the Ground in a Quadrangular
Figure, two Foot and a half square; I took four other Sticks,
and tyed them parallel at each Corner, about two Foot
from the Ground; and then I fastened my Handkerchief
to the nine Sticks that stood erect; and extended it on
all Sides, till it was as tight as the Top of a Drum; and
the four parallel Sticks rising about five Inches higher than
the Handkerchief, served as Ledges on each Side. When
I had finished my Work, I desired the Emperor to let a
Troop of his best Horse, Twenty-four in Number, come
and exercise upon this Plain. His Majesty approved of the
Proposal, and I took them up one by one in my Hands,
ready mounted and armed, with the proper Officers to
exercise them. As soon as they got into Order, they
divided into two Parties, performed mock Skirmishes,
discharged blunt Arrows, drew their Swords, fled and pursued, attacked and retired; and in short discovered the
best military Discipline I ever beheld. The parallel Sticks
secured them and their Horses from falling over the Stage;
and the Emperor was so much delighted, that he ordered
this Entertainment to be repeated several Days; and once
was pleased to be lifted up, and give the Word of Command; and, with great Difficulty, persuaded even the
Empress her self to let me hold her in her close Chair,
within two Yards of the Stage, from whence she was able
to take a full View of the whole Performance. It was my
good Fortune that no ill Accident happened in these
Entertainments; only once a fiery Horse that belonged
to one of the Captains, pawing with his Hoof struck a
Hole in my Handkerchief, and his Foot slipping, he over-
threw his Rider and himself; but I immediately relieved

them both: For covering the Hole with one Hand, I set down the Troop with the other, in the same Manner as I took them up. The Horse that fell was strained in the left Shoulder, but the Rider got no Hurt, and I repaired my Handkerchief as well as I could: However, I would not trust to the Strength of it any more in such dangerous Enterprizes.

About two or three Days before I was set at Liberty, as I was entertaining the Court with these Kinds of Feats, there arrived an Express to inform his Majesty, that some of his Subjects riding near the Place where I was first taken up, had seen a great black Substance lying on the Ground, very oddly shaped, extending its Edges round as wide as his Majesty's Bedchamber, and rising up in the Middle as high as a Man. That it was no living Creature, as they at first apprehended; for it lay on the Grass without Motion, and some of them had walked round it several Times: That by mounting upon each others Shoulders, they had got to the Top, which was flat and even; and, stamping upon it, they found it was hollow within: That they humbly conceived it might be something belonging to the *Man-Mountain*; and if his Majesty pleased, they would undertake to bring it with only five Horses. I presently knew what they meant; and was glad at Heart to receive this Intelligence. It seems, upon my first reaching the Shore, after our Shipwreck, I was in such Confusion, that before I came to the Place where I went to sleep, my Hat, which I had fastened with a String to my Head while I was rowing, and had stuck on all the Time I was swimming, fell off after I came to Land; the String, as I conjecture, breaking by some Accident which I never observed, but thought my Hat had been lost at Sea. I intreated his Imperial Majesty to give Orders it might be brought to me as soon as possible, describing to him the Use and the Nature of it: And the next Day the Waggoners arrived with it, but not in a very good Condition; they had bored two Holes in the Brim, within an Inch and a half of the Edge, and fastened two Hooks in the Holes; these Hooks were tyed by a long Cord to the

Harness, and thus my Hat was dragged along for above half an *English* Mile: but the Ground in that Country being extremely smooth and level, it received less Damage than I expected.

Two Days after this Adventure, the Emperor having ordered that Part of his Army, which quarters in and about his Metropolis, to be in a Readiness, took a fancy of diverting himself in a very singular Manner. He desired I would stand like a *Colossus*, with my Legs as far asunder as I conveniently could. He then commanded his General (who was an old experienced Leader, and a great Patron of mine) to draw up the Troops in close Order, and march them under me; the Foot by Twenty-four in a Breast, and the Horse by Sixteen, with Drums beating, Colours flying, and Pikes advanced. This Body consisted of three Thousand Foot, and a Thousand Horse. His Majesty gave Orders, upon Pain of Death, that every Soldier in his March should observe the strictest Decency, with regard to my Person; which, however, could not prevent some of the younger Officers from turning up their Eyes as they passed under me. And, to confess the Truth, my Breeches were at that Time in so ill a Condition, that they afforded some Opportunities for Laughter and Admiration.

I had sent so many Memorials and Petitions for my Liberty, that his Majesty at length mentioned the Matter first in the Cabinet, and then in a full Council; where it was opposed by none, except *Skyresh Bolgolam*, who was pleased, without any Provocation, to be my mortal Enemy. But it was carried against him by the whole Board, and confirmed by the Emperor. That Minister was *Galbet*, or Admiral of the Realm; very much in his Master's Confidence, and a Person well versed in Affairs, but of a morose and sour Complection. However, he was at length persuaded to comply; but prevailed that the Articles and Conditions upon which I should be set free, and to which I must swear, should be drawn up by himself. These Articles were brought to me by *Skyresh Bolgolam* in Person, attended by two under Secretaries, and several Persons of Distinction. After they were read, I was demanded to swear to the Performance of them; first in the Manner of my own Country, and afterwards in the Method prescribed by their Laws; which was to hold my right Foot in my left Hand, to place the middle Finger of my right Hand on the Crown of my Head, and my Thumb on the Tip of my right Ear. But, because the Reader may perhaps be curious to have some Idea of the Style and Manner of Expression peculiar to that People, as well as to know the Articles upon which I recovered my Liberty; I have made a Translation of the whole Instrument, Word for Word, as near as I was able; which I here offer to the Publick.

Golbasto Momaren Evlame Gurdilo Shefin Mully Ully Gue, most Mighty Emperor of *Lilliput*, Delight and Terror of the Universe, whose Dominions extend five Thousand Blustrugs, (about twelve Miles in Circumference) to the Extremities of the Globe: Monarch of all Monarchs: Taller than the Sons of Men; whose Feet press down to the Center, and whose Head strikes against the Sun: At whose Nod the Princes of the Earth shake their Knees; pleasant as the Spring, comfortable as the Summer, fruitful as Autumn, dreadful as Winter. His most sublime Majesty proposeth to the *Man-Mountain*, lately arrived at our Celestial Dominions, the following Articles, which by a solemn Oath he shall be obliged to perform.

First, The *Man-Mountain* shall not depart from our Dominions, without our Licence under our Great Seal.

Secondly, He shall not presume to come into our Metropolis, without our express Order; at which time, the Inhabitants shall have two Hours Warning, to keep within their Doors.

Thirdly, The said *Man-Mountain* shall confine his Walks to our principal high Roads; and not offer to walk or lie down in a Meadow, or Field of Corn.

Fourthly, As he walks the said Roads, he shall take

the utmost Care not to trample upon the Bodies of any of our loving Subjects, their Horses, or Carriages; nor take any of our said Subjects into his Hands, without their own Consent.

Fifthly, If an Express require extraordinary Dispatch; the *Man-Mountain* shall be obliged to carry in his Pocket the Messenger and Horse, a six Days Journey once in every Moon, and return the said Messenger back (if so required) safe to our Imperial Presence.

Sixthly, He shall be our Ally against our Enemies in the Island of *Blefuscu*, and do his utmost to destroy their Fleet, which is now preparing to invade Us.

Seventhly, That the said *Man-Mountain* shall, at his Times of Leisure, be aiding and assisting to our Workmen, in helping to raise certain great Stones, towards covering the Wall of the principal Park, and other our Royal Buildings.

Eighthly, That the said *Man-Mountain* shall, in two Moons Time, deliver in an exact survey of the Circumference of our Dominions, by a Computation of his own Paces round the Coast.

Lastly, That upon his solemn Oath to observe all the above Articles, the said *Man-Mountain* shall have a daily Allowance of Meat and Drink, sufficient for the Support of 1728 of our Subjects; with free Access to our Royal Person, and other Marks of our Favour. Given at our Palace at *Belfaborac* the Twelfth Day of the Ninety-first Moon of our Reign.

I swore and subscribed to these Articles with great Chearfulness and Content, although some of them were not so honourable as I could have wished; which proceeded wholly from the Malice of *Skyresh Bolgolam* the High Admiral: Whereupon my Chains were immediately unlocked, and I was at full Liberty: The Emperor himself, in Person, did me the Honour to be by at the whole

Ceremony. I made my Acknowledgments, by prostrating myself at his Majesty's Feet: But he commanded me to rise; and after many gracious Expressions, which, to avoid the Censure of Vanity, I shall not repeat; he added, that he hoped I should prove a useful Servant, and well deserve all the Favours he had already conferred upon me, or might do for the future.

The Reader may please to observe, that in the last Article for the Recovery of my Liberty, the Emperor stipulates to allow me a Quantity of Meat and Drink, sufficient for the Support of 1728 *Lilliputians*. Some time after, asking a Friend at Court how they came to fix on that determinate Number; he told me, that his Majesty's Mathematicians, having taken the Height of my Body by the Help of a Quadrant, and finding it to exceed theirs in the Proportion of Twelve to One, they concluded from the Similarity of their Bodies, that mine must contain at least 1728 of theirs, and consequently would require as much Food as was necessary to support that Number of *Lilliputians*. By which, the Reader may conceive an Idea of the Ingenuity of that People, as well as the prudent and exact Oeconomy of so great a Prince.

CHAPTER FOUR

MILDENDO, THE METROPOLIS OF LILLIPUT, DESCRIBED, TO-
GETHER WITH THE EMPEROR'S PALACE. A CONVERSATION
BETWEEN THE AUTHOR AND A PRINCIPAL SECRETARY, CON-
CERNING THE AFFAIRS OF THAT EMPIRE. THE AUTHOR'S
OFFERS TO SERVE THE EMPEROR IN HIS WARS.

THE first Request I made after I had obtained my Liberty, was, that I might have Licence to see *Mildendo*, the Metropolis; which the Emperor easily granted me, but with a special Charge to do no Hurt, either to the Inhabitants, or their Houses. The People had Notice by Proclamation of my Design to visit the Town. The Wall which encompassed it, is two Foot and an half high, and at least eleven Inches broad, so that a Coach and Horses may be driven very safely round it; and it is flanked with strong Towers at ten Foot Distance. I stept over the great *Western* Gate, and passed very gently, and sideling through the two principal Streets, only in my short Waistcoat, for fear of damaging the Roofs and Eves of the Houses with the Skirts of my Coat. I walked with the utmost Circumspection, to avoid treading on any Stragglers, who might remain in the Streets, although the Orders were very strict, that all People should keep in their Houses, at their own Peril. The Garret Windows and Tops of Houses were so crowded with Spectators, that I thought in all my Travels I had not seen a more populous Place. The City is an exact Square, each Side of the Wall being five Hundred Foot long. The two great Streets which run cross and divide it into four Quarters, are five Foot wide. The Lanes and Alleys which I could not enter, but only viewed them as I passed, are from Twelve to Eighteen Inches. The Town is capable of holding five Hundred Thousand Souls. The Houses are from three to five Stories. The Shops and Markets well provided.

The Emperor's Palace is in the Center of the City, where the two great Streets meet. It is inclosed by a Wall of two Foot high, and Twenty Foot distant from the Buildings. I had his Majesty's Permission to step over this Wall; and the Space being so wide between that and the Palace, I could easily view it on every Side. The outward Court is a Square of Forty Foot, and includes two other Courts: In the inmost are the Royal Apartments, which I was very desirous to see, but found it extremely difficult; for the great Gates, from one Square into another, were but Eighteen Inches high, and seven Inches wide. Now the Buildings of the outer Court were at least five Foot high; and it was impossible for me to stride over them, without infinite Damage to the Pile, although the Walls were strongly built of hewn Stone, and four Inches thick. At the same time, the Emperor had a great Desire that I should see the Magnificence of his Palace: But this I was not able to do till three Days after, which I spent in cutting

down with my Knife some of the largest Trees in the
Royal Park, about an Hundred Yards distant from the
City. Of these Trees I made two Stools, each about
three Foot high, and strong enough to bear my Weight.
The People having received Notice a second time, I went
again through the City to the Palace, with my two Stools
in my Hands. When I came to the Side of the outer Court,
I stood upon one Stool, and took the other in my Hand:
This I lifted over the Roof, and gently set it down on
the Space between the first and second Court, which
was eight Foot wide. I then stept over the Buildings very
conveniently from one Stool to the other, and drew up
the first after me with a hooked Stick. By this Contrivance I got into the inmost Court; and lying down upon
my Side, I applied my Face to the Windows of the middle
Stories, which were left open on Purpose, and discovered
the most splendid Apartments that can be imagined.
There I saw the Empress, and the young Princes in their
several Lodgings, with their chief Attendants about them.
Her Imperial Majesty was pleased to smile very graciously
upon me and gave me out of the Window her Hand to
kiss.

But I shall not anticipate the Reader with farther Descriptions of this Kind, because I reserve them for a greater
Work, which is now almost ready for the Press; containing a general Description of this Empire, from its first
Erection, through a long Series of Princes, with a particular Account of their Wars and Politicks, Laws, Learning,
and Religion; their Plants and Animals, their peculiar
Manners and Customs, with other Matters very curious
and useful; my chief Design at present being only to
relate such Events and Transactions as happened to the
Publick, or to my self, during a Residence of about nine
Months in that Empire.

One Morning, about a Fortnight after I had obtained
my Liberty, *Reldresal*, Principal Secretary (as they style
him) of private Affairs, came to my House, attended only
by one Servant. He ordered his Coach to wait at a Distance, and desired I would give him an Hour's Audience;

which I readily consented to, on Account of his Quality, and Personal Merits, as well as of the many good Offices he had done me during my Sollicitations at Court. I offered to lie down, that he might the more conveniently reach my Ear; but he chose rather to let me hold him in my Hand during our Conversation. He began with Compliments on my Liberty; said, he might pretend to some Merit in it; but, however, added, that if it had not been for the present Situation of things at Court, perhaps I might not have obtained it so soon. For, *said he*, as flourishing a Condition as we appear to be in to Foreigners, we labour under two mighty Evils; a violent Faction at home, and the Danger of an Invasion by a most potent Enemy from abroad. As to the first, you are to understand, that for above seventy Moons past, there have been two struggling Parties in this Empire, under the Names of *Tramecksan*, and *Slamecksan*, from the high and low Heels on their Shoes, by which they distinguish themselves.

It is alledged indeed, that the high Heels are most agreeable to our ancient Constitution: But however this be, his Majesty hath determined to make use of only low Heels in the Administration of the Government, and all Offices in the Gift of the Crown; as you cannot but observe; and particularly, that his Majesty's Imperial Heels are lower at least by a *Drurr* than any of his Court; (*Drurr* is a Measure about the fourteenth Part of an Inch.) The Animosities between these two Parties run so high, that they will neither eat nor drink, nor talk with each other. We compute the *Tramecksan*, or High-Heels, to exceed us in Number; but the Power is wholly on our Side. We apprehend his Imperial Highness, the Heir to the Crown, to have some Tendency towards the High-Heels; at least we can plainly discover one of his Heels higher than the other; which gives him a Hobble in his Gait. Now, in the midst of these intestine Disquiets, we are threatened with an Invasion from the Island of *Blefuscu*, which is the other great Empire of the Universe, almost as large and powerful as this of his Majesty. For as to what we have heard you affirm, that there are other Kingdoms and States in the World, inhabited by human Creatures as large as your self, our Philosophers are in much Doubt; and would rather conjecture that you dropt from the Moon, or one of the Stars; because it is certain, that an hundred Mortals of your Bulk, would, in a short Time, destroy all the Fruits and Cattle of his Majesty's Dominions. Besides, our Histories of six Thousand Moons make no Mention of any other Regions, than the two great Empires of *Lilliput* and *Blefuscu.* Which two mighty Powers have, as I was going to tell you, been engaged in a most obstinate War for six and thirty Moons past. It began upon the following Occasion. It is allowed on all Hands, that the primitive Way of breaking Eggs before we eat them, was upon the larger End: But his present Majesty's Grand-father, while he was a Boy, going to eat an Egg, and breaking it according to the ancient Practice, happened to cut one of his Fingers. Whereupon the Emperor his Father, published an Edict, commanding all his Subjects, upon great Penalties, to break the smaller End of their Eggs. The People so highly resented this Law, that our Histories tell us, there have been six Rebellions raised on that Account; wherein one Emperor lost his Life, and another his Crown. These civil Commotions were constantly fomented by the Monarchs of *Blefuscu*; and when they were quelled, the Exiles always fled for Refuge to that Empire. It is computed, that eleven Thousand Persons have, at several Times, suffered Death, rather than submit to break their Eggs at the smaller End. Many hundred large Volumes have been published upon this Controversy: But the Books of the *Big-Endians* have been long forbidden, and the whole Party rendred incapable by Law of holding Employments. During the Course of these Troubles, the Emperors of *Blefuscu* did frequently expostulate by their Ambassadors, accusing us of making a Schism in Religion, by offending against a fundamental Doctrine of our great Prophet *Lustrog*, in the fifty-fourth Chapter of the *Brundrecal*, (which is their *Alcoran.*) This, however, is thought to be a meer Strain upon the Text: For the Words are these; *That all true Believers shall break their Eggs at the convenient*

Low heels in favour

HERBERT COLE '99

End: and which is the convenient End, seems, in my humble Opinion, to be left to every Man's Conscience, or at least in the Power of the chief Magistrate to determine. Now the *Big-Endian* Exiles have found so much Credit in the Emperor of *Blefuscu's* Court; and so much private Assistance and Encouragement from their Party here at home, that a bloody War hath been carried on between the two Empires for six and thirty Moons with various Success; during which Time we have lost Forty Capital Ships, and a much greater Number of smaller Vessels, together with thirty thousand of our best Seamen and Soldiers; and the Damage received by the Enemy is reckoned to be somewhat greater than ours. However, they have now equipped a numerous Fleet, and are just preparing to make a Descent upon us: And his Imperial Majesty, placing great Confidence in your Valour and Strength, hath commanded me to lay this Account of his affairs before you.

I desired the Secretary to present my humble Duty to the Emperor, and to let him know, that I thought it would not become me, who was a Foreigner, to interfere with Parties; but I was ready, with the Hazard of my Life, to defend his Person and State against all Invaders.

CHAPTER FIVE

THE AUTHOR BY AN EXTRAORDINARY STRATAGEM PREVENTS AN INVASION. A HIGH TITLE OF HONOUR IS CONFERRED UPON HIM. AMBASSADORS ARRIVE FROM THE EMPEROR OF BLEFUSCU, AND SUE FOR PEACE. THE EMPRESS'S APARTMENT ON FIRE BY AN ACCIDENT; THE AUTHOR INSTRUMENTAL IN SAVING THE REST OF THE PALACE.

THE Empire of *Blefuscu*, is an Island situated to the North North-East Side of *Lilliput*, from whence it is parted only by a Channel of eight Hundred Yards wide. I had not yet seen it, and upon this Notice of an intended Invasion, I avoided appearing on that Side of the Coast,

for fear of being discovered by some of the Enemies Ships,
who had received no Intelligence of me; all intercourse
between the two Empires having been strictly forbidden
during the War, upon Pain of Death; and an Embargo laid
by our Emperor upon all Vessels whatsoever. I communicated to his Majesty a Project I had formed of seizing the
Enemies whole Fleet; which, as our Scouts assured us,
lay at Anchor in the Harbour ready to sail with the first
fair Wind. I consulted the most experienced Seamen,
upon the Depth of the Channel, which they had often
plummed; who told me, that in the Middle at high Water
it was seventy *Glumgluffs* deep, which is about six Foot of
European Measure; and the rest of it fifty *Glumgluffs* at most.
I walked to the North-East Coast over against *Blefuscu*;
where, lying down behind a Hillock, I took out my small
Pocket Perspective Glass, and viewed the Enemy's Fleet
at Anchor, consisting of about fifty Men of War, and a
great Number of Transports: I then came back to my
House, and gave Order (for which I had a Warrant) for
a great Quantity of the strongest Cable and Bars of Iron.
The Cable was about as thick as Packthread, and the Bars
of the Length and Size of a Knitting-Needle. I trebled the
Cable to make it stronger; and for the same Reason I
twisted three of the Iron Bars together, binding the Extremities into a Hook. Having thus fixed fifty Hooks to as
many Cables, I went back to the North-East Coast, and
putting off my Coat, Shoes, and Stockings, walked into
the Sea in my Leathern Jerken, about half an Hour before high Water. I waded with what Haste I could, and
swam in the Middle about thirty Yards until I felt the
Ground; I arrived at the Fleet in less than half an Hour.
The Enemy was so frighted when they saw me, that they
leaped out of their Ships, and swam to Shore; where there
could not be fewer than thirty thousand Souls. I then took
my Tackling, and fastning a Hook to the Hole at the Prow
of each, I tyed all the Cords together at the End. While
I was thus employed, the Enemy discharged several Thousand Arrows, many of which stuck in my Hands and Face;
and besides the excessive Smart, gave me much Disturb-

ance in my Work. My greatest Apprehension was for my
Eyes, which I should have infallibly lost, if I had not suddenly thought of an Expedient. I kept, among other little
Necessaries, a Pair of Spectacles in a private Pocket, which,
as I observed before, had escaped the Emperor's Searchers.
These I took out, and fastened as strongly as I could upon
my Nose; and thus armed went on boldly with my Work
in spight of the Enemy's Arrows; many of which struck
against the Glasses of my Spectacles, but without any
other Effect, further than a little to discompose them.
I had now fastened all the Hooks, and taking the Knot
in my Hand, began to pull; but not a Ship would stir, for
they were all too fast held by their Anchors; so that the
boldest Part of my Enterprize remained. I therefore let
go the Cord, and leaving the Hooks fixed to the Ships,
I resolutely cut with my Knife the Cables that fastened
the Anchors; receiving above two hundred Shots in my
Face and Hands: Then I took up the knotted End of the
Cables to which my Hooks were tyed; and with great
Ease drew fifty of the Enemy's largest Men of War after
me.

The *Blefuscudians*, who had not the least Imagination of
what I intended, were at first confounded with Astonishment. They had seen me cut the Cables, and thought
my Design was only to let the Ships run a-drift, or fall
foul on each other: But when they perceived the whole
Fleet moving in Order, and saw me pulling at the End;
they set up such a Scream of Grief and Dispair, that it is
almost impossible to describe or conceive. When I had
got out of Danger, I stopt a while to pick out the Arrows
that stuck in my Hands and Face, and rubbed on some
of the same Ointment that was given me at my first
Arrival, as I have formerly mentioned. I then took off my
Spectacles, and waiting about an Hour until the Tyde
was a little fallen, I waded through the Middle with my
Cargo, and arrived safe at the Royal Port of *Lilliput*.

The Emperor and his whole Court stood on the Shore,
expecting the Issue of this great Adventure. They saw the
Ships move forward in a large Half-Moon, but could not

discern me, who was up to my Breast in Water. When I advanced to the Middle of the Channel, they were yet more in Pain because I was under Water to my Neck. The Emperor concluded me to be drowned, and that the Enemy's Fleet was approaching in a hostile Manner: But he was soon eased of his Fears; for the Channel growing shallower every Step I made, I came in a short Time within Hearing; and holding up the End of the Cable by which the Fleet was fastened, I cryed in a loud Voice, *Long live the most puissant Emperor of Lilliput!* This great Prince received me at my Landing with all possible Encomiums, and created me a *Nardac* upon the Spot, which is the highest Title of Honour among them.

His Majesty desired I would take some other Opportunity of bringing all the rest of his Enemy's Ships into his Ports. And so unmeasurable is the Ambition of Princes, that he seemed to think of nothing less than reducing the whole Empire of *Blefuscu* into a Province, and governing it by a Viceroy; of destroying the *Big-Endian* Exiles, and compelling that People to break the smaller End of their Eggs; by which he would remain sole Monarch of the whole World. But I endeavoured to divert him from this Design, by many Arguments drawn from the Topicks of Policy as well as Justice: And I plainly protested, that I would never be an Instrument of bringing a free and brave People into Slavery: And when the Matter was debated in Council, the wisest Part of the Ministry were of my Opinion.

This open bold Declaration of mine was so opposite to the Schemes and Politicks of his Imperial Majesty, that he could never forgive me: He mentioned it in a very artful Manner at Council, where, I was told, that some of the wisest appeared, at least by their Silence, to be of my Opinion; but others, who were my secret Enemies, could not forbear some Expressions, which by a Side-wind reflected on me. And from this Time began an Intrigue between his Majesty, and a Junta of Ministers maliciously bent against me, which broke out in less than two Months, and had like to have ended in my utter Destruction. Of so little Weight are the greatest Services to Princes, when put into the Balance with a Refusal to gratify their Passions.

About three Weeks after this Exploit, there arrived a solemn Embassy from *Blefuscu*, with humble Offers of a Peace; which was soon concluded upon Conditions very advantageous to our Emperor; wherewith I shall not trouble the Reader. There were six Ambassadors, with a Train of about five Hundred Persons; and their Entry was very magnificent, suitable to the Grandeur of their Master, and the Importance of their Business. When their Treaty was finished, wherein I did them several good Offices by the Credit I now had, or at least appeared to have at Court; their Excellencies, who were privately told how much I had been their Friend, made me a Visit in Form. They began with many Compliments upon my Valour and Generosity; invited me to that Kingdom in the Emperor their Master's Name; and desired me to shew them some Proofs of my prodigious Strength, of which they had heard so many Wonders; wherein I readily obliged them, but shall not interrupt the Reader with the Particulars.

When I had for some time entertained their Excellencies to their infinite Satisfaction and Surprize, I desired they would do me the Honour to present my most humble Respects to the Emperor their Master, the Renown of whose Virtues had so justly filled the whole World with Admiration, and whose Royal Person I resolved to attend before I returned to my own Country. Accordingly, the next time I had the Honour to see our Emperor, I desired his general Licence to wait on the *Blefuscudian* Monarch, which he was pleased to grant me, as I could plainly perceive, in a very cold Manner; but could not guess the Reason, till I had a Whisper from a certain Person, that *Flimnap* and *Bolgolam* had represented my Intercourse with those Ambassadors, as a Mark of Disaffection, from which I am sure my Heart was wholly free. And this was the first time I began to conceive some imperfect Idea of Courts and Ministers.

It is to be observed, that these Ambassadors spoke to

me by an Interpreter; the Languages of both Empires differing as much from each other as any two in *Europe*, and each Nation priding itself upon the Antiquity, Beauty, and Energy of their own Tongues, with an avowed Contempt for that of their Neighbour: Yet our Emperor standing upon the Advantage he had got by the Seizure of their Fleet, obliged them to deliver their Credentials, and make their Speech in the *Lilliputian* Tongue. And it must be confessed, that from the great Intercourse of Trade and Commerce between both Realms; from the continual Reception of Exiles, which is mutual among them; and from the Custom in each Empire to send their young Nobility and richer Gentry to the other, in order to polish themselves, by seeing the World, and understanding Men and Manners; there are few Persons of Distinction, or Merchants, or Seamen, who dwell in the Maritime Parts, but what can hold Conversation in both Tongues; as I found some Weeks after, when I went to pay my Respects to the Emperor of *Blefuscu*, which in the Midst of great Misfortunes, through the Malice of my Enemies, proved a very happy Adventure to me, as I shall relate in its proper Place.

The Reader may remember, that when I signed those Articles upon which I recovered my Liberty, there were some which I disliked upon Account of their being too servile, neither could any thing but an extreme Necessity have forced me to submit. But being now a *Nardac*, of the highest Rank in that Empire, such Offices were looked upon as below my Dignity; and the Emperor (to do him Justice) never once mentioned them to me. However, it was not long before I had an Opportunity of doing his Majesty, at least, as I then thought, a most signal Service. I was alarmed at Midnight with the Cries of many Hundred People at my Door; by which being suddenly awaked, I was in some Kind of Terror. I heard the Word *Burglum* repeated incessantly; several of the Emperor's Court making their Way through the Croud, intreated me to come immediately to the Palace, where her Imperial Majesty's Apartment was on fire, by the Carelessness of a

Maid of Honour, who fell asleep while she was reading a Romance. I got up in an Instant; and Orders being given to clear the Way before me; and it being likewise a Moonshine Night, I made a shift to get to the Palace without trampling on any of the People. I found they had already applied Ladders to the Walls of the Apartment, and were well provided with Buckets, but the Water was at some Distance. These Buckets were about the Size of a large Thimble, and the poor People supplied me with them as fast as they could; but the Flame was so violent, that they did little Good. I might easily have stifled it with my Coat, which I unfortunately left behind me for haste, and came away only in my Leathern Jerkin. The Case seemed wholly desperate and deplorable; and this magnificent Palace would have infallibly been burnt down to the Ground, if, by a Presence of Mind, unusual to me, I had not suddenly thought of an Expedient. I had the Evening before drank plentifully of a most delicious Wine, called *Glimigrim*, (the *Blefuscudians* call it *Flunec*, but ours is esteemed the better Sort) which is very diuretick. By the luckiest Chance in the World, I had not discharged myself of any Part of it. The Heat I had contracted by coming very near the Flames, and by my labouring to quench them, made the Wine begin to operate by Urine; which I voided in such a Quantity, and applied so well to the proper Places, that in three Minutes the Fire was wholly extinguished; and the rest of that noble Pile, which had cost so many Ages in erecting, preserved from Destruction.

It was now Day-light, and I returned to my House, without waiting to congratulate with the Emperor; because, although I had done a very eminent Piece of Service, yet I could not tell how his Majesty might resent the Manner by which I had performed it: For, by the fundamental Laws of the Realm, it is Capital in any Person, of what Quality soever, to make water within the Precincts of the Palace. But I was a little comforted by a Message from his Majesty, that he would give Orders to the Grand Justiciary for passing my Pardon in Form; which, however, I could not obtain. And I was privately assured, that

the Empress conceiving the greatest Abhorrence of what
I had done, removed to the most distant Side of the Court,
firmly resolved that those Buildings should never be repaired
for her Use; and, in the Presence of her chief Confidents,
could not forbear vowing Revenge.

CHAPTER SIX

OF THE INHABITANTS OF LILLIPUT; THEIR LEARNING,
LAWS, AND CUSTOMS. THE MANNER OF EDUCATING THEIR
CHILDREN. THE AUTHOR'S WAY OF LIVING IN THAT
COUNTRY. HIS VINDICATION OF A GREAT LADY.

ALTHOUGH I intend to leave the Description of this
Empire to a particular Treatise, yet in the mean time
I am content to gratify the curious Reader with some general Ideas. As the common Size of the Natives is somewhat under six Inches, so there is an exact Proportion in
all other Animals, as well as Plants and Trees: For Instance, the tallest Horses and Oxen are between four and
five Inches in Height, the Sheep an Inch and a half, more
or less; their Geese about the Bigness of a Sparrow; and
so the several Gradations downwards, till you come to the
smallest, which, to my Sight, were almost invisible; but
Nature hath adapted the Eyes of the *Lilliputians* to all Objects proper for their View: They see with great Exactness,
but at no great Distance. And to show the Sharpness of
their Sight towards Objects that are near, I have been
much pleased with observing a Cook pulling a Lark,
which was not so large as a common Fly; and a young
Girl threading an invisible Needle with invisible Silk.
Their tallest Trees are about seven Foot high; I mean
some of those in the great Royal Park, the Tops whereof
I could but just reach with my Fist clinched. The other
Vegetables are in the same Proportion: But this I leave
to the Reader's Imagination.

I shall say but little at present of their Learning, which
for many Ages hath flourished in all its Branches among

them: But their Manner of Writing is very peculiar; being neither from the Left to the Right, like the *Europeans*; nor from the Right to the Left, like the *Arabians*; nor from up to down, like the *Chinese*; nor from down to up, like the *Cascagians*; but aslant from one Corner of the Paper to the other, like Ladies in *England*.

They bury their Dead with their Heads directly downwards; because they hold an Opinion, that in eleven Thousand Moons they are all to rise again; in which Period, the Earth (which they conceive to be flat) will turn upside down, and by this Means they shall, at their Resurrection, be found ready standing on their Feet. The Learned among them confess the Absurdity of this Doctrine; but the Practice still continues, in Compliance to the Vulgar.

There are some Laws and Customs in this Empire very peculiar; and if they were not so directly contrary to those of my own dear Country, I should be tempted to say a little in their Justification. It is only to be wished, that they were as well executed. The first I shall mention, relateth to Informers. All Crimes against the State, are punished here with the utmost Severity; but if the Person accused make his Innocence plainly to appear upon his Tryal, the Accuser is immediately put to an ignominious Death; and out of his Goods or Lands, the innocent Person is quadruply recompensed for the Loss of his Time, for the Danger he underwent, for the Hardship of his Imprisonment, and for all the Charges he hath been at in making his Defence. Or, if that Fund be deficient, it is largely supplyed by the Crown. The Emperor doth also confer on him some publick Mark of his Favour; and Proclamation is made of his Innocence through the wholly City.

They look upon Fraud as a greater Crime than Theft, and therefore seldom fail to punish it with Death: For they alledge, that Care and Vigilance, with a very common Understanding, may preserve a Man's Goods from Thieves; but Honesty hath no Fence against superior Cunning: And since it is necessary that there should be a perpetual Intercourse of buying and selling, and dealing upon Credit; where Fraud is permitted or connived at, or hath no Law to punish it, the honest Dealer is always undone, and the Knave gets the Advantage. I remember when I was once interceeding with the King for a Criminal who had wronged his Master of a great Sum of Money, which he had received by Order, and ran away with; and happening to tell his Majesty, by way of Extenuation, that it was only a Breach of Trust; the Emperor thought it monstrous in me to offer, as a Defence, the greatest Aggravation of the Crime: And truly, I had little to say in Return, farther than the common Answer, that different Nations had different Customs; for, I confess, I was heartily ashamed.

Although we usually call Reward and Punishment, the two Hinges upon which all Government turns; yet I could never observe this Maxim to be put in Practice by any Nation except that of *Lilliput*. Whoever can there bring sufficient Proof that he hath strictly observed the Laws of his Country for Seventy-three Moons, hath a Claim to certain Privileges, according to his Quality and Condition of Life, with a proportionable Sum of Money out of a Fund appropriated for that Use: He likewise acquires the Title of *Snilpall*, or *Legal*, which is added to his Name, but doth not descend to his Posterity. And these People thought it a prodigious Defect of Policy among us, when I told them that our Laws were enforced only by Penalties, without any Mention of Reward. It is upon this account that the Image of Justice, in their Courts of Judicature, is formed with six Eyes, two before, as many behind, and on each Side one, to signify Circumspection; with a Bag of Gold open in her right Hand, and a Sword sheathed in her left, to shew she is more disposed to reward than to punish.

In chusing Persons for all Employments, they have more Regard to good Morals than to great Abilities: For, since Government is necessary to Mankind, they believe that the common Size of human Understandings, is fitted to some Station or other; and that Providence never intended to make the Management of publick Affairs a Mystery, to be comprehended only by a few Persons of sublime Genius, of which there seldom are three born in an Age: But, they suppose Truth, Justice, Temperance, and the like, to be in every Man's Power; the Practice of which Virtues, assisted by Experience and a good Intention, would qualify any Man for the Service of his Country, except where a Course of Study is required. But they thought the Want of Moral Virtues was so far from being supplied by superior Endowments of the Mind, that Employments could never be put into such dangerous Hands as those of Persons so qualified; and at least, that the Mistakes committed by Ignorance in a virtuous Disposition, would never be of such fatal Consequence to the Publick Weal, as the Practices of a Man, whose Inclinations led him to be corrupt, and had great Abilities to manage, to multiply, and defend his Corruptions.

In like Manner, the Disbelief of a Divine Providence renders a Man uncapable of holding any publick Station: For, since Kings avow themselves to be the Deputies of Providence, the *Lilliputians* think nothing can be more absurd than for a Prince to employ such Men as disown the Authority under which he acteth.

In relating these and the following Laws, I would only be understood to mean the original Institutions, and not the most scandalous Corruptions into which these People are fallen by the degenerate Nature of Man. For as to that infamous Practice of acquiring great Employments by dancing on the Ropes, or Badges of Favour and Distinction by leaping over Sticks, and creeping under them; the Reader is to observe, that they were first introduced by the Grandfather of the Emperor now reigning; and grew to the present Height, by the gradual Increase of Party and Faction.

Ingratitude is among them a capital Crime, as we read it to have been in some other Countries: For they reason thus; that whoever makes ill Returns to his Benefactor, must needs be a common Enemy to the rest of Mankind, from whom they have received no Obligation; and therefore such a Man is not fit to live.

Their Notions relating to the Duties of Parents and Children differ extremely from ours. For, since the Conjunction of Male and Female is founded upon the great Law of Nature, in order to propagate and continue the Species; the *Lilliputians* will needs have it, that Men and Women are joined together like other Animals, by the Motives of Concupiscence; and that their Tenderness towards their Young, proceedeth from the like natural Principle: For which Reason they will never allow, that a Child is under any Obligation to his Father for begetting him, or to his Mother for bringing him into the World; which, considering the Miseries of human Life, was neither a Benefit in itself, nor intended so by his Parents, whose Thoughts in their Love-encounters were otherwise employed. Upon these, and the like Reasonings, their Opinion is, that Parents are the last of all others to be trusted with the Education of their own Children: And therefore they have in every Town publick Nurseries, where all Parents, except Cottagers and Labourers, are obliged to send their Infants of both Sexes to be reared and educated when they come to the Age of twenty Moons; at which Time they are supposed to have some Rudiments of Docility. These Schools are of several Kinds, suited to different Qualities, and to both Sexes. They have certain Professors well skilled in preparing Children for such a Condition of Life as befits the Rank of their Parents, and their own Capacities as well as Inclinations. I shall first say something of the Male Nurseries, and then of the Female.

The Nurseries for Males of Noble or Eminent Birth, are provided with grave and learned Professors, and their several Deputies. The Clothes and Food of the Children are plain and simple. They are bred up in the Principles of Honour, Justice, Courage, Modesty, Clemency, Religion, and Love of their Country: They are always employed in some Business, except in the Times of eating and sleeping, which are very short, and two Hours for Diversions, consisting of bodily Exercises. They are dressed by Men until four Years of Age, and then are obliged to dress themselves, although their Quality be ever so great; and the Women Attendants, who are aged proportionably to ours at fifty, perform only the most menial Offices. They are never suffered to converse with Servants, but go together in small or greater Numbers to take their Diversions, and always in the Presence of a Professor, or one of his Deputies; whereby they avoid those early bad Impressions of Folly and Vice to which our Children are subject. Their Parents are suffered to see them only twice a Year; the Visit is not to last above an Hour; they are allowed to kiss the Child at Meeting and Parting; but a Professor, who always standeth by on those Occasions, will not suffer them to whisper, or use any fondling Expressions, or bring any Presents of Toys, Sweet-meats, and the like.

The Pension from each Family for the Education and Entertainment of a Child, upon Failure of due Payment, is levyed by the Emperor's Officers.

The Nurseries for Children of ordinary Gentlemen, Merchants, Traders, and Handicrafts, are managed proportionably after the same Manner; only those designed for Trades, are put out Apprentices at seven Years old; whereas those of Persons of Quality continue in their Exercises until Fifteen, which answers to One and Twenty with us: But the Confinement is gradually lessened for the last three Years.

In the Female Nurseries, the young Girls of Quality are educated much like the Males, only they are dressed by orderly Servants of their own Sex, but always in the Presence of a Professor or Deputy, until they come to dress themselves, which is at five Years old. And if it be found that these Nurses ever presume to entertain the Girls with frightful or foolish Stories, or the common Follies practised by Chamber-Maids among us; they are publickly whipped thrice about the City, imprisoned for a Year, and banished for Life to the most desolate Parts of the Country. Thus the young Ladies there are as much ashamed of being Cowards and Fools, as the Men; and despise all personal Ornaments beyond Decency and

Cleanliness; neither did I perceive any Difference in
their Education, made by their Difference of Sex, only
that the Exercises of the Females were not altogether so
robust; and that some Rules were given them relating
to domestick Life, and a smaller Compass of Learning
was enjoyned them: For, their Maxim is, that among
People of Quality, a Wife should be always a reasonable
and agreeable Companion, because she cannot always be
young. When the Girls are twelve Years old, which among
them is the marriageable Age, their Parents or Guardians
take them home, with great Expressions of Gratitude to
the Professors, and seldom without Tears of the young
Lady and her Companions.

In the Nurseries of Females of the meaner Sort, the Children are instructed in all Kinds of Works proper for their
Sex, and their several Degrees: Those intended for Apprentices are dismissed at seven Years old, the rest are kept to
eleven.

The meaner Families who have Children at these Nurseries, are obliged, besides their annual Pension, which is
as low as possible, to return to the Steward of the Nursery
a small Monthly Share of their Gettings, to be a Portion
for the Child; and therefore all Parents are limited in
their Expences by the Law. For the *Lilliputians* think
nothing can be more unjust, than that People, in Sub-
servience to their own Appetites, should bring Children
into the World, and leave the Burthen of supporting
them on the Publick. As to Persons of Quality, they
give Security to appropriate a certain Sum for each
Child, suitable to their Condition; and these Funds are
always managed with good Husbandry, and the most exact
Justice.

The Cottagers and Labourers keep their Children at
home, their Business being only to till and cultivate the
Earth; and therefore their Education is of little Consequence to the Publick; but the Old and Diseased among
them are supported by Hospitals: For begging is a Trade
unknown in this Empire.

And here it may perhaps divert the curious Reader, to

give some Account of my Domestick, and my Manner of living in this Country, during a Residence of nine Months and thirteen Days. Having a Head mechanically turned, and being likewise forced by Necessity, I had made for myself a Table and Chair convenient enough, out of the largest Trees in the Royal Park. Two hundred Sempstresses were employed to make me Shirts, and Linnen for my Bed and Table, all of the strongest and coarsest kind they could get; which, however, they were forced to quilt together in several Folds; for the thickest was some Degrees finer than Lawn. Their Linnen is usually three Inches wide, and three Foot make a Piece. The Sempstresses took my Measure as I lay on the Ground, one standing at my Neck, and another at my Mid-Leg, with a strong Cord extended, that each held by the End, while the third measured the Length of the Cord with a Rule of an Inch long. Then they measured my right Thumb, and desired no more; for by a mathematical Computation, that twice round the Thumb is once round the Wrist, and so on to the Neck and the Waist; and by the Help of my old Shirt, which I displayed on the Ground before them for a Pattern, they fitted me exactly. Three hundred Taylors were employed in the same Manner to make me Clothes; but they had another Contrivance for taking my Measure. I kneeled down, and they raised a Ladder from the Ground to my Neck; upon this Ladder one of them mounted, and let fall a Plum-Line from my Collar to the Floor, which just answered the Length of my Coat; but my Waist and Arms I measured myself. When my Cloaths were finished, which was done in my House, (for the largest of theirs would not have been able to hold them) they looked like the Patch-work made by the Ladies in *England*, only that mine were all of a Colour.

I had three hundred Cooks to dress my Victuals, in little convenient Huts built about my House, where they and their Families lived, and prepared me two Dishes a-piece. I took up twenty Waiters in my Hand, and placed them on the Table; an hundred more attended below on the Ground, some with Dishes of Meat, and some with Bar-

rels of Wine, and other Liquors, slung on their Shoulders;
all which the Waiters above drew up as I wanted, in a
very ingenious Manner, by certain Cords, as we draw
the Bucket up a Well in *Europe*. A Dish of their Meat was
a good Mouthful, and a Barrel of their Liquor a reasonable Draught. Their Mutton yields to ours, but their
Beef is excellent. I have had a Sirloin so large, that
I have been forced to make three Bits of it; but this is
rare. My Servants were astonished to see me eat it Bones
and all, as in our Country we do the Leg of a Lark.
Their Geese and Turkeys I usually eat at a Mouthful,
and I must confess they far exceed ours. Of their smaller
Fowl I could take up twenty or thirty at the End of my
Knife.

One day his Imperial Majesty being informed of my
Way of living, desired that himself, and his Royal Consort,
with the young Princes of the Blood of both Sexes, might
have the Happiness (as he was pleased to call it) of dining
with me. They came accordingly, and I placed them upon
Chairs of State on my Table, just over against me, with
their Guards about them. *Flimnap* the Lord High Treasurer attended there likewise, with his white Staff; and I
observed he often looked on me with a sour Countenance,
which I would not seem to regard, but eat more than
usual, in Honour to my dear Country, as well as to fill
the Court with Admiration. I have some private Reasons
to believe, that this Visit from his Majesty gave *Flimnap*
an Opportunity of doing me ill Offices to his Master. That
Minister had always been my secret Enemy, although he
outwardly caressed me more than was usual to the Morose-
ness of his Nature. He represented to the Emperor the
low Condition of his Treasury; that he was forced to
take up Money at great Discount; that Exchequer Bills
would not circulate under nine *per Cent.* below Par; that
I had cost his Majesty about a Million and a half of
Sprugs, (their greatest Gold Coin, about the Bigness of a
Spangle;) and upon the whole, that it would be advise-
able in the Emperor to take the first fair Occasion of dismissing me.

I am here obliged to vindicate the Reputation of an excellent Lady, who was an innocent Sufferer upon my Account. The Treasurer took a Fancy to be jealous of his Wife, from the Malice of some evil Tongues, who informed him that her Grace had taken a violent Affection for my Person; and the Court-Scandal ran for some Time that she once came privately to my Lodging. This I solemnly declare to be a most infamous Falshood, without any Grounds, farther than that her Grace was pleased to treat me with all innocent Marks of Freedom and Friendship. I own she came often to my House, but always publickly, nor ever without three more in the Coach, who were usually her Sister, and young Daughter, and some particular Acquaintance; but this was common to many other Ladies of the Court. And I still appeal to my Servants round, whether they at any Time saw a Coach at my Door without knowing what Persons were in it. On those Occasions, when a Servant had given me Notice, my Custom was to go immediately to the Door; and after paying my Respects, to take up the Coach and two Horses very carefully in my Hands, (for if there were six Horses, the Postillion always unharnessed four) and place them on a Table, where I had fixed a moveable Rim quite round, of five Inches high, to prevent Accidents. And I have often had four Coaches and Horses at once on my Table full of Company, while I sat in my Chair leaning my Face towards them; and when I was engaged with one Sett, the Coachmen would gently drive the others round my Table. I have passed many an Afternoon very agreeably in these Conversations: But I defy the Treasurer, or his two Informers, (I will name them, and let them make their best of it) *Clustril* and *Drunlo*, to prove that any Person ever came to me *incognito*, except the Secretary *Reldresal*, who was sent by express Command of his Imperial Majesty, as I have before related. I should not have dwelt so long upon this Particular, if it had not been a Point wherein the Reputation of a great Lady is so nearly concerned; to say nothing of my own; although I had the Honour to be a *Nardac*, which the Treasurer himself is not; for all the World knows he is only a *Clumglum*, a Title inferior by one Degree, as that of a Marquess is to a Duke in *England*; yet I allow he preceded me in right of his Post. These false Informations, which I afterwards came to the Knowledge of, by an Accident not proper to mention, made the Treasurer shew his Lady for some Time an ill Countenance, and me a worse: For although he were at last undeceived and reconciled to her, yet I lost all Credit with him; and found my Interest decline very fast with the Emperor himself, who was indeed too much governed by that Favourite.

CHAPTER SEVEN

THE AUTHOR BEING INFORMED OF A DESIGN TO ACCUSE HIM OF HIGH TREASON, MAKES HIS ESCAPE TO BLEFUSCU. HIS RECEPTION THERE.

BEFORE I proceed to give an Account of my leaving this Kingdom, it may be proper to inform the Reader of a private Intrigue which had been for two Months forming against me.

I had been hitherto all my Life a Stranger to Courts, for which I was unqualified by the Meanness of my Condition. I had indeed heard and read enough of the Dispositions of great Princes and Ministers; but never expected to have found such terrible Effects of them in so remote a Country, governed, as I thought, by very different Maxims from those in *Europe*.

When I was just preparing to pay my Attendance on the Emperor of *Blefuscu*; a considerable Person at Court (to whom I had been very serviceable at a time when he lay under the highest Displeasure of his Imperial Majesty) came to my House very privately at Night in a close Chair, and without sending his Name, desired Admittance: The Chair-men were dismissed; I put the Chair, with his Lordship in it, into my Coat-Pocket; and giving Orders to a trusty Servant to say I was indisposed and gone to sleep, I fastened the Door of my House, placed the Chair on the Table, according to my usual Custom, and sat down by it.

After the common Salutations were over, observing his Lordship's Countenance full of Concern; and enquiring into the Reason, he desired I would hear him with Patience, in a Matter that highly concerned my Honour and my Life. His Speech was to the following Effect, for I took Notes of it as soon as he left me.

You are to know, said he, that several Committees of Council have been lately called in the most private Manner on your Account: And it is but two Days since his Majesty came to a full Resolution.

You are very sensible that *Skyris Bolgolam* (*Galbet*, or High Admiral) hath been your mortal Enemy almost ever since your Arrival. His original Reasons I know not; but his Hatred is much increased since your great Success against *Blefuscu*, by which his Glory, as Admiral, is obscured. This Lord, in Conjunction with *Flimnap* the High Treasurer, whose Enmity against you is notorious on Account of his Lady; *Limtoc* the General, *Lalcon* the Chamberlain, and *Balmuff* the grand Justiciary, have prepared Articles of Impeachment against you, for Treason, and other capital Crimes.

This Preface made me so impatient, being conscious of my own Merits and Innocence, that I was going to interrupt; when he intreated me to be silent; and thus proceeded.

Out of Gratitude for the Favours you have done me, I procured Information of the whole Proceedings, and a Copy of the Articles, wherein I venture my Head for your Service.

Articles of Impeachment against Quinbus Flestrin,

(*the* Man-Mountain).

ARTICLE 1

WHEREAS, by a Statute made in the Reign of his Imperial Majesty *Calin Deffar Plune*, it is enacted, That whoever shall make water within the Precincts of the

Royal Palace, shall be liable to the Pains and Penalties of High Treason: Notwithstanding, the said *Quinbus Flestrin*, in open Breach of the said Law, under Colour of extinguishing the Fire kindled in the Apartment of his Majesty's most dear Imperial Consort, did maliciously, traitorously, and devilishly, by discharge of his Urine, put out the said Fire kindled in the said Apartment, lying and being within the Precincts of the said Royal Palace; against the Statute in that Case provided, &c. against the Duty, &c.

ARTICLE 2

That the said *Quinbus Flestrin* having brought the Imperial Fleet of *Blefuscu* into the Royal Port, and being afterwards commanded by his Imperial Majesty to seize all the other Ships of the said Empire of *Blefuscu*, and reduce that Empire to a Province, to be governed by a Vice-Roy from hence; and to destroy and put to death not only all the *Big-Endian Exiles*, but likewise all the People of that Empire, who would not immediately forsake the *Big-Endian* Heresy: He the said *Flestrin*, like a false Traitor against his most Auspicious, Serene, Imperial Majesty, did petition to be excused from the said Service, upon Pretence of Unwillingness to force the Consciences, or destroy the Liberties and Lives of an innocent People.

ARTICLE 3

That, whereas certain Embassadors arrived from the Court of *Blefuscu* to sue for Peace in his Majesty's Court:

He the said *Flestrin* did, like a false Traitor, aid, abet, comfort, and divert the said Embassadors; although he knew them to be Servants to a Prince who was lately an open Enemy to his Imperial Majesty, and in open War against his said Majesty.

ARTICLE 4

That the said *Quinbus Flestrin*, contrary to the Duty of a faithful Subject, is now preparing to make a Voyage to the Court and Empire of *Blefuscu*, for which he hath received only verbal Licence from his Imperial Majesty; and under Colour of the said Licence, doth falsly and traitorously intend to take the said Voyage, and thereby to aid, comfort, and abet the Emperor of *Blefuscu*, so late an Enemy, and in open War with his Imperial Majesty aforesaid.

There are some other Articles, but these are the most important, of which I have read you an Abstract.

In the several Debates upon this Impeachment, it must be confessed that his Majesty gave many Marks of his great *Lenity*; often urging the Services you had done him, and endeavouring to extenuate your Crimes. The Treasurer and Admiral insisted that you should be put to the most painful and ignominious Death, by setting Fire on your House at Night; and the General was to attend with Twenty Thousand Men armed with poisoned Arrows, to shoot you on the Face and Hands. Some of your Servants were to have private Orders to strew a poisonous Juice on your Shirts and Sheets, which would soon make you tear your own Flesh, and die in the utmost Torture. The General came into the same Opinion; so that for a long time there was a Majority against you. But his Majesty resolving, if possible, to spare your Life, at last brought off the Chamberlain.

Upon this Incident, *Reldresal*, principal Secretary for private Affairs, who always approved himself your true Friend, was commanded by the Emperor to deliver his Opinion, which he accordingly did; and therein justified the good Thoughts you have of him. He allowed your Crimes to be great; but that still there was room for Mercy, the most commendable Virtue in a Prince, and for which his Majesty was so justly celebrated. He said, the Friendship between you and him was so well known to the World, that perhaps the most honourable Board might think him partial: However, in Obedience to the Command he had received, he would freely offer his Sentiments. That if his Majesty, in Consideration of your

Services, and pursuant to his own merciful Disposition, would please to spare your Life, and only give order to put out both your Eyes; he humbly conceived, that by this Expedient, Justice might in some measure be satisfied, and all the World would applaud the *Lenity* of the Emperor, as well as the fair and generous Proceedings of those who have the Honour to be his Counsellors. That the Loss of your Eyes would be no Impediment to your bodily Strength, by which you might still be useful to his Majesty. That Blindness is an Addition to Courage, by concealing Dangers from us; that the Fear you had for your Eyes, was the greatest Difficulty in bringing over the Enemy's Fleet; and it would be sufficient for you to see by the Eyes of the Ministers, since the greatest Princes do no more.

This Proposal was received with the utmost Disapprobation by the whole Board. *Bolgolam*, the Admiral, could not preserve his Temper; but rising up in Fury, said, he wondered how the Secretary durst presume to give his Opinion for preserving the Life of a Traytor: That the Services you had performed, were, by all true Reasons of State, the great Aggravation of your Crimes; that you, who were able to extinguish the Fire, by discharge of Urine in her Majesty's Apartment (which he mentioned with Horror) might, at another time, raise an Inundation by the same Means, to drown the whole Palace; and the same Strength which enabled you to bring over the Enemy's Fleet, might serve, upon the first Discontent, to carry it back; That he had good Reasons to think you were a *Big-Endian* in your Heart; and as Treason begins in the Heart before it appears in Overt-Acts; so he accused you as a Traytor on that Account, and therefore insisted you should be put to death.

The Treasurer was of the same Opinion; he shewed to what Streights his Majesty's Revenue was reduced by the Charge of maintaining you, which would soon grow insupportable: That the Secretary's Expedient of putting out your Eyes, was so far from being a Remedy against this Evil, that it would probably increase it; as it is

manifest from the common Practice of blinding some
Kind of Fowl, after which they fed the faster, and grew
sooner fat: That his sacred Majesty, and the Council,
who are your Judges, were in their own Consciences fully
convinced of your Guilt; which was a sufficient Argu-
ment to condemn you to death, without the *formal Proofs
required by the strict Letter of the Law.*

But his Imperial Majesty fully determined against capital
Punishment, was graciously pleased to say, that since the
Council thought the Loss of your Eyes too easy a Censure,
some other may be inflicted hereafter. And your Friend
the Secretary humbly desiring to be heard again, in Answer
to what the Treasurer had objected concerning the great
Charge his Majesty was at in maintaining you; said, that
his Excellency, who had the sole Disposal of the Emperor's
Revenue, might easily provide against this Evil, by gradually lessening your Establishment; by which, for want of
sufficient Food, you would grow weak and faint, and lose
your Appetite, and consequently decay and consume in a
few Months; neither would the Stench of your Carcass be
then so dangerous, when it should become more than half
diminished; and immediately upon your Death, five or six
Thousand of his Majesty's Subjects might, in two or three
Days, cut your Flesh from your Bones, take it away by
Cart-loads, and bury it in distant Parts to prevent Infect-
ion; leaving the Skeleton as a Monument of Admiration
to Posterity.

Thus by the great Friendship of the Secretary, the whole
Affair was compromised. It was strictly enjoined, that the
Project of starving you by Degrees should be kept a
Secret; but the Sentence of putting out your Eyes was
entered on the Books; none dissenting except *Bolgolam*
the Admiral, who being a Creature of the Empress, was
perpetually instigated by her Majesty to insist upon your
Death; she having born perpetual Malice against you,
on Account of that infamous and illegal Method you took
to extinguish the Fire in her Apartment.

In three Days your Friend the Secretary will be directed
to come to your House, and read before you the Articles

of Impeachment; and then to signify the great *Lenity* and Favour of his Majesty and Council; whereby you are only condemned to the Loss of your Eyes, which his Majesty doth not question you will gratefully and humbly submit to; and Twenty of his Majesty's Surgeons will attend, in order to see the Operation well performed, by discharging very sharp pointed Arrows into the Balls of your Eyes, as you lie on the Ground.

I leave to your Prudence what Measures you will take; and to avoid Suspicion, I must immediately return in as private a Manner as I came.

His Lordship did so, and I remained alone, under many Doubts and Perplexities of Mind.

It was a Custom introduced by this Prince and his Ministry, (very different, as I have been assured, from the Practices of former Times) that after the Court had decreed any cruel Execution, either to gratify the Monarch's Resentment, or the Malice of a Favourite; the Emperor always made a Speech to his whole Council, expressing his *great Lenity and Tenderness, as Qualities known and confessed by all the World*. This Speech was immediately published through the Kingdom; nor did any thing terrify the People so much as those Encomiums on his Majesty's Mercy; because it was observed, that the more these Praises were enlarged and insisted on, the more *inhuman* was the Punishment, and the *Sufferer more innocent*. Yet, as to myself, I must confess, having never been designed for a Courtier, either by my Birth or Education, I was so ill a Judge of Things, that I could not discover the *Lenity* and Favour of this Sentence; but conceived it (perhaps erroneously) rather to be rigorous than gentle. I sometimes thought of standing my Tryal; for although I could not deny the Facts alledged in the several Articles, yet I hoped they would admit of some Extenuations. But having in my Life perused many State-Tryals, which I ever observed to terminate as the Judges thought fit to direct; I durst not rely on so dangerous a Decision, in so critical a Juncture, and against such powerful Enemies. Once I was strongly bent upon Resistance: For while I had

Liberty, the whole Strength of that Empire could hardly subdue me, and I might easily with Stones pelt the Metropolis to Pieces: But I soon rejected that Project with Horror, by remembering the Oath I had made to the Emperor, the Favours I received from him, and the high Title of *Nardac* he conferred upon me. Neither had I so soon learned the Gratitude of Courtiers, to persuade myself that his Majesty's *present Severities acquitted me of all past Obligations.*

At last I fixed upon a Resolution, for which it is probable I may incur some Censure, and not unjustly; for I confess I owe the preserving my Eyes, and consequently my Liberty, to my own great Rashness and Want of Experience: Because if I had then known the Nature of Princes and Ministers, which I have since observed in many other Courts, and their Methods of treating Criminals less obnoxious than myself; I should with great Alacrity and Readiness have submitted to so *easy* a Punishment. But hurried on by the Precipitancy of Youth; and having his Imperial Majesty's Licence to pay my Attendance upon the Emperor of *Blefuscu*; I took this Opportunity, before the three Days were elapsed, to send a Letter to my Friend the Secretary, signifying my Resolution of setting out that Morning for *Blefuscu*, pursuant to the Leave I had got; and without waiting for an Answer, I went to that Side of the Island where our Fleet lay. I seized a large Man of War, tied a Cable to the Prow, and lifting up the Anchors, I stript myself, put my Cloaths (together with my Coverlet, which I carryed under my Arm) into the Vessel; and drawing it after me, between wading and swimming, arrived at the Royal Port of *Blefuscu*, where the People had long expected me: They lent me two Guides to direct me to the Capital City, which is of the same Name; I held them in my Hands until I came within two Hundred Yards of the Gate; and desired them to signify my Arrival to one of the Secretaries, and let him know, I there waited his Majesty's Commands. I had an Answer in about an Hour, that his Majesty, attended by the Royal Family, and great Officers of the Court, was coming out to receive

me. I advanced a Hundred Yards; the Emperor, and his
Train, alighted from their Horses, the Empress and Ladies
from their Coaches; and I did not perceive they were in
any Fright or Concern. I lay on the Ground to kiss his
Majesty's and the Empress's Hand. I told his Majesty,
that I was come according to my Promise, and with the
Licence of the Emperor my Master, to have the Honour
of seeing so mighty a Monarch, and to offer him any Service in my Power, consistent with my Duty to my own
Prince; not mentioning a Word of my Disgrace, because
I had hitherto no regular Information of it, and might
suppose myself wholly ignorant of any such Design;
neither could I reasonably conceive that the Emperor
would discover the Secret while I was out of his Power:
Wherein, however, it soon appeared I was deceived.

I shall not trouble the Reader with the particular
Account of my Reception at this Court, which was suitable
to the Generosity of so great a Prince; nor of the Difficulties I was in for want of a House and Bed, being forced
to lie on the Ground, wrapt up in my Coverlet.

CHAPTER EIGHT

THE AUTHOR, BY A LUCKY ACCIDENT, FINDS MEANS TO LEAVE BLEFUSCU; AND, AFTER SOME DIFFICULTIES, RETURNS SAFE TO HIS NATIVE COUNTRY.

THREE Days after my Arrival, walking out of Curiosity
to the North-East Coast of the Island; I observed,
about half a League off, in the Sea, somewhat that
looked like a Boat overturned: I pulled off my Shoes and
Stockings, and wading two or three Hundred Yards, I
found the Object to approach nearer by Force of the Tide;
and then plainly saw it to be a real Boat, which I supposed
might, by some Tempest, have been driven from a Ship.
Whereupon I returned immediately towards the City, and
desired his Imperial Majesty to lend me Twenty of the
tallest Vessels he had left after the Loss of his Fleet, and
three Thousand Seamen under the Command of his Vice-

Admiral. This Fleet sailed round, while I went back the
shortest Way to the Coast where I first discovered the Boat;
I found the Tide had driven it still nearer; the Seamen
were all provided with Cordage, which I had beforehand
twisted to a sufficient Strength. When the Ships came up,
I stript myself, and waded till I came within an Hundred
Yards of the Boat; after which I was forced to swim till
I got up to it. The Seamen threw me the End of the Cord,
which I fastened to a Hole in the fore-part of the Boat,
and the other End to a Man of War: But I found all my
Labour to little Purpose; for being out of my Depth,
I was not able to work. In this Necessity, I was forced
to swim behind, and push the Boat forwards as often as
I could, with one of my Hands; and the Tide favouring
me, I advanced so far, that I could just hold up my Chin
and feel the Ground. I rested two or three Minutes,
and then gave the Boat another Shove, and so on till
the Sea was no higher than my Arm-pits. And now the
most laborious Part being over, I took out my other
Cables which were stowed in one of the Ships, and fastening them first to the Boat, and then to nine of the Vessels
which attended me; the Wind being favourable, the
Seamen towed, and I shoved till we arrived within forty
Yards of the Shore; and waiting till the Tide was out, I
got dry to the Boat, and by the Assistance of two Thousand
Men, with Ropes and Engines, I made a shift to turn it
on its Bottom, and found it was but little damaged.

I shall not trouble the Reader with the Difficulties I was
under by the Help of certain Paddles, which cost me ten
Days making, to get my Boat to the Royal Port of *Blefuscu*;
where a mighty Concourse of People appeared upon my
Arrival, full of Wonder at the Sight of so prodigious a
Vessel. I told the Emperor, that my good Fortune had
thrown this Boat in my Way, to carry me to some Place
from whence I might return into my native Country;
and begged his Majesty's Orders for getting Materials to
fit it up; together with his Licence to depart; which,
after some kind Expostulations, he was pleased to grant.

I did very much wonder, in all this Time, not to have

heard of any Express relating to me from our Emperor to the Court of *Blefuscu*. But I was afterwards given privately to understand, that his Imperial Majesty, never imagining I had the least Notice of his Designs, believed I was only gone to *Blefuscu* in Performance of my Promise, according to the Licence he had given me, which was well known at our Court; and would return in a few Days when that Ceremony was ended. But he was at last in pain at my long absence; and, after consulting with the Treasurer, and the rest of that Cabal; a Person of Quality was dispatched with the Copy of the Articles against me. This Envoy had Instructions to represent to the Monarch of *Blefuscu*, the great *Lenity* of his Master, who was content to punish me no further than with the Loss of my Eyes: That I had fled from Justice, and if I did not return in two Hours, I should be deprived of my Title of *Nardac*, and declared a Traitor. The Envoy further added; that in order to maintain the Peace and Amity between both Empires, his Master expected, that his Brother of *Blefuscu* would give Orders to have me sent back to *Lilliput*, bound Hand and Foot, to be punished as a Traitor.

The Emperor of *Blefuscu* having taken three Days to consult, returned an Answer consisting of many Civilities and Excuses. He said, that as for sending me bound, his Brother knew it was impossible; that although I had deprived him of his Fleet, yet he owed great Obligations to me for many good Offices I had done him in making the Peace. That however, both their Majesties would soon be made easy; for I had found a prodigious Vessel on the Shore, able to carry me on the Sea, which he had given order to fit up with my own Assistance and Direction; and he hoped in a few Weeks both Empires would be freed from so insupportable an Incumbrance.

With this Answer the Envoy returned to *Lilliput*, and the Monarch of *Blefuscu* related to me all that had past; offering me at the same time (but under the strictest Confidence) his gracious Protection, if I would continue in his Service, wherein although I believed him sincere, yet I resolved never more to put any Confidence in Princes or

Ministers, where I could possibly avoid it; and therefore, with all due Acknowledgments for his favourable Intentions, I humbly begged to be excused. I told him, that since Fortune, whether good or evil, had thrown a Vessel in my Way; I was resolved to venture myself in the Ocean, rather than be an Occasion of Difference between two such mighty Monarchs. Neither did I find the Emperor at all displeased; and I discovered by a certain Accident, that he was very glad of my Resolution, and so were most of his Ministers.

These Considerations moved me to hasten my Departure somewhat sooner than I intended; to which the Court, impatient to have me gone, very readily contributed. Five hundred Workmen were employed to make two Sails to my Boat, according to my Directions, by quilting thirteen fold of their strongest Linnen together. I was at the Pains of making Ropes and Cables, by twisting ten, twenty or thirty of the thickest and strongest of theirs. A great Stone that I happened to find, after a long Search by the Seashore, served me for an Anchor. I had the Tallow of three hundred Cows for greasing my Boat, and other Uses. I was at incredible Pains in cutting down some of the largest Timber Trees for Oars and Masts, wherein I was, however, much assisted by his Majesty's Ship-Carpenters, who helped me in smoothing them, after I had done the rough Work.

In about a Month, when all was prepared, I sent to receive his Majesty's Commands, and to take my leave. The Emperor and Royal Family came out of the Palace; I lay down on my Face to kiss his Hand, which he very graciously gave me; so did the Empress, and young Princes of the Blood. His Majesty presented me with fifty Purses of two hundred *Sprugs* a-piece, together with his Picture at full length, which I put immediately into one of my Gloves, to keep it from being hurt. The Ceremonies at my Departure were too many to trouble the Reader with at this time.

I stored the Boat with the Carcasses of an hundred Oxen, and three hundred Sheep, with Bread and Drink proportionable, and as much Meat ready dressed as four hundred

Cooks could provide. I took with me six Cows and two
Bulls alive, with as many Yews and Rams, intending to
carry them into my own Country and propagate the Breed.
And to feed them on board, I had a good Bundle of Hay,
and a Bag of Corn. I would gladly have taken a Dozen of
the Natives; but this was a thing the Emperor would by
no Means permit; and besides a diligent Search into my
Pockets, his Majesty engaged my Honour not to carry away
any of his Subjects, although with their own Consent and
Desire.

Having thus prepared all things as well as I was able; I
set sail on the Twenty-fourth Day of *September* 1701, at
six in the Morning; and when I had gone about four
Leagues to the Northward, the Wind being at South-
East; at six in the Evening, I descryed a small Island about
half a League to the North West. I advanced forward,
and cast Anchor on the Lee-side of the Island, which
seemed to be uninhabited. I then took some Refreshment,
and went to my Rest. I slept well, and as I conjecture at
least six Hours; for I found the Day broke in two Hours
after I awaked. It was a clear Night; I eat my Breakfast
before the Sun was up; and heaving Anchor, the Wind
being favourable, I steered the same Course that I had
done the Day before, wherein I was directed by my Pocket-
Compass. My Intention was to reach, if possible, one of
those Islands, which I had reason to believe lay to the
North-East of *Van Diemen's* Land. I discovered nothing
all that Day; but upon the next, about three in the Afternoon, when I had by my Computation made Twenty-
four Leagues from *Blefuscu*, I descryed a Sail steering to
the South-East; my Course was due East. I hailed her,
but could get no Answer; yet I found I gained upon her,
for the Wind slackened. I made all the Sail I could, and
in half an Hour she spyed me, then hung out her Antient,
and discharged a Gun. It is not easy to express the Joy
I was in upon the unexpected Hope of once more seeing
my beloved Country, and the dear Pledges I had left
in it. The Ship slacked her Sails, and I came up with her
between five and six in the Evening, *September* 26; but my

Heart leapt within me to see her *English* Colours. I put my Cows and Sheep into my Coat-Pockets, and got on board with all my Cargo of Provisions. The Vessel was an *English* Merchant-man, returning from *Japan* by the *North* and *South Seas*; the Captain, Mr. *John Biddel* of *Deptford*, a very civil Man, and an excellent Sailor. We were now in the Latitude of 30 Degrees South; there were about fifty Men in the Ship; and here I met an old Comrade of mine, one *Peter Williams*, who gave me a good Character to the Captain. This Gentleman treated me with Kindness, and desired I would let him know what Place I came from last, and whither I was bound; which I did in few Words; but he thought I was raving, and that the Dangers I underwent had disturbed my Head; whereupon I took my black Cattle and Sheep out of my Pocket, which, after great Astonishment, clearly convinced him of my Veracity. I then shewed him the Gold given me by the Emperor of *Blefuscu*, together with his Majesty's Picture at full Length, and some other Rarities of that Country. I gave him two Purses of two Hundred *Sprugs* each, and promised, when we arrived in *England*, to make him a Present of a Cow and a Sheep big with Young.

I shall not trouble the Reader with a particular Account of this Voyage; which was very prosperous for the most Part. We arrived in the *Downs* on the 13th of *April* 1702. I had only one Misfortune, that the Rats on board carried away one of my Sheep; I found her Bones in a Hole, picked clean from the Flesh. The rest of my Cattle I got safe on Shore, and set them a grazing in a Bowling-Green at *Greenwich*, where the Fineness of the Grass made them feed very heartily, although I had always feared the contrary: Neither could I possibly have preserved them in so long a Voyage, if the Captain had not allowed me some of his best Bisket, which rubbed to Powder, and mingled with Water, was their constant Food. The short Time I continued in *England*, I made a considerable Profit by shewing my Cattle to many Persons of Quality, and others: And before I began my second Voyage, I sold them for six Hundred Pounds. Since my last Return, I find the Breed is considerably increased, especially the Sheep; which I hope will prove much to the Advantage of the Woollen Manufacture, by the Fineness of the Fleeces.

I stayed but two Months with my Wife and Family; for my insatiable Desire of seeing foreign Countries would suffer me to continue no longer. I left fifteen Hundred Pounds with my Wife, and fixed her in a good House at *Redriff*. My remaining Stock I carried with me, Part in Money, and Part in Goods, in Hopes to improve my Fortunes. My eldest Uncle, *John*, had left me an Estate in Land, near *Epping*, of about Thirty Pounds a Year; and I had a long Lease of the *Black-Bull* in *Fetter-Lane*, which yielded me as much more: So that I was not in any Danger of leaving my Family upon the Parish. My Son *Johnny*, named so after his Uncle, was at the Grammar School, and a towardly Child. My Daughter *Betty* (who is now well married, and has Children) was then at her Needle-Work. I took Leave of my Wife, and Boy and Girl, with Tears on both Sides; and went on board the *Adventure*, a Merchant-Ship of three Hundred Tons, bound for *Surat*, Captain *John Nicholas* of *Liverpool*, Commander. But my Account of this Voyage must be referred to the second Part of my Travels.

The End of the First Part

PART TWO

A VOYAGE TO BROBDINGNAG

BROBDINGNAG

Flanflasnic

Lorbrulgrud

Discovered A.D. 1703

NORTH AMERICA

Streights of Anian

C. Blanco

St. Sebastian

C. Mendocino

Pt° Sᵗ Francis Drake

Mount St. Martin

P. Monterey

CHAPTER ONE

A GREAT STORM DESCRIBED. THE LONG BOAT SENT TO
FETCH WATER, THE AUTHOR GOES WITH IT TO DISCOVER
THE COUNTRY. HE IS LEFT ON SHOAR, IS SEIZED BY ONE
OF THE NATIVES, AND CARRIED TO A FARMER'S HOUSE.
HIS RECEPTION THERE, WITH SEVERAL ACCIDENTS THAT
HAPPENED THERE. A DESCRIPTION OF THE INHABITANTS.

HAVING been condemned by Nature and Fortune to
an active and restless Life; in two Months after my
Return, I again left my native Country, and took Shipping in the *Downs* on the 20th Day of *June* 1702, in the
Adventure, Capt. *John Nicholas*, a *Cornish* Man, Commander,
bound for *Surat*. We had a very prosperous Gale till we
arrived at the *Cape* of *Good-hope*, where we landed for
fresh Water; but discovering a Leak we unshipped our
Goods, and wintered there; for the Captain falling sick
of an Ague, we could not leave the *Cape* till the End of
March. We then set sail, and had a good Voyage till
we passed the *Streights* of *Madagascar*; but having got
Northward of that Island, and to about five Degrees
South Latitude, the Winds, which in those Seas are observed to blow a constant equal Gale between the North
and West, from the Beginning of *December* to the Beginning
of *May*, on the 19th of *April* began to blow with much
greater Violence, and more Westerly than usual; continuing so for twenty Days together, during which time
we were driven a little to the East of the *Molucca* Islands,
and about three Degrees Northward of the Line, as our
Captain found by an Observation he took the 2d of
May, at which time the Wind ceased, and it was a perfect
Calm, whereat I was not a little rejoyced. But he being
a Man well experienced in the Navigation of those Seas,
bid us all prepare against a Storm, which accordingly
happened the Day following: For a Southern Wind,
called the Southern *Monsoon*, began to set in.

Finding it was like to overblow, we took in our Sprit-
sail, and stood by to hand the Fore-sail; but making foul

Weather, we looked the Guns were all fast, and handed the
Missen. The Ship lay very broad off, so we thought it
better spooning before the Sea, than trying or hulling.
We reeft the Foresail and set him, we hawled aft the Fore-
sheet; the Helm was hard a Weather. The Ship wore
bravely. We belay'd the Foredown-hall; but the Sail
was split, and we hawl'd down the Yard, and got the
Sail into the Ship, and unbound all the things clear of
it. It was a very fierce Storm; the Sea broke strange and
dangerous. We hawl'd off upon the Lanniard of the
Wipstaff, and helped the Man at Helm. We would not
get down our Top-Mast, but let all stand, because she
scudded before the Sea very well, and we knew that the
Top-Mast being aloft, the Ship was the wholesomer, and
made better way through the Sea, seeing we had Sea room.
When the Storm was over, we set Fore-sail and Main-
sail, and brought the Ship too. Then we set the Missen, Maintop-Sail and the Foretop-Sail. Our Course was
East North-east, the Wind was at South-west. We got the
Star-board Tack aboard, we cast off our Weather-braces
and Lifts; we set in the Lee-braces, and hawl'd forward
by the Weather-bowlings, and hawl'd them tight, and
belayed them, and hawl'd over the Missen Tack to Wind-
ward, and kept her full and by as near as she would lye.

During this Storm, which was followed by a strong
Wind West South-west, we were carried by my Computation about five hundred Leagues to the East, so that
the oldest Sailor on Board could not tell in what part of
the World we were. Our Provisions held out well, our
Ship was staunch, and our Crew all in good Health; but
we lay in the utmost Distress for Water. We thought it
best to hold on the same Course rather than turn more
Northerly, which might have brought us to the North-
west Parts of great *Tartary*, and into the frozen Sea.

On the 16*th* Day of *June* 1703, a Boy on the Top-mast
discovered Land. On the 17*th* we came in full View of a
great Island or Continent, (for we knew not whether) on
the South-side whereof was a small Neck of Land jutting
out into the Sea, and a Creek too shallow to hold a Ship

of above one hundred Tuns. We cast Anchor within a League of this Creek, and our Captain sent a dozen of his Men well armed in the Long Boat, with Vessels for Water if any could be found. I desired his leave to go with them, that I might see the Country, and make what Discoveries I could. When we came to Land we saw no River or Spring, nor any Sign of Inhabitants. Our Men therefore wandered on the Shore to find out some fresh Water near the Sea, and I walked alone about a Mile on the other Side, where I observed the Country all barren and rocky. I now began to be weary, and seeing nothing to entertain my Curiosity, I returned gently down towards the Creek; and the Sea being full in my View, I saw our Men already got into the Boat, and rowing for Life to the Ship. I was going to hollow after them, although it had been to little purpose, when I observed a huge Creature walking after them in the Sea, as fast as he could: He walked not much deeper than his Knees, and took prodigious strides: But our Men had the start of him half a League, and the Sea thereabouts being full of sharp pointed Rocks, the Monster was not able to overtake the Boat. This I was afterwards told, for I durst not stay to see the Issue of that Adventure; but run as fast as I could the Way I first went; and then climbed up a steep Hill, which gave me some Prospect of the Country. I found it fully cultivated; but that which first surprized me was the Length of the Grass, which in those Grounds that seemed to be kept for Hay, was above twenty Foot high.

I fell into a high Road, for so I took it to be, although it served to the Inhabitants only as a foot Path through a Field of Barley. Here I walked on for sometime, but could see little on either Side, it being now near Harvest, and the Corn rising at least forty Foot. I was an Hour walking to the end of this Field; which was fenced in with a Hedge of at least one hundred and twenty Foot high, and the Trees so lofty that I could make no Computation of their Altitude. There was a Stile to pass from this Field into the next: It had four Steps, and a Stone to cross

over when you came to the utmost. It was impossible for
me to climb this Stile, because every Step was six Foot
high, and the upper Stone above twenty. I was endeavouring to find some Gap in the Hedge; when I discovered
one of the Inhabitants in the next Field advancing towards
the Stile, of the same Size with him whom I saw in the
Sea pursuing our Boat. He appeared as Tall as an ordinary Spire-steeple; and took about ten Yards at every
Stride, as near as I could guess. I was struck with the
utmost Fear and Astonishment, and ran to hide my self
in the Corn, from whence I saw him at the Top of the
Stile, looking back into the next Field on the right Hand;
and heard him call in a Voice many Degrees louder than
a speaking Trumpet; but the Noise was so High in the
Air, that at first I certainly thought it was Thunder. Whereupon seven Monsters like himself came towards him with
Reaping-Hooks in their Hands, each Hook about the
largeness of six Scythes. These People were not so well clad
as the first, whose Servants or Labourers they seemed to
be. For, upon some Words he spoke, they went to reap
the Corn in the Field where I lay. I kept from them at as
great a Distance as I could, but was forced to move with
extream Difficulty; for the Stalks of the Corn were sometimes not above a Foot distant, so that I could hardly
squeeze my Body betwixt them. However, I made a shift
to go forward till I came to a part of the Field where the
Corn had been laid by the Rain and Wind: Here it was
impossible for me to advance a step; for the Stalks were
so interwoven that I could not creep through, and the
Beards of the fallen Ears so strong and pointed, that they
pierced through my Cloaths into my Flesh. At the same
time I heard the Reapers not above an hundred Yards
behind me. Being quite dispirited with Toil, and wholly
overcome by Grief and Despair, I lay down between two
Ridges, and heartily wished I might there end my Days.
I bemoaned my desolate Widow, and Fatherless Children:
I lamented my own Folly and Wilfulness in attempting a
second Voyage against the Advice of all my Friends and
Relations. In this terrible Agitation of Mind I could not

forbear thinking of *Lilliput*, whose Inhabitants looked upon
me as the greatest Prodigy that ever appeared in the
World; where I was able to draw an Imperial Fleet in
my Hand, and perform those other Actions which will be
recorded for ever in the Chronicles of that Empire, while
Posterity shall hardly believe them, although attested by
Millions. I reflected what a Mortification it must prove
to me to appear as inconsiderable in this Nation, as one
single *Lilliputian* would be among us. But, this I conceived
was to be the least of my Misfortunes: For, as human
Creatures are observed to be more Savage and cruel in
Proportion to their Bulk; what could I expect but to be
a Morsel in the Mouth of the first among these enormous
Barbarians who should happen to seize me? Undoubtedly
Philosophers are in the Right when they tell us, that nothing is great or little otherwise than by Comparison: It
might have pleased Fortune to let the *Lilliputians* find some
Nation, where the People were as diminutive with respect
to them, as they were to me. And who knows but that
even this prodigious Race of Mortals might be equally
overmatched in some distant Part of the World, whereof
we have yet no Discovery?

Scared and confounded as I was, I could not forbear
going on with these Reflections; when one of the Reapers
approaching within ten Yards of the Ridge where I lay,
made me apprehend that with the next Step I should be
squashed to Death under his Foot, or cut in two with his
Reaping Hook. And therefore when he was again about
to move, I screamed as loud as Fear could make me.
Whereupon the huge Creature trod short, and looking
round about under him for some time, at last espied me
as I lay on the Ground. He considered a while with the
Caution of one who endeavours to lay hold on a small
dangerous Animal in such a Manner that it shall not be
able either to scratch or to bite him; as I my self have
sometimes done with a *Weasel* in *England*. At length he
ventured to take me up behind by the middle between
his Fore-finger and Thumb, and brought me within three
Yards of his Eyes, that he might behold my Shape more

perfectly. I guessed his Meaning; and my good Fortune gave me so much Presence of Mind, that I resolved not to struggle in the least as he held me in the Air above sixty Foot from the Ground; although he grievously pinched my Sides, for fear I should slip through his Fingers. All I ventured was to raise my Eyes towards the Sun, and place my Hands together in a supplicating Posture, and to speak some Words in an humble melancholy Tone, suitable to the Condition I then was in. For, I apprehended every Moment that he would dash me against the Ground, as we usually do any little hateful Animal which we have a Mind to destroy. But my good Star would have it, that he appeared pleased with my Voice and Gestures, and began to look upon me as a Curiosity; much wondering to hear me pronounce articulate Words, although he could not understand them. In the mean time I was not able to forbear Groaning and shedding Tears, and turning my Head towards my Sides; letting him know, as well as I could, how cruelly I was hurt by the Pressure of his Thumb and Finger. He seemed to apprehend my Meaning; for, lifting up the Lappet of his Coat, he put me gently into it, and immediately ran along with me to his Master, who was a substantial Farmer, and the same Person I had first seen in the Field.

The Farmer having (as I supposed by their Talk) received such an Account of me as his Servant could give him, took a piece of a small Straw, about the Size of a walking Staff, and therewith lifted up the Lappets of my Coat; which it seems he thought to be some kind of Covering that Nature had given me. He blew my Hairs aside to take a better View of my Face. He called his Hinds about him, and asked them (as I afterwards learned) whether they had ever seen in the Fields any little Creature that resembled me. He then placed me softly on the Ground upon all four; but I got immediately up, and walked slowly backwards and forwards, to let those People see I had no Intent to run away. They all sate down in a Circle about me, the better to observe my Motions. I pulled off my Hat, and made a low Bow towards the

Farmer: I fell on my Knees, and lifted up my Hands and Eyes, and spoke several Words as loud as I could: I took a Purse of Gold out of my Pocket, and humbly presented it to him. He received it on the Palm of his Hand, then applied it close to his Eye, to see what it was, and afterwards turned it several times with the Point of a Pin, (which he took out of his Sleeve,) but could make nothing of it. Whereupon I made a Sign that he should place his Hand on the Ground: I then took the Purse, and opening it, poured all the Gold into his Palm. There were six *Spanish*-Pieces of four Pistoles each, besides twenty or thirty smaller Coins. I saw him wet the Tip of his little Finger upon his Tongue, and take up one of my largest Pieces, and then another; but he seemed to be wholly ignorant what they were. He made me a Sign to put them again into my Purse, and the Purse again into my Pocket; which after offering to him several times, I thought it best to do.

The Farmer by this time was convinced I must be a rational Creature. He spoke often to me, but the Sound of his Voice pierced my Ears like that of a Water-Mill; yet his Words were articulate enough. I answered as loud as I could in several Languages; and he often laid his Ear within two Yards of me, but all in vain, for we were wholly unintelligible to each other. He then sent his Servants to their Work, and taking his Handkerchief out of his Pocket, he doubled and spread it on his Hand, which he placed flat on the Ground with the Palm upwards, making me a Sign to step into it, as I could easily do, for it was not above a Foot in thickness. I thought it my part to obey; and for fear of falling, laid my self at full Length upon the Handkerchief, with the Remainder of which he lapped me up to the Head for further Security; and in this Manner carried me home to his House. There he called his Wife, and shewed me to her; but she screamed and ran back as Women in *England* do at the Sight of a Toad or a Spider. However, when she had a while seen my Behaviour, and how well I observed the Signs her Husband made, she was soon reconciled, and by Degrees grew extreamly tender of me.

It was about twelve at Noon, and a Servant brought in
Dinner. It was only one substantial Dish of Meat (fit for
the plain Condition of an Husband-Man) in a Dish of
about four and twenty Foot Diameter. The Company were
the Farmer and Wife, three Children, and an old Grand-
mother: When they were sat down, the Farmer placed me
at some Distance from him on the Table, which was thirty
Foot high from the Floor. I was in a terrible Fright, and
kept as far as I could from the Edge, for fear of falling.
The Wife minced a bit of Meat, then crumbled some Bread
on a Trencher, and placed it before me. I made her a
low Bow, took out my Knife and Fork, and fell to eat;
which gave them exceeding Delight. The Mistress sent
her Maid for a small Dram-cup, which held about two
Gallons; and filled it with Drink: I took up the Vessel
with much difficulty in both Hands, and in a most respectful
Manner drank to her Lady-ship's Health, expressing the
Words as loud as I could in *English*; which made the
Company laugh so heartily, that I was almost deafened
with the Noise. This Liquour tasted like a small Cyder,
and was not unpleasant. Then the Master made me a
Sign to come to his Trencher side; but as I walked on the
Table, being in great surprize all the time, as the indulgent
Reader will easily conceive and excuse, I happened to
stumble against a Crust, and fell flat on my Face, but
received no hurt. I got up immediately, and observing
the good People to be in much Concern, I took my Hat
(which I held under my Arm out of good Manners) and
waving it over my Head, made three Huzza's, to shew
I had got no Mischief by the Fall. But advancing forwards
toward my Master (as I shall henceforth call him) his
youngest Son who sate next him, an arch Boy of about
ten Years old, took me up by the Legs, and held me so
high in the Air, that I trembled every Limb; but his
Father snatched me from him; and at the same time gave
him such a Box on the left Ear, as would have felled an
European Troop of Horse to the Earth; ordering him to
be taken from the Table. But, being afraid the Boy might
owe me a Spight; and well remembring how mischievous

all Children among us naturally are to Sparrows, Rabbits, young Kittens, and Puppy-Dogs; I fell on my Knees, and pointing to the Boy, made my Master understand, as well as I could, that I desired his Son might be pardoned. The Father complied, and the Lad took his Seat again; whereupon I went to him and kissed his Hand, which my Master took, and made him stroak me gently with it.

In the Midst of Dinner my Mistress's favourite Cat leapt into her Lap. I heard a Noise behind me like that of a Dozen Stocking-Weavers at work; and turning my Head, I found it proceeded from the Purring of this Animal, who seemed to be three Times larger than an Ox, as I computed by the View of her Head, and one of her Paws, while her Mistress was feeding and stroaking her. The Fierceness of this Creature's Countenance altogether discomposed me; although I stood at the further End of the Table, above fifty Foot off; and although my Mistress held her fast for fear she might give a Spring, and seize me in her Talons. But it happened there was no Danger; for the Cat took not the least Notice of me when my Master placed me within three Yards of her. And as I have been always told, and found true by Experience in my Travels, that flying, or discovering Fear before a fierce Animal, is a certain Way to make it pursue or attack you; so I resolved in this dangerous Juncture to shew no Manner of Concern. I walked with Intrepidity five or six Times before the very Head of the Cat, and came within half a Yard of her; whereupon she drew her self back, as if she were more afraid of me: I had less Apprehension concerning the Dogs, whereof three or four came into the Room, as it is usual in Farmers Houses; one of which was a Mastiff equal in Bulk to four Elephants, and a Grey-hound somewhat taller than the Mastiff, but not so large.

When Dinner was almost done, the Nurse came in with a Child of a Year old in her Arms; who immediately spyed me, and began a Squall that you might have heard from *London-Bridge* to *Chelsea*; after the usual Oratory of Infants, to get me for a Play-thing. The Mother out of pure Indulgence took me up, and put me towards the Child, who presently seized me by the Middle, and got my Head in his Mouth, where I roared so loud that the Urchin was frighted, and let me drop; and I should infallibly have broke my Neck, if the Mother had not held her Apron under me. The Nurse to quiet her Babe made use of a Rattle, which was a Kind of hollow Vessel filled with great Stones, and fastned by a Cable to the Child's Waist: But all in vain, so that she was forced to apply the last Remedy by giving it suck. I must confess no Object ever disgusted me so much as the Sight of her monstrous Breast, which I cannot tell what to compare with, so as to give the curious Reader an Idea of its Bulk, Shape and Colour. It stood prominent six Foot, and could not be less than sixteen in Circumference. The Nipple was about half the Bigness of my Head, and the Hue both of that and the Dug so varified with Spots, Pimples and Freckles, that nothing could appear more nauseous: For I had a near Sight of her, she sitting down the more conveniently to give Suck, and I standing on the Table. This made me reflect upon the fair Skins of our *English* Ladies, who appear so beautiful to us, only because they are of our own Size, and their Defects not to be seen but through a magnifying Glass, where we find by Experiment that the smoothest and whitest Skins look rough and coarse, and ill coloured.

I remember when I was at *Lilliput,* the Complexions of those diminutive People appeared to me the fairest in the World: And talking upon this Subject with a Person of Learning there, who was an intimate Friend of mine; he said, that my Face appeared much fairer and smoother when he looked on me from the Ground, than it did upon a nearer View when I took him up in my Hand, and brought him close; which he confessed was at first a very shocking Sight. He said, he could discover great Holes in my Skin; that the Stumps of my Beard were ten Times stronger than the Bristles of a Boar; and my Complexion made up of several Colours altogether disagreeable: Although I must beg Leave to say for my self, that I am as fair as most of my Sex and Country, and very little Sunburnt by all my Travels. On the other Side, discoursing of the Ladies in that Emperor's Court, he used to tell me, one had Freckles, another too wide a Mouth, a third too large a Nose; nothing of which I was able to distinguish. I confess this Reflection was obvious enough; which, however, I could not forbear, lest the Reader might think those vast Creatures were actually deformed: For I must do them Justice to say they are a comely Race of People; and particularly the Features of my Master's Countenance, although he were but a Farmer, when I beheld him from the Height of sixty Foot, appeared very well proportioned.

When Dinner was done, my Master went out to his Labourers; and as I could discover by his Voice and Gesture, gave his Wife a strict Charge to take Care of me. I was very much tired and disposed to sleep, which my Mistress perceiving, she put me on her own Bed, and covered me with a clean white Handkerchief, but larger and coarser than the Main Sail of a Man of War.

I slept about two Hours, and dreamed I was at home with my Wife and Children, which aggravated my Sorrows when I awaked and found my self alone in a vast Room, between two and three Hundred Foot wide, and above two Hundred high; lying in a Bed twenty Yards wide. My Mistress was gone about her houshold Affairs, and had locked me in. The Bed was eight Yards from the Floor. Some natural Necessities required me to get down: I durst not presume to call, and if I had, it would have been in vain with such a Voice as mine at so great a Distance from the Room where I lay, to the Kitchen where the Family kept. While I was under these Circumstances, two Rats crept up the Curtains, and ran smelling backwards and forwards on the Bed: One of them came up almost to my Face; whereupon I rose in a Fright, and drew out my Hanger to defend my self. These horrible Animals had the Boldness to attack me on both Sides, and one of them held his Fore-feet at my Collar; but I had the good Fortune to rip up his Belly before he could do me any Mischief. He fell down at my Feet; and the other seeing the Fate of his Comrade, made his Escape, but not without one good Wound on the Back, which I gave

him as he fled, and made the Blood run trickling from
him. After this Exploit I walked gently to and fro on the
Bed, to recover my Breath and Loss of Spirits. These
Creatures were of the Size of a large Mastiff, but infinitely
more nimble and fierce; so that if I had taken off my Belt
before I went to sleep, I must have infallibly been torn to
Pieces and devoured. I measured the Tail of the dead
Rat, and found it to be two Yards long, wanting an Inch;
but it went against my Stomach to drag the Carcass off
the Bed, where it lay still bleeding; I observed it had
yet some Life, but with a strong Slash cross the Neck, I
thoroughly dispatched it.

Soon after, my Mistress came into the Room, who seeing
me all bloody, ran and took me up in her Hand. I pointed
to the dead *Rat*, smiling and making other Signs to shew
I was not hurt; whereat she was extremely rejoyced,
calling the Maid to take up the dead *Rat* with a Pair of
Tongs, and throw it out of the Window. Then she set me
on a Table, where I shewed her my Hanger all bloody,
and wiping it on the Lappet of my Coat, returned it to the
Scabbard. I was pressed to do more than one Thing, which
another could not do for me; and therefore endeavoured
to make my Mistress understand that I desired to be set
down on the Floor; which after she had done, my Bash-
fulness would not suffer me to express my self farther than
by pointing to the Door, and bowing several Times. The
good Woman with much Difficulty at last perceived what I
would be at; and taking me up again in her Hand, walked
into the Garden where she set me down. I went on one
Side about two Hundred Yards; and beckoning to her not
to look or follow me, I hid my self between two Leaves of
Sorrel, and there discharged the Necessities of Nature.

I hope, the gentle Reader will excuse me for dwelling on
these and the like Particulars; which however insignificant
they may appear to grovelling vulgar Minds, yet will certainly help a Philosopher to enlarge his Thoughts and Imagination, and apply them to the Benefit of publick as well
as private Life; which was my sole Design in presenting
this and other Accounts of my Travels to the World;

wherein I have been chiefly studious of Truth, without affecting any Ornaments of Learning, or of Style. But the whole Scene of this Voyage made so strong an Impression on my Mind, and is so deeply fixed in my Memory, that in committing it to Paper, I did not omit one material Circumstance: However, upon a strict Review, I blotted out several Passages of less Moment which were in my first Copy, for fear of being censured as tedious and trifling, whereof Travellers are often, perhaps not without Justice, accused.

CHAPTER TWO

A DESCRIPTION OF THE FARMER'S DAUGHTER. THE AUTHOR
CARRIED TO A MARKET-TOWN, AND THEN TO THE METRO-
POLIS. THE PARTICULARS OF HIS JOURNEY.

My Mistress had a Daughter of nine Years old, a Child of towardly Parts for her Age, very dextrous at her Needle, and skilful in dressing her Baby. Her Mother and she contrived to fit up the Baby's Cradle for me against Night: The Cradle was put into a small Drawer of a Cabinet, and the Drawer placed upon a hanging Shelf for fear of the *Rats*. This was my Bed all the Time I stayed with those People, although made more convenient by Degrees, as I began to learn their Language, and make my Wants known. This young Girl was so handy, that after I had once or twice pulled off my Cloaths before her, she was able to dress and undress me, although I never gave her that Trouble when she would let me do either my self. She made me seven Shirts, and some other Linnen of as fine Cloth as could be got, which indeed was coarser than Sackcloth; and these she constantly washed for me with her own Hands. She was likewise my School-Mistress to teach me the Language: When I pointed to any thing, she told me the Name of it in her own Tongue, so that in a few Days I was able to call for whatever I had a mind to. She was very good natured, and not above forty Foot high, being little for her Age. She gave me the Name of

Grildrig, which the Family took up, and afterwards the
whole Kingdom. The Word imports what the *Latins* call
Nanunculus, the *Italians Homunceletino*, and the *English
Mannikin*. To her I chiefly owe my Preservation in that
Country: We never parted while I was there; I called
her my *Glumdalclitch*, or little Nurse: And I should be
guilty of great Ingratitude if I omitted this honourable
Mention of her Care and Affection towards me, which I
heartily wish it lay in my Power to requite as she deserves,
instead of being the innocent but unhappy Instrument of
her Disgrace, as I have too much Reason to fear.

It now began to be known and talked of in the Neighbourhood, that my Master had found a strange Animal
in the Fields, about the Bigness of a *Splacknuck*, but exactly
shaped in every Part like a human Creature; which it likewise imitated in all its Actions; seemed to speak in a little
Language of its own, had already learned several Words of
theirs, went erect upon two Legs, was tame and gentle,
would come when it was called, do whatever it was bid,
had the finest Limbs in the World, and a Complexion fairer
than a Nobleman's Daughter of three Years old. Another
Farmer who lived hard by, and was a particular Friend of
my Master, came on a Visit on Purpose to enquire into
the Truth of this Story. I was immediately produced, and
placed upon a Table; where I walked as I was commanded,
drew my Hanger, put it up again, made my Reverence to
my Master's Guest, asked him in his own Language how
he did, and told him he was welcome; just as my little
Nurse had instructed me. This Man, who was old and
dimsighted, put on his Spectacles to behold me better, at
which I could not forbear laughing very heartily; for his
Eyes appeared like the Full-Moon shining into a Chamber
at two Windows. Our People, who discovered the Cause
of my Mirth, bore me Company in Laughing; at which the
old Fellow was Fool enough to be angry and out of Countenance. He had the Character of a great Miser; and to
my Misfortune he well deserved it by the cursed Advice
he gave my Master, to shew me as a Sight upon a Market-
Day in the next Town, which was half an Hour's Riding,

about two and twenty Miles from our House. I guessed there was some Mischief contriving, when I observed my Master and his Friend whispering long together, sometimes pointing at me; and my Fears made me fancy that I overheard and understood some of their Words. But, the next Morning *Glumdalclitch* my litte Nurse told me the whole Matter, which she had cunningly picked out from her Mother. The poor Girl laid me on her Bosom, and fell a weeping with Shame and Grief. She apprehended some Mischief would happen to me from rude vulgar Folks, who might squeeze me to Death, or break one of my Limbs by taking me in their Hands. She had also observed how modest I was in my Nature, how nicely I regarded my Honour; and what an Indignity I should conceive it to be exposed for Money as a publick Spectacle to the meanest of the People. She said, her *Papa* and *Mamma* had promised that *Grildrig* should be hers; but now she found they meant to serve her as they did last Year, when they pretended to give her a Lamb; and yet, as soon as it was fat, sold it to a Butcher. For my own Part, I may truly affirm that I was less concerned than my Nurse. I had a strong Hope which never left me, that I should one Day recover my Liberty; and as to the Ignominy of being carried about for a Monster, I considered my self to be a perfect Stranger in the Country; and that such a Misfortune could never be charged upon me as a Reproach if ever I should return to *England*; since the King of *Great Britain* himself, in my Condition, must have undergone the same Distress.

My Master, pursuant to the Advice of his Friend, carried me in a Box the next Market-Day to the neighbouring Town; and took along with him his little Daughter my Nurse upon a Pillion behind me. The Box was close on every Side, with a little Door for me to go in and out, and a few Gimlet-holes to let in Air. The Girl had been so careful to put the Quilt of her Baby's Bed into it, for me to lye down on. However, I was terribly shaken and discomposed in this Journey, although it were but of half an Hour. For the Horse went about forty Foot at every Step;

and trotted so high, that the Agitation was equal to the rising and falling of a Ship in a great Storm, but much more frequent: Our Journey was somewhat further than from *London* to St. *Albans*. My Master alighted at an Inn which he used to frequent; and after consulting a while with the Inn-keeper, and making some necessary Preparations, he hired the *Grultrud*, or Cryer, to give Notice through the Town, of a strange Creature to be seen at the Sign of the Green *Eagle*, not so big as a *Splacknuck*, (an Animal in that Country very finely shaped, about six Foot long) and in every Part of the Body resembling an human Creature; could speak several Words, and perform an Hundred diverting Tricks.

I was placed upon a Table in the largest Room of the Inn, which might be near three Hundred Foot square. My little Nurse stood on a low Stool close to the Table, to take care of me, and direct what I should do. My Master, to avoid a Croud, would suffer only Thirty People at a Time to see me. I walked about on the Table as the Girl commanded; she asked me Questions as far as she knew my Understanding of the Language reached, and I answered them as loud as I could. I turned about several Times to the Company, paid my humble Respects, said they were welcome; and used some other Speeches I had been taught. I took up a Thimble filled with Liquor, which *Glumdalclitch* had given me for a Cup, and drank their Health. I drew out my Hanger, and flourished with it after the Manner of Fencers in *England*. My Nurse gave me Part of a Straw, which I exercised as a Pike, having learned the Art in my Youth. I was that Day shewn to twelve Sets of Company; and as often forced to go over again with the same Fopperies, till I was half dead with Weariness and Vexation. For, those who had seen me, made such wonderful Reports, that the People were ready to break down the Doors to come in. My Master for his own Interest would not suffer any one to touch me, except my Nurse; and, to prevent Danger, Benches were set round the Table at such a Distance, as put me out of every Body's Reach. However, an unlucky School-

Boy aimed a Hazel-Nut directly at my Head, which very narrowly missed me; otherwise, it came with so much Violence, that it would have infallibly knocked out my Brains; for it was almost as large as a small Pumpion: But I had the Satisfaction to see the young Rogue well beaten, and turned out of the Room.

My Master gave publick Notice, that he would shew me again the next Market-Day: And in the mean time, he prepared a more convenient Vehicle for me, which he had Reason enough to do; for I was so tired with my first Journey, and with entertaining Company eight Hours together, that I could hardly stand upon my Legs, or speak a Word. It was at least three Days before I recovered my Strength; and that I might have no rest at home, all the neighbouring Gentlemen from an Hundred Miles round, hearing of my Fame, came to see me at my Master's own House. There could not be fewer than thirty Persons with their Wives and Children; (for the Country is very populous;) and my Master demanded the Rate of a full Room whenever he shewed me at Home, although it were only to a single Family. So that for some time I had but little Ease every Day of the Week, (except *Wednesday*, which is their Sabbath) although I were not carried to the Town.

My Master finding how profitable I was like to be, resolved to carry me to the most considerable Cities of the Kingdom. Having therefore provided himself with all things necessary for a long Journey, and settled his Affairs at Home; he took Leave of his Wife; and upon the 17*th* of *August* 1703, about two Months after my Arrival, we set out for the Metropolis, situated near the Middle of that Empire, and about three Thousand Miles distance from our House: My Master made his Daughter *Glumdalclitch* ride behind him. She carried me on her Lap in a Box tied about her Waist. The Girl had lined it on all Sides with the softest Cloth she could get, well quilted underneath; furnished it with her Baby's Bed, provided me with Linnen and other Necessaries; and made every thing as convenient as she could. We had no other Company but a Boy of the House, who rode after us with the Luggage.

My Master's Design was to shew me in all the Towns by the Way, and to step out of the Road for Fifty or an Hundred Miles, to any Village or Person of Quality's House where he might expect Custom. We made easy Journies of not above seven or eight Score Miles a Day: For *Glumdalclitch*, on Purpose to spare me, complained she was tired with the trotting of the Horse. She often took me out of my Box at my own Desire, to give me Air, and shew me the Country; but always held me fast by Leading-strings. We passed over five or six Rivers many Degrees broader and deeper than the *Nile* or the *Ganges*; and there was hardly a Rivulet so small as the *Thames* at *London-Bridge*. We were ten Weeks in our Journey; and I was shewn in Eighteen large Towns, besides many Villages and private Families.

On the 26th Day of *October*, we arrived at the Metropolis, called in their Language *Lorbrulgrud*, or *Pride of the Universe*. My Master took a Lodging in the principal Street of the City, not far from the Royal Palace; and put out Bills in the usual Form, containing an exact Description of my Person and Parts. He hired a large Room between three and four Hundred Foot wide. He provided a Table sixty Foot in Diameter, upon which I was to act my Part; and pallisadoed it round three Foot from the Edge, and as many high, to prevent my falling over. I was shewn ten Times a Day to the Wonder and Satisfaction of all People. I could now speak the Language tolerably well; and perfectly understood every Word that was spoken to me. Besides, I had learned their Alphabet, and could make a shift to explain a Sentence here and there; for *Glumdalclitch* had been my Instructer while we were at home, and at leisure Hours during our Journey. She carried a little Book in her Pocket, not much larger than a *Sanson's Atlas*; it was a common Treatise for the use of young Girls, giving a short Account of their Religion; out of this she taught me my Letters, and interpreted the Words.

CHAPTER THREE

THE AUTHOR SENT FOR TO COURT. THE QUEEN BUYS HIM
OF HIS MASTER THE FARMER, AND PRESENTS HIM TO THE
KING. HE DISPUTES WITH HIS MAJESTY'S GREAT SCHOLARS.
AN APARTMENT AT COURT PROVIDED FOR THE AUTHOR. HE
IS IN HIGH FAVOUR WITH THE QUEEN. HE STANDS UP FOR
THE HONOUR OF HIS OWN COUNTRY. HIS QUARRELS WITH
THE QUEEN'S DWARF.

THE frequent Labours I underwent every Day, made
in a few Weeks a very considerable Change in my
Health: The more my Master got by me, the more
unsatiable he grew. I had quite lost my Stomach, and was
almost reduced to a Skeleton. The Farmer observed it;
and concluding I soon must die, resolved to make as good
a Hand of me as he could. While he was thus reasoning
and resolving with himself; a *Slardral*, or Gentleman Usher,
came from Court, commanding my Master to bring me
immediately thither for the Diversion of the Queen and
her Ladies. Some of the latter had already been to see me;
and reported strange Things of my Beauty, Behaviour,
and good Sense. Her Majesty and those who attended her,
were beyond Measure delighted with my Demeanor. I fell
on my Knees, and begged the Honour of kissing her Imperial Foot; but this Gracious Princess held out her little
Finger towards me (after I was set on a Table) which I
embraced in both my Arms, and put the Tip of it, with
the utmost Respect, to my Lip. She made me some general Questions about my Country and my Travels, which
I answered as distinctly and in as few Words as I could.
She asked, whether I would be content to live at Court.
I bowed down to the Board of the Table, and humbly
answered, that I was my Master's Slave; but if I were
at my own Disposal, I should be proud to devote my Life
to her Majesty's Service. She then asked my Master
whether he were willing to sell me at a good Price. He,
who apprehended I could not live a Month, was ready

enough to part with me; and demanded a Thousand
Pieces of Gold; which were ordered him on the Spot, each
Piece being about the Bigness of eight Hundred Moydores:
But, allowing for the Proportion of all Things between
that Country and *Europe*, and the high Price of Gold
among them; was hardly so great a Sum as a Thousand
Guineas would be in *England*. I then said to the Queen;
since I was now her Majesty's most humble Creature and
Vassal, I must beg the Favour, that *Glumdalclitch*, who had
always tended me with so much Care and Kindness, and
understood to do it so well, might be admitted into her
Service, and continue to be my Nurse and Instructor. Her
Majesty agreed to my Petition; and easily got the Farmer's
Consent, who was glad enough to have his Daughter preferred at Court: And the poor Girl herself was not able to
hide her Joy. My late Master withdrew, bidding me farewell, and saying he had left me in a good Service; to which
I replyed not a Word, only making him a slight Bow.

The Queen observed my Coldness; and when the
Farmer was gone out of the Apartment, asked me the
Reason. I made bold to tell her Majesty, that I owed no
other Obligation to my late Master, than his not dashing
out the Brains of a poor harmless Creature found by Chance
in his Field; which Obligation was amply recompenced by
the Gain he had made in shewing me through half the
Kingdom, and the Price he had now sold me for. That the
Life I had since led, was laborious enough to kill an
Animal of ten Times my Strength. That my Health was
much impaired by the continual Drudgery of entertaining
the Rabble every Hour of the Day; and that if my Master
had not thought my Life in Danger, her Majesty perhaps
would not have got so cheap a Bargain. But as I was out
of all fear of being ill treated under the Protection of so
great and good an Empress, the Ornament of Nature, the
Darling of the World, the Delight of her Subjects, the
Phoenix of the Creation; so, I hoped my late Master's
Apprehensions would appear to be groundless; for I
already found my Spirits to revive by the Influence of her
most August Presence.

This was the Sum of my Speech, delivered with great Improprieties and Hesitation; the latter Part was altogether framed in the Style peculiar to that People, whereof I learned some Phrases from *Glumdalclitch*, while she was carrying me to Court.

The Queen giving great Allowance for my Defectiveness in speaking, was however surprised at so much Wit and good Sense in so diminutive an Animal. She took me in her own Hand, and carried me to the King, who was then retired to his Cabinet. His Majesty, a Prince of much Gravity, and austere Countenance, not well observing my Shape at first View, asked the Queen after a cold Manner, how long it was since she grew fond of a *Splacknuck*; for such it seems he took me to be, as I lay upon my Breast in her Majesty's right Hand. But this Princess, who hath an infinite deal of Wit and Humour, set me gently on my Feet upon the Scrutore; and commanded me to give His Majesty an Account of my self, which I did in a very few Words; and *Glumdalclitch*, who attended at the Cabinet Door, and could not endure I should be out of her Sight, being admitted; confirmed all that had passed from my Arrival at her Father's House.

The King, although he be as learned a Person as any in his Dominions; and had been educated in the Study of Philosophy, and particularly Mathematicks; yet when he observed my Shape exactly, and saw me walk erect, before I began to speak, conceived I might be a piece of Clockwork, (which is in that Country arrived to a very great Perfection) contrived by some ingenious Artist. But, when he heard my Voice, and found what I delivered to be regular and rational, he could not conceal his Astonishment. He was by no means satisfied with the Relation I gave him of the Manner I came into his Kingdom; but thought it a Story concerted between *Glumdalclitch* and her Father, who had taught me a Sett of Words to make me sell at a higher Price. Upon this Imagination he put several other Questions to me, and still received rational Answers, no otherwise defective than by a Foreign Accent, and an imperfect Knowledge in the Language; with some rustick

Phrases which I had learned at the Farmer's House, and did not suit the polite Style of a Court.

His Majesty sent for three great Scholars who were then in their weekly waiting (according to the Custom in that Country.) These Gentlemen, after they had a while examined my Shape with much Nicety, were of different Opinion concerning me. They all agreed that I could not be produced according to the regular Laws of Nature; because I was not framed with a Capacity of preserving my Life, either by Swiftness, or climbing of Trees, or digging Holes in the Earth. They observed by my Teeth, which they viewed with great Exactness, that I was a carnivorous Animal; yet most Quadrupeds being an Overmatch for me; and Field-Mice, with some others, too nimble, they could not imagine how I should be able to support my self, unless I fed upon Snails and other Insects; which they offered by many learned Arguments to evince that I could not possibly do. One of them seemed to think that I might be an Embrio, or abortive Birth. But this Opinion was rejected by the other two, who observed my Limbs to be perfect and finished; and that I had lived several Years, as it was manifested from my Beard; the Stumps whereof they plainly discovered through a Magnifying-Glass. They would not allow me to be a Dwarf, because my Littleness was beyond all Degrees of Comparison; for the Queen's favourite Dwarf, the smallest ever known in that Kingdom, was near thirty Foot high. After much Debate, they concluded unanimously that I was only *Relplum Scalcath*, which is interpreted literally *Lusus Naturae*; a Determination exactly agreeable to the Modern Philosophy of *Europe*: whose Professors, disdaining the old Evasion of *occult Causes*, whereby the Followers of *Aristotle* endeavour in vain to disguise their Ignorance; have invented this wonderful Solution of all Difficulties, to the unspeakable Advancement of human Knowledge.

After this decisive Conclusion, I entreated to be heard a Word or two. I applied my self to the King, and assured His Majesty, that I came from a Country which abounded with several Millions of both Sexes, and of my own Stature;

where the Animals, Trees, and Houses were all in Proportion; and where by Consequence I might be as able to defend my self, and to find Sustenance, as any of his Majesty's
Subjects could do here; which I took for a full Answer to
those Gentlemens Arguments. To this they only replied
with a Smile of Contempt; saying, that the Farmer had
instructed me very well in my Lesson. The King, who had
a much better Understanding, dismissing his learned Men,
sent for the Farmer, who by good Fortune was not yet gone
out of Town: Having therefore first examined him privately, and then confronted him with me and the young
Girl; his Majesty began to think that what we told him
might possibly be true. He desired the Queen to order, that
a particular Care should be taken of me; and was of Opinion, that *Glumdalclitch* should still continue in her Office of
tending me, because he observed we had a great Affection
for each other. A convenient Apartment was provided for
her at Court; she had a sort of Governess appointed to take
care of her Education, a Maid to dress her, and two other
Servants for menial Offices; but, the Care of me was wholly
appropriated to her self. The Queen commanded her own
Cabinet-maker to contrive a Box that might serve me for a
Bed-chamber, after the Model that *Glumdalclitch* and I
should agree upon. This Man was a most ingenious Artist;
and according to my Directions, in three Weeks finished for
me a wooden Chamber of sixteen Foot square, and twelve
High; with Sash Windows, a Door, and two Closets, like a
London Bed-chamber. The Board that made the Cieling
was to be lifted up and down by two Hinges, to put in a
Bed ready furnished by her Majesty's Upholsterer; which
Glumdalclitch took out every Day to air, made it with her
own Hands, and letting it down at Night, locked up the
Roof over me. A Nice Workman, who was famous for little
Curiosities, undertook to make me two Chairs, with Backs
and Frames, of a Substance not unlike Ivory; and two
Tables, with a Cabinet to put my Things in. The Room
was quilted on all Sides, as well as the Floor and the Cieling,
to prevent any Accident from the Carelessness of those who
carried me; and to break the Force of a Jolt when I went

in a Coach. I desired a Lock for my Door to prevent Rats and Mice from coming in: The Smith after several Attempts made the smallest that was ever seen among them; for I have known a larger at the Gate of a Gentleman's House in *England*. I made a shift to keep the Key in a Pocket of my own, fearing *Glumdalclitch* might lose it. The Queen likewise ordered the thinnest Silks that could be gotten, to make me Cloaths; not much thicker than an *English* Blanket, very cumbersome till I was accustomed to them. They were after the Fashion of the Kingdom, partly resembling the *Persian*, and partly the *Chinese*; and are a very grave decent Habit.

The Queen became so fond of my Company, that she could not dine without me. I had a Table placed upon the same at which her Majesty eat, just at her left Elbow; and a Chair to sit on. *Glumdalclitch* stood upon a Stool on the Floor, near my Table, to assist and take Care of me. I had an entire set of Silver Dishes and Plates, and other Necessaries, which in Proportion to those of the Queen, were not much bigger than what I have seen in a *London* Toy-shop, for the Furniture of a Baby-house: These my little Nurse kept in her Pocket, in a Silver Box, and gave me at Meals as I wanted them; always cleaning them her self. No Person dined with the Queen but the two Princesses Royal; the elder sixteen Years old, and the younger at that time thirteen and a Month. Her Majesty used to put a Bit of Meat upon one of my Dishes, out of which I carved for my self; and her Diversion was to see me eat in Miniature. For the Queen (who had indeed but a weak Stomach) took up at one Mouthful, as much as a dozen *English* Farmers could eat at a Meal, which to me was for some time a very nauseous Sight. She would craunch the Wing of a Lark, Bones and all, between her Teeth, although it were nine Times as large as that of a full grown Turkey; and put a Bit of Bread in her Mouth, as big as two twelve-penny Loves. She drank out of a Golden Cup, above a Hogshead at a Draught. Her Knives were twice as long as a Scythe set strait upon the Handle. The Spoons, Forks, and other Instruments were all in the same Proportion. I remember

when *Glumdalclitch* carried me out of Curiosity to see some
of the Tables at Court, where ten or a dozen of these enormous Knives and Forks were lifted up together; I thought
I had never till then beheld so terrible a Sight.

It is the Custom, that every *Wednesday*, (which as I have
before observed, was their Sabbath) the King and Queen,
with the Royal Issue of both Sexes, dine together in the
Apartment of his Majesty; to whom I was now become a
Favourite; and at these Times my little Chair and Table
were placed at his left Hand before one of the Salt-sellers.
This Prince took a Pleasure in conversing with me; enquiring into the Manners, Religion, Laws, Government, and
Learning of *Europe*, wherein I gave him the best Account
I was able. His Apprehension was so clear, and his Judgment so exact, that he made very wise Reflexions and Observations upon all I said. But, I confess, that after I had
been a little too copious in talking of my own beloved
Country; of our Trade, and Wars by Sea and Land, of our
Schisms in Religion, and Parties in the State; the Prejudices of his Education prevailed so far, that he could not
forbear taking me up in his right Hand, and stroaking me
gently with the other; after an hearty Fit of laughing, asked
me whether I were a *Whig* or a *Tory*. Then turning to his
first Minister, who waited behind him with a white Staff,
near as tall as the Main-mast of the Royal *Sovereign*; he observed, how contemptible a Thing was human Grandeur,
which could be mimicked by such diminutive Insects as I:
And yet, said he, I dare engage, those Creatures have their
Titles and Distinctions of Honour; they contrive little
Nests and Burrows, that they call Houses and Cities; they
make a Figure in Dress and Equipage; they love, they
fight, they dispute, they cheat, they betray. And thus he
continued on, while my Colour came and went several
Times, with Indignation to hear our noble Country, the
Mistress of Arts and Arms, the Scourge of *France*, the
Arbitress of *Europe*, the Seat of Virtue, Piety, Honour
and Truth, the Pride and Envy of the World, so contempt-
uously treated.

But, as I was not in a Condition to resent Injuries, so,

upon mature Thoughts, I began to doubt whether I were injured or no. For, after having been accustomed several Months to the Sight and Converse of this People, and observed every Object upon which I cast my Eyes, to be of proportionable Magnitude; the Horror I had first conceived from their Bulk and Aspect was so far worn off, that if I then beheld a Company of *English* Lords and Ladies in their Finery and Birth-day Cloaths, acting their several Parts in the most courtly Manner of Strutting, and Bowing and Prating; to say the Truth, I should have been strongly tempted to laugh as much at them as this King and his Grandees did at me. Neither indeed could I forbear smiling at my self, when the Queen used to place me upon her Hand towards a Looking-Glass, by which both our Persons appeared before me in full View together; and there could nothing be more ridiculous than the Comparison: So that I really began to imagine my self dwindled many Degrees below my usual Size.

Nothing angred and mortified me so much as the Queen's Dwarf, who being of the lowest Stature that was ever in that Country, (for I verily think he was not full Thirty Foot high) became so insolent at seeing a Creature so much beneath him, that he would always affect to swagger and look big as he passed by me in the Queen's Antichamber, while I was standing on some Table talking with the Lords or Ladies of the Court; and he seldom failed of a smart Word or two upon my Littleness; against which I could only revenge my self by calling him *Brother*, challenging him to wrestle; and such Repartees as are usual in the Mouths of *Court Pages*. One Day at Dinner, this malicious little Cubb was so nettled with something I had said to him, that raising himself upon the Frame of her Majesty's Chair, he took me up by the Middle, as I was sitting down, not thinking any Harm, and let me drop into a large Silver Bowl of Cream; and then ran away as fast as he could. I fell over Head and Ears, and if I had not been a good Swimmer, it might have gone very hard with me; for *Glumdalclitch* in that Instant happened to be at the other End of the Room; and the Queen was in such a Fright, that she wanted Pres-

Nothing angered and mortified me so much as the Queen's Dwarf

ence of Mind to assist me. But my little Nurse ran to my
Relief; and took me out, after I had swallowed above a
Quart of Cream. I was put to Bed; however I received no
other Damage than the Loss of a Suit of Cloaths, which
was utterly spoiled. The Dwarf was soundly whipped, and
as a further Punishment, forced to drink up the Bowl of
Cream, into which he had thrown me; neither was he ever
restored to Favour: For, soon after the Queen bestowed
him to a Lady of high Quality; so that I saw him no more,
to my very great Satisfaction; for I could not tell to what
Extremitys such a malicious Urchin might have carried his
Resentment.

He had before served me a scurvy Trick, which set
the Queen a laughing, although at the same time she were
heartily vexed, and would have immediately cashiered him,
if I had not been so generous as to intercede. Her Majesty
had taken a Marrow-bone upon her Plate; and after
knocking out the Marrow, placed the Bone again in the
Dish erect as it stood before; the Dwarf watching his Opportunity, while *Glumdalclitch* was gone to the Side-board,
mounted the Stool that she stood on to take care of me at
Meals; took me up in both Hands, and squeezing my Legs
together, wedged them into the Marrow-bone above my
Waist; where I stuck for some time, and made a very ridiculous Figure. I believe it was near a Minute before any
one knew what was become of me; for I thought it below
me to cry out. But, as Princes seldom get their Meat hot,
my Legs were not scalded, only my Stockings and Breeches
in a sad Condition. The Dwarf at my Entreaty had no
other Punishment than a sound whipping.

I was frequently raillied by the Queen upon Account of
my Fearfulness; and she used to ask me whether the People
of my Country were as great Cowards as my self. The
Occasion was this. The Kingdom is much pestered with
Flies in Summer; and these odious Insects, each of them
as big as a *Dunstable* Lark, hardly gave me any Rest while
I sat at Dinner, with their continual Humming and Buzzing
about my Ears. They would sometimes alight upon my
Victuals, and leave their loathsome Excrement or Spawn

behind, which to me was very visible, although not to the Natives of that Country, whose large Opticks were not so acute as mine in viewing smaller Objects. Sometimes they would fix upon my Nose or Forehead, where they stung me to the Quick, smelling very offensively; and I could easily trace that viscous Matter, which our Naturalists tell us enables those Creatures to walk with their Feet upwards upon a Cieling. I had much ado to defend my self against these detestable Animals, and could not forbear starting when they came on my Face. It was the common Practice of the Dwarf to catch a Number of these Insects in his Hand, as School-boys do among us, and let them out suddenly under my Nose, on Purpose to frighten me, and divert the Queen. My Remedy was to cut them in Pieces with my Knife as they flew in the Air; wherein my Dexterity was much admired.

I remember one Morning when *Glumdalclitch* had set me in my Box upon a Window, as she usually did in fair Days to give me Air, (for I durst not venture to let the Box be hung on a Nail out of the Window, as we do with Cages in *England*) after I had lifted up one of my Sashes, and sat down at my Table to eat a Piece of Sweet-Cake for my Breakfast; above twenty Wasps, allured by the Smell, came flying into the Room, humming louder than the Drones of as many Bagpipes. Some of them seized my Cake, and carried it piecemeal away; others flew about my Head and Face, confounding me with the Noise, and putting me in the utmost Terror of their Stings. However I had the Courage to rise and draw my Hanger, and attack them in the Air. I dispatched four of them, but the rest got away; and I presently shut my Window. These Insects were as large as Partridges; I took out their Stings, found them an Inch and a half long, and as sharp as Needles. I carefully preserved them all, and having since shewn them with some other Curiosities in several Parts of *Europe*; upon my Return to *England* I gave three of them to *Gresham College*, and kept the fourth for my self.

CHAPTER FOUR

THE COUNTRY DESCRIBED. A PROPOSAL FOR CORRECTING
MODERN MAPS. THE KING'S PALACE, AND SOME ACCOUNT OF
THE METROPOLIS. THE AUTHOR'S WAY OF TRAVELLING.
THE CHIEF TEMPLE DESCRIBED.

I NOW intend to give the Reader a short Description of
this Country, as far as I travelled in it, which was not
above two thousand Miles round *Lorbrulgrud* the Metropolis. For, the Queen, whom I always attended, never
went further when she accompanied the King in his Progresses; and there staid till his Majesty returned from viewing his Frontiers. The whole Extent of this Prince's Dominions reacheth about six thousand Miles in Length, and
from three to five in Breadth. From whence I cannot but
conclude, that our Geographers of *Europe* are in a great
Error, by supposing nothing but Sea between *Japan* and
California: For it was ever my Opinion, that there must be
a Balance of Earth to counterpoise the great Continent of
Tartary; and therefore they ought to correct their Maps
and Charts, by joining this vast Tract of Land to the
North-west Parts of *America*; wherein I shall be ready to
lend them my Assistance.

The Kingdom is a Peninsula, terminated to the North-
east by a Ridge of Mountains thirty Miles high which are
altogether impassable by Reason of the Volcanoes upon the
Tops. Neither do the most Learned know what sort of
Mortals inhabit beyond those Mountains, or whether they
be inhabited at all. On the three other Sides it is bounded
by the Ocean. There is not one Sea-port in the whole Kingdom; and those Parts of the Coasts into which the Rivers
issue, are so full of pointed Rocks, and the Sea generally so
rough, that there is no venturing with the smallest of their
Boats; so that these People are wholly excluded from any
Commerce with the rest of the World. But the large Rivers
are full of Vessels, and abound with excellent Fish; for they
seldom get any from the Sea, because the Sea-fish are of

the same Size with those in *Europe*, and consequently not worth catching; whereby it is manifest, that Nature in the Production of Plants and Animals of so extraordinary a Bulk, is wholly confined to this Continent; of which I leave the Reasons to be determined by Philosophers. However, now and then they take a Whale that happens to be dashed against the Rocks, which the common People feed on heartily. These Whales I have known so large that a Man could hardly carry one upon his Shoulders; and sometimes for Curiosity they are brought in Hampers to *Lorbrulgrud*: I saw one of them in a Dish at the King's Table, which passed for a Rarity; but I did not observe he was fond of it; for I think indeed the Bigness disgusted him, although I have seen one somewhat larger in *Greenland*.

The Country is well inhabited, for it contains fifty one Cities, near an hundred walled Towns, and a great Number of Villages. To satisfy my curious Reader, it may be sufficient to describe *Lorbrulgrud*. This City stands upon almost two equal Parts on each Side the River that passes through. It contains above eighty thousand Houses. It is in Length three *Glonglungs* (which make about fifty four English Miles) and two and a half in Breadth, as I measured it myself in the Royal Map made by the King's Order, which was laid on the Ground on purpose for me, and extended an hundred Feet; I paced the Diameter and Circumference several times Bare-foot, and computing by the Scale, measured it pretty exactly.

The King's Palace is no regular Edifice, but an Heap of Buildings about seven Miles round: The chief Rooms are generally two hundred and forty Foot high, and broad and long in Proportion. A Coach was allowed to *Glumdalclitch* and me, wherein her Governess frequently took her out to see the Town, or go among the Shops; and I was always of the Party, carried in my Box; although the Girl at my own Desire would often take me out, and hold me in her Hand, that I might more conveniently view the Houses and the People as we passed along the Streets. I reckoned our Coach to be about a Square of *Westminster-Hall*, but not altogether so high; however, I cannot be very exact. One

Day the Governess ordered our Coachman to stop at several Shops; where the Beggars watching their Opportunity, crouded to the Sides of the Coach, and gave me the most horrible Spectacles that ever an *European* Eye beheld. There was a Woman with a Cancer in her Breast, swelled to a monstrous Size, full of Holes, in two or three of which I could have easily crept, and covered my whole Body. There was a Fellow with a Wen in his Neck, larger than five Woolpacks; and another with a couple of wooden Legs, each about twenty Foot high. But, the most hateful Sight of all was the Lice crawling on their Cloaths: I could see distinctly the Limbs of these Vermin with my naked Eye, much better than those of an *European* Louse through a Microscope; and their Snouts with which they rooted like Swine. They were the first I ever beheld; and I should have been curious enough to dissect one of them, if I had proper Instruments (which I unluckily left behind me in the Ship) although indeed the Sight was so nauseous, that it perfectly turned my Stomach.

Beside the large Box in which I was usually carried, the Queen ordered a smaller one to be made for me, of about twelve Foot Square, and ten high, for the Convenience of Travelling; because the other was somewhat too large for *Glumdalclitch's* Lap, and cumbersom in the Coach; it was made by the same Artist, whom I directed in the whole Contrivance. This travelling Closet was an exact Square with a Window in the Middle of three of the Squares, and each Window was latticed with Iron Wire on the outside, to prevent Accidents in long Journeys. On the fourth Side, which had no Window, two strong Staples were fixed, through which the Person that carried me, when I had a Mind to be on Horseback, put in a Leathern Belt, and buckled it about his Waist. This was always the Office of some grave trusty Servant in whom I could confide, whether I attended the King and Queen in their Progresses, or were disposed to see the Gardens, or pay a Visit to some great Lady or Minister of State in the Court, when *Glumdalclitch* happened to be out of Order: For I soon began to be known and esteemed among the greatest Officers, I suppose more upon Account of their Majesty's Favour, than any Merit of my own. In Journeys, when I was weary of the Coach, a Servant on Horseback would buckle my Box, and place it on a Cushion before him; and there I had a full Prospect of the Country on three Sides from my three Windows. I had in this Closet a Field-Bed and a Hammock hung from the Cieling, two Chairs and a Table, neatly screwed to the Floor, to prevent being tossed about by the Agitation of the Horse or the Coach. And having been long used to Sea-Voyages, those Motions, although sometimes very violent, did not much discompose me.

Whenever I had a Mind to see the Town, it was always in my Travelling-Closet; which *Glumdalclitch* held in her Lap in a kind of open Sedan, after the Fashion of the Country, born by four Men, and attended by two others in the Queen's Livery. The People who had often heard of me, were very curious to croud about the Sedan; and the Girl was complaisant enough to make the Bearers stop, and to take me in her Hand that I might be more conveniently seen.

I was very desirious to see the chief Temple, and particularly the Tower belonging to it, which is reckoned the highest in the Kingdom. Accordingly one Day my Nurse carried me thither, but I may truly say I came back disappointed; for, the Height is not above three thousand Foot, reckoning from the Ground to the highest Pinnacle top; which allowing for the Difference between the Size of those People, and us in *Europe*, is no great matter for Admiration, nor at all equal in Proportion, (if I rightly remember) to *Salisbury* Steeple. But, not to detract from a Nation to which during my Life I shall acknowledge myself extremely obliged; it must be allowed, that whatever this famous Tower wants in Height, is amply made up in Beauty and Strength. For the Walls are near an hundred Foot thick, built of hewn Stone, whereof each is about forty Foot square, and adorned on all Sides with Statues of Gods and Emperors cut in Marble larger than the Life, placed in their several Niches. I measured a little Finger which had fallen down from one of these Statues, and lay unperceived among some Rubbish; and found it exactly four Foot and an Inch in Length. *Glumdalclitch* wrapped it up in a Handkerchief, and carried it home in her Pocket to keep among other Trinkets, of which the Girl was very fond, as Children at her Age usually are.

The King's Kitchen is indeed a noble Building, vaulted at Top, and about six hundred Foot high. The great Oven is not so wide by ten Paces as the Cupola at St. *Paul's*: For I measured the latter on purpose after my Return. But if I should describe the Kitchen-grate, the prodigious Pots and Kettles, the Joints of Meat turning on the Spits, with many other Particulars; perhaps I should be hardly believed; at least a severe Critick would be apt to think I enlarged a little, as Travellers are often suspected to do. To avoid which Censure, I fear I have run too much into the other Extream; and that if this Treatise should happen to be translated into the Language of *Brobdingnag*, (which is the general Name of that Kingdom) and transmitted thither; the King and his People would have Reason to complain; that I had done them an Injury by a false and diminutive Representation.

His Majesty seldom keeps above six hundred Horses in his Stables: They are generally from fifty four to sixty Foot high. But, when he goes abroad on solemn Days, he is attended for State by a Militia Guard of five hundred Horse, which indeed I thought was the most splendid Sight that could be ever beheld, till I saw part of his Army in Battalia ; whereof I shall find another Occasion to speak.

CHAPTER FIVE

SEVERAL ADVENTURES THAT HAPPENED TO THE AUTHOR.
THE EXECUTION OF A CRIMINAL. THE AUTHOR SHEWS HIS
SKILL IN NAVIGATION.

I SHOULD have lived happy enough in that Country, if my Littleness had not exposed me to several ridiculous and troublesome Accidents; some of which I shall venture to relate. *Glumdalclitch* often carried me into the Gardens of the Court in my smaller Box, and would sometimes take me out of it and hold me in her Hand, or set me down to walk. I remember, before the Dwarf left the Queen, he followed us one Day into those Gardens; and my Nurse having set me down, he and I being close together, near some Dwarf Apple-trees, I must need shew my Wit by a silly Allusion between him and the Trees, which happens to hold in their Language as it doth in ours. Whereupon, the malicious Rogue watching his Opportunity, when I was walking under one of them, shook it directly over my Head, by which a dozen Apples, each of them near as large as a *Bristol* Barrel, came tumbling about my Ears; one of them hit me on the Back as I chanced to stoop, and knocked me down flat on my Face, but I received no other Hurt; and the Dwarf was pardoned at my Desire, because I had given the Provocation.

Another Day, *Glumdalclitch* left me on a smooth Grass-plot to divert my self while she walked at some Distance with her Governess. In the mean time, there suddenly fell such a violent Shower of Hail, that I was immediately by the Force of it struck to the Ground: And when I was down, the Hail-stones gave me such cruel Bangs all over the Body, as if I had been pelted with Tennis-Balls; however I made a Shift to creep on all four, and shelter my self by lying flat on my Face on the Lee-side of a Border of Lemmon Thyme; but so bruised from Head to Foot, that I could not go abroad in ten Days. Neither is this at all to be wondered at; because Nature in that Country observing the same Proportion through all her Operations, a Hail-stone is near Eighteen Hundred Times as large as one in *Europe*; which I can assert upon Experience, having been so curious to weigh and measure them.

But, a more dangerous Accident happened to me in the same Garden, when my little Nurse, believing she had put me in a secure Place, which I often entreated her to do, that I might enjoy my own Thoughts; and having left my Box at home to avoid the Trouble of carrying it, went to another Part of the Gardens with her Governess and some Ladies of her Acquaintance. While she was absent and out of hearing, a small white Spaniel belonging to one of the chief Gardiners, having got by Accident into the Garden, happened to range near the Place where I lay. The Dog following the Scent, came directly up, and taking me in his Mouth, ran strait to his Master, wagging his Tail, and set me gently on the Ground. By good Fortune he had been so well taught, that I was carried between his Teeth without the least Hurt, or even tearing my Cloaths. But, the poor Gardiner, who knew me well, and had a great Kindness for me, was in a terrible Fright. He gently took me up in both his Hands, and asked me how I did; but I was so amazed and out of Breath, that I could not speak a Word. In a few Minutes I came to my self, and he carried me safe to my little Nurse, who by this time had returned to the Place where she left me, and was in cruel Agonies when I did not appear, nor answer when she called; she severely reprimanded the Gardiner on Account of his Dog. But, the Thing was hushed up, and never known at Court; for the Girl was afraid of the Queen's Anger; and truly as to my self, I thought it would not be for my Reputation that such a Story should go about.

This Accident absolutely determined *Glumdalclitch* never to trust me abroad for the future out of her Sight. I had been long afraid of this Resolution; and therefore concealed from her some little unlucky Adventures that happened in those Times when I was left by my self. Once a Kite hovering over the Garden, made a Stoop at me, and if I had not resolutely drawn my Hanger, and run under a thick Espalier, he would have certainly carried me away in his Talons. Another time, walking to the Top of a fresh Molehill, I fell to my Neck, in the Hole through which that Animal had cast up the Earth; and coined some Lye not worth remembring, to excuse my self for spoiling my Cloaths. I likewise broke my right Shin against the Shell of a Snail, which I happened to stumble over, as I was walking alone, and thinking on poor *England*.

I cannot tell whether I were more pleased or mortified to observe in those solitary Walks, that the smaller Birds did not appear to be at all afraid of me; but would hop about within a Yard Distance, looking for Worms, and other Food, with as much Indifference and Security as if no Creature at all were near them. I remember, a Thrush had the Confidence to snatch out of my Hand with his Bill, a Piece of Cake that *Glumdalclitch* had just given me for my Breakfast. When I attempted to catch any of these Birds, they would boldly turn against me, endeavouring to pick my Fingers, which I durst not venture within their Reach; and then they would hop back unconcerned to hunt for Worms or Snails, as they did before. But, one Day I took a thick Cudgel, and threw it with all my Strength so luckily at a Linnet, that I knocked him down, and seizing him by the Neck with both my Hands, ran with him in Triumph to my Nurse. However, the Bird who had only been stunned, recovering himself, gave me so many Boxes with his Wings on both Sides of my Head and Body, although I held him at Arms Length, and was out of the Reach of his Claws, that I was twenty Times thinking to let him go. But I was soon relieved by one of our Servants, who wrung off the Bird's Neck; and I had him next Day for Dinner by the Queen's Command. This Linnet, as near as I can remember, seemed to be somewhat larger than an *English* Swan.

The Maids of Honour often invited *Glumdalclitch* to their Apartments, and desired she would bring me along with her, on Purpose to have the Pleasure of seeing and touching me. They would often strip me naked from Top to Toe, and lay me at full Length in their Bosoms; wherewith I was much disgusted; because, to say the Truth, a very offensive Smell came from their Skins; which I do not mention or intend to the Disadvantage of those excellent Ladies, for whom I have all Manner of Respect: But, I conceive, that my Sense was more acute in Proportion to my Littleness; and that those illustrious Persons were no more disagreeable to their Lovers, or to each other, than People of the same Quality are with us in *England*. And, after all, I found their natural Smell was much more supportable than when they used Perfumes, under which I immediately swooned away. I cannot forget, that an intimate Friend of mine in

Lilliput took the Freedom in a warm Day, when I had used a good deal of Exercise, to complain of a strong Smell about me; although I am as little faulty that way as most of my Sex: But I suppose, his Faculty of Smelling was as nice with regard to me, as mine was to that of this People. Upon this Point, I cannot forbear doing Justice to the Queen my Mistress, and *Glumdalclitch* my Nurse; whose Persons were as sweet as those of any Lady in *England*.

That which gave me most Uneasiness among these Maids of Honour, when my Nurse carried me to visit them, was to see them use me without any Manner of Ceremony, like a Creature who had no Sort of Consequence. For, they would strip themselves to the Skin, and put on their Smocks in my Presence, while I was placed on their Toylet directly before their naked Bodies; which, I am sure, to me was very far from being a tempting Sight, or from giving me any other Motions than those of Horror and Disgust. Their Skins appeared so coarse and uneven, so variously coloured when I saw them near, with a Mole here and there as broad as a Trencher, and Hairs hanging from it thicker than Pack-threads; to say nothing further concerning the rest of their Persons. Neither did they at all scruple while I was by, to discharge what they had drunk, to the Quantity of at least two Hogsheads, in a Vessel that held above three Tuns. The handsomest among these Maids of Honour, a pleasant frolicksome Girl of sixteen, would sometimes set me astride upon one of her Nipples; with many other Tricks, wherein the Reader will excuse me for not being over particular. But, I was so much displeased, that I entreated *Glumdalclitch* to contrive some Excuse for not seeing that young Lady any more.

One Day, a young Gentleman who was Nephew to my Nurse's Governess, came and pressed them both to see an Execution. It was of a Man who had murdered one of that Gentleman's intimate Acquaintance. *Glumdalclitch* was prevailed on to be of the Company, very much against her Inclination, for she was naturally tender hearted: And, as for my self, although I abhorred such Kind of Spectacles; yet my Curiosity tempted me to see something that I thought must be extraordinary. The Malefactor was fixed in a Chair upon a Scaffold erected for the Purpose; and his Head cut off at one Blow with a Sword of about forty Foot long. The Veins and Arteries spouted up such a prodigious Quantity of Blood, and so high in the Air, that the great *Jet d'Eau* at *Versailles* was not equal for the Time it lasted; and the Head when it fell on the Scaffold Floor, gave such a Bounce, as made me start, although I were at least an *English* Mile distant.

The Queen, who often used to hear me talk of my Sea-Voyages, and took all Occasions to divert me when I was melancholy, asked me whether I understood how to handle a Sail or an Oar; and whether a little Exercise of Rowing might not be convenient for my Health. I answered, that I understood both very well. For although my proper Employment had been to be Surgeon or Doctor to the Ship; yet often upon a Pinch, I was forced to work like a common Mariner. But, I could not see how this could be done in their Country, where the smallest Wherry was equal to a first Rate Man of War among us; and such a Boat as I could manage, would never live in any of their Rivers: Her Majesty said, if I would contrive a Boat, her own Joyner should make it, and she would provide a Place for me to sail in. The Fellow was an ingenious Workman, and by my Instructions in ten Days finished a Pleasure-Boat with all its Tackling, able conveniently to hold eight *Europeans*. When it was finished, the Queen was so delighted, that she ran with it in her Lap to the King, who ordered it to be put in a Cistern full of Water, with me in it, by way of Tryal; where I could not manage my two Sculls or little Oars for want of Room. But, the Queen had before contrived another Project. She ordered the Joyner to make a wooden Trough of three Hundred Foot long, fifty broad, and eight deep; which being well pitched to prevent leaking, was placed on the Floor along the Wall, in an outer Room of the Palace. It had a Cock near the Bottom, to let out the Water when it began to grow stale; and two Servants could easily fill it in half an Hour. Here I often used to row for my Diversion, as well as that of the Queen

and her Ladies, who thought themselves agreeably entertained with my Skill and Agility. Sometimes I would put
up my Sail, and then my Business was only to steer, while
the Ladies gave me a Gale with their Fans; and when they
were weary, some of the Pages would blow my Sail forward
with their Breath, while I shewed my Art by steering Star-
board or Larboard as I pleased. When I had done, *Glumdalclitch* always carried back my Boat into her Closet, and
hung it on a Nail to dry.

In this Exercise I once met an Accident which had like
to have cost me my Life. For, one of the Pages having put
my Boat into the Trough; the Governess who attended
Glumdalclitch, very officiously lifted me up to place me in the
Boat; but I happened to slip through her Fingers, and
should have infallibly fallen down forty Foot upon the
Floor, if by the luckiest Chance in the World, I had not
been stop'd by a Corking-pin that stuck in the good Gentlewoman's Stomacher; the Head of the Pin passed between
my Shirt and the Waistband of my Breeches; and thus I
was held by the Middle in the Air, till *Glumdalclitch* ran to
my Relief.

Another time, one of the Servants, whose Office it was
to fill my Trough every third Day with fresh Water; was so
careless to let a huge Frog (not perceiving it) slip out of his
Pail. The Frog lay concealed till I was put into my Boat,
but then seeing a resting Place, climbed up, and made it
lean so much on one Side, that I was forced to balance it
with all my Weight on the other, to prevent overturning.
When the Frog was got in, it hopped at once half the
Length of the Boat, and then over my Head, backwards
and forwards, dawbing my Face and Cloaths with its odious
Slime. The Largeness of its Features made it appear the
most deformed Animal that can be conceived. However, I
desired *Glumdalclitch* to let me deal with it alone. I banged
it a good while with one of my Sculls, and at last forced it
to leap out of the Boat.

But, the greatest Danger I ever underwent in that Kingdom, was from a Monkey, who belonged to one of the
Clerks of the Kitchen. *Glumdalclitch* had locked me up in

her Closet, while she went somewhere upon Business, or a
Visit. The Weather being very warm, the Closet Window
was left open, as well as the Windows and the Door of my
bigger Box, in which I usually lived, because of its Largeness and Conveniency. As I sat quietly meditating at my
Table, I heard something bounce in at the Closet Window,
and skip about from one Side to the other; whereat,
although I were much alarmed, yet I ventured to look out,
but not stirring from my Seat; and then I saw this frolicksome Animal, frisking and leaping up and down, till at last
he came to my Box, which he seemed to view with great
Pleasure and Curiosity, peeping in at the Door and every
Window. I retreated to the farther Corner of my Room,
or Box; but the Monkey looking in at every Side, put me
into such a Fright, that I wanted Presence of Mind to conceal my self under the Bed, as I might easily have done.
After some time spent in peeping, grinning, and chattering,
he at last espyed me; and reaching one of his Paws in at
the Door, as a Cat does when she plays with a Mouse,
although I often shifted Place to avoid him; he at length
seized the Lappet of my Coat (which being made of that
Country Silk, was very thick and strong) and dragged me
out. He took me up in his right Fore-foot, and held me
as a Nurse doth a Child she is going to suckle; just as I
have seen the same Sort of Creature do with a Kitten in
Europe: And when I offered to struggle, he squeezed me
so hard, that I thought it more prudent to submit. I have
good Reason to believe that he took me for a young one of
his own Species, by his often stroaking my Face very gently
with his other Paw. In these Diversions he was interrupted
by a Noise at the Closet Door, as if some Body were opening it; whereupon he suddenly leaped up to the Window
at which he had come in, and thence upon the Leads and
Gutters, walking upon three Legs, and holding me in the
fourth, till he clambered up to a Roof that was next to ours.
I heard *Glumdalclitch* give a Shriek at the Moment he was
carrying me out. The poor Girl was almost distracted:
That Quarter of the Palace was all in an Uproar; the
Servants ran for Ladders; the Monkey was seen by Hun-

dreds in the Court, sitting upon the Ridge of a Building, holding me like a Baby in one of his Fore-Paws, and feeding me with the other, by cramming into my Mouth some Victuals he had squeezed out of the Bag on one Side of his Chaps, and patting me when I would not eat; whereat many of the Rabble below could not forbear laughing; neither do I think they justly ought to be blamed; for without Question, the Sight was ridiculous enough to every Body but my self. Some of the People threw up Stones, hoping to drive the Monkey down; but this was strictly forbidden, or else very probably my Brains had been dashed out.

The Ladders were now applied, and mounted by several Men; which the Monkey observing, and finding himself almost encompassed; not being able to make Speed enough with his three Legs, let me drop on a Ridge-Tyle, and made his Escape. Here I sat for some time five Hundred Yards from the Ground, expecting every Moment to be blown down by the Wind, or to fall by my own Giddiness, and come tumbling over and over from the Ridge to the Eves. But an honest Lad, one of my Nurse's Footmen, climbed up, and putting me into his Breeches Pocket, brought me down safe.

I was almost choaked with the filthy Stuff the Monkey had crammed down my Throat; but, my dear little Nurse picked it out of my Mouth with a small Needle; and then I fell a vomiting, which gave me great Relief. Yet I was so weak and bruised in the Sides with the Squeezes given me by this odious Animal, that I was forced to keep my Bed a Fortnight. The King, Queen, and all the Court, sent every Day to enquire after my Health; and her Majesty made me several Visits during my Sickness. The Monkey was killed, and an Order made that no such Animal should be kept about the Palace.

When I attended the King after my Recovery, to return him Thanks for his Favours, he was pleased to railly me a good deal upon this Adventure. He asked me what my Thoughts and Speculations were while I lay in the Monkey's Paw; how I liked the Victuals he gave me, his Man-

ner of Feeding; and whether the fresh Air on the Roof had
sharpened my Stomach. He desired to know what I would
have done upon such an Occasion in my own Country. I
told his Majesty, that in *Europe* we had no Monkies, except
such as were brought for Curiosities from other Places, and
so small, that I could deal with a Dozen of them together,
if they presumed to attack me. And as for that monstrous
Animal with whom I was so lately engaged, (it was indeed
as large as an Elephant) if my Fears had suffered me to
think so far as to make Use of my Hanger (looking fiercely,
and clapping my Hand upon the Hilt as I spoke) when he
poked his Paw into my Chamber, perhaps I should have
given him such a Wound, as would have made him glad to
withdraw it with more Haste than he put it in. This I delivered in a firm Tone, like a Person who was jealous lest
his Courage should be called in Question. However, my
Speech produced nothing else besides a loud Laughter;
which all the Respect due to his Majesty from those about
him, could not make them contain. This made me reflect,
how vain an Attempt it is for a Man to endeavour doing
himself Honour among those who are out of all Degree of
Equality or Comparison with him. And yet I have seen
the Moral of my own Behaviour very frequent in *England*
since my Return; where a little contemptible Varlet, without the least Title to Birth, Person, Wit, or common Sense,
shall presume to look with Importance, and put himself
upon a Foot with the greatest Persons of the Kingdom.

I was every Day furnishing the Court with some ridiculous Story; and *Glumdalclitch*, although she loved me to
Excess, yet was arch enough to inform the Queen, whenever I committed any Folly that she thought would be
diverting to her Majesty. The Girl who had been out of
Order, was carried by her Governess to take the Air about
an Hour's Distance, or thirty Miles from Town. They
alighted out of the Coach near a small Foot-path in a Field;
and *Glumdalclitch* setting down my travelling Box, I went
out of it to walk. There was a Cow-dung in the Path, and
I must needs try my Activity by attempting to leap over it.
I took a Run, but unfortunately jumped short, and found

my self just in the Middle up to my Knees. I waded through
with some Difficulty, and one of the Footmen wiped me as
clean as he could with his Handkerchief; for I was filthily
bemired, and my Nurse confined me to my Box until we
returned home; where the Queen was soon informed of what
had passed, and the Footmen spread it about the Court; so
that all the Mirth, for some Days, was at my Expence.

CHAPTER SIX

SEVERAL CONTRIVANCES OF THE AUTHOR TO PLEASE THE
KING AND QUEEN. HE SHEWS HIS SKILL IN MUSICK. THE KING
ENQUIRES INTO THE STATE OF EUROPE, WHICH THE AUTHOR
RELATES TO HIM. THE KING'S OBSERVATIONS THEREON.

I USED to attend the King's Levee once or twice a Week,
and had often seen him under the Barber's Hand, which
indeed was at first very terrible to behold. For, the Razor
was almost twice as long as an ordinary Scythe. His Majesty, according to the Custom of the Country, was only
shaved twice a Week. I once prevailed on the Barber to give
me some of the Suds or Lather, out of which I picked Forty
or Fifty of the strongest Stumps of Hair, I then took a Piece
of fine Wood, and cut it like the Back of Comb, making
several Holes in it at equal Distance, with as small a Needle
as I could get from *Glumdalclitch*. I fixed in the Stumps so
artificially, scraping and sloping them with my Knife towards the Points, that I made a very tolerable Comb;
which was a seasonable Supply, my own being so much
broken in the Teeth, that it was almost useless: Neither
did I know any Artist in that Country so nice and exact,
as would undertake to make me another.

And this puts me in mind of an Amusement wherein I
spent many of my leisure Hours. I desired the Queen's
Woman to save for me the Combings of her Majesty's Hair,
whereof in time I got a good Quantity; and consulting
with my Friend the Cabinet-maker, who had received general Orders to do little Jobbs for me; I directed him to

make two Chair-frames, no larger than those I had in my Box, and then to bore little Holes with a fine Awl round those Parts where I designed the Backs and Seats; through these Holes I wove the strongest Hairs I could pick out, just after the Manner of Cane-chairs in *England*. When they were finished, I made a Present of them to her Majesty, who kept them in her Cabinet, and used to shew them for Curiosities; as indeed they were the Wonder of every one who beheld them. The Queen would have had me sit upon one of these Chairs, but I absolutely refused to obey her; protesting I would rather dye a Thousand Deaths than place a dishonourable Part of my Body on those precious Hairs that once adorned her Majesty's Head. Of these Hairs (as I had always a Mechanical Genius) I likewise made a neat little Purse about five Foot long, with her Majesty's Name decyphered in Gold Letters; which I gave to *Glumdalclitch*, by the Queen's Consent. To say the Truth, it was more for Shew than Use, being not of Strength to bear the Weight of the larger Coins; and therefore she kept nothing in it, but some little Toys that Girls are fond of.

The King, who delighted in Musick, had frequent Consorts at Court, to which I was sometimes carried, and set in my Box on a Table to hear them: But, the Noise was so great, that I could hardly distinguish the Tunes. I am confident, that all the Drums and Trumpets of a Royal Army, beating and sounding together just at your Ears, could not equal it. My Practice was to have my Box removed from the Places where the Performers sat, as far as I could; then to shut the Doors and Windows of it, and draw the Window-Curtains; after which I found their Musick not disagreeable.

I had learned in my Youth to play a little upon the Spinet; *Glumdalclitch* kept one in her Chamber, and a Master attended twice a Week to teach her: I call it a Spinet, because it somewhat resembled that Instrument, and was play'd upon in the same Manner. A Fancy came into my Head, that I would entertain the King and Queen with an *English* Tune upon this Instrument. But this ap-

peared extremely difficult: For, the Spinet was near sixty
Foot long, each Key being almost a Foot wide; so that,
with my Arms extended, I could not reach to above five
Keys; and to press them down required a good smart
stroak with my Fist, which would be too great a Labour,
and to no purpose. The Method I contrived was this. I
prepared two round Sticks about the Bigness of common
Cudgels; they were thicker at one End than the other;
and I covered the thicker End with a Piece of a Mouse's
Skin, that by rapping on them, I might neither Damage
the Tops of the Keys, nor interrupt the Sound. Before
the Spinet, a Bench was placed about four Foot below the
Keys, and I was put upon the Bench. I ran sideling
upon it that way and this, as fast as I could, banging the
proper Keys with my two Sticks; and made a shift to play
a Jigg to the great Satisfaction of both their Majesties: But,
it was the most violent Exercise I ever underwent, and yet
I could not strike above sixteen Keys, nor, consequently,
play the Bass and Treble together, as other Artists do;
which was a great Disadvantage to my Performance.

The King, who as I before observed, was a Prince of excellent Understanding, would frequently order that I
should be brought in my Box, and set upon the Table in
his Closet. He would then command me to bring one of
my Chairs out of the Box, and sit down within three Yards
Distance upon the Top of the Cabinet; which brought me
almost to a Level with his Face. In this Manner I had
several Conversations with him. I one Day took the Freedom to tell his Majesty, that the Contempt he discovered
towards *Europe*, and the rest of the World, did not seem
answerable to those excellent Qualities of Mind, that he
was Master of. That, Reason did not extend itself with the
Bulk of the Body: On the contrary, we observed in our
Country, that the tallest Persons were usually least provided with it. That among other Animals, Bees and Ants
had the Reputation of more Industry, Art, and Sagacity
than many of the larger Kinds. And that, as inconsiderable as he took me to be, I hoped I might live to do his
Majesty some signal Service.   The King heard me with

Attention; and began to conceive a much better Opinion of me than he had ever before. He desired I would give him as exact an Account of the Government of *England* as I possibly could; because, as fond as Princes commonly are of their own Customs (for so he conjectured of other Monarchs by my former Discourses) he should be glad to hear of any thing that might deserve Imitation.

Imagine with thy self, courteous Reader, how often I then wished for the Tongue of *Demosthenes* or *Cicero*, that might have enabled me to celebrate the Praise of my own dear native Country in a Style equal to its Merits and Felicity.

I began my Discourse by informing his Majesty, that our Dominions consisted of two Islands, which composed three mighty Kingdoms under one Sovereign, besides our Plantations in *America*. I dwelt long upon the Fertility of our Soil, and the Temperature of our Climate. I then spoke at large upon the Constitution of an *English* Parliament, partly made up of an illustrious Body called the House of Peers, Persons of the noblest Blood, and of the most ancient and ample Patrimonies. I described that extraordinary Care always taken of their Education in Arts and Arms, to qualify them for being Counsellors born to the King and Kingdom; to have a Share in the Legislature, to be Members of the highest Court of Judicature from whence there could be no Appeal; and to be Champions always ready for the Defence of their Prince and Country by their Valour, Conduct and Fidelity. That these were the Ornament and Bulwark of the Kingdom; worthy Followers of their most renowned Ancestors, whose Honour had been the Reward of their Virtue; from which their Posterity were never once known to degenerate. To these were joined several holy Persons, as part of that Assembly, under the Title of Bishops; whose peculiar Business it is, to take care of Religion, and of those who instruct the People therein. These were searched and sought out through the whole Nation, by the Prince and wisest Counsellors, among such of the Priesthood, as were most deservedly distinguished by the Sanctity of their Lives, and the Depth of their Erudi-

tion; who were indeed the spiritual Fathers of the Clergy
and the People.

That, the other Part of the Parliament consisted of an
Assembly called the House of Commons; who were all
principal Gentlemen, *freely* picked and culled out by the
People themselves, for their great Abilities, and Love of
their Country, to represent the Wisdom of the whole
Nation. And, these two Bodies make up the most august
Assembly in *Europe*; to whom, in Conjunction with the
Prince, the whole Legislature is committed.

I then descended to the Courts of Justice, over which
the Judges, those venerable Sages and Interpreters of the
Law, presided, for determining the disputed Rights and
Properties of Men, as well as for the Punishment of Vice,
and Protection of Innocence. I mentioned the prudent
Management of our Treasury; the Valour and Atchieve-
ments of our Forces by Sea and Land. I computed the
Number of our People, by reckoning how many Millions
there might be of each Religious Sect, or Political Party
among us. I did not omit even our Sports and Pastimes,
or any other Particular which I thought might redound to
the Honour of my Country. And, I finished all with a brief
historical Account of Affairs and Events in *England* for
about an hundred Years past.

This Conversation was not ended under five Audiences,
each of several Hours; and the King heard the whole with
great Attention; frequently taking Notes of what I spoke,
as well as Memorandums of what Questions he intended to
ask me.

When I had put an End to these long Discourses, his
Majesty in a sixth Audience consulting his Notes, proposed
many Doubts, Queries, and Objections, upon every Article.
He asked, what Methods were used to cultivate the Minds
and Bodies of our young Nobility; and in what kind of
Business they commonly spent the first and teachable Part
of their Lives. What Course was taken to supply that
Assembly, when any noble Family became extinct. What
Qualifications were necessary in those who are to be crea-
ted new Lords: Whether the Humour of the Prince, a Sum

of Money to a Court-Lady, or a Prime Minister; or a Design of strengthening a Party opposite to the publick Interest, ever happened to be Motives in those Advancements.
What Share of Knowledge these Lords had in the Laws of
their Country, and how they came by it, so as to enable
them to decide the Properties of their Fellow-Subjects in
the last Resort. Whether they were always so free from
Avarice, Partialities, or Want, that a Bribe, or some other
sinister View, could have no Place among them. Whether
those holy Lords I spoke of, were constantly promoted to
that Rank upon Account of their Knowledge in religious
Matters, and the Sanctity of their Lives; had never been
Compliers with the Times, while they were common Priests;
or slavish prostitute Chaplains to some Nobleman, whose
Opinions they continued servilely to follow after they were
admitted into that Assembly.

He then desired to know, what Arts were practised in
electing those whom I called Commoners. Whether, a
Stranger with a strong Purse might not influence the vulgar
Voters to chuse him before their own Landlords, or the
most considerable Gentleman in the Neighbourhood. How
it came to pass, that People were so violently bent upon
getting into this Assembly, which I allowed to be a great
Trouble and Expence, often to the Ruin of their Families,
without any Salary or Pension: Because this appeared such
an exalted Strain of Virtue and publick Spirit, that his
Majesty seemed to doubt it might possibly not be always
sincere: And he desired to know, whether such zealous Gentlemen could have any Views of refunding themselves for the
Charges and Trouble they were at, by sacrificing the publick Good to the Designs of a weak and vicious Prince, in
Conjunction with a corrupted Ministry. He multiplied his
Questions, and sifted me thoroughly upon every Part of
this Head; proposing numberless Enquiries and Objections, which I think it not prudent or convenient to repeat.

Upon what I said in relation to our Courts of Justice,
his Majesty desired to be satisfied in several Points: And,
this I was the better able to do, having been formerly almost
ruined by a long Suit in Chancery, which was decreed for

me with Costs. He asked, what Time was usually spent in determining between Right and Wrong; and what Degree of Expence. Whether Advocates and Orators had Liberty to plead in Causes manifestly known to be unjust, vexatious, or oppressive. Whether Party in Religion or Politicks were observed to be of any Weight in the Scale of Justice. Whether those pleading Orators were Persons educated in the general Knowledge of Equity; or only in provincial, national, and other local Customs. Whether they or their Judges had any Part in penning those Laws, which they assumed the Liberty of interpreting and glossing upon at their Pleasure. Whether they had ever at different Times pleaded for and against the same Cause, and cited Precedents to prove contrary Opinions. Whether they were a rich or a poor Corporation. Whether they received any pecuniary Reward for pleading or delivering their Opinions. And particularly whether they were ever admitted as Members in the lower Senate.

He fell next upon the Management of our Treasury; and said, he thought my Memory had failed me, because I computed our Taxes at about five or six Millions a Year; and when I came to mention the Issues, he found they sometimes amounted to more than double; for, the Notes he had taken were very particular in this Point; because he hoped, as he told me, that the Knowledge of our Conduct might be useful to him; and he could not be deceived in his Calculations. But, if what I told him were true, he was still at a Loss how a Kingdom could run out of its Estate like a private Person. He asked me, who were our Creditors? and, where we found Money to pay them? He wondered to hear me talk of such chargeable and extensive Wars; that, certainly we must be a quarrelsome People, or live among very bad Neighbours; and that our Generals must needs be richer than our Kings. He asked, what Business we had out of our own Islands, unless upon the Score of Trade or Treaty, or to defend the Coasts with our Fleet. Above all, he was amazed to hear me talk of a mercenary standing Army in the Midst of Peace, and among a free People. He said, if we were governed by our own Consent

in the Persons of our Representatives, he could not imagine
of whom we were afraid, or against whom we were to fight;
and would hear my Opinion, whether a private Man's
House might not better be defended by himself, his Children, and Family; than by half a Dozen Rascals picked up
at a Venture in the Streets, for small Wages, who might
get an Hundred Times more by cutting their Throats.

He laughed at my odd Kind of Arithmetick (as he was
pleased to call it) in reckoning the Numbers of our People
by a Computation drawn from the several Sects among us
in Religion and Politicks. He said, he knew no Reason,
why those who entertain Opinions prejudicial to the Publick, should be obliged to change, or should not be obliged
to conceal them. And, as it was Tyranny in any Government to require the first, so it was Weakness not to enforce
the second: For, a Man may be allowed to keep Poisons in
his Closet, but not to vend them about as Cordials.

He observed, that among the Diversions of our Nobility
and Gentry, I had mentioned Gaming. He desired to know
at what Age this Entertainment was usually taken up, and
when it was laid down. How much of their Time it employed; whether it ever went so high as to affect their Fortunes. Whether mean vicious People, by their Dexterity in
that Art, might not arrive at great Riches, and sometimes
keep our very Nobles in Dependance, as well as habituate
them to vile Companions; wholly take them from the Improvement of their Minds, and force them by the Losses
they received, to learn and practice that infamous Dexterity upon others.

He was perfectly astonished with the historical Account
I gave him of our Affairs during the last Century; protesting
it was only an Heap of Conspiracies, Rebellions, Mur-
ders, Massacres, Revolutions, Banishments; the very worst
Effects that Avarice, Faction, Hypocrisy, Perfidiousness,
Cruelty, Rage, Madness, Hatred, Envy, Lust, Malice, and
Ambition could produce.

His Majesty in another Audience, was at the Pains to
recapitulate the Sum of all I had spoken; compared the
Questions he made, with the Answers I had given; then

taking me into his Hands, and stroaking me gently, delivered himself in these Words, which I shall never forget, nor the Manner he spoke them in. My little Friend *Grildrig*; you have made a most admirable Panegyrick upon your Country. You have clearly proved that Ignorance, Idleness, and Vice are the proper Ingredients for qualifying a Legislator. That Laws are best explained, interpreted, and applied by those whose Interest and Abilities lie in perverting, confounding, and eluding them. I observe among you some Lines of an Institution, which in its Original might have been tolerable; but these half erased, and the rest wholly blurred and blotted by Corruptions. It doth not appear from all you have said, how any one Perfection is required towards the Procurement of any one Station among you; much less that Men are ennobled on Account of their Virtue, that Priests are advanced for their Piety or Learning, Soldiers for their Conduct or Valour, Judges for their Integrity, Senators for the Love of their Country, or Counsellors for their Wisdom. As for yourself (continued the King) who have spent the greatest Part of your Life in travelling; I am well disposed to hope you may hitherto have escaped many Vices of your Country. But, by what I have gathered from your own Relation, and the Answers I have with much Pains wringed and extorted from you; I cannot but conclude the Bulk of your Natives, to be the most pernicious Race of little odious Vermin that Nature ever suffered to crawl upon the Surface of the Earth.

CHAPTER SEVEN

THE AUTHOR'S LOVE OF HIS COUNTRY. HE MAKES A PROPOSAL OF MUCH ADVANTAGE TO THE KING; WHICH IS REJECTED. THE KING'S GREAT IGNORANCE IN POLITICKS. THE LEARNING OF THAT COUNTRY VERY IMPERFECT AND CONFINED. THEIR LAWS, AND MILITARY AFFAIRS, AND PARTIES IN THE STATE.

NOTHING but an extreme Love of Truth could have hindered me from concealing this Part of my Story. It was in vain to discover my Resentments, which were always turned into Ridicule: And I was forced to rest with Patience, while my noble and most beloved Country was so injuriously treated. I am heartily sorry as any of my Readers can possibly be, that such an Occasion was given: But this Prince happened to be so curious and inquisitive upon every Particular, that it could not consist either with Gratitude or good Manners to refuse giving him what Satisfaction I was able. Yet thus much I may be allowed to say in my own Vindication; that I artfully eluded many of his Questions; and gave to every Point a more favourable turn by many Degrees than the strictness of Truth would allow. For, I have always born that laudable Partiality to my own Country, which *Dionysius Halicarnassensis* with so much Justice recommends to an Historian. I would hide the Frailties and Deformities of my Political Mother, and place her Virtues and Beauties in the most advantageous Light. This was my sincere Endeavour in those many Discourses I had with that mighty Monarch, although it unfortunately failed of Success.

But, great Allowances should be given to a King who lives wholly secluded from the rest of the World, and must therefore be altogether unacquainted with the Manners and Customs that most prevail in other Nations: The want of which Knowledge will ever produce many *Prejudices*, and a certain *Narrowness of Thinking*; from which we and the politer Countries of *Europe* are wholly exempted. And it would be hard indeed, if so remote a Prince's Notions of Virtue and Vice were to be offered as a Standard for all Mankind.

To confirm what I have now said, and further to shew the miserable Effects of a *confined Education*; I shall here insert a Passage which will hardly obtain Belief. In hopes to ingratiate my self farther into his Majesty's Favour, I told him of an Invention discovered between three and four hundred Years ago, to make a certain Powder; into an heap of which the smallest Spark of Fire falling, would kindle the whole in a Moment, although it were as big as a Mountain; and make it all fly up in the Air together, with a Noise and Agitation greater than Thunder. That,

HERBERT COLE. 1899.

He was amazed

a proper Quantity of this Powder rammed into an hollow Tube of Brass or Iron, according to its Bigness, would drive a Ball of Iron or Lead with such Violence and Speed, as nothing was able to sustain its Force. That, the largest Balls thus discharged, would not only Destroy whole Ranks of an Army at once; but batter the strongest Walls to the Ground; sink down Ships with a thousand Men in each, to the Bottom of the Sea; and when linked together by a Chain, would cut through Masts and Rigging; divide Hundreds of Bodies in the Middle, and lay all Waste before them. That we often put this Powder into large hollow Balls of Iron, and discharged them by an Engine into some City we were besieging; which would rip up the Pavement, tear the Houses to Pieces, burst and throw Splinters on every Side, dashing out the Brains of all who came near. That I knew the Ingredients very well, which were Cheap, and common; I understood the Manner of compounding them, and could direct his Workmen how to make those Tubes of a Size proportionable to all other Things in his Majesty's Kingdom; and the largest need not be above two hundred Foot long; twenty or thirty of which Tubes, charged with the proper Quantity of Powder and Balls, would batter down the Walls of the strongest Town in his Dominions in a few Hours; or destroy the whole Metropolis, if ever it should pretend to dispute his absolute Commands. This I humbly offered to his Majesty, as a small Tribute of Acknowledgment in return of so many Marks that I had received of his Royal Favour and Protection.

The King was struck with Horror at the Description I had given of those terrible Engines, and the Proposal I had made. He was amazed how so impotent and groveling an Insect as I (these were his Expressions) could entertain such inhuman Ideas, and in so familiar a Manner as to appear wholly unmoved at all the Scenes of Blood and Desolation, which I had painted as the common Effects of those destructive Machines; whereof he said, some evil Genius, Enemy to Mankind, must have been the first Contriver. As for himself, he protested, that although few Things delighted him so much as new Discoveries in Art or in

Nature; yet he would rather lose Half his Kingdom than be privy to such a Secret; which he commanded me, as I valued my Life, never to mention any more.

A strange Effect of *narrow Principles* and *short Views*! that a Prince possessed of every Quality which procures Veneration, Love and Esteem; of strong Parts, great Wisdom and profound Learning; endued with admirable Talents for Government, and almost adored by his Subjects; should from a *nice unnecesssary Scruple*, whereof in *Europe* we can have no Conception, let slip an Opportunity put into his Hands, that would have made him absolute Master of the Lives, the Liberties, and the Fortunes of his People. Neither do I say this with the least Intention to detract from the many Virtues of that excellent King; whose Character I am sensible will on this Account be very much lessened in the Opinion of an *English* Reader: But, I take this Defect among them to have risen from their Ignorance; by not having hitherto reduced *Politicks* into a *Science*, as the more acute Wits of *Europe* have done. For, I remember very well, in a Discourse one Day with the King; when I happened to say, there were several thousand Books among us written upon the *Art of Government*; it gave him (directly contrary to my Intention) a very mean Opinion of our Understandings. He professed both to abominate and despise all *Mystery, Refinement*, and *Intrigue*, either in a Prince or a Minister. He could not tell what I meant by *Secrets of State*, where an Enemy or some Rival Nation were not in the Case. He confined the Knowledge of governing within very *narrow Bounds*; to common Sense and Reason, to Justice and Lenity, to the Speedy Determination of Civil and criminal Causes; with some other obvious Topicks which are not worth considering. And, he gave it for his Opinion; that whoever could make two Ears of Corn, or two Blades of Grass to grow upon a Spot of Ground where only one grew before; would deserve better of Mankind, and do more essential Service to his Country, than the whole Race of Politicians put together.

The Learning of this People is very defective; consisting only in Morality, History, Poetry and Mathematicks; wherein they must be allowed to excel. But, the last of these is wholly applied to what may be useful in Life; to the Improvement of Agriculture and all mechanical Arts; so that among us it would be little esteemed. And as to Ideas, Entities, Abstractions and Transcendentals, I could never drive the least Conception into their Heads.

No Law of that Country must exceed in Words the Number of Letters in their Alphabet; which consists only of two and twenty. But indeed, few of them extend even to that Length. They are expressed in the most plain and simple Terms, wherein those People are not Mercurial enough to discover above one Interpretation. And, to write a Comment upon any Law, is a capital Crime. As to the Decision of civil Causes, or Proceedings against Criminals, their Precedents are so few, that they have little Reason to boast of any extraordinary Skill in either.

They have had the Art of Printing, as well as the *Chinese*, Time out of Mind. But their Libraries are not very large; for that of the King's, which is reckoned the largest, doth not amount to above a thousand Volumes; placed in a Gallery of twelve hundred Foot long; from whence I had Liberty to borrow what Books I pleased. The Queen's Joyner had contrived in one of *Glumdalclitch's* Rooms a Kind of wooden Machine five and twenty Foot high, formed like a standing Ladder; the Steps were each fifty Foot long: it was indeed a moveable Pair of Stairs, the lowest End placed at ten Foot Distance from the Wall of the Chamber. The Book I had a Mind to read was put up leaning against the Wall. I first mounted to the upper Step of the Ladder, and turning my Face towards the Book, began at the Top of the Page, and so walking to the Right and Left about eight or ten Paces according to the Length of the Lines, till I had gotten a little below the Level of my Eyes; and then descending gradually till I came to the Bottom: After which I mounted again, and began the other Page in the same Manner, and so turned over the Leaf, which I could easily do with both my Hands, for it was as thick and stiff as a Paste-board, and in the largest Folio's not above eighteen or twenty Foot long.

Their Stile is clear, masculine, and smooth, but not Florid; for they avoid nothing more than multiplying unnecessary Words, or using various Expressions. I have perused many of their Books, especially those in History and Morality. Among the latter I was much diverted with a little old Treatise, which always lay in *Glumdalclitch's* Bed-chamber, and belonged to her Governess, a grave elderly Gentlewoman, who dealt in Writings of Morality and Devotion. The Book treats of the Weakness of Human kind; and is in little Esteem except among Women and the Vulgar. However, I was curious to see what an Author of that Country could say upon such a Subject. This Writer went through all the usual Topicks of *European* Moralists; shewing how diminutive, contemptible, and helpless an Animal was Man in his own Nature; how unable to defend himself from the Inclemencies of the Air, or the Fury of wild Beasts: How much he was excelled by one Creature in Strength, by another in Speed, by a third in Foresight, by a fourth in Industry. He added, that Nature was degenerated in these latter declining Ages of the World, and could now produce only small abortive Births in Comparison of those in ancient Times. He said, it was very reasonable to think, not only that the Species of Men were originally much larger, but also that there must have been Giants in former Ages; which, as it is asserted by History and Tradition, so it hath been confirmed by huge Bones and Sculls casually dug up in several Parts of the Kingdom, far exceeding the common dwindled Race of Man in our Days. He argued, that the very Laws of Nature absolutely required we should have been made in the Beginning, of a Size more large and robust, not so liable to Destruction from every little Accident of a Tile falling from an House, or a Stone cast from the Hand of a Boy, or of being drowned in a little Brook. From this Way of Reasoning the Author drew several moral Applications useful in the Conduct of Life, but needless here to repeat. For my own Part, I could not avoid reflecting, how universally this Talent was spread of drawing Lectures in Morality, or indeed rather Matter of Discontent and repining, from the

Quarrels we raise with Nature. And, I believe upon a strict
Enquiry, those Quarrels might be shewn as ill-grounded
among us, as they are among that People.

As to their military Affairs; they boast that the King's
Army consists of an hundred and seventy six thousand
Foot, and thirty two thousand Horse: If that may be called
an Army, which is made up of Tradesmen in the several
Cities, and Farmers in the Country, whose Commanders
are only the Nobility and Gentry, without Pay or Reward.
They are indeed perfect enough in their Exercises; and
under very good Discipline, wherein I saw no great Merit:
For, how should it be otherwise, where every Farmer is
under the Command of his own Landlord, and every Citi-
zen under that of the principal Men in his own City, chosen
after the Manner of *Venice* by *Ballot*?

I have often seen the Militia of *Lorbrulgrud* drawn out
to Exercise in a great Field near the City, of twenty Miles
Square. They were in all not above twenty five thousand
Foot, and six thousand Horse; but it was impossible for me
to compute their Number, considering the Space of Ground
they took up. A *Cavalier* mounted on a large Steed might
be about Ninety Foot high. I have seen this Whole Body
of Horse upon the Word of Command draw their Swords
at once, and brandish them in the Air. Imagination can
Figure nothing so Grand, so surprising and so astonishing.
It looked as if ten thousand Flashes of Lightning were dart-
ing at the same time from every Quarter of the Sky.

I was curious to know how this Prince, to whose Dominions there is no Access from any other Country, came
to think of Armies, or to teach his People the Practice of
military Discipline. But I was soon informed, both by Conversation, and Reading their Histories. For, in the Course
of many Ages they have been troubled with the same
Disease, to which the whole Race of Mankind is Subject;
the Nobility often contending for Power, the People for
Liberty, and the King for absolute Dominion. All which,
however happily tempered by the Laws of that Kingdom,
have been sometimes violated by each of the three Parties;
and have more than once occasioned Civil Wars, the last

whereof was happily put an End to by this Prince's Grand-
father in a general Composition; and the Militia then
settled with common Consent hath been ever since kept
in the strictest Duty.

CHAPTER EIGHT

THE KING AND QUEEN MAKE A PROGRESS TO THE FRONTIERS.
THE AUTHOR ATTENDS THEM. THE MANNER IN WHICH HE
LEAVES THE COUNTRY VERY PARTICULARLY RELATED. HE
RETURNS TO ENGLAND.

I HAD always a strong Impulse that I should some time
recover my Liberty, although it were impossible to conjecture by what Means, or to form any Project with the
least Hope of succeeding. The Ship in which I sailed was
the first ever known to be driven within Sight of that Coast;
and the King had given strict Orders, that if at any Time
another appeared, it should be taken ashore, and with all
its Crew and Passengers brought in a Tumbril to *Lorbrulgrud.* He was strongly bent to get me a Woman of my own
Size, by whom I might propagate the Breed: But I think
I should rather have died than undergone the Disgrace of
leaving a Posterity to be kept in Cages like tame Canary
Birds; and perhaps in time sold about the Kingdom to Persons of Quality for Curiosities. I was indeed treated with
much Kindness; I was the Favourite of a great King and
Queen, and the Delight of the whole Court; but it was
upon such a Foot as ill became the Dignity of human Kind.
I could never forget those domestick Pledges I had left behind me. I wanted to be among People with whom I could
converse upon even Terms; and walk about the Streets
and Fields without Fear of being trod to Death like a Frog
or young Puppy. But, my Deliverance came sooner than
I expected, and in a Manner not very common: The whole
Story and Circumstances of which I shall faithfully relate.

I had now been two Years in this Country; and, about
the Beginning of the third, *Glumdalclitch* and I attended the
King and Queen in Progress to the South Coast of the

Kingdom. I was carried as usual in my Travelling-Box, which, as I have already described, was a very convenient Closet of twelve Foot wide. I had ordered a Hammock to be fixed by silken Ropes from the four Corners at the Top; to break the Jolts, when a Servant carried me before him on Horseback, as I sometimes desired; and would often sleep in my Hammock while we were upon the Road. On the Roof of my Closet, set not directly over the Middle of the Hammock, I ordered the Joyner to cut out a Hole of a Foot square to give me Air in hot Weather as I slept; which Hole I shut at pleasure with a Board that drew backwards and forwards through a Groove.

When we came to our Journey's End, the King thought proper to pass a few Days at a Palace he hath near *Flanflasnic*, a City within eighteen *English* Miles of the Sea-side. *Glumdalclitch* and I were much fatigued: I had gotten a small Cold; but the poor Girl was so ill as to be confined to her Chamber. I longed to see the Ocean, which must be the only Scene of my Escape, if ever it should happen. I pretended to be worse than I really was; and desired leave to take the fresh Air of the Sea, with a Page whom I was very fond of, and who had sometimes been trusted with me. I shall never forget with what Unwillingness *Glumdalclitch* consented; nor the strict Charge she gave the Page to be careful of me; bursting at the same time into a Flood of Tears, as if she had some Foreboding of what was to happen. The Boy took me out in my Box about Half an Hour's Walk from the Palace, towards the Rocks on the Sea-shore. I ordered him to set me down; and lifting up one of my Sashes, cast many a wistful melancholy Look towards the Sea. I found myself not very well; and told the Page that I had a Mind to take a Nap in my Hammock, which I hoped would do me good. I got in, and the Boy shut the Window close down, to keep out the Cold. I soon fell asleep: And all I can conjecture is, that while I slept, the Page, thinking no Danger could happen, went among the Rocks to look for Birds Eggs; having before observed him from my Window searching about, and picking up one or two in the Clefts. Be that as it will; I found my self

suddenly awaked with a violent Pull upon the Ring which
was fastned at the Top of my Box for the Conveniency of
Carriage. I felt the Box raised very high in the Air, and
then born forward with prodigious Speed. The first Jolt
had like to have shaken me out of my Hammock; but afterwards the Motion was easy enough. I called out several
times as loud as I could raise my Voice, but all to no purpose. I looked towards my Windows, and could see nothing but the Clouds and Sky. I heard a Noise just over my
Head like the clapping of Wings; and then began to perceive the woful Condition I was in; that some Eagle had
got the Ring of my Box in his Beak, with an Intent to let it
fall on a Rock, like a Tortoise in a Shell, and then pick out
my Body and devour it. For the Sagacity and Smell of
this Bird enable him to discover his Quarry at a great Distance, although better concealed than I could be within a
two Inch Board.

In a little time I observed the Noise and flutter of Wings
to encrease very fast; and my Box was tossed up and down
like a Sign-post in a windy Day. I heard several Bangs or
Buffets, as I thought, given to the Eagle (for such I am certain it must have been that held the Ring of my Box in his
Beak) and then all on a sudden felt my self falling perpen-
dicularly down for above a Minute; but with such incredible Swiftness that I almost lost my Breath. My Fall was
stopped by a terrible Squash, that sounded louder to my
Ears than the Cataract of *Niagara*; after which I was quite
in the Dark for another Minute, and then my Box began
to rise so high that I could see Light from the Tops of my
Windows. I now perceived that I was fallen into the Sea.
My Box, by the Weight of my Body, the Goods that were
in, and the broad Plates of Iron fixed for Strength at the
four Corners of the Top and Bottom, floated about five
Foot deep in Water. I did then, and do now suppose, that
the Eagle which flew away with my Box was pursued by
two or three others, and forced to let me drop while he was
defending himself against the Rest, who hoped to share in
the Prey. The Plates of Iron fastned at the Bottom of the
Box, (for those were the strongest) preserved the Balance

while it fell; and hindred it from being broken on the Surface of the Water. Every Joint of it was well grooved, and the Door did not move on Hinges, but up and down like a Sash; which kept my Closet so tight that very little Water came in. I got with much Difficulty out of my Hammock, having first ventured to draw back the Slip board on the Roof already mentioned, contrived on purpose to let in Air; for want of which I found my self almost stifled.

How often did I then wish my self with my dear *Glumdalclitch*, from whom one single Hour had so far divided me! And I may say with Truth, that in the midst of my own Misfortune, I could not forbear lamenting my poor Nurse, the Grief she would suffer for my Loss, the Displeasure of the Queen, and the Ruin of her Fortune. Perhaps many Travellers have not been under greater Difficulties and Distress than I was at this Juncture; expecting every Moment to see my Box dashed in Pieces, or at least overset by the first violent Blast, or a rising Wave. A Breach in one single Pane of Glass would have been immediate Death: Nor could any thing have preserved the Windows but the strong Lattice Wires placed on the outside against Accidents in Travelling. I saw the Water ooze in at several Crannies, although the Leaks were not considerable; and I endeavoured to stop them as well as I could. I was not able to lift up the Roof of my Closet, which otherwise I certainly should have done, and sat on the Top of it, where I might at least preserve myself from being shut up, as I may call it, in the Hold. Or, if I escaped these Dangers for a Day or two, what could I expect but a miserable Death of Cold and Hunger! I was four Hours under these Circumstances, expecting and indeed wishing every Moment to be my last.

I have already told the Reader, that there were two strong Staples fixed upon the Side of my Box which had no Window, and into which the Servant, who used to carry me on Horseback, would put a Leathern Belt, and buckle it about his Waist. Being in this disconsolate State, I heard, or at least thought I heard some kind of grating Noise on that Side of my Box where the Staples were fixed; and

soon after I began to fancy that the Box was pulled, or
towed along in the Sea; for I now and then felt a sort of
tugging, which made the Waves rise near the Tops of my
Windows, leaving me almost in the Dark. This gave me
some faint Hopes of Relief, although I were not able to
imagine how it could be brought about. I ventured to
unscrew one of my Chairs, which were always fastned to the
Floor; and having made a hard shift to screw it down
again directly under the Slipping-board that I had lately
opened; I mounted on the Chair, and putting my Mouth
as near as I could to the Hole, I called for Help in a loud
Voice, and in all the Languages I understood. I then fastned my Handkerchief to a Stick I usually carried, and
thrusting it up the Hole, waved it several times in the Air;
that if any Boat or Ship were near, the Seamen might conjecture some unhappy Mortal to be shut up in the Box.

I found no Effect from all I could do, but plainly perceived my Closet to be moved along; and in the Space of
an Hour, or better, that Side of the Box where the Staples
were, and had no Window, struck against something that
was hard. I apprehended it to be a Rock, and found my
self tossed more than ever. I plainly heard a Noise upon
the Cover of my Closet, like that of a Cable, and the grating of it as it passed through the Ring. I then found my
self hoisted up by Degrees at least three Foot higher than
I was before. Whereupon, I again thrust up my Stick and
Handkerchief, calling for Help till I was almost hoarse.
In return to which, I heard a great Shout repeated three
times, giving me such Transports of Joy as are not to be
conceived but by those who feel them. I now heard a
trampling over my Head; and somebody calling through
the Hole with a loud Voice in the *English* Tongue: *If there
be any Body below, let them speak.* I answered, I was an *Englishman*, drawn by ill Fortune into the greatest Calamity
that ever any Creature underwent; and begged, by all that
was moving, to be delivered out of the Dungeon I was in.
The Voice replied, I was safe, for my Box was fastned to
their Ship; and the Carpenter should immediately come,
and saw an Hole in the Cover, large enough to pull me

out. I answered, that was needless, and would take up too much Time; for there was no more to be done, but let one of the Crew put his Finger into the Ring, and take the Box out of the Sea into the Ship, and so into the Captain's Cabbin. Some of them upon hearing me talk so wildly, thought I was mad; others laughed; for indeed it never came into my Head, that I was now got among People of my own Stature and Strength. The Carpenter came, and in a few Minutes sawed a Passage about four Foot square; then let down a small Ladder, upon which I mounted, and from thence was taken into the Ship in a very weak Condition.

The Sailors were all in Amazement, and asked me a thousand Questions, which I had no Inclination to answer. I was equally confounded at the Sight of so many Pigmies; for such I took them to be, after having so long accustomed my Eyes to the monstrous Objects I had left. But the Captain, Mr. *Thomas Wilcocks*, an honest worthy *Shropshire* Man, observing I was ready to faint, took me into his Cabbin, gave me a Cordial to comfort me, and made me *turn in* upon his own Bed; advising me to take a little Rest, of which I had great need. Before I went to sleep I gave him to understand, that I had some valuable Furniture in my Box too good to be lost; a fine Hammock, an handsome Field-Bed, two Chairs, a Table and a Cabinet: That my Closet was hung on all Sides, or rather quilted with Silk and Cotton: That if he would let one of the Crew bring my Closet into his Cabbin, I would open it before him, and shew him my Goods. The Captain hearing me utter these Absurdities, concluded I was raving: However, (I suppose to pacify me) he promised to give Order as I desired; and going upon Deck, sent some of his Men down into my Closet, from whence (as I afterwards found) they drew up all my Goods, and stripped off the Quilting; but the Chairs, Cabinet and Bed-sted being screwed to the Floor, were much damaged by the Ignorance of the Seamen, who tore them up by Force. Then they knocked off some of the Boards for the Use of the Ship; and when they had got all they had a Mind for, let the Hulk drop into the Sea,

which by Reason of many Breaches made in the Bottom
and Sides, sunk *to rights*. And indeed I was glad not to have
been a Spectator of the Havock they made; because I am
confident it would have sensibly touched me, by bringing
former Passages into my Mind, which I had rather forget.

I slept some Hours, but perpetually disturbed with
Dreams of the Place I had left, and the Dangers I had
escaped. However, upon waking I found my self much recovered. It was now about eight a Clock at Night, and
the Captain ordered Supper immediately, thinking I had
already fasted too long. He entertained me with great
Kindness, observing me not to look wildly, or talk incon-
sistently; and when we were left alone, desired I would
give him a Relation of my Travels, and by what Accident I
came to be set adrift in that monstrous wooden Chest. He
said, that about twelve a Clock at Noon, as he was looking
through his Glass, he spied it at a Distance, and thought
it was a Sail, which he had a Mind to make; being not
much out of his Course, in hopes of buying some Biscuit,
his own beginning to fall short. That, upon coming nearer,
and finding his Error, he sent out his Long-boat to discover
what I was; that his Men came back in a Fright, swearing
they had seen a swimming House. That he laughed at their
Folly, and went himself in the Boat, ordering his Men to
take a strong Cable along with them. That the Weather
being calm, he rowed round me several times, observed my
Windows, and the Wire Lattices that defended them. That
he discovered two Staples upon one Side, which was all
of Boards, without any Passage for Light. He then commanded his Men to row up to that Side; and fastning a
Cable to one of the Staples, ordered his Men to tow my
Chest (as he called it) towards the Ship. When it was there,
he gave Directions to fasten another Cable to the Ring
fixed in the Cover, and to raise up my Chest with Pullies,
which all the Sailors were not able to do above two or three
Foot. He said, they saw my Stick and Handkerchief thrust
out of the Hole, and concluded, that some unhappy Man
must be shut up in the Cavity. I asked whether he or the
Crew had seen any prodigious Birds in the Air about the

Time he first discovered me: To which he answered, that discoursing this Matter with the Sailors while I was asleep, one of them said he had *observed* three Eagles flying towards the North; but remarked nothing of their being larger than the usual Size; which I suppose must be imputed to the great Height they were at: And he could not guess the Reason of my Question. I then asked the Captain how far he reckoned we might be from Land; he said, by the best Computation he could make, we were at least an hundred Leagues. I assured him, that he must be mistaken by almost half; for I had not left the Country from whence I came, above two Hours before I dropt into the Sea. Whereupon he began again to think that my Brain was disturbed, of which he gave me a Hint, and advised me to go to Bed in a Cabin he had provided. I assured him I was well refreshed with his good Entertainment and Company, and as much in my Senses as ever I was in my Life. He then grew serious, and desired to ask me freely whether I were not troubled in Mind by the Consciousness of some enormous Crime, for which I was punished at the Command of some Prince, by exposing me in that Chest; as great Criminals in other Countries have been forced to Sea in a leaky Vessel without Provisions: For, although he should be sorry to have taken so ill a Man into his Ship, yet he would engage his Word to set me safe on Shore in the first Port where we arrived. He added, that his Suspicions were much increased by some very absurd Speeches I had delivered at first to the Sailors, and afterwards to himself, in relation to my Closet or Chest, as well as by my odd Looks and Behaviour while I was at Supper.

I begged his Patience to hear me tell my Story; which I faithfully did from the last Time I left *England*, to the Moment he first discovered me. And, as Truth always forceth its Way into rational Minds; so, this honest worthy Gentleman, who had some Tincture of Learning, and very good Sense, was immediately convinced of my Candor and Veracity. But, further to confirm all I had said, I entreated him to give Order that my Cabinet should be brought, of which I kept the Key in my Pocket, (for he had already informed me how the Seamen disposed of my Closet) I opened it in his Presence, and shewed him the small Collection of Rarities I made in the Country from whence I had been so strangely delivered. There was the Comb I had contrived out of the Stumps of the King's Beard; and another of the same Materials, but fixed into a paring of her Majesty's Thumb-nail, which served for the Back. There was a Collection of Needles and Pins from a Foot to half a Yard long. Four Wasp-Stings, like Joyners Tacks: Some Combings of the Queen's Hair: A Gold Ring which one Day she made me a Present of in a most obliging Manner, taking it from her little Finger, and throwing it over my Head like a Collar. I desired the Captain would please to accept this Ring in Return of his Civilities; which he absolutely refused. I shewed him a Corn that I had cut off with my own Hand from a Maid of Honour's Toe; it was about the Bigness of a *Kentish* Pippin, and grown so hard, that when I returned to *England*, I got it hollowed into a Cup and set in Silver. Lastly, I desired him to see the Breeches I had then on, which were made of a Mouse's Skin.

I could force nothing on him but a Footman's Tooth, which I observed him to examine with great Curiosity, and found he had a Fancy for it. He received it with abundance of Thanks, more than such a Trifle could deserve. It was drawn by an unskilful Surgeon in a Mistake from one of *Glumdalclitch's* Men, who was afflicted with the Tooth-ach; but it was as sound as any in his Head. I got it cleaned, and put it into my Cabinet. It was about a Foot long, and four Inches in Diameter.

The Captain was very well satisfied with this plain Relation I had given him; and said, he hoped when we returned to *England*, I would oblige the World by putting it in Paper, and making it publick. My Answer was, that I thought we were already over-stocked with Books of Travels: That nothing could now pass which was not extraordinary; wherein I doubted, some Authors less consulted Truth than their own Vanity or Interest, or the Diversion of ignorant Readers. That my Story could contain little besides common Events, without those ornamental Descriptions of strange Plants, Trees, Birds, and other Animals; or the barbarous Customs and Idolatry of savage People, with which most Writers abound. However, I thanked him for his good Opinion, and promised to take the Matter into my Thoughts.

He said, he wondered at one Thing very much; which was, to hear me speak so loud; asking me whether the King or Queen of that Country were thick of Hearing. I told him it was what I had been used to for above two Years past; and that I admired as much at the Voices of him and his Men, who seemed to me only to whisper, and yet I could hear them well enough. But, when I spoke in that Country, it was like a Man talking in the Street to another looking out from the Top of a Steeple, unless when I was placed on a Table, or held in any Person's Hand. I told him, I had likewise observed another Thing; that when I first got into the Ship, and the Sailors stood all about me, I thought they were the most little contemptible Creatures I had ever beheld. For, indeed, while I was in that Prince's Country, I could never endure to look in a Glass after my Eyes had been accustomed to such prodigious Objects; because the Comparison gave me so despicable a Conceit of my self. The Captain said, that while we were at Supper, he observed me to look at every thing with a Sort of Wonder; and that I often seemed hardly able to contain my Laughter; which he knew not well how to take, but imputed it to some Disorder in my Brain. I answered, it was very true; and I wondered how I could forbear, when I saw his Dishes of the Size of a Silver Three-pence, a Leg of Pork hardly a Mouthful, a Cup not so big as a Nutshell: And so I went on, describing the rest of his Houshold stuff and Provisions after the same Manner. For although the Queen had ordered a little Equipage of all Things necessary for me while I was in her Service; yet my Ideas were wholly taken up with what I saw on every Side of me; and I winked at my own Littleness, as People do at their own Faults. The Captain understood my Raillery very well, and merrily replied with the old *English* Proverb, that he doubted, my Eyes were bigger than my Belly; for he did not observe my Stomach so good, although I had fasted all Day: And continuing in his Mirth, protested he would have gladly given an Hundred Pounds to have seen my Closet in the Eagle's Bill, and afterwards in its Fall from so great an Height into the Sea; which would certainly have been a most astonishing Object, worthy to have the Description of it transmitted to future Ages: And the Comparison of *Phaeton* was so obvious, that he could not forbear applying it, although I did not much admire the Conceit.

The Captain having been at *Tonquin*, was in his Return to *England* driven North Eastward to the Latitude of 44 Degrees, and of Longitude 143. But meeting a Trade Wind two Days after I came on board him, we sailed Southward a long Time, and coasting *New-Holland*, kept our Course West-south-west, and then South-south-west till we doubled the *Cape of Good-hope*. Our Voyage was very prosperous, but I shall not trouble the Reader with a Journal of it. The Captain called in at one or two Ports, and sent in his Longboat for Provisions and fresh Water; but I never went out of the Ship till we came into the *Downs*, which was on the 3d Day of *June* 1706, about nine Months after my Escape. I offered to leave my Goods in Security for Payment of my Freight; but the Captain protested he would not receive one Farthing. We took kind Leave of each other; and I made him promise he would come to see me at my House in *Redriff*. I hired a Horse and Guide for five Shillings, which I borrowed of the Captain.

As I was on the Road; observing the Littleness of the Houses, the Trees, the Cattle and the People, I began to think my self in *Lilliput*. I was afraid of trampling on every Traveller I met; and often called aloud to have them stand out of the Way; so that I had like to have gotten one or two broken Heads for my Impertinence.

When I came to my own House, for which I was forced to enquire, one of the Servants opening the Door, I bent down to go in (like a Goose under a Gate) for fear of striking my Head. My Wife ran out to embrace me, but I stooped lower than her Knees, thinking she could otherwise never be able to reach my Mouth. My Daughter kneeled to ask me Blessing, but I could not see her till she arose; having been so long used to stand with my Head and Eyes erect to above Sixty Foot; and then I went to take her up with one Hand, by the Waist. I looked down upon the Servants, and one or two Friends who were in the House, as if they had been Pigmies, and I a Giant. I told my Wife, she had been too thrifty; for I found she had starved herself and her Daughter to nothing. In short, I behaved my self so unaccountably, that they were all of the Captain's Opinion when he first saw me; and concluded I had lost my Wits. This I mention as an Instance of the great Power of Habit and Prejudice.

In a little Time I and my Family and Friends came to a right Understanding: But my Wife protested I should never go to Sea any more; although my evil Destiny so ordered, that she had not Power to hinder me; as the Reader may know hereafter. In the mean Time, I here conclude the second Part of my unfortunate Voyages.

The End of the Second Part

PART THREE

A VOYAGE TO LAPUTA, BALNIBARBI, LUGGNAGG, GLUBBDUBDRIB, AND JAPAN

Parts Unknown

LAND OF
St. James B.
Robbin I.
LESSO
Solmon B.
C. Canal

Companys
Land

Stats I.

Sea of
Corea
Sandō I.
Torpia
Nivalo
Meaco Yedo
JAPON
Osacca Surungo
Tonsa I.
Bungo I.
Dimeris Straits
I. Tanaxima

Toy Pt.
Red Pt.
Busho Pt.
Barnevelts
Ongeluckig I.
South I.
Sialo
Glangun
Maldoneda

LUGN-AGG
Traldragdul

Clamrgnig

I. Desarte

Glubbdubdrib

Urac
Timal

Laputa

BALNIBARBI
Lagado

Discovered
A.D. 1701

CHAPTER ONE

THE AUTHOR SETS OUT ON HIS THIRD VOYAGE. IS TAKEN
BY PYRATES. THE MALICE OF A DUTCHMAN. HIS ARRIVAL
AT AN ISLAND. HE IS RECEIVED INTO LAPUTA.

I HAD not been at home above ten Days, when Captain
William Robinson, a *Cornish* Man, Commander of the
Hopewell, a stout Ship of three Hundred Tuns, came to
my House. I had formerly been Surgeon of another Ship
where he was Master, and a fourth Part Owner, in a
Voyage to the *Levant*. He had always treated me more
like a Brother than an inferior Officer; and hearing of my
Arrival made me a Visit, as I apprehended only out of
Friendship, for nothing passed more than what is usual
after long Absence. But repeating his Visits often, expressing his Joy to find me in good Health, asking whether
I were now settled for Life, adding that he intended a
Voyage to the *East-Indies*, in two Months, at last he plainly invited me, although with some Apologies, to be Surgeon of the Ship. That I should have another Surgeon
under me, besides our two Mates; that my Sallary should
be double to the usual Pay; and that having experienced
my Knowledge in Sea-Affairs to be at least equal to his,
he would enter into any Engagement to follow my Advice,
as much as if I had Share in the Command.

He said so many other obliging things, and I knew him
to be so honest a Man, that I could not reject his Proposal;
the Thirst I had of seeing the World, notwithstanding my
past Misfortunes, continuing as violent as ever. The only
Difficulty that remained, was to persuade my Wife, whose
Consent however I at last obtained, by the Prospect of
Advantage she proposed to her Children.

We set out the 5th Day of *August*, 1706, and arrived at
Fort St. *George*, the 11th of *April* 1707. We stayed there
three Weeks to refresh our Crew, many of whom were sick.
From thence we went to *Tonquin*, where the Captain resolved to continue some time; because many of the Goods

he intended to buy were not ready, nor could he expect to be dispatched in several Months. Therefore in hopes to defray some of the Charges he must be at, he bought a Sloop, loaded it with several Sorts of Goods, wherewith the *Tonquinese* usually trade to the neighbouring Islands; and putting Fourteen Men on Board, whereof three were of the Country, he appointed me Master of the Sloop, and gave me Power to traffick, while he transacted his Affairs at *Tonquin.*

We had not sailed above three Days, when a great Storm arising, we were driven five Days to the North-North-East, and then to the East; after which we had fair Weather, but still with a pretty strong Gale from the West. Upon the tenth Day we were chased by two Pyrates, who soon overtook us; for my Sloop was so deep loaden, that she sailed very slow; neither were we in a Condition to defend our selves.

We were boarded about the same Time by both the Pyrates, who entered furiously at the Head of their Men; but finding us all prostrate upon our Faces, (for so I gave Order), they pinioned us with strong Ropes, and setting a Guard upon us, went to search the Sloop.

I observed among them a *Dutchman*, who seemed to be of some Authority, although he were not Commander of either Ship. He knew us by our Countenances to be *Englishmen*, and jabbering to us in his own Language, swore we should be tyed Back to Back, and thrown into the Sea. I spoke *Dutch* tolerably well; I told him who we were, and begged him in Consideration of our being Christians and Protestants, of neighbouring Countries, in strict Alliance, that he would move the Captains to take some Pity on us. This inflamed his Rage; he repeated his Threatnings, and turning to his Companions, spoke with great Vehemence, in the *Japanese* Language, as I suppose; often using the Word *Christianos.*

The largest of the two Pyrate Ships was commanded by a *Japanese* Captain, who spoke a little *Dutch*, but very imperfectly. He came up to me, and after several Questions, which I answered in great Humility, he said we should not die. I made the Captain a very low Bow, and then turning to the *Dutchman*, said, I was sorry to find more Mercy in a Heathen, than in a Brother Christian. But I had soon Reason to repent those foolish Words; for that malicious Reprobate, having often endeavoured in vain to persuade both the Captains that I might be thrown into the Sea, (which they would not yield to after the Promise made me, that I should not die) however prevailed so far as to have a Punishment inflicted on me, worse in all human Appearance than Death it self. My Men were sent by an equal Division into both the Pyrate-Ships, and my Sloop new manned. As to my self, it was determined that I should be set a-drift, in a small Canoe, with Paddles and a Sail, and four Days Provisions; which last the *Japanese* Captain was so kind to double out of his own Stores, and would permit no Man to search me. I got down into the Canoe, while the *Dutchman* standing upon the Deck, loaded me with all the Curses and injurious Terms his Language could afford.

About an Hour before we saw the Pyrates, I had taken an Observation, and found we were in the Latitude of 46 N. and of Longitude 183. When I was at some Distance from the Pyrates, I discovered by my Pocket-Glass several Islands to the South-East. I set up my Sail, the Wind being fair, with a Design to reach the nearest of those Islands, which I made a Shift to do in about three Hours. It was all rocky; however I got many Birds Eggs; and striking Fire, I kindled some Heath and dry Sea Weed, by which I roasted my Eggs. I eat no other Supper, being resolved to spare my Provisions as much as I could. I passed the Night under the Shelter of a Rock, strowing some Heath under me, and slept pretty well.

The next Day I sailed to another Island, and thence to a third and fourth, sometimes using my Sail, and sometimes my Paddles. But not to trouble the Reader with a particular Account of my Distresses; let it suffice, that on the 5th Day, I arrived at the last Island in my Sight, which lay South-South-East to the former.

This Island was at a greater Distance than I expected, and I did not reach it in less than five Hours. I encompassed it almost round before I could find a convenient

Place to land in, which was a small Creek, about three Times the Wideness of my Canoe. I found the Island to be all rocky, only a little intermingled with Tufts of Grass, and sweet smelling Herbs. I took out my small Provisions, and after having refreshed myself, I secured the Remainder in a Cave, whereof there were great Numbers. I gathered Plenty of Eggs upon the Rocks, and got a Quantity of dry Sea-weed, and parched Grass, which I designed to kindle the next Day, and roast my Eggs as well as I could. (For I had about me my Flint, Steel, Match, and Burning-glass.) I lay all Night in the Cave where I had lodged my Provisions. My Bed was the same dry Grass and Sea-weed which I intended for Fewel. I slept very little; for the Disquiets of my Mind prevailed over my Wearyness, and kept me awake. I considered how impossible it was to preserve my Life, in so desolate a Place; and how miserable my End must be. Yet I found my self so listless and desponding, that I had not the Heart to rise; and before I could get Spirits enough to creep out of my Cave, the Day was far advanced. I walked a while among the Rocks, the Sky was perfectly clear, and the Sun so hot, that I was forced to turn my Face from it: When all on a Sudden it became obscured, as I thought, in a Manner very different from what happens by the Interposition of a Cloud. I turned back, and perceived a vast Opake Body between me and the Sun, moving forwards towards the Island: It seemed to be about two Miles high, and hid the Sun six or seven Minutes, but I did not observe the Air to be much colder, or the Sky more darkned, than if I had stood under the Shade of a Mountain. As it approached nearer over the Place where I was, it appeared to be a firm Substance, the Bottom flat, smooth, and shining very bright from the Reflexion of the Sea below. I stood upon a Height about two Hundred Yards from the Shoar, and saw this vast Body descending almost to a Parallel with me, at less than an *English* Mile Distance. I took out my Pocket-Perspective, and could plainly discover Numbers of People moving up and down the

Sides of it, which appeared to be sloping, but what those People were doing, I was not able to distinguish.

The natural Love of Life gave me some inward Motions of Joy; and I was ready to entertain a Hope, that this Adventure might some Way or other help to deliver me from the desolate Place and Condition I was in. But, at the same Time, the Reader can hardly conceive my Astonishment, to behold an Island in the Air, inhabited by Men, who were able (as it should seem) to raise, or sink, or put it into a progressive Motion, as they pleased. But not being, at that Time, in a Disposition to philosophise upon this Phaenomenon, I rather chose to observe what Course the Island would take; because it seemed for a while to stand still. Yet soon after it advanced nearer; and I could see the Sides of it, encompassed with several Gradations of Galleries and Stairs, at certain Intervals, to descend from one to the other. In the lowest Gallery, I beheld some People fishing with long Angling Rods, and others looking on. I waved my Cap, (for my Hat was long since worn out), and my Handkerchief towards the Island; and upon its nearer Approach, I called and shouted with the utmost Strength of my Voice; and then looking circumspectly, I beheld a Crowd gathered to that Side which was most in my View. I found by their pointing towards me and to each other, that they plainly discovered me, although they made no Return to my Shouting: But I could see four or five Men running in great Haste up the Stairs to the Top of the Island, who then disappeared. I happened rightly to conjecture, that these were sent for Orders to some Person in Authority upon this Occasion.

The Number of People increased; and in less than Half an Hour, the Island was moved and raised in such a Manner, that the lowest Gallery appeared in a Parallel of less than an Hundred Yards Distance from the Height where I stood. I then put my self into the most supplicating Postures, and spoke in the humblest Accent, but received no Answer. Those who stood nearest over-against me, seemed to be Persons of Distinction, as I supposed by their Habit. They conferred earnestly with each other, looking often upon me. At length one of them called out in a clear, polite, smooth Dialect, not unlike in Sound to the *Italian*; and therefore I returned an Answer in that Language, hoping at least that the Cadence might be more agreeable to his Ears. Although neither of us understood the other, yet my Meaning was easily known, for the People saw the Distress I was in.

They made Signs for me to come down from the Rock, and go towards the Shoar, which I accordingly did; and the flying Island being raised to a convenient Height, the Verge directly over me, a Chain was let down from the lowest Gallery, with a Seat fastned to the Bottom, to which I fixed my self, and was drawn up by Pullies.

CHAPTER TWO

THE HUMOURS AND DISPOSITIONS OF THE LAPUTIANS DE-
SCRIBED. AN ACCOUNT OF THEIR LEARNING. OF THE KING
AND HIS COURT. THE AUTHOR'S RECEPTION THERE. THE
INHABITANTS SUBJECT TO FEARS AND DISQUIETUDES. AN
ACCOUNT OF THE WOMEN.

AT my alighting I was surrounded by a Crowd of People, but those who stood nearest seemed to be of better Quality. They beheld me with all the Marks and Circumstances of Wonder; neither indeed was I much in their Debt; having never till then seen a Race of Mortals so singular in their Shapes, Habits, and Countenances. Their Heads were all reclined to the Right, or the Left; one of their Eyes turned inward, and the other directly up to the Zenith. Their outward Garments were adorned with the Figures of Suns, Moons, and Stars, interwoven with those of Fiddles, Flutes, Harps, Trumpets, Harpsicords, and many more Instruments of Musick, unknown to us in *Europe*. I observed here and there many in the Habit of Servants, with a blown Bladder fastned like a Flail to the End of a short Stick, which they carried in their Hands. In each Bladder was a small Quantity of dried Pease, or little Pebbles, (as I was afterwards informed.) With these Bladders they now and then flapped the Mouths and Ears of those who stood near them, of which Practice I could not then conceive the Meaning. It seems, the Minds of these People are so taken up with intense Speculations, that they neither can speak, or attend to the Discourses of others, without being rouzed by some external Taction upon the Organs of Speech and Hearing; for which Reason, those Persons who are able to afford it, always keep a *Flapper*, (the Original is *Climenole*) in their Family, as one of their Domesticks; nor ever walk abroad or make Visits without him. And the Business of this Officer is, when two or more Persons are in Company, gently to strike with his Bladder the Mouth of him who is to speak, and the Right Ear of him or them to whom the Speaker addresseth himself. This *Flapper* is likewise employed diligently to attend his Master in his Walks, and upon Occasion to give him a soft Flap on his Eyes; because he is always so wrapped up in Cogitation, that he is in manifest Danger of falling down every Precipice, and bouncing his Head against every Post; and in the Streets, of jostling others, or being jostled himself into the Kennel.

It was necessary to give the Reader this Information, without which he would be at the same Loss with me, to understand the Proceedings of these People, as they conducted me up the Stairs, to the Top of the Island, and from thence to the Royal Palace. While we were ascending, they forgot several Times what they were about, and left me to my self, till their Memories were again rouzed by their *Flappers*; for they appeared altogether unmoved by the Sight of my foreign Habit and Countenance, and by the Shouts of the Vulgar, whose Thoughts and Minds were more disengaged.

At last we entered the Palace, and proceeded into the Chamber of Presence; where I saw the King seated on his Throne, attended on each Side by Persons of prime Quality. Before the Throne, was a large Table filled with

Globes and Spheres, and Mathematical Instruments of all
Kinds. His Majesty took not the least Notice of us, although our Entrance were not without sufficient Noise,
by the Concourse of all Persons belonging to the Court.
But, he was then deep in a Problem, and we attended
at least an Hour, before he could solve it. There stood
by him on each Side, a young Page, with Flaps in their
Hands; and when they saw he was at Leisure, one of
them gently struck his Mouth, and the other his Right
Ear; at which he started like one awaked on the sudden,
and looking towards me, and the Company I was in,
recollected the Occasion of our coming, whereof he had
been informed before. He spoke some Words; whereupon immediately a young Man with a Flap came up to
my Side, and flapt me gently on the Right Ear; but I
made Signs as well as I could, that I had no Occasion for
such an Instrument; which as I afterwards found, gave
his Majesty and the whole Court a very mean Opinion
of my Understanding. The King, as far as I could conjecture, asked me several Questions, and I addressed my
self to him in all the Languages I had. When it was
found, that I could neither understand nor be understood, I was conducted by his Order to an Apartment
in his Palace, (this Prince being distinguished above all
his Predecessors for his Hospitality to Strangers,) where
two Servants were appointed to attend me. My Dinner
was brought, and four Persons of Quality, whom I re-
membered to have seen very near the King's Person, did
me the Honour to dine with me. We had two Courses,
of three Dishes each. In the first Course, there was a
Shoulder of Mutton, cut into an Æquilateral Triangle;
a Piece of Beef into a Rhomboides; and a Pudding into
a Cycloid. The second Course was two Ducks, trussed
up into the Form of Fiddles; Sausages and Puddings resembling Flutes and Haut-boys, and a Breast of Veal in
the Shape of a Harp. The Servants cut our Bread into
Cones, Cylinders, Parallelograms, and several other
Mathematical Figures.

While we were at Dinner, I made bold to ask the Names

of several Things in their Language; and those noble Persons, by the Assistance of their *Flappers*, delighted to give me Answers, hoping to raise my Admiration of their great Abilities, if I could be brought to converse with them. I was soon able to call for Bread, and Drink, or whatever else I wanted.

After Dinner my Company withdrew, and a Person was sent to me by the King's Order, attended by a *Flapper*. He brought with him Pen, Ink, and Paper, and three or four Books; giving me to understand by Signs, that he was sent to teach me the Language. We sat together four Hours, in which Time I wrote down a great Number of Words in Columns, with the Translations over against them. I likewise made a Shift to learn several short Sentences. For my Tutor would order one of my Servants to fetch something, to turn about, to make a Bow, to sit, or stand, or walk, and the like. Then I took down the Sentence in Writing. He shewed me also in one of his Books, the Figures of the Sun, Moon, and Stars, the Zodiack, the Tropics and Polar Circles, together with the Denominations of many Figures of Planes and Solids. He gave me the Names and Descriptions of all the Musical Instruments, and the general Terms of Art in playing on each of them. After he had left me, I placed all my Words with their Interpretations in alphabetical Order. And thus in a few Days, by the Help of a very faithful Memory, I got some Insight into their Language.

The Word, which I interpret the *Flying* or *Floating Island*, is in the Original *Laputa*; whereof I could never learn the true Etymology. *Lap* in the old obsolete Language signifieth *High*, and *Untuh* a *Governor*; from which they say by Corruption was derived *Laputa* from *Lapuntuh*. But I do not approve of this Derivation, which seems to be a little strained. I ventured to offer to the Learned among them a Conjecture of my own, that *Laputa* was *quasi Lap outed*; *Lap* signifying properly the dancing of the Sun Beams in the Sea; and *outed* a Wing, which however I shall not obtrude, but submit to the judicious Reader.

Those to whom the King had entrusted me, observing

how ill I was clad, ordered a Taylor to come next Morning, and take my Measure for a Suit of Cloths. This Operator did his Office after a different Manner from those of his Trade in *Europe*. He first took my Altitude by a Quadrant, and then with Rule and Compasses, described the Dimensions and Out-Lines of my whole Body; all which he entred upon Paper, and in six Days brought my Cloths very ill made, and quite out of Shape, by happening to mistake a Figure in the Calculation. But my Comfort was, that I observed such Accidents very frequent, and little regarded.

During my Confinement for want of Cloaths, and by an Indisposition that held me some Days longer, I much enlarged my Dictionary; and when I went next to Court, was able to understand many Things the King spoke, and to return him some Kind of Answers. His Majesty had given Orders, that the Island should move North-East and by East, to the vertical Point over *Lagado*, the Metropolis of the whole Kingdom, below upon the firm Earth. It was about Ninety Leagues distant, and our Voyage lasted four Days and an Half. I was not in the least sensible of the progressive Motion made in the Air by the Island. On the second Morning, about Eleven o'Clock, the King himself in Person, attended by his Nobility, Courtiers, and Officers, having prepared all their Musical Instruments, played on them for three Hours without Intermission; so that I was quite stunned with the Noise; neither could I possibly guess the Meaning, till my Tutor informed me. He said, that the People of their Island had their Ears adapted to hear the Musick of the Spheres, which always played at certain Periods; and the Court was now prepared to bear their Part in whatever Instrument they most excelled.

In our Journey towards *Lagado* the Capital City, his Majesty ordered that the Island should stop over certain Towns and Villages, from whence he might receive the Petitions of his Subjects. And to this Purpose, several Packthreads were let down with small Weights at the Bottom. On these Packthreads the People strung their Petitions, which mounted up directly like the Scraps of

Paper fastned by School-boys at the End of the String that holds their Kite. Sometimes we received Wine and Victuals from below, which were drawn up by Pullies.

The Knowledge I had in Mathematicks gave me great Assistance in acquiring their Phraseology, which depended much upon that Science and Musick; and in the latter I was not unskilled. Their Ideas are perpetually conversant in Lines and Figures. If they would, for Example, praise the Beauty of a Woman, or any other Animal, they describe it by Rhombs, Circles, Parallelograms, Ellipses, and other Geometrical Terms; or else by Words of Art drawn from Musick, needless here to repeat. I observed in the King's Kitchen all Sorts of Mathematical and Musical Instruments, after the Figures of which they cut up the Joynts that were served to his Majesty's Table.

Their Houses are very ill built, the Walls bevil, without one right Angle in any Apartment; and this Defect ariseth from the Contempt they bear for practical Geometry; which they despise as vulgar and mechanick, those Instructions they give being too refined for the Intellectuals of their Workmen; which occasions perpetual Mistakes. And although they are dextrous enough upon a Piece of Paper, in the Management of the Rule, the Pencil, and the Divider, yet in the common Actions and Behaviour of Life, I have not seen a more clumsy, awkward, and unhandy People, nor so slow and perplexed in their Conceptions upon all other Subjects, except those of Mathematicks and Musick. They are very bad Reasoners, and vehemently given to Opposition, unless when they happen to be of the right Opinion, which is seldom their Case. Imagination, Fancy, and Invention, they are wholly Strangers to, nor have any Words in their Language by which those Ideas can be expressed; the whole Compass of their Thoughts and Mind, being shut up within the two forementioned Sciences.

Most of them, and especially those who deal in the Astronomical Part, have great Faith in judicial Astrology, although they are ashamed to own it publickly. But, what I chiefly admired, and thought altogether unaccountable,

was the strong Disposition I observed in them towards
News and Politicks; perpetually enquiring into publick
Affairs, giving their Judgments in Matters of State; and
passionately disputing every Inch of a Party Opinion. I
have indeed observed the same Disposition among most
of the Mathematicians I have known in *Europe*; although
I could never discover the least Analogy between the two
Sciences; unless those People suppose, that because the
smallest Circle hath as many Degrees as the largest, therefore the Regulation and Management of the World require
no more Abilities than the handling and turning of a
Globe. But, I rather take this Quality to spring from a
very common Infirmity of human Nature, inclining us to
be more curious and conceited in Matters where we have
least Concern, and for which we are least adapted either
by Study or Nature.

These People are under continual Disquietudes, never
enjoying a Minute's Peace of Mind; and their Disturbances proceed from Causes which very little affect the rest
of Mortals. Their Apprehensions arise from several Changes they dread in the Celestial Bodies. For instance; that
the Earth by the continual Approaches of the Sun towards
it, must in Course of Time be absorbed or swallowed up.
That the Face of the Sun will by Degrees be encrusted
with its own Effluvia, and give no more Light to the
World. That, the Earth very narrowly escaped a Brush
from the Tail of the last Comet, which would have infallibly reduced it to Ashes; and that the next, which they
have calculated for One and Thirty Years hence, will
probably destroy us. For, if in its Perihelion it should
approach within a certain Degree of the Sun, (as by their
Calculations they have Reason to dread) it will conceive
a Degree of Heat ten Thousand Times more intense than
that of red hot glowing Iron; and in its Absence from
the Sun, carry a blazing Tail Ten Hundred Thousand
and Fourteen Miles long; through which if the Earth
should pass at the Distance of one Hundred Thousand
Miles from the *Nucleus*, or main Body of the Comet, it
must in its Passage be set on Fire, and reduced to Ashes.

That the Sun daily spending its Rays without any Nutriment to supply them, will at last be wholly consumed and annihilated; which must be attended with the Destruction of this Earth, and of all the Planets that receive their Light from it.

They are so perpetually alarmed with the Apprehensions of these and the like impending Dangers, that they can neither sleep quietly in their Beds, nor have any Relish for the common Pleasures or Amusements of Life. When they meet an Acquaintance in the Morning, the first Question is about the Sun's Health; how he looked at his Setting and Rising, and what Hopes they have to avoid the Stroak of the approaching Comet. This Conversation they are apt to run into with the same Temper that Boys discover, in delighting to hear terrible Stories of Sprites and Hobgoblins, which they greedily listen to, and dare not go to Bed for fear.

The Women of the Island have Abundance of Vivacity; they contemn their Husbands, and are exceedingly fond of Strangers, whereof there is always a considerable Number from the Continent below, attending at Court, either upon Affairs of the several Towns and Corporations, or their own particular Occasions; but are much despised, because they want the same Endowments. Among these the Ladies chuse their Gallants: But the Vexation is, that they act with too much Ease and Security; for the Husband is always so wrapped in Speculation, that the Mistress and Lover may proceed to the greatest Familiarities before his Face, if he be but provided with Paper and Implements, and without his *Flapper* at his Side.

The Wives and Daughters lament their Confinement to the Island, although I think it the most delicious Spot of Ground in the World; and although they live here in the greatest Plenty and Magnificence, and are allowed to do whatever they please: They long to see the World, and take the Diversions of the Metropolis, which they are not allowed to do without a particular Licence from the King; and this is not easy to be obtained, because the People of Quality have found by frequent Experience, how hard it

is to persuade their Women to return from below. I was
told, that a great Court Lady, who had several Children,
is married to the prime Minister, the richest Subject in
the Kingdom, a very graceful Person, extremely fond of
her, and lives in the finest Palace of the Island; went
down to *Lagado*, on the Pretence of Health, there hid her
self for several Months, till the King sent a Warrant to
search for her; and she was found in an obscure Eating-
House all in Rags, having pawned her Cloths to maintain
an old deformed Footman, who beat her every Day, and
in whose Company she was taken much against her Will.
And although her Husband received her with all possible
Kindness, and without the least Reproach; she soon after
contrived to steal down again with all her Jewels, to the
same Gallant, and hath not been heard of since.

This may perhaps pass with the Reader rather for an
European or *English* Story, than for one of a Country so
remote. But he may please to consider, that the Caprices
of Womankind are not limited by any Climate or Nation;
and that they are much more uniform than can be easily
imagined.

In about a Month's Time I had made a tolerable Proficiency in their Language, and was able to answer most of
the King's Questions, when I had the Honour to attend
him. His Majesty discovered not the least Curiosity to
enquire into the Laws, Government, History, Religion, or
Manners of the Countries where I had been; but confined
his Questions to the State of Mathematicks, and received
the Account I gave him, with great Contempt and Indifference, though often rouzed by his *Flapper* on each Side

CHAPTER THREE

A PHÆNOMENON SOLVED BY MODERN PHILOSOPHY AND
ASTRONOMY. THE LAPUTIANS GREAT IMPROVEMENTS IN THE
LATTER. THE KING'S METHOD OF SUPPRESSING INSURRECTIONS.

I DESIRED Leave of this Prince to see the Curiosities of
the Island; which he was graciously pleased to grant,
and ordered my Tutor to attend me. I chiefly wanted to
know to what Cause in Art or in Nature, it owed its several
Motions; whereof I will now give a philosophical Account
to the Reader.

The flying or floating Island is exactly circular; its
Diameter 7837 Yards, or about four Miles and an Half,
and consequently contains ten Thousand Acres. It is three
Hundred Yards thick. The Bottom, or under Surface,
which appears to those who view it from below, is one even
regular Plate of Adamant, shooting up to the Height of
about two Hundred Yards. Above it lye the several Minerals in their usual Order; and over all is a Coat of rich
Mould ten or twelve Foot deep. The Declivity of the upper
Surface, from the Circumference to the Center, is the natural Cause why all the Dews and Rains which fall upon
the Island, are conveyed in small Rivulets towards the
Middle, where they are emptied into four large Basons,
each of about Half a Mile in Circuit, and two Hundred
Yards distant from the Center. From these Basons the
Water is continually exhaled by the Sun in the Day-time,
which effectually prevents their overflowing. Besides, as it
is in the Power of the Monarch to raise the Island above
the Region of Clouds and Vapours, he can prevent the
falling of Dews and Rains whenever he pleases. For the
highest Clouds cannot rise above two Miles, as Naturalists
agree, at least they were never known to do so in that
Country.

At the Center of the *Island* there is a Chasm about fifty
Yards in Diameter, from whence the Astronomers descend
into a large Dome, which is therefore called *Flandona*

Gagnole, or the *Astronomers Cave*; situated at the Depth of an Hundred Yards beneath the upper Surface of the Adamant. In this Cave are Twenty Lamps continually burning, which from the Reflection of the Adamant cast a strong Light into every Part. The Place is stored with great Variety of Sextants, Quadrants, Telescopes, Astrolabes, and other Astronomical Instruments. But the greatest Curiosity, upon which the Fate of the Island depends, is a Load-stone of a prodigious Size, in Shape resembling a Weaver's Shuttle. It is in Length six Yards, and in the thickest Part at least three Yards over. This Magnet is sustained by a very strong Axle of Adamant, passing through its Middle, upon which it plays, and is poized so exactly that the weakest Hand can turn it. It is hooped round with an hollow Cylinder of Adamant, four Foot deep, as many thick, and twelve Yards in Diameter, placed horizontally, and supported by Eight Adamantine Feet, each Six Yards high. In the Middle of the Concave Side there is a Groove Twelve Inches deep, in which the Extremities of the Axle are lodged, and turned round as there is Occasion.

This Stone cannot be moved from its Place by any Force, because the Hoop and its Feet are one continued Piece with that Body of Adamant which constitutes the Bottom of the Island.

By Means of this Load-stone, the Island is made to rise and fall, and move from one Place to another. For, with respect to that Part of the Earth over which the Monarch presides, the Stone is endued at one of its Sides with an attractive Power, and at the other with a repulsive. Upon placing the Magnet erect with its attracting End towards the Earth, the Island descends; but when the repelling Extremity points downwards, the Island mounts directly upwards. When the Position of the Stone is oblique, the Motion of the Island is so too. For in this Magnet the Forces always act in Lines parallel to its Direction.

By this oblique Motion the Island is conveyed to different Parts of the Monarch's Dominions. To explain the Manner of its Progress, let *A B* represent a Line drawn

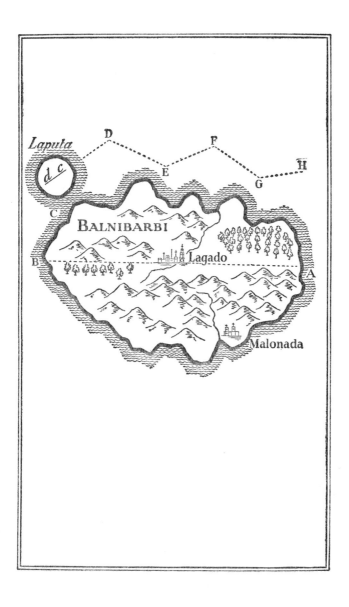

cross the Dominions of *Balnibarbi*; let the Line *c d* represent the Load-stone, of which let *d* be the repelling End, and *c* the attracting End, the Island being over *C*; let the Stone be placed in the Position *c d* with its repelling End downwards; then the Island will be driven upwards obliquely towards *D*. When it is arrived at *D*, let the Stone be turned upon its Axle till its attracting End points towards *E*, and then the Island will be carried obliquely towards *E*; where if the Stone be again turned upon its Axle till it stands in the Position *E F*, with its repelling Point downwards, the Island will rise obliquely towards *F*, where by directing the attracting End towards *G*, the Island may be carried to *G*, and from *G* to *H*, by turning the Stone, so as to make its repelling Extremity point directly downwards. And thus by changing the Situation of the Stone as often as there is Occasion, the Island is made to rise and fall by Turns in an oblique Direction; and by those alternate Risings and Fallings (the Obliquity being not considerable) is conveyed from one Part of the Dominions to the other.

But it must be observed, that this Island cannot move beyond the Extent of the Dominions below; nor can it rise above the Height of four Miles. For which the Astronomers (who have written large Systems concerning the Stone) assign the following Reason: That the Magnetick Virtue does not extend beyond the Distance of four Miles, and that the Mineral which acts upon the Stone in the Bowels of the Earth, and in the Sea about six Leagues distant from the Shoar, is not diffused through the whole Globe, but terminated with the Limits of the King's Dominions: And it was easy from the great Advantage of such a superior Situation, for a Prince to bring under his Obedience whatever Country lay within the Attraction of that Magnet.

When the Stone is put parallel to the Plane of the Horizon, the Island standeth still; for in that Case, the Extremities of it being at equal Distance from the Earth, act with equal Force, the one in drawing downwards, the other in pushing upwards; and consequently no Motion can ensue.

This Load-stone is under the Care of certain Astronomers, who from Time to Time give it such Positions as the Monarch directs. They spend the greatest Part of their Lives in observing the celestial Bodies, which they do by the Assistance of Glasses, far excelling ours in Goodness. For, although their largest Telescopes do not exceed three Feet, they magnify much more than those of a Hundred with us, and shew the Stars with greater Clearness. This Advantage hath enabled them to extend their Discoveries much farther than our Astronomers in *Europe*. They have made a Catalogue of ten Thousand fixed Stars, whereas the largest of ours do not contain above one third Part of that Number. They have likewise discovered two lesser Stars, or *Satellites*, which revolve about *Mars*; whereof the innermost is distant from the Center of the primary Planet exactly three of his Diameters, and the outermost five; the former revolves in the Space of ten Hours, and the latter in Twenty-one and an Half; so that the Squares of their periodical Times, are very near in the same Proportion with the Cubes of their Distance from the Center of *Mars*; which evidently shews them to be governed by the same Law of Gravitation, that influences the other heavenly Bodies.

They have observed Ninety-three different Comets, and settled their Periods with great Exactness. If this be true, (and they affirm it with great Confidence) it is much to be wished that their Observations were made publick; whereby the Theory of Comets, which at present is very lame and defective, might be brought to the same Perfection with other Parts of Astronomy.

The King would be the most absolute Prince in the Universe, if he could but prevail on a Ministry to join with him; but these having their Estates below on the Continent, and considering that the Office of a Favourite hath a very uncertain Tenure, would never consent to the enslaving their Country.

If any Town should engage in Rebellion or Mutiny,

fall into violent Factions, or refuse to pay the usual Tribute; the King hath two Methods of reducing them to Obedience. The first and the mildest Course is by keeping the Island hovering over such a Town, and the Lands about it; whereby he can deprive them of the Benefit of the Sun and the Rain, and consequently afflict the Inhabitants with Dearth and Diseases. And if the Crime deserve it, they are at the same time pelted from above with great Stones, against which they have no Defence, but by creeping into Cellars or Caves, while the Roofs of their Houses are beaten to Pieces. But if they still continue obstinate, or offer to raise Insurrections; he proceeds to the last Remedy, by letting the Island drop directly upon their Heads, which makes a universal Destruction both of Houses and Men. However, this is an Extremity to which the Prince is seldom driven, neither indeed is he willing to put it in Execution; nor dare his Ministers advise him to an Action, which as it would render them odious to the People, so it would be a great Damage to their own Estates that lie all below; for the Island is the King's Demesn.

But there is still indeed a more weighty Reason, why the Kings of this Country have been always averse from executing so terrible an Action, unless upon the utmost Necessity. For if the Town intended to be destroyed should have in it any tall Rocks, as it generally falls out in the larger Cities; a Situation probably chosen at first with a View to prevent such a Catastrophe: Or if it abound in high Spires or Pillars of Stone, a sudden Fall might endanger the Bottom or under Surface of the Island, which although it consist as I have said, of one entire Adamant two hundred Yards thick, might happen to crack by too great a Choque, or burst by approaching too near the Fires from the Houses below; as the Backs both of Iron and Stone will often do in our Chimneys. Of all this the People are well apprized, and understand how far to carry their Obstinacy, where their Liberty or Property is concerned. And the King, when he is highest provoked, and most determined to press a City to Rubbish, orders the Island to descend with great Gentleness, out of a Pretence of

Tenderness to his People, but indeed for fear of breaking the Adamantine Bottom; in which Case it is the Opinion of all their Philosophers, that the Load-stone could no longer hold it up, and the whole Mass would fall to the Ground.

By a fundamental Law of this Realm, neither the King nor either of his two elder Sons, are permitted to leave the Island; nor the Queen till she is past Child-bearing.

CHAPTER FOUR

THE AUTHOR LEAVES LAPUTA, IS CONVEYED TO BALNIBARBI, ARRIVES AT THE METROPOLIS. A DESCRIPTION OF THE METRO- POLIS AND THE COUNTRY ADJOINING. THE AUTHOR HOSPIT- ABLY RECEIVED BY A GREAT LORD. HIS CONVERSATION WITH THAT LORD.

ALTHOUGH I cannot say that I was ill treated in this Island, yet I must confess I thought my self too much neglected, not without some Degree of Contempt. For neither Prince nor People appeared to be curious in any Part of Knowledge, except Mathematicks and Musick, wherein I was far their inferior, and upon that Account very little regarded.

On the other Side, after having seen all the Curiosities of the Island, I was very desirous to leave it, being heartily weary of those People. They were indeed excellent in two Sciences for which I have great Esteem, and wherein I am not unversed; but at the same time so abstracted and involved in Speculation, that I never met with such dis- agreeable Companions. I conversed only with Women, Tradesmen, *Flappers*, and Court-Pages, during two Months of my Abode there; by which at last I rendered my self extremely contemptible; yet these were the only People from whom I could ever receive a reasonable Answer.

I had obtained by hard Study a good Degree of Know- ledge in their Language: I was weary of being confined to an Island where I received so little Countenance; and resolved to leave it with the first Opportunity.

There was a great Lord at Court, nearly related to the King, and for that Reason alone used with Respect. He was universally reckoned the most ignorant and stupid Person among them. He had performed many eminent Services for the Crown, had great natural and acquired Parts, adorned with Integrity and Honour; but so ill an Ear for Musick, that his Detractors reported he had been often known to beat Time in the wrong Place; neither could his Tutors without extreme Difficulty teach him to demonstrate the most easy Proposition in the Mathematicks. He was pleased to shew me many Marks of Favour, often did me the Honour of a Visit, desired to be informed in the Affairs of *Europe*, the Laws and Customs, the Manners and Learning of the several Countries where I had travelled. He listened to me with great Attention, and made very wise Observations on all I spoke. He had two *Flappers* attending him for State, but never made use of them except at Court, and in Visits of Ceremony; and would always command them to withdraw when we were alone together.

I intreated this illustrious Person to intercede in my Behalf with his Majesty for Leave to depart; which he accordingly did, as he was pleased to tell me, with Regret: For, indeed he had made me several Offers very advantageous, which however I refused with Expressions of the highest Acknowledgment.

On the 16th Day of *February*, I took Leave of his Majesty and the Court. The King made me a Present to the Value of about two Hundred Pounds *English*; and my Protector his Kinsman as much more, together with a Letter of Recommendation to a Friend of his in *Lagado*, the Metropolis: The Island being then hovering over a Mountain about two Miles from it, I was let down from the lowest Gallery, in the same Manner as I had been taken up.

The Continent, as far as it is subject to the Monarch of the *Flying Island*, passeth under the general Name of *Balnibarbi*; and the Metropolis, as I said before, is called *Lagado*. I felt some little Satisfaction in finding my self on firm Ground. I walked to the City without any Concern, being clad like one of the Natives, and sufficiently instructed to converse with them. I soon found out the Person's House to whom I was recommended; presented my Letter from his Friend the Grandee in the Island, and was received with much Kindness. This great Lord, whose Name was *Munodi*, ordered me an Apartment in his own House, where I continued during my Stay, and was entertained in a most hospitable Manner.

The next Morning after my Arrival he took me in his Chariot to see the Town, which is about half the Bigness of *London*; but the Houses very strangely built, and most of them out of Repair. The People in the Streets walked fast, looked wild, their Eyes fixed, and were generally in Rags. We passed through one of the Town Gates, and went about three Miles into the Country, where I saw many Labourers working with several Sorts of Tools in the Ground, but was not able to conjecture what they were about; neither did I observe any Expectation either of Corn or Grass, although the Soil appeared to be excellent. I could not forbear admiring at these odd Appearances both in Town and Country; and I made bold to desire my Conductor, that he would be pleased to explain to me what could be meant by so many busy Heads, Hands and Faces, both in the Streets and the Fields, because I did not discover any good Effects they produced; but on the contrary, I never knew a Soil so unhappily cultivated, Houses so ill contrived and so ruinous, or a People whose Countenances and Habit expressed so much Misery and Want.

This Lord *Munodi* was a Person of the first Rank, and had been some Years Governor of *Lagado*; but by a Cabal of Ministers was discharged for Insufficiency. However the King treated him with Tenderness, as a wellmeaning Man, but of a low contemptible Understanding.

When I gave that free Censure of the Country and its Inhabitants, he made no further Answer than by telling me, that I had not been long enough among them to form a Judgment; and that the different Nations of the

World had different Customs; with other common Topicks to the same Purpose. But when we returned to his
Palace, he asked me how I liked the Building, what
Absurdities I observed, and what Quarrel I had with
the Dress or Looks of his Domesticks. This he might
safely do; because every Thing about him was magnificent, regular and polite. I answered, that his Excellency's Prudence, Quality, and Fortune, had exempted
him from those Defects which Folly and Beggary had
produced in others. He said, if I would go with him to
his Country House about Twenty Miles distant, where his
Estate lay, there would be more Leisure for this Kind of
Conversation. I told his Excellency, that I was entirely at
his Disposal; and accordingly we set out next Morning.

During our Journey, he made me observe the several
Methods used by Farmers in managing their Lands;
which to me were wholly unaccountable: For except in
some very few Places, I could not discover one Ear of
Corn, or Blade of Grass. But, in three Hours travelling,
the Scene was wholly altered; we came into a most
beautiful Country; Farmers Houses at small Distances,
neatly built, the Fields enclosed, containing Vineyards,
Corn-grounds and Meadows. Neither do I remember to
have seen a more delightful Prospect. His Excellency
observed my Countenance to clear up; he told me with
a Sigh, that there his Estate began, and would continue
the same till we should come to his House. That his
Countrymen ridiculed and despised him for managing
his Affairs no better, and for setting so ill an Example to
the Kingdom; which however was followed by very few,
such as were old and wilful, and weak like himself.

We came at length to the House, which was indeed a
noble Structure, built according to the best Rules of ancient
Architecture. The Fountains, Gardens, Walks, Avenues,
and Groves were all disposed with exact Judgment and
Taste. I gave due Praises to every Thing I saw, whereof
his Excellency took not the least Notice till after Supper;
when, there being no third Companion, he told me with
a very melancholy Air, that he doubted he must throw

down his Houses in Town and Country, to rebuild them
after the present Mode; destroy all his Plantations, and
cast others into such a Form as modern Usage required;
and give the same Directions to all his Tenants, unless he
would submit to incur the Censure of Pride, Singularity,
Affectation, Ignorance, Caprice; and perhaps encrease
his Majesty's Displeasure.

That the Admiration I appeared to be under, would
cease or diminish when he had informed me of some Particulars, which probably I never heard of at Court, the
People there being too much taken up in their own Speculations, to have Regard to what passed here below.

The Sum of his Discourse was to this Effect. That about
Forty Years ago, certain Persons went up to *Laputa*, either
upon Business or Diversion; and after five Months Continuance, came back with a very little Smattering in Mathematicks, but full of Volatile Spirits acquired in that
Airy Region. That these Persons upon their Return, began to dislike the Management of every Thing below;
and fell into Schemes of putting all Arts, Sciences, Languages, and Mechanics upon a new Foot. To this End
they procured a Royal Patent for erecting an Academy
of PROJECTORS in *Lagado*: And the Humour prevailed so
strongly among the People, that there is not a Town of
any Consequence in the Kingdom without such an Academy. In these Colleges, the Professors contrive new
Rules and Methods of Agriculture and Building, and new
Instruments and Tools for all Trades and Manufactures,
whereby, as they undertake, one Man shall do the Work
of Ten; a Palace may be built in a Week, of Materials so
durable as to last for ever without repairing. All the
Fruits of the Earth shall come to Maturity at whatever
Season we think fit to chuse, and increase an Hundred
Fold more than they do at present; with innumerable
other happy Proposals. The only Inconvenience is, that
none of these Projects are yet brought to Perfection; and
in the mean time, the whole Country lies miserably waste,
the Houses in Ruins, and the People without Food or
Cloaths. By all which, instead of being discouraged, they

are Fifty Times more violently bent upon prosecuting their Schemes, driven equally on by Hope and Despair: That, as for himself, being not of an enterprizing Spirit, he was content to go on in the old Forms; to live in the Houses his Ancestors had built, and act as they did in every Part of Life without Innovation. That, some few other Persons of Quality and Gentry had done the same; but were looked on with an Eye of Contempt and ill Will, as Enemies to Art, ignorant, and ill Commonwealthsmen, preferring their own Ease and Sloth before the general Improvement of their Country.

His Lordship added, that he would not by any further Particulars prevent the Pleasure I should certainly take in viewing the grand Academy, whither he was resolved I should go. He only desired me to observe a ruined Building upon the Side of a Mountain about three Miles distant, of which he gave me this Account. That he had a very convenient Mill within Half a Mile of his House, turned by a Current from a large River, and sufficient for his own Family as well as a great Number of his Tenants. That, about seven Years ago, a Club of those Projectors came to him with Proposals to destroy this Mill, and build another on the Side of that Mountain, on the long Ridge whereof a long Canal must be cut for a Repository of Water, to be conveyed up by Pipes and Engines to supply the Mill: Because the Wind and Air upon a Height agitated the Water, and thereby made it fitter for Motion: And because the Water descending down a Declivity would turn the Mill with half the Current of a River whose Course is more upon a Level. He said, that being then not very well with the Court, and pressed by many of this Friends, he complyed with the Proposal; and after employing an Hundred Men for two Years, the Work miscarryed, the Projectors went off, laying the Blame intirely upon him; railing at him ever since, and putting others upon the same Experiment, with equal Assurance of Success, as well as equal Disappointment.

In a few Days we came back to Town; and his Excellency, considering the bad Character he had in the Academy, would not go with me himself, but recommended me to a Friend of his to bear me Company thither. My Lord was pleased to represent me as a great Admirer of Projects, and a Person of much Curiosity and easy Belief; which indeed was not without Truth; for I had my self been a Sort of Projector in my younger Days.

CHAPTER FIVE

THE AUTHOR PERMITTED TO SEE THE GRAND ACADEMY OF LAGADO. THE ACADEMY LARGELY DESCRIBED. THE ARTS WHEREIN THE PROFESSORS EMPLOY THEMSELVES.

THIS Academy is not an entire single Building, but a Continuation of several Houses on both Sides of a Street; which growing waste, was purchased and applyed to that Use.

I was received very kindly by the Warden and went for many Days to the Academy. Every Room hath in it one or more Projectors; and I believe I could not be in fewer than five Hundred Rooms.

The first Man I saw was of a meagre Aspect, with sooty Hands and Face, his Hair and Beard long, ragged and singed in several Places. His Clothes, Shirt, and Skin were all of the same Colour. He had been Eight Years upon a Project for extracting Sun-Beams out of Cucumbers, which were to be put into Vials hermetically sealed, and let out to warm the Air in raw inclement Summers. He told me, he did not doubt in Eight Years more, that he should be able to supply Governors Gardens with Sun-shine at a reasonable Rate; but he complained that his Stock was low, and intreated me to give him something as an Encouragement to Ingenuity, especially since this had been a very dear Season for Cucumbers. I made him a small Present, for my Lord had furnished me with Money on purpose, because he knew their Practice of begging from all who go to see them.

I went into another Chamber, but was ready to hasten

back, being almost overcome with a horrible Stink. My Conductor pressed me forward, conjuring me in a Whisper to give no Offence, which would be highly resented; and therefore I durst not so much as stop my Nose. The Projector of this Cell was the most ancient Student of the Academy. His Face and Beard were of a pale Yellow; his Hands and Clothes dawbed over with Filth. When I was presented to him, he gave me a very close Embrace, (a Compliment I could well have excused). His Employment from his first coming into the Academy, was an Operation to reduce human Excrement to its original Food, by separating the several Parts, removing the Tincture which it receives from the Gall, making the Odour exhale, and scumming off the Saliva. He had a weekly Allowance from the Society, of a Vessel filled with human Ordure, about the Bigness of a *Bristol* Barrel.

I saw another at work to calcine Ice into Gunpowder; who likewise shewed me a Treatise he had written concerning the Malleability of Fire, which he intended to publish.

There was a most ingenious Architect who had contrived a new Method for building Houses, by beginning at the Roof, and working downwards to the Foundation; which he justified to me by the like Practice of those two prudent Insects the Bee and the Spider.

There was a Man born blind, who had several Apprentices in his own Condition: Their Employment was to mix Colours for Painters, which their Master taught them to distinguish by feeling and smelling. It was indeed my Misfortune to find them at that Time not very perfect in their Lessons; and the Professor himself happened to be generally mistaken: This Artist is much encouraged and esteemed by the whole Fraternity.

In another Apartment I was highly pleased with a Projector, who had found a Device of plowing the Ground with Hogs, to save the Charges of Plows, Cattle, and Labour. The Method is this: In an Acre of Ground you bury at six Inches Distance, and eight deep, a Quantity of Acorns, Dates, Chesnuts, and other Masts or Vegetables whereof these Animals are fondest; then you drive six Hundred or more of them into the Field, where in a few Days they will root up the whole Ground in search of their Food, and make it fit for sowing, at the same time manuring it with their Dung. It is true, upon Experiment they found the Charge and Trouble very great, and they had little or no Crop. However, it is not doubted that this Invention may be capable of great Improvement.

I went into another Room, where the Walls and Ceiling were all hung round with Cobwebs, except a narrow Passage for the Artist to go in and out. At my Entrance he called aloud to me not to disturb his Webs. He lamented the fatal Mistake the World had been so long in of using Silk-Worms, while we had such plenty of domestick Insects, who infinitely excelled the former, because they understood how to weave as well as spin. And he proposed farther, that by employing Spiders, the Charge of dying Silks would be wholly saved; whereof I was fully convinced when he shewed me a vast Number of Flies most beautifully coloured, wherewith he fed his Spiders; assuring us, that the Webs would take a Tincture from them; and as he had them of all Hues, he hoped to fit every Body's Fancy, as soon as he could find proper Food for the Flies, of certain Gums, Oyls, and other glutinous Matter, to give a Strength and Consistence to the Threads.

There was an Astronomer who had undertaken to place a Sun-Dial upon the great Weather-Cock on the Town-House, by adjusting the annual and diurnal Motions of the Earth and Sun, so as to answer and coincide with all accidental Turnings of the Wind.

I was complaining of a small Fit of the Cholick; upon which my Conductor led me into a Room, where a great Physician resided, who was famous for curing that Disease by contrary Operations from the same Instrument. He had a large Pair of Bellows, with a long slender Muzzle of Ivory. This he conveyed eight Inches up the Anus, and drawing in the Wind, he affirmed he could make the Guts as lank as a dried Bladder. But when the Disease was more stubborn and violent, he let in the Muzzle while the Bellows was full of Wind, which he discharged into the Body of the Patient; then withdrew the Instrument to replenish it, clapping his Thumb strongly against the Orifice of the Fundament; and this being repeated three or four Times, the adventitious Wind would rush out, bringing the noxious along with it (like Water put into a Pump) and the Patient recovers. I saw him try both Experiments upon a Dog, but could not discern any Effect from the former. After the latter, the Animal was ready to burst, and made so violent a Discharge, as was very offensive to me and my Companions. The Dog died on the Spot, and we left the Doctor endeavouring to recover him by the same Operation.

I visited many other Apartments, but shall not trouble my Reader with all the Curiosities I observed, being studious of Brevity.

I had hitherto seen only one Side of the Academy, the other being appropriated to the Advancers of speculative Learning; of whom I shall say something when I have mentioned one illustrious Person more, who is called among them *the universal Artist*. He told us, he had been Thirty Years employing his Thoughts for the Improvement of human Life. He had two large Rooms full of wonderful Curiosities, and Fifty Men at work. Some were condensing Air into a dry tangible Substance, by extracting the Nitre, and letting the aqueous or fluid Particles percolate: Others softening Marble for Pillows and Pincushions; others petrifying the Hoofs of a living Horse to preserve them from foundring. The Artist himself was at that Time busy upon two great Designs: The first, to sow Land with Chaff, wherein he affirmed the true seminal Virtue to be contained, as he demonstrated by several Experiments which I was not skilful enough to comprehend. The other was, by a certain Composition of Gums, Minerals, and Vegetables outwardly applied, to prevent the Growth of Wool upon two young Lambs; and he hoped in a reasonable Time to propagate the Breed of naked Sheep all over the Kingdom.

We crossed a Walk to the other Part of the Academy,

where, as I have already said, the Projectors in speculative Learning resided.

The first Professor I saw was in a very large Room, with Forty Pupils about him. After Salutation, observing me to look earnestly upon a Frame, which took up the greatest Part of both the Length and Breadth of the Room; he said, perhaps I might wonder to see him employed in a Project for improving speculative Knowledge by practical and mechanical Operations. But the World would soon be sensible of its Usefulness; and he flattered himself, that a more noble exalted Thought never sprang in any other Man's Head. Every one knew how laborious the usual Method is of attaining to Arts and Sciences; whereas by his Contrivance, the most ignorant Person at a reasonable Charge, and with a little bodily Labour, may write Books in Philosophy, Poetry, Politicks, Law, Mathematicks and Theology, without the least Assistance from Genius or Study. He then led me to the Frame, about the Sides whereof all his Pupils stood in Ranks. It was Twenty Foot square, placed in the Middle of the Room. The Superficies was composed of several Bits of Wood, about the Bigness of a Dye, but some larger than others. They were all linked together by slender Wires. These Bits of Wood were covered on every Square with Papers pasted on them; and on these Papers were written all the Words of their Language in their several Moods, Tenses, and Declensions, but without any Order. The Professor then desired me to observe, for he was going to set his Engine at work. The Pupils at his Command took each of them hold of an Iron Handle, whereof there were Forty fixed round the Edges of the Frame; and giving them a sudden Turn, the whole Disposition of the Words was entirely changed. He then commanded Six and Thirty of the Lads to read the several Lines softly as they appeared upon the Frame; and where they found three or four Words together that might make Part of a Sentence, they dictated to the four remaining Boys who were Scribes. This Work was repeated three or four Times, and at every Turn the Engine was so contrived, that the Words shifted into new

Places, as the square Bits of Wood moved upside down.

Six Hours a-Day the young Students were employed in this Labour; and the Professor shewed me several Volumes in large Folio already collected, of broken Sentences, which he intended to piece together; and out of those rich Materials to give the World a compleat Body of all Arts and Sciences; which however might be still improved, and much expedited, if the Publick would raise a Fund for making and employing five Hundred such Frames in

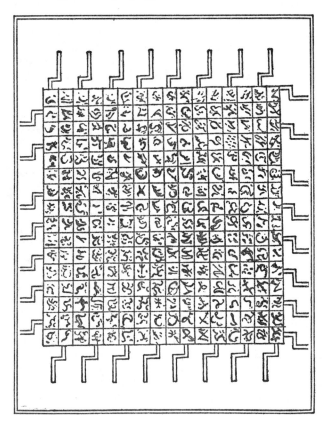

Lagado, and oblige the Managers to contribute in common their several Collections.

He assured me, that this Invention had employed all his Thoughts from his Youth; that he had emptyed the whole Vocabulary into his Frame, and made the strictest Computation of the general Proportion there is in Books between the Numbers of Particles, Nouns, and Verbs, and other Parts of Speech.

I made my humblest Acknowledgments to this illustrious Person for his great Communicativeness; and promised if ever I had the good Fortune to return to my native Country, that I would do him Justice, as the sole Inventor of this wonderful Machine; the Form and Contrivance of which I desired Leave to delineate upon Paper as in the Figure here annexed. I told him, although it were the Custom of our Learned in *Europe* to steal Inventions from each other, who had thereby at least this Advantage, that it became a Controversy which was the right Owner; yet I would take such Caution, that he should have the Honour entire without a Rival.

We next went to the School of Languages, where three Professors sat in Consultation upon improving that of their own Country.

The first Project was to shorten Discourse by cutting Polysyllables into one, and leaving out Verbs and Participles; because in Reality all things imaginable are but Nouns.

The other, was a Scheme for entirely abolishing all Words whatsoever: And this was urged as a great Advantage in Point of Health as well as Brevity. For, it is plain, that every Word we speak is in some Degree a Diminution of our Lungs by Corrosion; and consequently contributes to the shortning of our Lives. An Expedient was therefore offered, that since Words are only Names for *Things,* it would be more convenient for all Men to carry about them, such *Things* as were necessary to express the particular Business they are to discourse on. And this Invention would certainly have taken Place, to the great Ease as well as Health of the Subject, if the Women in Conjunction with

the Vulgar and Illiterate had not threatned to raise a Rebellion, unless they might be allowed the Liberty to speak
with their Tongues, after the Manner of their Forefathers:
Such constant irreconcileable Enemies to Science are the
common People. However, many of the most Learned and
Wise adhere to the new Scheme of expressing themselves by
Things; which hath only this Inconvenience attending it;
that if a Man's Business be very great, and of various Kinds,
he must be obliged in Proportion to carry a greater Bundle
of *Things* upon his Back, unless he can afford one or two
strong Servants to attend him. I have often beheld two of
those Sages almost sinking under the Weight of their Packs,
like Pedlars among us, who when they met in the Streets,
would lay down their Loads, open their Sacks, and hold
Conversation for an Hour together; then put up their Implements, help each other to resume their Burthens, and
take their Leave.

But, for short Conversations a Man may carry Implements in his Pockets and under his Arms, enough to supply
him, and in his House he cannot be at a Loss; therefore
the Room where Company meet who practice this Art,
is full of all *Things* ready at Hand, requisite to furnish
Matter for this Kind of artificial Converse.

Another great Advantage proposed by this Invention,
was, that it would serve as an universal Language to be
understood in all civilized Nations, whose Goods and Uten-
sils are generally of the same Kind, or nearly resembling,
so that their Uses might easily be comprehended. And
thus, Embassadors would be qualified to treat with foreign
Princes or Ministers of State, to whose Tongues they were
utter Strangers.

I was at the Mathematical School, where the Master
taught his Pupils after a Method scarce imaginable to us in
Europe. The Proposition and Demonstration were fairly
written on a thin Wafer, with Ink composed of a Cephalick
Tincture. This the Student was to swallow upon a fasting
Stomach, and for three Days following eat nothing but
Bread and Water. As the Wafer digested, the Tincture
mounted to his Brain, bearing the Proposition along with

it. But the Success hath not hitherto been answerable, partly by some Error in the *Quantum* or Composition, and partly by the Perverseness of Lads; to whom this Bolus is so nauseous, that they generally steal aside, and discharge it upwards before it can operate; neither have they been yet persuaded to use so long an Abstinence as the Prescription requires.

CHAPTER SIX

A FURTHER ACCOUNT OF THE ACADEMY. THE AUTHOR PROPOSETH SOME IMPROVEMENTS, WHICH ARE HONOURABLY RECEIVED.

IN the School of political Projectors I was but ill entertained; the Professors appearing in my Judgment wholly out of their Senses; which is a Scene that never fails to make me melancholy. These unhappy People were proposing Schemes for persuading Monarchs to chuse Favourites upon the Score of their Wisdom, Capacity and Virtue; of teaching Ministers to consult the publick Good; of rewarding Merit, great Abilities, and eminent Services; of instructing Princes to know their true Interest, by placing it on the same Foundation with that of their People: Of chusing for Employments Persons qualified to exercise them; with many other wild impossible Chimæras, that never entered before into the Heart of Man to conceive; and confirmed in me the old Observation, that there is nothing so extravagant and irrational which some Philosophers have not maintained for Truth.

But, however I shall so far do Justice to this Part of the Academy, as to acknowledge that all of them were not so visionary. There was a most ingenious Doctor who seemed to be perfectly versed in the whole Nature and System of Government. This illustrious Person had very usefully employed his Studies in finding out effectual Remedies for all Diseases and Corruptions, to which the several Kinds of publick Administration are subject by the Vices or Infirmities of those who govern, as well as by the Licentiousness

of those who are to obey. For Instance: Whereas all
Writers and Reasoners have agreed, that there is a strict
universal Resemblance between the natural and the political Body; can there be any thing more evident, than
that the Health of both must be preserved, and the Diseases cured by the same Prescriptions? It is allowed,
that Senates and great Councils are often troubled with
redundant, ebullient, and other peccant Humours; with
many Diseases of the Head, and more of the Heart;
with strong Convulsions, with grievous Contractions of
the Nerves and Sinews in both Hands, but especially the
Right: With Spleen, Flatus, Vertigoes and Deliriums; with
scrophulous Tumours full of fœtid purulent Matter; with
sower frothy Ructations; with Canine Appetites and Crudeness of Digestion; besides many others needless to mention. This Doctor therefore proposed, that upon the meeting of a Senate, certain Physicians should attend at the
three first Days of their sitting, and at the Close of each
Day's Debate, feel the Pulses of every Senator; after
which having maturely considered, and consulted upon
the Nature of the several Maladies, and the Methods of
Cure; they should on the fourth Day return to the Senate-
House, attended by their Apothecaries stored with proper
Medicines; and before the Members sat, administer to
each of them Lenitives, Aperitives, Abstersives, Corrosives,
Restringents, Palliatives, Laxatives, Cephalalgicks, Icter-
icks, Apophlegmaticks, Acousticks, as their several Cases
required; and according as these Medicines should
operate, repeat, alter, or omit them at the next Meeting.

This Project could not be of any great Expence to the
Publick; and might in my poor Opinion, be of much Use
for the Dispatch of Business in those Countries where
Senates have any Share in the legislative Power; beget
Unanimity, shorten Debates, open a few Mouths which are
now closed, and close many more which are now open;
curb the Petulancy of the Young, and correct the Positiveness of the Old; rouze the Stupid, and damp the Pert.

Again; Because it is a general Complaint that the Favourites of Princes are troubled with short and weak Mem-

ories; the same Doctor proposed, that whoever attended a first Minister, after having told his Business with the utmost Brevity, and in the plainest Words; should at his Departure give the said Minister a Tweak by the Nose, or a Kick in the Belly, or tread on his Corns, or lug him thrice by both Ears, or run a Pin into his Breech, or pinch his Arm black and blue; to prevent Forgetfulness: And at every Levee Day repeat the same Operation, till the Business were done or absolutely refused.

He likewise directed, that every Senator in the great Council of a Nation, after he had delivered his Opinion, and argued in the Defence of it, should be obliged to give his Vote directly contrary; because if that were done, the Result would infallibly terminate in the Good of the Publick.

When Parties in a State are violent, he offered a wonderful Contrivance to reconcile them. The Method is this. You take an Hundred Leaders of each Party; you dispose them into Couples of such whose Heads are nearest of a Size; then let two nice Operators saw off the *Occiput* of each Couple at the same Time, in such a Manner that the Brain may be equally divided. Let the *Occiputs* thus cut off be interchanged, applying each to the Head of his opposite Party-man. It seems indeed to be a Work that requireth some Exactness; but the Professor assured us, that if it were dextrously performed, the Cure would be infallible. For he argued thus; that the two half Brains being left to debate the Matter between themselves within the Space of one Scull, would soon come to a good Understanding, and produce that Moderation as well as Regularity of Thinking, so much to be wished for in the Heads of those, who imagine they came into the World only to watch and govern its Motion: And as to the Difference of Brains in Quantity or Quality, among those who are Directors in Faction; the Doctor assured us from his own Knowledge, that it was a perfect Trifle.

I heard a very warm Debate between two Professors, about the most commodious and effectual Ways and Means of raising Money without grieving the Subject. The first affirmed, the justest Method would be to lay a certain Tax upon Vices and Folly; and the Sum fixed upon every Man, to be rated after the fairest Manner by a Jury of his Neighbours. The second was of an Opinion directly contrary; to tax those Qualities of Body and Mind for which Men chiefly value themselves; the Rate to be more or less according to the Degrees of excelling; the Decision whereof should be left entirely to their own Breast. The highest Tax was upon Men, who are the greatest Favourites of the other Sex; and the Assessments according to the Number and Natures of the Favours they have received; for which they are allowed to be their own Vouchers. Wit, Valour, and Politeness were likewise proposed to be largely taxed, and collected in the same Manner, by every Person giving his own Word for the Quantum of what he possessed. But, as to Honour, Justice, Wisdom and Learning, they should not be taxed at all; because, they are Qualifications of so singular a Kind, that no Man will either allow them in his Neighbour, or value them in himself.

The Women were proposed to be taxed according to their Beauty and Skill in Dressing; wherein they had the same Privilege with the Men, to be determined by their own Judgment. But Constancy, Chastity, good Sense, and good Nature were not rated, because they would not bear the Charge of Collecting.

To keep Senators in the Interest of the Crown, it was proposed that the Members should raffle for Employments; every Man first taking an Oath, and giving Security that he would vote for the Court, whether he won or no; after which the Losers had in their Turn the Liberty of raffling upon the next Vacancy. Thus, Hope and Expectation would be kept alive; none would complain of broken Promises, but impute their Disappointments wholly to Fortune, whose Shoulders are broader and stronger than those of a Ministry.

Another Professor shewed me a large Paper of Instructions for discovering Plots and Conspiracies against the Government. He advised great Statesmen to examine into the Dyet of all suspected Persons; their Times of eating; upon which Side they lay in Bed; with which Hand they wiped their Posteriors; to take a strict View of their Excrements, and from the Colour, the Odour, the Taste, the Consistence, the Crudeness, or Maturity of Digestion, form a Judgment of their Thoughts and Designs: Because Men are never so serious, thoughtful, and intent, as when they are at Stool; which he found by frequent Experiment: For in such Conjunctures, when he used merely as a Trial to consider which was the best Way of murdering the King, his Ordure would have a Tincture of Green; but quite different when he thought only of raising an Insurrection, or burning the Metropolis.

The whole Discourse was written with great Acuteness, containing many Observations both curious and useful for Politicians, but as I conceived not altogether compleat. This I ventured to tell the Author, and offered if he pleased to supply him with some Additions. He received my Proposition with more Compliance than is usual among Writers, especially those of the Projecting Species; professing he would be glad to receive farther Information.

I told him, that in the Kingdon of *Tribnia*, by the Natives called *Langden*, where I had long sojourned, the Bulk of the People consisted wholly of Discoverers, Witnesses, Informers, Accusers, Prosecutors, Evidences, Swearers; together with their several subservient and subaltern Instruments; all under the Colours, the Conduct, and pay of Ministers and their Deputies. The Plots in that Kingdom are usually the Workmanship of those Persons who desire to raise their own Characters of profound Politicians; to restore new Vigour to a crazy Administration; to stifle or divert general Discontents; to fill their Coffers with Forfeitures; and raise or sink the Opinion of publick Credit, as either shall best answer their private Advantage. It is first agreed and settled among them, what suspected Persons shall be accused of a Plot: Then, effectual Care is taken to secure all their Letters and other Papers, and put the Owners in Chains. These Papers are delivered to a Set of Artists very dextrous in finding out the mysterious Meanings of Words, Syllables and Letters. For Instance, they can decypher a Close-stool to signify a Privy-Council; a Flock of Geese, a Senate; a lame Dog, an Invader; the Plague, a standing Army; a Buzard, a Minister; the Gout, a High Priest; a Gibbet, a Secretary of State; a Chamber pot, a Committee of Grandees; a Sieve, a Court Lady; a Broom, a Revolution; a Mouse-trap, an Employment; a bottomless Pit, the Treasury; a Sink, a C[our]t; a Cap and Bells, a Favourite; a broken Reed, a Court of Justice; an empty Tun, a General; a running Sore, the Administration.

When this Method fails, they have two others more effectual; which the Learned among them call Acrosticks, and Anagrams. *First,* they can decypher all initial Letters into political Meanings: Thus, *N,* shall signify a Plot; *B,* a Regiment of Horse; *L,* a Fleet at Sea. Or, *secondly,* by transposing the Letters of the Alphabet, in any suspected Paper, they can lay open the deepest Designs of a discontented Party. So for Example, if I should say in a Letter to a Friend, *Our Brother* Tom *hath just got the Piles*; a Man of Skill in this Art would discover how the same Letters which compose that Sentence, may be analysed into the following Words; *Resist,*——a *Plot is brought home* —— *The Tour.* And this is the Anagrammatick Method.

The Professor made me great Acknowledgments for communicating these Observations, and promised to make honourable mention of me in his Treatise.

I saw nothing in this Country that could invite me to a longer Continuance; and began to think of returning home to *England.*

CHAPTER SEVEN

THE Continent of which this Kingdom is a part, ex- tends itself, as I have Reason to believe, Eastward to that unknown Tract of *America*, Westward of *California*, and North to the Pacifick Ocean, which is not above an hundred and fifty Miles from *Lagado*; where there is a good Port and much Commerce with the great Island of *Luggnagg*; situated to the North-West about 29 Degrees North Latitude, and 140 Longitude. This Island of *Lugg- nagg* stands South Eastwards of *Japan*, about an hundred Leagues distant. There is a strict Alliance between the *Japanese* Emperor and the King of *Luggnagg*, which affords frequent Opportunities of sailing from one Island to the other. I determined therefore to direct my Course this Way, in order to my Return to *Europe*. I hired two Mules with a Guide to shew me the Way, and carry my small Baggage. I took leave of my noble Protector, who had shewn me so much Favour, and made me a generous Present at my Departure.

My Journey was without any Accident or Adventure worth relating. When I arrived at the Port of *Maldonada*, (for so it is called) there was no Ship in the Harbour bound for *Luggnagg*, nor like to be in some Time. The Town is about as large as *Portsmouth*. I soon fell into some Ac- quaintance, and was very hospitably received. A Gentle- man of Distinction said to me, that since the Ships bound for *Luggnagg* could not be ready in less than a Month, it might be no disagreeable Amusement for me to take a Trip to the little Island of *Glubbdubdrib*, about five Leagues off to the South-West. He offered himself and a Friend to accompany me, and that I should be provided with a small convenient Barque for the Voyage.

GLUBBDUBDRIB, as nearly as I can interpret the

Word, signifies the Island of *Sorcerers or Magicians*. It is about one third as large as the Isle of *Wight*, and extreamly fruitful: It is governed by the Head of a certain Tribe, who are all Magicians. This Tribe marries only among each other; and the eldest in Succession is Prince or Governor. He hath a noble Palace, and a Park of about three thousand Acres, surrounded by a Wall of hewn Stone twenty Foot high. In this Park are several small Inclosures for Cattle, Corn and Gardening.

The Governor and his Family are served and attended by Domesticks of a Kind somewhat unusual. By his Skill in Necromancy, he hath Power of calling whom he pleaseth from the Dead, and commanding their Service for twenty four Hours, but no longer; nor can he call the same Persons up again in less than three Months, except upon very extraordinary Occasions.

When we arrived at the Island, which was about Eleven in the Morning, one of the Gentlemen who accompanied me, went to the Governor, and desired Admittance for a Stranger, who came on purpose to have the Honour of attending on his Highness. This was immediately granted, and we all three entered the Gate of the Palace between two Rows of Guards, armed and dressed after a very antick Manner, and something in their Countenances that made my Flesh creep with a Horror I cannot express. We passed through several Apartments between Servants of the same Sort, ranked on each Side as before, till we came to the Chamber of Presence, where after three profound Obeysances, and a few general Questions, we were permitted to sit on three Stools near the lowest Step of his Highness's Throne. He understood the Language of *Balnibarbi*, although it were different from that of his Island. He desired me to give him some Account of my Travels; and to let me see that I should be treated without Ceremony, he dismissed all his Attendants with a Turn of his Finger, at which to my great Astonishment they vanished in an Instant, like Visions in a Dream, when we awake on a sudden. I could not recover myself in some Time, till the Governor assured me that I should receive no Hurt;

and observing my two Companions to be under no Concern, who had been often entertained in the same Manner, I began to take Courage; and related to his Highness a short History of my several Adventures, yet not without some Hesitation, and frequently looking behind me to the Place where I had seen those domestick Spectres. I had the Honour to dine with the Governor, where a new Set of Ghosts served up the Meat, and waited at Table. I now observed myself to be less terrified than I had been in the Morning. I stayed till Sun-set, but humbly desired his Highness to excuse me for not accepting his Invitation of lodging in the Palace. My two Friends and I lay at a private House in the Town adjoining, which is the Capital of this little Island; and the next Morning we returned to pay our Duty to the Governor, as he was pleased to command us.

After this Manner we continued in the Island for ten Days, most Part of every Day with the Governor, and at Night in our Lodging. I soon grew so familiarized to the Sight of Spirits, that after the third or fourth Time they gave me no Emotion at all; or if I had any Apprehensions left, my Curiosity prevailed over them. For his Highness the Governor ordered me to call up whatever Persons I would chuse to name, and in whatever Numbers among all the Dead from the Beginning of the World to the present Time, and command them to answer any Questions I should think fit to ask; with this Condition, that my Questions must be confined within the Compass of the Times they lived in. And one Thing I might depend upon, that they would certainly tell me Truth; for Lying was a Talent of no Use in the lower World.

I made my humble Acknowledgments to his Highness for so great a Favour. We were in a Chamber, from whence there was a fair Prospect into the Park. And because my first Inclination was to be entertained with Scenes of Pomp and Magnificence, I desired to see *Alexander* the Great, at the Head of his Army just after the Battle of *Arbela*; which upon a Motion of the Governor's Finger immediately appeared in a large Field under the Window, where we stood. *Alexander* was called up into the Room: It was with great Difficulty that I understood his *Greek*, and had but little of my own. He assured me upon his Honour that he was not poisoned, but dyed of a Fever by excessive Drinking.

Next I saw *Hannibal* passing the *Alps*, who told me he had not a Drop of Vinegar in his Camp.

I saw *Cæsar* and *Pompey* at the Head of their Troops just ready to engage. I saw the former in his last great Triumph. I desired that the Senate of *Rome* might appear before me in one large Chamber, and a modern Representative, in Counterview, in another. The first seemed to be an Assembly of Heroes and Demy-Gods; the other a Knot of Pedlars, Pick-pockets, Highwaymen and Bullies. The Governor at my Request gave the Sign for *Cæsar* and *Brutus* to advance towards us. I was struck with a profound Veneration at the Sight of *Brutus*; and could easily discover the most consummate Virtue, the greatest Intrepidity, and Firmness of Mind, the truest Love of his Country, and general Benevolence for Mankind in every Lineament of his Countenance. I observed with much Pleasure, that these two Persons were in good Intelligence with each other; and *Cæsar* freely confessed to me, that the greatest Actions of his own Life were not equal by many Degrees to the Glory of taking it away. I had the Honour to have much Conversation with *Brutus*; and was told that his Ancestor *Junius*, *Socrates*, *Epaminondas*, *Cato* the Younger, Sir *Thomas More* and himself, were perpetually together: A *Sextumvirate* to which all the Ages of the World cannot add a Seventh.

It would be tedious to trouble the Reader with relating what vast Numbers of illustrious Persons were called up, to gratify that insatiable Desire I had to see the World in every Period of Antiquity placed before me. I chiefly fed my Eyes with beholding the Destroyers of Tyrants and Usurpers, and the Restorers of Liberty to oppressed and injured Nations. But it is impossible to express the Satisfaction I received in my own Mind, after such a Manner as to make it a suitable Entertainment to the Reader.

CHAPTER EIGHT

A FURTHER ACCOUNT OF GLUBBDUBDRIB. ANTIENT AND MODERN HISTORY CORRECTED.

HAVING a Desire to see those Antients, who were most renowned for Wit and Learning, I set apart one Day on purpose. I proposed that *Homer* and *Aristotle* might appear at the Head of all their Commentators; but these were so numerous, that some Hundreds were forced to attend in the Court and outward Rooms of the Palace. I knew and could distinguish those two Heroes at first Sight, not only from the Croud, but from each other. *Homer* was the taller and comelier Person of the two, walked very erect for one of his Age, and his Eyes were the most quick and piercing I ever beheld. *Aristotle* stooped much, and made use of a Staff. His Visage was meager, his Hair lank and thin, and his Voice hollow. I soon discovered, that both of them were perfect Strangers to the rest of the Company, and had never seen or heard of them before. And I had a Whisper from a Ghost, who shall be nameless, that these Commentators always kept in the most distant Quarters from their Principals in the lower World, through a Consciousness of Shame and Guilt, because they had so horribly misrepresented the Meaning of those Authors to Posterity. I introduced *Didymus* and *Eustathius* to *Homer*, and prevailed on him to treat them better than perhaps they deserved; for he soon found they wanted a Genius to enter into the Spirit of a Poet. But *Aristotle* was out of all Patience with the Account I gave him of *Scotus* and *Ramus*, as I presented them to him; and he asked them whether the rest of the Tribe were as great Dunces as themselves.

I then desired the Governor to call up *Descartes* and *Gassendi*, with whom I prevailed to explain their Systems to *Aristotle*. This great Philosopher freely acknowledged his own Mistakes in Natural Philosophy, because he proceeded in many things upon Conjecture, as all Men must do; and he found, that *Gassendi*, who had made the Doctrine of *Epicurus* as palatable as he could, and the *Vortices* of *Descartes*, were equally exploded. He predicted the same Fate to *Attraction*, whereof the present Learned are such zealous Asserters. He said, that new Systems of Nature were but new Fashions, which would vary in every Age; and even those who pretend to demonstrate them from Mathematical Principles, would flourish but a short Period of Time, and be out of Vogue when that was determined.

I spent five Days in conversing with many others of the antient Learned. I saw most of the first *Roman* Emperors. I prevailed on the Governor to call up *Eliogabalus's* Cooks to dress us a Dinner; but they could not shew us much of their Skill, for want of Materials. A *Helot* of *Agesilaus* made us a Dish of *Spartan* Broth, but I was not able to get down a second Spoonful.

The two Gentlemen who conducted me to the Island were pressed by their private Affairs to return in three Days, which I employed in seeing some of the modern Dead, who had made the greatest Figure for two or three Hundred Years past in our own and other Countries of *Europe*; and having been always a great Admirer of old illustrious Families, I desired the Governor would call up a Dozen or two of Kings with their Ancestors in order, for eight or nine Generations. But my Disappointment was grievous and unexpected. For, instead of a long Train with Royal Diadems, I saw in one Family two Fidlers, three spruce Courtiers, and an *Italian* Prelate. In another, a Barber, an Abbot, and two Cardinals. I have too great a Veneration for crowned Heads to dwell any longer on so nice a Subject: But as to Counts, Marquesses, Dukes, Earls, and the like, I was not so scrupulous. And I confess it was not without some Pleasure that I found my self able to trace the particular Features, by which certain Families are distinguished up to their Originals. I could plainly discover from whence one Family derives a long Chin; why a second hath abounded with Knaves for two Generations, and Fools for two

I proposed that Homer *and* Aristotle *might appear*

more; why a third happened to be crack-brained, and a fourth to be Sharpers. Whence it came, what *Polydore Virgil* says of a certain great House, *Nec Vir fortis, nec Fœmina Casta.* How Cruelty, Falshood, and Cowardice grew to be Characteristicks by which certain Families are distinguished as much as by their Coat of Arms. Who first brought the Pox into a noble House, which hath lineally descended in scrophulous Tumours to their Posterity. Neither could I wonder at all this, when I saw such an Interruption of Lineages by Pages, Lacqueys, Valets, Coachmen, Gamesters, Fidlers, Players, Captains, and Pickpockets.

I was chiefly disgusted with modern History. For having strictly examined all the Persons of greatest Name in the Courts of Princes for an Hundred Years past, I found how the World had been misled by prostitute Writers, to ascribe the greatest Exploits in War to Cowards, the wisest Counsel to Fools, Sincerity to Flatterers, *Roman* Virtue to Betrayers of their Country, Piety to Atheists, Chastity to Sodomites, Truth to Informers. How many innocent and excellent Persons had been condemned to Death or Banishment, by the practising of great Ministers upon the Corruption of Judges, and the Malice of Factions. How many Villains had been exalted to the highest Places of Trust, Power, Dignity, and Profit: How great a Share in the Motions and Events of Courts, Councils, and Senates might be challenged by Bawds, Whores, Pimps, Parasites, and Buffoons: How low an Opinion I had of human Wisdom and Integrity, when I was truly informed of the Springs and Motives of great Enterprizes and Revolutions in the World, and of the contemptible Accidents to which they owed their Success.

Here I discovered the Roguery and Ignorance of those who pretend to write *Anecdotes*, or secret History; who send so many Kings to their Graves with a Cup of Poison; will repeat the Discourse between a Prince and chief Minister, where no Witness was by; unlock the Thoughts and Cabinets of Embassadors and Secretaries of State; and have the perpetual Misfortune to be mistaken. Here

I discovered the true Causes of many great Events that
have surprized the World: How a Whore can govern
the Back-stairs, the Back-stairs a Council, and the Council
a Senate. A General confessed in my Presence that he
got a Victory purely by the Force of Cowardice and ill
Conduct: And an Admiral, that for want of proper Intelligence, he beat the Enemy to whom he intended to
betray the Fleet. Three Kings protested to me, that in
their whole Reigns they did never once prefer any Person
of Merit, unless by Mistake or Treachery of some Minister
in whom they confided: Neither would they do it if they
were to live again; and they shewed with great Strength
of Reason, that the Royal Throne could not be supported
without Corruption; because, that positive, confident,
restive Temper, which Virtue infused into Man, was a
perpetual Clog to publick Business.

I had the Curiosity to enquire in a particular Manner,
by what Method great Numbers had procured to themselves high Titles of Honour, and prodigious Estates; and
I confined my Enquiry to a very modern Period: However,
without grating upon present Times, because I would be
sure to give no Offence even to Foreigners (for I hope
the Reader need not be told that I do not in the least
intend my own Country in what I say upon this Occasion)
a great Number of Persons concerned were called up, and
upon a very slight Examination, discovered such a Scene
of Infamy, that I cannot reflect upon it without some
Seriousness. Perjury, Oppression, Subornation, Fraud,
Pandarism, and the like *Infirmities* were amongst the most
excusable Arts they had to mention; and for these I
gave, as it was reasonable, due Allowance. But when
some confessed, they owed their Greatness and Wealth
to Sodomy or Incest; others to the prostituting of their
own Wives and Daughters; others to the betraying their
Country or their Prince; some to poisoning, more to
the perverting of Justice in order to destroy the Innocent:
I hope I may be pardoned if these Discoveries inclined
me a little to abate of that profound Veneration which
I am naturally apt to pay to Persons of high Rank, who

ought to be treated with the utmost Respect due to their
sublime Dignity, by us their Inferiors.

I had often read of some great Services done to Princes
and States, and desired to see the Persons by whom those
Services were performed. Upon Enquiry I was told, that
their Names were to be found on no Record, except a
few of them whom History hath represented as the vilest
Rogues and Traitors. As to the rest, I had never once
heard of them. They all appeared with dejected Looks,
and in the meanest Habit; most of them telling me they
died in Poverty and Disgrace, and the rest on a Scaffold
or a Gibbet.

Among others there was one Person whose Case ap-
peared a little singular. He had a Youth about Eighteen
Years old standing by his Side. He told me, he had for
many Years been Commander of a Ship; and in the Sea
Fight at *Actium*, had the good Fortune to break through
the Enemy's great Line of Battle, sink three of their Capital
Ships, and take a fourth, which was the sole Cause of
Antony's Flight, and of the Victory that ensued: That the
Youth standing by him, his only Son, was killed in the
Action. He added, that upon the Confidence of some
Merit, the War being at an End, he went to *Rome*, and solic-
ited at the Court of *Augustus* to be preferred to a greater
Ship, whose Commander had been killed; but without
any regard to his Pretensions, it was given to a Boy who
had never seen the Sea, the Son of a *Libertina*, who waited
on one of the Emperor's Mistresses. Returning back to
his own Vessel, he was charged with Neglect of Duty,
and the Ship given to a favourite Page of *Publicola* the
Vice-Admiral; whereupon he retired to a poor Farm, at
a great Distance from *Rome*, and there ended his Life.
I was so curious to know the Truth of this Story, that
I desired *Agrippa* might be called, who was Admiral in
that Fight. He appeared, and confirmed the whole Account, but with much more Advantage to the Captain,
whose Modesty had extenuated or concealed a great Part
of his Merit.

I was surprized to find Corruption grown so high and

so quick in that Empire, by the Force of Luxury so lately introduced; which made me less wonder at many parallel Cases in other Countries, where Vices of all Kinds have reigned so much longer, and where the whole Praise as well as Pillage hath been engrossed by the chief Commander, who perhaps had the least Title to either.

As every Person called up made exactly the same Appearance he had done in the World, it gave me melancholy Reflections to observe how much the Race of human Kind was degenerate among us, within these Hundred Years past. How the Pox under all its Consequences and Denominations had altered every Lineament of an *English* Countenance; shortened the Size of Bodies, unbraced the Nerves, relaxed the Sinews and Muscles, introduced a sallow Complexion, and rendered the Flesh loose and *rancid*.

I descended so low as to desire that some *English* Yeomen of the old Stamp, might be summoned to appear; once so famous for the Simplicity of their Manners, Dyet and Dress; for Justice in their Dealings; for their true Spirit of Liberty; for their Valour and Love of their Country. Neither could I be wholly unmoved after comparing the Living with the Dead, when I considered how all these pure native Virtues were prostituted for a Piece of Money by their Grand-children; who in selling their Votes, and managing at Elections have acquired every Vice and Corruption that can possibly be learned in a Court.

CHAPTER NINE

THE AUTHOR'S RETURN TO MALDONADA. SAILS TO THE KINGDOM OF LUGGNAGG. THE AUTHOR CONFINED. HE IS SENT FOR TO COURT. THE MANNER OF HIS ADMITTANCE. THE KING'S GREAT LENITY TO HIS SUBJECTS.

THE Day of our Departure being come, I took leave of his Highness the Governor of *Glubbdubdrib*, and returned with my two Companions to *Maldonada*, where after a Fortnight's waiting, a Ship was ready to sail for

Luggnagg. The two Gentlemen and some others were so generous and kind as to furnish me with Provisions, and see me on Board. I was a Month in Voyage. We had one violent Storm, and were under a Necessity of steering Westward to get into the Trade-Wind, which holds for above sixty Leagues. On the 21st of *April,* 1708, we sailed in the River of *Clumegnig,* which is a Sea-port Town, at the South-East Point of *Luggnagg.* We cast Anchor within a League of the Town, and made a Signal for a Pilot. Two of them came on Board in less than half an Hour, by whom we were guided between certain Shoals and Rocks, which are very dangerous in the Passage, to a large Basin, where a Fleet may ride in Safety within a Cable's Length of the Town-Wall.

Some of our Sailors, whether out of Treachery or Inadvertence, had informed the Pilots that I was a Stranger and a great Traveller, whereof these gave Notice to a Custom-House Officer, by whom I was examined very strictly upon my landing. This Officer spoke to me in the Language of *Balnibarbi,* which by the Force of much Commerce is generally understood in that Town, especially by Seamen, and those employed in the Customs. I gave him a short Account of some Particulars, and made my Story as plausible and consistent as I could; but I thought it necessary to disguise my Country, and call my self a *Hollander*; because my Intentions were for *Japan,* and I knew the *Dutch* were the only *Europeans* permitted to enter into that Kingdom. I therefore told the Officer, that having been shipwrecked on the Coast of *Balnibarbi,* and cast on a Rock, I was received up into *Laputa,* or the flying Island (of which he had often heard) and was now endeavouring to get to *Japan,* from whence I might find a Convenience of returning to my own Country. The Officer said, I must be confined till he could receive Orders from Court, for which he would write immediately, and hoped to receive an Answer in a Fortnight. I was carried to a convenient Lodging, with a Centry placed at the Door; however I had the Liberty of a large Garden, and was treated with Humanity enough, being maintained all the Time at the King's Charge. I was invited by several Persons, chiefly out of Curiosity, because it was reported I came from Countries very remote, of which they had never heard.

I hired a young Man who came in the same Ship to be an Interpreter; he was a Native of *Luggnagg*, but had lived some Years at *Maldonada*, and was a perfect Master of both Languages. By his Assistance I was able to hold a Conversation with those that came to visit me; but this consisted only of their Questions and my Answers.

The Dispatch came from Court about the Time we expected. It contained a Warrant for conducting me and my Retinue to *Traldragdubh* or *Trildrogdrib*, (for it is pronounced both Ways as near as I can remember) by a Party of Ten Horse. All my Retinue was that poor Lad for an Interpreter, whom I persuaded into my Service. At my humble Request we had each of us a Mule to ride on. A Messenger was dispatched half a Day's Journey before us, to give the King Notice of my Approach, and to desire that his Majesty would please to appoint a Day and Hour, when it would be his gracious Pleasure that I might have the Honour to *lick the Dust before his Footstool.* This is the Court Style, and I found it to be more than Matter of Form: For upon my Admittance two Days after my Arrival, I was commanded to crawl upon my Belly, and lick the Floor as I advanced; but on account of my being a Stranger, Care was taken to have it so clean that the Dust was not offensive. However, this was a peculiar Grace, not allowed to any but Persons of the highest Rank, when they desire an Admittance: Nay, sometimes the Floor is strewed with Dust on purpose, when the Person to be admitted happens to have powerful Enemies at Court: And I have seen a great Lord with his Mouth so crammed, that when he had crept to the proper Distance from the Throne, he was not able to speak a Word. Neither is there any Remedy, because it is capital for those who receive an Audience to spit or wipe their Mouths in his Majesty's Presence. There is indeed another Custom, which I cannot altogether approve of. When the King hath a

Mind to put any of his Nobles to Death in a gentle indulgent Manner; he commands to have the Floor strowed with
a certain brown Powder, of a deadly Composition, which
being licked up infallibly kills him in twenty-four Hours.
But in Justice to this Prince's great Clemency, and the
Care he hath of his Subjects Lives, (wherein it were much
to be wished that the Monarchs of *Europe* would imitate
him) it must be mentioned for his Honour, that strict
Orders are given to have the infected Parts of the Floor
well washed after every such Execution; which if his
Domesticks neglect, they are in Danger of incurring his
Royal Displeasure. I my self heard him give Directions,
that one of his Pages should be whipt, whose Turn it
was to give Notice about washing the Floor after an
Execution, but maliciously had omitted it; by which
Neglect a young Lord of great Hopes coming to an Audience, was unfortunately poisoned, although the King
at that Time had no Design against his Life. But this
good Prince was so gracious, as to forgive the Page his
Whipping, upon Promise that he would do so no more,
without special Orders.

To return from this Digression; when I had crept within
four Yards of the Throne, I raised my self gently upon my
Knees, and then striking my Forehead seven Times against
the Ground, I pronounced the following Words, as they
had been taught me the Night before, *Ickpling Gloffthrobb
Squutserumm blhiop Mlashnalt Zwin tnodbalkguffh Slhiophad
Gurdlubh Asht.* This is the Compliment established by the
Laws of the Land for all Persons admitted to the King's
Presence. It may be rendered into *English* thus: *May your
cœlestial Majesty out-live the Sun, eleven Moons and an half.*
To this the King returned some Answer, which although
I could not understand, yet I replied as I had been directed; *Fluft drin Yalerick Dwuldum prastrad mirplush,* which
properly signifies, *My Tongue is in the Mouth of my Friend;*
and by this Expression was meant that I desired leave to
bring my Interpreter; whereupon the young Man already
mentioned was accordingly introduced; by whose Inter-
vention I answered as many Questions as his Majesty

could put in above an Hour. I spoke in the *Balnibarbian*
Tongue, and my Interpreter delivered my Meaning in
that of *Luggnagg*.

The King was much delighted with my Company, and
ordered his *Bliffmarklub* or High Chamberlain to appoint
a Lodging in the Court for me and my Interpreter, with a
daily Allowance for my Table, and a large Purse of Gold
for my common Expences.

I stayed three Months in this Country out of perfect
Obedience to his Majesty, who was pleased highly to favour
me, and made me very honourable Offers. But I thought
it more consistent with Prudence and Justice to pass the
Remainder of my Days with my Wife and Family.

CHAPTER TEN

THE LUGGNUGGIANS COMMENDED. A PARTICULAR DESCRIP-
TION OF THE STRULDBRUGS, WITH MANY CONVERSATIONS
BETWEEN THE AUTHOR AND SOME EMINENT PERSONS UPON
THAT SUBJECT.

THE *Luggnuggians* are a polite and generous People,
and although they are not without some Share of that
Pride which is peculiar to all *Eastern* Countries, yet they
shew themselves courteous to Strangers, especially such
who are countenanced by the Court. I had many Acquaintance among Persons of the best Fashion, and being always
attended by my Interpreter, the Conversation we had was
not disagreeable.

One Day in much good Company, I was asked by a Person of Quality, whether I had seen any of their *Struldbrugs*
or *Immortals*. I said I had not; and desired he would explain to me what he meant by such an Appellation, applyed to a mortal Creature. He told me, that sometimes,
although very rarely, a Child happened to be born in a
Family with a red circular Spot in the Forehead, directly
over the left Eye-brow, which was an infallible Mark that
it should never dye. The Spot, as he described it, was

about the Compass of a Silver Threepence, but in the Course of Time grew larger, and changed its Colour; for at Twelve Years old it became green, so continued till Five and Twenty, then turned to a deep blue; at Five and Forty it grew coal black, and as large as an *English* Shilling; but never admitted any farther Alteration. He said these Births were so rare, that he did not believe there could be above Eleven Hundred *Struldbrugs* of both Sexes in the whole Kingdom, of which he computed about Fifty in the Metropolis, and among the rest a young Girl born about three Years ago. That, these Productions were not peculiar to any Family, but a meer Effect of Chance; and the Children of the *Struldbruggs* themselves, were equally mortal with the rest of the People.

I freely own myself to have been struck with inexpressible Delight upon hearing this Account: And the Person who gave it me happening to understand the *Balnibarbian* Language, which I spoke very well, I could not forbear breaking out into Expressions perhaps a little too extravagant. I cryed out as in a Rapture; Happy Nation, where every Child hath at least a Chance for being immortal! Happy People who enjoy so many living Examples of antient Virtue, and have Masters ready to instruct them in the Wisdom of all former Ages! But, happiest beyond all Comparison are those excellent *Struldbruggs*, who being born exempt from that universal Calamity of human Nature, have their Minds free and disingaged, without the Weight and Depression of Spirits caused by the continual Apprehension of Death. I discovered my Admiration that I had not observed any of these illustrious Persons at Court; the black Spot on the Fore-head, being so remarkable a Distinction, that I could not have easily overlooked it: And it was impossible that his Majesty, a most judicious Prince, should not provide himself with a good Number of such wise and able Counsellors. Yet perhaps the Virtue of those Reverend Sages was too strict for the corrupt and libertine Manners of a Court. And we often find by Experience, that young Men are too opinionative and volatile to be guided by the sober Dictates of their Seniors. However, since the King was pleased to allow me Access to his Royal Person, I was resolved upon the very first Occasion to deliver my Opinion to him on this Matter freely, and at large by the Help of my Interpreter; and whether he would please to take my Advice or no, yet in one Thing I was determined, that his Majesty having frequently offered me an Establishment in this Country, I would with great Thankfulness accept the Favour, and pass my Life here in the Conversation of those superiour Beings the *Struldbruggs*, if they would please to admit me.

The Gentleman to whom I addressed my Discourse, because (as I have already observed) he spoke the Language of *Balnibarbi*, said to me with a Sort of a Smile, which usually ariseth from Pity to the Ignorant, that he was glad of any Occasion to keep me among them, and desired my Permission to explain to the Company what I had spoke. He did so; and they talked together for some time in their own Language, whereof I understood not a Syllable, neither could I observe by their Countenances what Impression my Discourse had made on them. After a short Silence, the same Person told me, that his Friends and mine (so he thought fit to express himself) were very much pleased with the judicious Remarks I had made on the great Happiness and Advantages of immortal Life; and they were desirous to know in a particular Manner, what Scheme of Living I should have formed to myself, if it had fallen to my Lot to have been born a *Struldbrugg*.

I answered, it was easy to be eloquent on so copious and delightful a Subject, especially to me who have been often apt to amuse myself with Visions of what I should do if I were a King, a General, or a great Lord: And upon this very Case I had frequently run over the whole System how I should employ myself, and pass the Time if I were sure to live for ever.

That, if it had been my good Fortune to come into the World a *Struldbrugg*; as soon as I could discover my own Happiness by understanding the Difference between Life and Death, I would first resolve by all Arts and Methods whatsoever to procure myself Riches: In the Pursuit of which, by Thrift and Management, I might reasonably expect in about two Hundred Years, to be the wealthiest Man in the Kingdom. In the second Place, I would from my earliest Youth apply myself to the Study of Arts and Sciences, by which I should arrive in time to excel all others in Learning. Lastly, I would carefully record every Action and Event of Consequence that happened in the Publick, impartially draw the Characters of the several Successions of Princes, and great Ministers of State; with my own Observations on every Point. I would exactly set down the several Changes in Customs, Languages, Fashions of Dress, Dyet and Diversions. By all which Acquirements, I should be a living Treasury of Knowledge and Wisdom, and certainly become the Oracle of the Nation.

I would never marry after Threescore, but live in an hospitable Manner, yet still on the saving Side. I would entertain myself in forming and directing the Minds of hopeful young Men, by convincing them from my own Remembrance, Experience and Observation, fortified by numerous Examples, of the Usefulness of Virtue in publick and private Life. But, my choise and constant Companions should be a Sett of my own immortal Brotherhood, among whom I would elect a Dozen from the most ancient down to my own Contemporaries. Where any of these wanted Fortunes, I would provide them with convenient Lodges round my own Estate, and have some of them always at my Table, only mingling a few of the most valuable among you Mortals, whom Length of Time would harden me to lose with little or no Reluctance, and treat your Posterity after the same Manner; just as a Man diverts himself with the annual Succession of Pinks and Tulips in his Garden, without regretting the Loss of those which withered the preceding Year.

These *Struldbruggs* and I would mutually communicate our Observations and Memorials through the Course of Time; remark the several Gradations by which Corruption steals into the World, and oppose it in every Step, by giving perpetual Warning and Instruction to Mankind; which, added to the strong Influence of our own Example, would probably prevent that continual Degeneracy of human Nature, so justly complained of in all Ages.

Add to all this, the Pleasure of seeing the various Revolutions of States and Empires; the Changes in the lower and upper World; antient Cities in Ruins, and obscure Villages become the Seats of Kings. Famous Rivers lessening into shallow Brooks; the Ocean leaving one Coast dry, and overwhelming another: The Discovery of many Countries yet unknown. Barbarity over-running the politest Nations, and the most barbarous becoming civilized. I should then see the Discovery of the *Longitude*, the *perpetual Motion*, the *universal Medicine*, and many other great Inventions brought to the utmost Perfection.

What wonderful Discoveries should we make in Astronomy, by outliving and confirming our own Predictions; by observing the Progress and Returns of Comets, with the Changes of Motion in the Sun, Moon and Stars.

I enlarged upon many other Topicks, which the natural Desire of endless Life and sublunary Happiness could easily furnish me with. When I had ended, and the Sum of my Discourse had been interpreted as before, to the rest of the Company, there was a good Deal of Talk among them in the Language of the Country, not without some Laughter at my Expence. At last the same Gentleman who had been my Interpreter, said, he was desired by the rest to set me right in a few Mistakes, which I had fallen into through the common Imbecility of human Nature, and upon that Allowance was less answerable for them. That, this Breed of *Struldbruggs* was peculiar to their Country, for there were no such People either in *Balnibarbi* or *Japan*, where he had the Honour to be Embassador from his Majesty, and found the Natives in both those Kingdoms very hard to believe that the Fact was possible; and it appeared from my Astonishment when he first mentioned the Matter to me, that I received it as a Thing wholly new, and scarcely to be credited. That in the two Kingdoms above-mentioned, where during his Residence he had conversed very much, he observed long Life to be the universal Desire and Wish of Mankind. That, whoever had one Foot in the Grave, was sure to hold back the other as strongly as he could. That the oldest had still Hopes of living one Day longer, and looked on Death as the greatest Evil, from which Nature always prompted him to retreat; only in this Island of *Luggnagg*, the Appetite for living was not so eager, from the continual Example of the *Struldbruggs* before their Eyes.

That the System of Living contrived by me was unreasonable and unjust, because it supposed a Perpetuity of Youth, Health, and Vigour, which no Man could be so foolish to hope, however extravagant he might be in his Wishes. That, the Question therefore was not whether a Man would chuse to be always in the Prime of Youth, attended with Prosperity and Health; but how he would pass a perpetual Life under all the usual Disadvantages which old Age brings along with it. For although few Men will avow their Desires of being immortal upon such hard Conditions, yet in the two Kingdoms before mentioned of *Balnibarbi* and *Japan*, he observed that every Man desired to put off Death for sometime longer, let it approach ever so late; and he rarely heard of any Man who died willingly, except he were incited by the Extremity of Grief or Torture. And he appealed to me whether in those Countries I had travelled as well as my own, I had not observed the same general Disposition.

After this Preface, he gave me a particular Account of the *Struldbruggs* among them. He said they commonly acted like Mortals, till about Thirty Years old, after which by Degrees they grew melancholy and dejected, increasing in both till they came to Fourscore. This he learned from their own Confession; for otherwise there not being above two or three of that Species born in an Age, they were too few to form a general Observation by. When they came to Fourscore Years, which is reckoned the Extremity of living in this Country, they had not only all the Follies and Infirmities of other old Men, but many more which arose from the dreadful Prospect of never dying. They were not only opinionative, peevish, covetous, morose, vain, talkative; but uncapable of Friendship, and

dead to all natural Affection, which never descended below their Grand-children. Envy and impotent Desires,
are their prevailing Passions. But those Objects against
which their Envy seems principally directed, are the Vices
of the younger Sort, and the Deaths of the old. By reflecting on the former, they find themselves cut off from all
Possibility of Pleasure; and whenever they see a Funeral,
they lament and repine that others are gone to an Harbour
of Rest, to which they themselves never can hope to arrive.
They have no Remembrance of any thing but what they
learned and observed in their Youth and middle Age,
and even that is very imperfect: And for the Truth or
Particulars of any Fact, it is safer to depend on common
Traditions than upon their best Recollections. The least
miserable among them, appear to be those who turn to
Dotage, and entirely lose their Memories; these meet
with more Pity and Assistance, because they want many
bad Qualities which abound in others.

If a *Struldbrugg* happen to marry one of his own Kind,
the Marriage is dissolved of Course by the Courtesy of
the Kingdom, as soon as the younger of the two comes to be
Fourscore. For the Law thinks it a reasonable Indulgence,
that those who are condemned without any Fault of their
own to a perpetual Continuance in the World, should
not have their Misery doubled by the Load of a Wife.

As soon as they have compleated the Term of Eighty
Years, they are looked on as dead in Law; their Heirs immediately succeed to their Estates, only a small Pittance is
reserved for their Support; and the poor ones are maintained at the publick Charge. After that Period they are
held incapable of any Employement of Trust or Profit;
they cannot purchase Lands, or take Leases, neither are
they allowed to be Witnesses in any Cause, either Civil or
Criminal, not even for the Decision of Meers and Bounds.

At Ninety they lose their Teeth and Hair; they have at
that Age no Distinction of Taste, but eat and drink whatever they can get, without Relish or Appetite. The Diseases they were subject to, still continue without encreasing
or diminishing. In talking they forget the common Appel-

lation of Things, and the Names of Persons, even of those who are their nearest Friends and Relations. For the same Reason they never can amuse themselves with reading, because their Memory will not serve to carry them from the Beginning of a Sentence to the End; and by this Defect they are deprived of the only Entertainment whereof they might otherwise be capable.

The Language of this Country being always upon the Flux, the *Struldbruggs* of one Age do not understand those of another; neither are they able after two Hundred Years to hold any Conversation (farther than by a few general Words) with their Neighbours the Mortals; and thus they lye under the Disadvantage of living like Foreigners in their own Country.

This was the Account given me of the *Struldbruggs*, as near as I can remember. I afterwards saw five or six of different Ages, the youngest not above two Hundred Years old, who were brought to me at several Times by some of my Friends; but although they were told that I was a great Traveller, and had seen all the World, they had not the least Curiosity to ask me a Question; only desired I would give them *Slumskudask*, or a Token of Remembrance; which is a modest Way of begging, to avoid the Law that strictly forbids it, because they are provided for by the Publick, although indeed with a very scanty Allowance.

They are despised and hated by all Sorts of People: When one of them is born, it is reckoned ominous, and their Birth is recorded very particularly; so that you may know their Age by consulting the Registry, which however hath not been kept above a Thousand Years past, or at least hath been destroyed by Time or publick Disturbances. But the usual Way of computing how old they are, is, by asking them what Kings or great Persons they can remember, and then consulting History; for infallibly the last Prince in their Mind did not begin his Reign after they were Fourscore Years old.

They were the most mortifying Sight I ever beheld; and the Women more horrible than the Men. Besides the usual Deformities in extreme old Age, they acquired an additional Ghastliness in Proportion to their Number of Years, which is not to be described; and among half a Dozen I soon distinguished which was the eldest, although there were not above a Century or two between them.

The Reader will easily believe, that from what I had heard and seen, my keen Appetite for Perpetuity of Life was much abated. I grew heartily ashamed of the pleasing Visions I had formed; and thought no Tyrant could invent a Death into which I would not run with Pleasure from such a Life. The King heard of all that had passed between me and my Friends upon this Occasion, and raillied me very pleasantly; wishing I would send a Couple of *Struldbruggs* to my own Country, to arm our People against the Fear of Death; but this it seems is forbidden by the fundamental Laws of the Kingdom; or else I should have been well content with the Trouble and Expence of transporting them.

I could not but agree, that the Laws of this Kingdom relating to the *Struldbruggs*, were founded upon the strongest Reasons, and such as any other Country would be under the Necessity of enacting in the like Circumstances. Otherwise, as Avarice is the necessary Consequent of old Age, those Immortals would in time become Proprietors of the whole Nation, and engross the Civil Power; which, for want of Abilities to manage, must end in the Ruin of the Publick.

CHAPTER ELEVEN

THE AUTHOR LEAVES LUGGNAGG AND SAILS TO JAPAN. FROM
THENCE HE RETURNS IN A DUTCH SHIP TO AMSTERDAM,
AND FROM AMSTERDAM TO ENGLAND.

I THOUGHT this Account of the *Struldbruggs* might be some Entertainment to the Reader, because it seems to be a little out of the common Way; at least, I do not remember to have met the like in any Book of Travels that hath come to my Hands: And if I am deceived, my Excuse must be, that it is necessary for Travellers, who describe the same Country, very often to agree in dwelling on the same Particulars, without deserving the Censure of having borrowed or transcribed from those who wrote before them.

There is indeed a perpetual Commerce between this Kingdom and the great Empire of *Japan*; and it is very probable that the *Japanese* Authors may have given some Account of the *Struldbruggs*; but my Stay in *Japan* was so short, and I was so entirely a Stranger to the Language, that I was not qualified to make any Enquiries. But I hope the *Dutch* upon this Notice will be curious and able enough to supply my Defects.

His Majesty having often pressed me to accept some Employment in his Court, and finding me absolutely determined to return to my Native Country; was pleased to give me his Licence to depart; and honoured me with a Letter of Recommendation under his own Hand to the Emperor of *Japan*. He likewise presented me with four Hundred forty-four large Pieces of Gold (this Nation delighting in even Numbers) and a red Diamond which I sold in *England* for Eleven Hundred Pounds.

On the 6th Day of *May*, 1709, I took a solemn Leave of his Majesty, and all my Friends. This Prince was so gracious as to order a Guard to conduct me to *Glanguenstald*, which is a Royal Port to the *South-West* Part of the Island. In six Days I found a Vessel ready to carry me to *Japan*; and spent fifteen Days in the Voyage. We landed at a small Port-Town called *Xamoschi*, situated on the *South-East* Part of *Japan*. The Town lies on the *Western* Part, where there is a narrow Streight, leading *Northward* into a long Arm of the Sea, upon the *North-West* Part of which *Yedo* the Metropolis stands. At landing I shewed the Custom-House Officers my Letter from the King of *Luggnagg* to his Imperial Majesty: They knew the Seal perfectly well; it was as broad as the Palm of my Hand. The Impression was, *A King lifting up a lame Beggar from the Earth*. The Magistrates of the Town hearing of my Letter,

received me as a publick Minister; they provided me with
Carriages and Servants, and bore my Charges to *Yedo*,
where I was admitted to an Audience, and delivered my
Letter; which was opened with great Ceremony, and ex-
plained to the Emperor by an Interpreter, who gave me
Notice of his Majesty's Order, that I should signify my
Request; and whatever it were, it should be granted for
the sake of his Royal Brother of *Luggnagg*. This Inter-
preter was a Person employed to transact Affairs with the
Hollanders: He soon conjectured by my Countenance that
I was an *European*, and therefore repeated his Majesty's
Commands in *Low-Dutch*, which he spoke perfectly well.
I answered, (as I had before determined) that I was a *Dutch*
Merchant, shipwrecked in a very remote Country, from
whence I travelled by Sea and Land to *Luggnagg*, and then
took Shipping for *Japan*, where I knew my Countrymen
often traded, and with some of these I hoped to get an
Opportunity of returning into *Europe*: I therefore most
humbly entreated his Royal Favour to give Order, that I
should be conducted in Safety to *Nangasac*. To this I added
another Petition, that for the sake of my Patron the King
of *Luggnagg*, his Majesty would condescend to excuse my
performing the Ceremony imposed on my Countrymen, of
trampling upon the Crucifix; because I had been thrown into
his Kingdom by my Misfortunes, without any Intention
of trading. When this latter Petition was interpreted to
the Emperor, he seemed a little surprised; and said, he
believed I was the first of my Countrymen who ever made
any Scruple in this Point; and that he began to doubt
whether I were a real *Hollander* or no; but rather suspected
I must be a Christian. However, for the Reasons I had
offered, but chiefly to gratify the King of *Luggnagg*, by an
uncommon Mark of his Favour, he would comply with the
singularity of my Humour; but the Affair must be managed
with Dexterity, and his Officers should be commanded to
let me pass as it were by Forgetfulness. For he assured me,
that if the Secret should be discovered by my Countrymen, the *Dutch*, they would cut my Throat in the Voyage.
I returned my Thanks by the Interpreter for so unusual a

Favour; and some Troops being at that Time on their March to *Nangasac*, the Commanding Officer had Orders to convey me safe thither, with particular Instructions about the Business of the *Crucifix*.

On the 9th Day of *June*, 1709, I arrived at *Nangasac*, after a very long and troublesome Journey. I soon fell into Company of some *Dutch* Sailors belonging to the *Amboyna* of *Amsterdam*, a stout Ship of 450 Tuns. I have lived long in *Holland*, pursuing my Studies at *Leyden*, and I spoke *Dutch* well: The Seamen soon knew from whence I came last; they were curious to enquire into my Voyages and Course of Life. I made up a Story as short and probable as I could, but concealed the greatest Part. I knew many Persons in *Holland*; I was able to invent Names for my Parents, whom I pretended to be obscure People in the Province of *Guelderland*. I would have given the Captain (one *Theodorus Vangrult*) what he pleased to ask for my Voyage to *Holland*; but, understanding I was a Surgeon, he was contented to take half the usual Rate, on Condition that I would serve him in the Way of my Calling. Before we took Shipping, I was often asked by some of the Crew, whether I had performed the Ceremony above-mentioned? I evaded the Question by general Answers, that I had satisfied the Emperor and Court in all Particulars. However, a malicious Rogue of a Skipper went to an Officer, and pointing to me, told him, I had not yet *trampled on the Crucifix*: But the other, who had received Instructions to let me pass, gave the Rascal twenty Strokes on the Shoulders with a Bamboo; after which I was no more troubled with such Questions.

Nothing happened worth mentioning in this Voyage. We sailed with a fair Wind to the *Cape of Good Hope*, where we staid only to take in fresh Water. On the 16th of *April* we arrived safe at *Amsterdam*, having lost only three Men by Sickness in the Voyage, and a fourth who fell from the Fore-mast into the Sea, not far from the Coast of *Guinea*. From *Amsterdam* I soon after set sail for *England* in a small Vessel belonging to that City.

On the 20th of *April*, 1710, we put in at the *Downs*. I landed the next Morning, and saw once more my Native Country after an Absence of five Years and six Months compleat. I went strait to *Redriff*, whither I arrived the same Day at two in the Afternoon, and found my Wife and Family in good Health.

The End of the Third Part

PART FOUR

A VOYAGE TO THE COUNTRY
OF THE HOUYHNHNMS

Nuyts Land

Edels Land
Lewins Land

I. St. Francol

I. St. Pieter

Sweers I.

I. Maelsuyker
De Wits I.

HOUYHNHNMS LAND

Discovered, A.D. 1711

CHAPTER ONE

THE AUTHOR SETS OUT AS CAPTAIN OF A SHIP. HIS MEN
CONSPIRE AGAINST HIM, CONFINE HIM A LONG TIME TO HIS
CABBIN, SET HIM ON SHORE IN AN UNKNOWN LAND. HE
TRAVELS UP INTO THE COUNTRY. THE YAHOOS, A STRANGE
SORT OF ANIMAL, DESCRIBED. THE AUTHOR MEETS TWO
HOUYHNHNMS.

I CONTINUED at home with my Wife and Children about
five Months in a very happy Condition, if I could have
learned the Lesson of knowing when I was well. I left my
poor Wife big with Child, and accepted an advantageous
Offer made me to be Captain of the *Adventure*, a stout
Merchant-man of 350 Tuns: For I understood Navigation
well, and being grown weary of a Surgeon's Employment
at Sea, which however I could exercise upon Occasion,
I took a skilful young Man of that Calling, one *Robert
Purefoy*, into my Ship. We set sail from *Portsmouth* upon
the 7th Day of *September*, 1710; on the 14th we met with
Captain *Pocock* of *Bristol*, at *Tenariff*, who was going to
the Bay of *Campeachy*, to cut Logwood. On the 16th he
was parted from us by a Storm: I heard since my Return,
that his Ship foundered, and none escaped, but one Cab-
bin-Boy. He was an honest Man, and a good Sailor, but
a little too positive in his own Opinions, which was the
Cause of his Destruction, as it hath been of several others.
For if he had followed my Advice, he might at this Time
have been safe at home with his Family as well as my self.

I had several Men died in my Ship of Calentures, so that
I was forced to get Recruits out of *Barbadoes*, and the *Lee-
ward Islands*, where I touched by the Direction of the Merchants who employed me; which I had soon too much
Cause to repent; for I found afterwards that most of them
had been Buccaneers. I had fifty Hands on Board; and
my Orders were, that I should trade with the *Indians* in
the *South-Sea*, and make what Discoveries I could. These
Rogues whom I had picked up, debauched my other Men,
and they all formed a Conspiracy to seize the Ship and

secure me; which they did one Morning, rushing into my Cabbin, and binding me Hand and Foot, threatening to throw me overboard, if I offered to stir. I told them, I was their Prisoner, and would submit. This they made me swear to do, and then unbound me, only fastening one of my Legs with a Chain near my Bed; and placed a Centry at my Door with his Piece charged, who was commanded to shoot me dead if I attempted my Liberty. They sent me down Victuals and Drink, and took the Government of the Ship to themselves. Their Design was to turn Pirates, and plunder the *Spaniards*, which they could not do, till they got more Men. But first they resolved to sell the Goods in the Ship, and then go to *Madagascar* for Recruits, several among them having died since my Confinement. They sailed many Weeks, and traded with the *Indians*; but I knew not what Course they took, being kept close Prisoner in my Cabbin, and expecting nothing less than to be murdered, as they often threatened me.

Upon the 9th Day of *May*, 1711, one *James Welch* came down to my Cabbin; and said he had Orders from the Captain to set me ashore. I expostulated with him, but in vain; neither would he so much as tell me who their new Captain was. They forced me into the Long-boat, letting me put on my best Suit of Cloaths, which were as good as new, and a small Bundle of Linnen, but no Arms except my Hanger; and they were so civil as not to search my Pockets, into which I conveyed what Money I had, with some other little Necessaries. They rowed about a League; and then set me down on a Strand. I desired them to tell me what Country it was: They all swore, they knew no more than my self, but said, that the Captain (as they called him) was resolved, after they had sold the Lading, to get rid of me in the first Place where they discovered Land. They pushed off immediately, advising me to make haste, for fear of being overtaken by the Tide; and bade me farewell.

In this desolate Condition I advanced forward, and soon got upon firm Ground, where I sat down on a Bank to rest my self, and consider what I had best to do. When I was a little refreshed, I went up into the Country, resolving to deliver my self to the first Savages I should meet; and purchase my Life from them by some Bracelets, Glass Rings, and other Toys, which Sailors usually provide themselves with in those Voyages, and whereof I had some about me: The Land was divided by long Rows of Trees, not regularly planted, but naturally growing; there was great Plenty of Grass, and several Fields of Oats. I walked very circumspectly for fear of being surprised, or suddenly shot with an Arrow from behind, or on either Side. I fell into a beaten Road, where I saw many Tracks of human Feet, and some of Cows, but most of Horses. At last I beheld several Animals in a Field, and one or two of the same Kind sitting in Trees. Their Shape was very singular, and deformed, which a little discomposed me, so that I lay down behind a Thicket to observe them better. Some of them coming forward near the Place where I lay, gave me an Opportunity of distinctly marking their Form. Their Heads and Breasts were covered with a thick Hair, some frizzled and others lank; they had Beards like Goats, and a long Ridge of Hair down their Backs, and the fore Parts of their Legs and Feet; but the rest of their Bodies were bare, so that I might see their Skins, which were of a brown Buff Colour. They had no Tails, nor any Hair at all on their Buttocks, except about the *Anus*; which, I presume Nature had placed there to defend them as they sat on the Ground; for this Posture they used, as well as lying down, and often stood on their hind Feet. They climbed high Trees, as nimbly as a Squirrel, for they had strong extended Claws before and behind, terminating on sharp Points, hooked. They would often spring, and bound, and leap with prodigious Agility. The Females were not so large as the Males; they had long lank Hair on their Heads, and only a Sort of Down on the rest of their Bodies, except about the *Anus*, and *Pudenda*. Their Dugs hung between their fore Feet, and often reached almost to the Ground as they walked. The Hair of both Sexes was of several Colours, brown, red, black and yellow. Upon the whole, I never beheld in all my Travels so disagreeable

an Animal, or one against which I naturally conceived
so strong an Antipathy. So that thinking I had seen enough,
full of Contempt and Aversion, I got up and pursued the
beaten Road, hoping it might direct me to the Cabbin of
some *Indian*. I had not gone far when I met one of these
Creatures full in my Way, and coming up directly to me.
The ugly Monster, when he saw me, distorted several
Ways every Feature of his Visage, and stared as at an Object he had never seen before; then approaching nearer,
lifted up his fore Paw, whether out of Curiosity or Mischief,
I could not tell: But I drew my Hanger, and gave him a
good Blow with the flat Side of it; for I durst not strike
him with the Edge, fearing the Inhabitants might be provoked against me, if they should come to know, that I had
killed or maimed any of their Cattle. When the Beast felt
the Smart, he drew back, and roared so loud, that a Herd
of at least forty came flocking about me from the next
Field, howling and making odious Faces; but I ran to
the Body of a Tree, and leaning my Back against it, kept
them off, by waving my Hanger. Several of this cursed
Brood getting hold of the Branches behind, leaped up into
the Tree, from whence they began to discharge their
Excrements on my Head: However, I escaped pretty well,
by sticking close to the Stem of the Tree, but was almost
stifled with the Filth, which fell about me on every Side.

In the Midst of this Distress, I observed them all to run
away on a sudden as fast as they could; at which I ventured to leave the Tree, and pursue the Road, wondering
what it was that could put them into this Fright. But looking on my Left-Hand, I saw a Horse walking softly in the
Field; which my Persecutors having sooner discovered,
was the Cause of their Flight. The Horse started a little
when he came near me, but soon recovering himself,
looked full in my Face with manifest Tokens of Wonder:
He viewed my Hands and Feet, walking round me several times. I would have pursued my Journey, but he
placed himself directly in the Way, yet looking with a
very mild Aspect, never offering the least Violence. We
stood gazing at each other for some time; at last I took

the Boldness, to reach my Hand towards his Neck, with a Design to stroak it; using the common Style and Whistle of Jockies when they are going to handle a strange Horse. But, this Animal seeming to receive my Civilities with Disdain, shook his Head, and bent his Brows, softly raising up his Left Fore-Foot to remove my Hand. Then he neighed three or four times, but in so different a Cadence, that I almost began to think he was speaking to himself in some Language of his own.

While He and I were thus employed, another Horse came up; who applying himself to the first in a very formal Manner, they gently struck each others Right Hoof before, neighing several times by Turns, and varying the Sound, which seemed to be almost articulate. They went some Paces off, as if it were to confer together, walking Side by Side, backward and forward, like Persons deliberating upon some Affair of Weight; but often turning their Eyes towards me, as it were to watch that I might not escape. I was amazed to see such Actions and Behaviour in Brute Beasts; and concluded with myself, that if the Inhabitants of this Country were endued with a proportionable Degree of Reason, they must needs be the wisest People upon Earth. This Thought gave me so much Comfort, that I resolved to go forward untill I could discover some House or Village, or meet with any of the Natives; leaving the two Horses to discourse together as they pleased. But the first, who was a Dapple-Grey, observing me to steal off, neighed after me in so expressive a Tone, that I fancied myself to understand what he meant; whereupon I turned back, and came near him, to expect his farther Commands; but concealing my Fear as much as I could; for I began to be in some Pain, how this Adventure might terminate; and the Reader will easily believe I did not much like my present Situation.

The two Horses came up close to me, looking with great Earnestness upon my Face and Hands. The grey Steed rubbed my Hat all round with his Right Fore-hoof, and discomposed it so much, that I was forced to adjust it better, by taking it off, and settling it again; whereat both he and his Companion (who was a brown Bay) appeared to be much surprized; the latter felt the Lappet of my Coat, and finding it to hang loose about me, they both looked with new Signs of Wonder. He stroked my Right Hand, seeming to admire the Softness, and Colour; but he squeezed it so hard between his Hoof and his Pastern, that I was forced to roar; after which they both touched me with all possible Tenderness. They were under great Perplexity about my Shoes and Stockings, which they felt very often, neighing to each other, and using various Gestures, not unlike those of a Philospher, when he would attempt to solve some new and difficult Phænomenon.

Upon the whole, the Behaviour of these Animals was so orderly and rational, so acute and judicious, that I at last concluded, they must needs be Magicians, who had thus metamorphosed themselves upon some Design; and seeing a Stranger in the Way, were resolved to divert themselves with him; or perhaps were really amazed at the Sight of a Man so very different in Habit, Feature and Complexion from those who might probably live in so remote a Climate. Upon the Strength of this Reasoning, I ventured to address them in the following Manner: Gentlemen, if you be Conjurers, as I have good Cause to believe, you can understand any Language; therefore I make bold to let your Worships know, that I am a poor distressed *Englishman*, driven by his Misfortunes upon your Coast; and I entreat one of you, to let me ride upon his Back, as if he were a real Horse, to some House or Village, where I can be relieved. In return of which Favour, I will make you a Present of this Knife and Bracelet, (taking them out of my Pocket.) The two Creatures stood silent while I spoke, seeming to listen with great Attention; and when I had ended, they neighed frequently towards each other, as if they were engaged in serious Conversation. I plainly observed, that their Language expressed the Passions very well, and the Words might with little

Pains be resolved into an Alphabet more easily than the *Chinese*.

I could frequently distinguish the Word *Yahoo*, which was repeated by each of them several times; and although it were impossible for me to conjecture what it meant, yet while the two Horses were busy in Conversation, I endeavoured to practice this Word upon my Tongue; and as soon as they were silent, I boldly pronounced *Yahoo* in a loud Voice, imitating, at the same time, as near as I could, the Neighing of a Horse; at which they were both visibly surprized, and the Grey repeated the same Word twice, as if he meant to teach me the right Accent, wherein I spoke after him as well as I could, and found myself perceivably to improve every time, although very far from any Degree of Perfection. Then the Bay tried me with a second Word, much harder to be pronounced; but reducing it to the *English Orthography*, may be spelt thus, *Houyhnhym*. I did not succeed in this so well as the former, but after two or three farther Trials, I had better Fortune; and they both appeared amazed at my Capacity.

After some farther Discourse, which I then conjectured might relate to me, the two Friends took their Leaves, with the same Compliment of striking each other's Hoof; and the Grey made me Signs that I should walk before him; wherein I thought it prudent to comply, till I could find a better Director. When I offered to slacken my Pace, he would cry *Hhuun, Hhuun*; I guessed his Meaning, and gave him to understand, as well as I could, that I was weary, and not able to walk faster; upon which, he would stand a while to let me rest.

CHAPTER TWO

THE AUTHOR CONDUCTED BY A HOUYHNHNM TO HIS HOUSE.
THE HOUSE DESCRIBED. THE AUTHOR'S RECEPTION. THE
FOOD OF THE HOUYHNHNMS. THE AUTHOR IN DISTRESS FOR
WANT OF MEAT, IS AT LAST RELIEVED. HIS MANNER OF FEEDING
IN THAT COUNTRY.

HAVING travelled about three Miles, we came to a
long Kind of Building, made of Timber, stuck in
the Ground, and wattled a-cross; the Roof was low, and
covered with Straw. I now began to be a little comforted;
and took out some Toys, which Travellers usually carry
for Presents to the Savage *Indians* of *America* and other
Parts, in hopes the People of the House would be thereby
encouraged to receive me kindly. The Horse made me a
Sign to go in first; it was a large Room with a smooth
Clay Floor, and a Rack and Manger extending the whole
Length on one Side. There were three Nags, and two
Mares, not eating, but some of them sitting down upon
their Hams, which I very much wondered at; but wondered more to see the rest employed in domestick Business:
The last seemed but ordinary Cattle; however this confirmed my first Opinion, that a People who could so far
civilize brute Animals, must needs excel in Wisdom all
the Nations of the World. The Grey came in just after,
and thereby prevented any ill Treatment, which the others
might have given me. He neighed to them several times
in a Style of Authority, and received Answers.

Beyond this Room there were three others, reaching the
Length of the House, to which you passed through three
Doors, opposite to each other, in the Manner of a Vista:
We went through the second Room towards the third;
here the Grey walked in first, beckoning me to attend:
I waited in the second Room, and got ready my Presents,
for the Master and Mistress of the House: They were two
Knives, three Bracelets of false Pearl, a small Looking
Glass and a Bead Necklace. The Horse neighed three

or four Times, and I waited to hear some answers in a
human Voice, but I heard no other Returns than in the
same Dialect, only one of two a little shriller than his.
I began to think that this House must belong to some
Person of great Note among them, because there appeared
so much Ceremony before I could gain Admittance. But,
that a Man of Quality should be served all by Horses, was
beyond my Comprehension. I feared my Brain was disturbed by my Sufferings and Misfortunes: I roused my self,
and looked about me in the Room where I was left alone;
this was furnished as the first, only after a more elegant
Manner. I rubbed my Eyes often, but the same Objects
still occurred. I pinched my Arms and Sides, to awake
my self, hoping I might be in a Dream. I then absolutely
concluded, that all these Appearances could be nothing
else but Necromancy and Magick. But I had no Time
to pursue these Reflections; for the Grey Horse came to
the Door, and made me a Sign to follow him into the
third Room; where I saw a very comely Mare, together
with a Colt and Fole, sitting on their Haunches, upon
Mats of Straw, not unartfully made, and perfectly neat and
clean.

The Mare soon after my Entrance, rose from her Mat,
and coming up close, after having nicely observed my
Hands and Face, gave me a most contemptuous Look;
then turning to the Horse, I heard the Word *Yahoo* often
repeated betwixt them; the meaning of which Word I
could not then comprehend, although it were the first I
had learned to pronounce; but I was soon better informed,
to my everlasting Mortification: For the Horse beckoning
to me with his Head, and repeating the Word *Hhuun,*
Hhuun, as he did upon the Road, which I understood was
to attend him, led me out into a kind of Court, where
was another Building at some Distance from the House.
Here we entered, and I saw three of those detestable
Creatures, which I first met after my landing, feeding upon
Roots, and the Flesh of some Animals, which I afterwards
found to be that of Asses and Dogs, and now and then a
Cow dead by Accident or Disease. They were all tied

by the Neck with strong Wyths, fastened to a Beam; they held their Food between the Claws of their fore Feet, and tore it with their Teeth.

The Master Horse ordered a Sorrel Nag, one of his Servants, to untie the largest of these Animals, and take him into a Yard. The Beast and I were brought close together; and our Countenances diligently compared, both by Master and Servant, who thereupon repeated several Times the Word *Yahoo*. My Horror and Astonishment are not to be described, when I observed, in this abominable Animal, a perfect human Figure; the Face of it indeed was flat and broad, the Nose depressed, the Lips large, and the Mouth wide: But these Differences are common to all savage Nations, where the Lineaments of the Countenance are distorted by the Natives suffering their Infants to lie grovelling on the Earth, or by carrying them on their Backs, nuzzling with their Face against the Mother's Shoulders. The Fore-feet of the *Yahoo* differed from my Hands in nothing else, but the Length of the Nails, the Coarseness and Brownness of the Palms, and the Hairiness on the Backs. There was the same Resemblance between our Feet, with the same Differences, which I knew very well, although the Horses did not, because of my Shoes and Stockings; the same in every Part of our Bodies, except as to Hairiness and Colour, which I have already described.

The great Difficulty that seemed to stick with the two Horses, was, to see the rest of my Body so very different from that of a *Yahoo*, for which I was obliged to my Cloaths, whereof they had no Conception: The Sorrel Nag offered me a Root, which he held (after their Manner, as we shall describe in its proper Place) between his Hoof and Pastern; I took it in my Hand, and having smelt it, returned it to him again as civilly as I could. He brought out of the *Yahoo's* Kennel a Piece of Ass's Flesh, but it smelt so offensively that I turned from it with loathing; he then threw it to the *Yahoo*, by whom it was greedily devoured. He afterwards shewed me a Wisp of Hay, and a Fettlock full of Oats; but I shook

my Head, to signify that neither of these were Food for me.
And indeed, I now apprehended, that I must absolutely
starve, if I did not get to some of my own Species: For
as to those filthy *Yahoos*, although there were few greater
Lovers of Mankind, at that time, than myself; yet I confess I never saw any sensitive Being so detestable on all
Accounts; and the more I came near them, the more
hateful they grew, while I stayed in that Country. This
the Master Horse observed by my Behaviour, and therefore
sent the *Yahoo* back to his Kennel. He then put his Fore-
hoof to his Mouth, at which I was much surprized, although he did it with Ease, and with a Motion that
appear'd perfectly natural; and made other Signs to
know what I would eat; but I could not return him
such an Answer as he was able to apprehend; and if he
had understood me, I did not see how it was possible to
contrive any way for finding myself Nourishment. While
we were thus engaged, I observed a Cow passing by;
whereupon I pointed to her, and expressed a Desire to
let me go and milk her. This had its Effect; for he led
me back into the House, and ordered a Mare-servant to
open a Room, where a good Store of Milk lay in Earthen
and Wooden Vessels, after a very orderly and cleanly
Manner. She gave me a large Bowl full, of which I drank
very heartily, and found myself well refreshed.

About Noon I saw coming towards the House a Kind
of Vehicle, drawn like a Sledge by four *Yahoos*. There was
in it an old Steed, who seemed to be of Quality; he alighted with his Hind-feet forward, having by Accident got
a Hurt in his Left Fore-foot. He came to dine with our
Horse, who received him with great Civility. They dined
in the best Room, and had Oats boiled in Milk for the
second Course, which the old Horse eat warm, but the
rest cold. Their Mangers were placed circular in the
Middle of the Room, and divided into several Partitions,
round which they sat on their Haunches upon Bosses of
Straw. In the Middle was a large Rack with Angles answering to every Partition of the Manger. So that each
Horse and Mare eat their own Hay, and their own Mash

of Oats and Milk, with much Decency and Regularity. The Behaviour of the young Colt and Fole appeared very modest; and that of the Master and Mistress extremely chearful and complaisant to their Guest. The Grey ordered me to stand by him; and much Discourse passed between him and his Friend concerning me, as I found by the Stranger's often looking on me, and the frequent Repetition of the Word *Yahoo*.

I happened to wear my Gloves; which the Master Grey observing, seemed perplexed; discovering Signs of Wonder what I had done to my Fore-feet; he put his Hoof three or four times to them, as if he would signify, that I should reduce them to their former Shape, which I presently did, pulling off both my Gloves, and putting them into my Pocket. This occasioned farther Talk, and I saw the Company was pleased with my Behaviour, whereof I soon found the good Effects. I was ordered to speak the few Words I understood; and while they were at Dinner, the Master taught me the Names for Oats, Milk, Fire, Water, and some others; which I could readily pronounce after him; having from my Youth a great Facility in learning Languages.

When Dinner was done, the Master Horse took me aside, and by Signs and Words made me understand the Concern he was in, that I had nothing to eat. Oats in their Tongue are called *Hlunnh*. This Word I pronounced two or three times; for although I had refused them at first, yet upon second Thoughts, I considered that I could contrive to make a Kind of Bread, which might be sufficient with Milk to keep me alive, till I could make my Escape to some other Country, and to Creatures of my own Species. The Horse immediately ordered a white Mare-servant of his Family to bring me a good Quantity of Oats in a Sort of wooden Tray. These I heated before the Fire as well as I could, and rubbed them till the Husks came off, which I made a shift to winnow from the Grain; I ground and beat them between two Stones, then took Water, and made them into a Paste or Cake, which I toasted at the Fire, and eat warm with Milk.

It was at first a very insipid Diet, altough common enough in many Parts of *Europe*, but grew tolerable by Time; and having been often reduced to hard Fare in my Life, this was not the first Experiment I had made how easily Nature is satisfied. And I cannot but observe, that I never had one Hour's Sickness, while I staid in this Island. It is true, I sometimes made a shift to catch a Rabbet, or Bird, by Springes made of *Yahoos* Hairs; and I often gathered wholesome Herbs, which I boiled, or eat as Salades with my Bread; and now and then, for a Rarity, I made a little Butter, and drank the Whey. I was at first at a great Loss for Salt; but Custom soon reconciled the Want of it; and I am confident that the frequent Use of Salt among us is an Effect of Luxury, and was first introduced only as a Provocative to Drink; except where it is necessary for preserving of Flesh in long Voyages, or in Places remote from great Markets. For we observe no Animal to be fond of it but Man: And as to myself, when I left this Country, it was a great while before I could endure the Taste of it in any thing that I eat.

This is enough to say upon the Subject of my Dyet, wherewith other Travellers fill their Books, as if the Readers were personally concerned, whether we fare well or ill. However, it was necessary to mention this Matter, lest the World should think it impossible that I could find Sustenance for three Years in such a Country, and among such Inhabitants.

When it grew towards Evening, the Master Horse ordered a Place for me to lodge in; it was but Six Yards from the House, and separated from the Stable of the *Yahoos*. Here I got some Straw, and covering myself with my own Cloaths, slept very sound. But I was in a short time better accommodated, as the Reader shall know hereafter, when I come to treat more particularly about my Way of living.

CHAPTER THREE

THE AUTHOR STUDIOUS TO LEARN THE LANGUAGE, THE HOUY-
HNHNM HIS MASTER ASSISTS IN TEACHING HIM. THE LAN-
GUAGE DESCRIBED. SEVERAL HOUYHNHNMS OF QUALITY COME
OUT OF CURIOSITY TO SEE THE AUTHOR. HE GIVES HIS MASTER
A SHORT ACCOUNT OF HIS VOYAGE.

M Y principal Endeavour was to learn the Language,
which my Master (for so I shall henceforth call
him) and his Children, and every Servant of his House
were desirous to teach me. For they looked upon it as a
Prodigy, that a brute Animal should discover such Marks
of a rational Creature. I pointed to every thing, and
enquired the Name of it, which I wrote down in my
Journal Book when I was alone, and corrected my bad
Accent, by desiring those of the Family to pronounce it
often. In this Employment, a Sorrel Nag, one of the
under Servants, was very ready to assist me.

In speaking, they pronounce through the Nose and
Throat, and their Language approaches nearest to the
High Dutch or *German*, of any I know in *Europe*; but is
much more graceful and significant. The Emperor *Charles*
V. made almost the same Observation, when he said,
That if he were to speak to his Horse, it should be in
High Dutch.

The Curiosity and Impatience of my Master were so
great, that he spent many Hours of his Leisure to instruct
me. He was convinced (as he afterwards told me) that I
must be a *Yahoo*, but my Teachableness, Civility and
Cleanliness astonished him; which were Qualities altogether so opposite to those Animals. He was most perplexed about my Cloaths, reasoning sometimes with himself, whether they were a Part of my Body; for I never
pulled them off till the Family were asleep, and got them
on before they waked in the Morning. My Master was
eager to learn from whence I came; how I acquired those
Appearances of Reason, which I discovered in all my

Actions; and to know my Story from my own Mouth, which he hoped he should soon do by the great Proficiency I made in learning and pronouncing their Words and Sentences. To help my Memory, I formed all I learned into the *English* Alphabet, and writ the Words down with the Translations. This last, after some time, I ventured to do in my Master's Presence. It cost me much Trouble to explain to him what I was doing; for the Inhabitants have not the least Idea of Books or Literature.

In about ten Weeks time I was able to understand most of his Questions; and in three Months could give him some tolerable Answers. He was extremely curious to know from what Part of the Country I came, and how I was taught to imitate a rational Creature; because the *Yahoos*, (whom he saw I exactly resembled in my Head, Hands and Face, that were only visible,) with some Appearance of Cunning, and the strongest Disposition to Mischief, were observed to be the most unteachable of all Brutes. I answered; that I came over the Sea, from a far Place, with many others of my own Kind, in a great hollow Vessel made of the Bodies of Trees: That, my Companions forced me to land on this Coast, and then left me to shift for myself. It was with some Difficulty, and by the Help of many Signs, that I brought him to understand me. He replied, That I must needs be mistaken, or that I *said the thing which was not*. (For they have no Word in their Language to express Lying or Falshood.) He knew it was impossible that there could be a Country beyond the Sea, or that a Parcel of Brutes could move a wooden Vessel whither they pleased upon Water. He was sure no *Houyhnhnm* alive could make such a Vessel, or would trust *Yahoos* to manage it.

The Word *Houyhnhnm*, in their Tongue, signifies a *Horse*; and in its Etymology, *the Perfection of Nature*. I told my Master, that I was at a Loss for Expression, but would improve as fast as I could; and hoped in a short time I should be able to tell him Wonders: He was pleased to direct his own Mare, his Colt and Fole, and the Servants of the Family to take all Opportunities of instructing me;

and every Day for two or three Hours, he was at the same
Pains himself: Several Horses and Mares of Quality in
the Neighbourhood came often to our House, upon the
Report spread of a wonderful *Yahoo*, that could speak like
a *Houyhnhnm*, and seemed in his Words and Actions to
discover some Glimmerings of Reason. These delighted
to converse with me; they put many Questions, and
received such Answers, as I was able to return. By all
which Advantages, I made so great a Progress, that in
five Months from my Arrival, I understood whatever was
spoke, and could express myself tolerably well.

The *Houyhnhnms* who came to visit my Master, out of a
Design of seeing and talking with me, could hardly believe
me to be a right *Yahoo*, because my Body had a different
Covering from others of my Kind. They were astonished to observe me without the usual Hair or Skin, except
on my Head, Face and Hands: but I discovered that
Secret to my Master, upon an Accident, which happened
about a Fortnight before.

I have already told the Reader, that every Night when
the Family were gone to Bed, it was my Custom to strip
and cover myself with my Cloaths: It happened one Morning early, that my Master sent for me, by the Sorrel Nag,
who was his Valet; when he came, I was fast asleep, my
Cloaths fallen off on one Side, and my Shirt above my
Waste. I awaked at the Noise he made, and observed him
to deliver his Message in some Disorder; after which he
went to my Master, and in a great Fright gave him a very
confused Account of what he had seen: This I presently
discovered; for going as soon as I was dressed, to pay my
Attendance upon his Honour, he asked me the Meaning of
what his Servant had reported; that I was not the same
Thing when I slept as I appeared to be at other times;
that his Valet assured him, some Part of me was white,
some yellow, at least not so white, and some brown.

I had hitherto concealed the Secret of my Dress, in order
to distinguish myself as much as possible, from that cursed
Race of *Yahoos*; but now I found it in vain to do so any
longer. Besides, I considered that my Cloaths and Shoes

would soon wear out, which already were in a declining Condition, and must be supplied by some Contrivance from the Hides of *Yahoos*, or other Brutes; whereby the whole Secret would be known. I therefore told my Master, that in the Country from whence I came, those of my Kind always covered their Bodies with the Hairs of certain Animals prepared by Art, as well for Decency, as to avoid Inclemencies of Air both hot and cold; of which, as to my own Person I would give him immediate Conviction, if he pleased to command me; only desiring his Excuse, if I did not expose those Parts that Nature taught us to conceal. He said, my Discourse was all very strange, but especially the last Part; for he could not understand why Nature should teach us to conceal what Nature had given. That neither himself nor Family were ashamed of any Parts of their Bodies; but however I might do as I pleased. Whereupon, I first unbuttoned my Coat, and pulled it off. I did the same with my Waste-coat; I drew off my Shoes, Stockings and Breeches. I let my Shirt down to my Waste, and drew up the Bottom, fastening it like a Girdle about my Middle to hide my Nakedness.

My Master observed the whole Performance with great Signs of Curiosity and Admiration. He took up all my Cloaths in his Pastern, one Piece after another, and examined them diligently; he then stroaked my Body very gently, and looked round me several Times; after which he said, it was plain I must be a perfect *Yahoo*; but that I differed very much from the rest of my Species, in the Whiteness, and Smoothness of my Skin, my want of Hair in several Parts of my Body, the Shape and Shortness of my Claws behind and before, and my Affectation of walking continually on my two hinder Feet. He desired to see no more; and gave me leave to put on my Cloaths again, for I was shuddering with Cold.

I expressed my Uneasiness at his giving me so often the Appellation of *Yahoo*, an odious Animal, for which I had so utter an Hatred and Contempt. I begged he would forbear applying that Word to me, and take the same Order in his Family, and among his Friends whom he suffered to see me. I requested likewise, that the Secret of my having a false Covering to my Body might be known to none but himself, at least as long as my present Cloathing should last: For as to what the Sorrel Nag his Valet had observed, his Honour might command him to conceal it.

All this my Master very graciously consented to; and thus the Secret was kept till my Cloaths began to wear out, which I was forced to supply by several Contrivances, that shall hereafter be mentioned. In the mean Time, he desired I would go on with my utmost Diligence to learn their Language, because he was more astonished at my Capacity for Speech and Reason, than at the Figure of my Body, whether it were covered or no; adding, that he waited with some Impatience to hear the Wonders which I promised to tell him.

From thenceforward he doubled the Pains he had been at to instruct me; he brought me into all Company, and made them treat me with Civility, because, as he told them privately, this would put me into good Humour, and make me more diverting.

Every Day when I waited on him, beside the Trouble he was at in teaching, he would ask me several Questions concerning my self, which I answered as well as I could; and by those Means he had already received some general Ideas, although very imperfect. It would be tedious to relate the several Steps, by which I advanced to a more regular Conversation: But the first Account I gave of my self in any Order and Length, was to this Purpose:

That, I came from a very far Country, as I already had attempted to tell him, with about fifty more of my own Species; that we travelled upon the Seas, in a great hollow Vessel made of Wood, and larger than his Honour's House. I described the Ship to him in the best Terms I could; and explained by the Help of my Handkerchief displayed, how it was driven forward by the Wind. That, upon a Quarrel among us, I was set on Shoar on this Coast, where I walked forward without knowing whither, till he delivered me from the Persecution of those execrable *Yahoos*. He asked me, Who made the Ship, and how it was possible that the *Houyhnhnms* of my Country would leave it to the Management of Brutes? My Answer was, that I durst proceed no farther in my Relation, unless he would give me his Word and Honour that he would not be offended; and then I would tell him the Wonders I had so often promised. He agreed; and I went on by assuring him, that the Ship was made by Creatures like myself, who in all the Countries I had travelled, as well as in my own, were the only governing, rational Animals; and that upon my Arrival hither, I was as much astonished to see the *Houyhnhnms* act like rational Beings, as he or his Friends could be in finding some Marks of Reason in a Creature he was pleased to call a *Yahoo*; to which I owned my Resemblance in every Part, but could not account for their degenerate and brutal Nature. I said farther, That if good Fortune ever restored me to my native Country, to relate my Travels hither, as I resolved to do; every Body would believe that I *said the Thing which was not*; that I invented the Story out of my own Head: And with all possible Respect to Himself, his Family, and Friends, and under his Promise of not being offended, our Countrymen would hardly think it probable, that a *Houyhnhnm* should be the presiding Creature of a Nation, and a *Yahoo* the Brute.

CHAPTER FOUR

THE HOUYHNHNMS NOTION OF TRUTH AND FALSHOOD. THE AUTHOR'S DISCOURSE DISAPPROVED BY HIS MASTER. THE AUTHOR GIVES A MORE PARTICULAR ACCOUNT OF HIMSELF, AND THE ACCIDENTS OF HIS VOYAGE.

MY Master heard me with great Appearances of Uneasiness in his Countenance; because *Doubting* or *not believing*, are so little known in this Country, that the Inhabitants cannot tell how to behave themselves under such Circumstances. And I remember in frequent Discourses with my Master concerning the Nature of Manhood, in other Parts of the World; having Occasion to talk of *Lying*, and *false Representation*, it was with much Difficulty that he comprehended what I meant; although he had otherwise a most acute Judgment. For he argued thus; That the Use of Speech was to make us understand one another, and to receive Information of Facts; now if any one *said the Thing which was not*, these Ends were defeated; because I cannot properly be said to understand him; and I am so far from receiving Information, that he leaves me worse than in Ignorance; for I am led to believe a Thing *Black* when it is *White*, and *Short* when it is *Long*. And these were all the Notions he had concerning that Faculty of *Lying*, so perfectly well understood, and so universally practised among human Creatures.

To return from this Digression; when I asserted that the *Yahoos* were the only governing Animals in my Country, which my Master said was altogether past his Conception, he desired to know, whether we had *Houyhnhnms* among us, and what was their Employment: I told him, we had great Numbers; that in Summer they grazed in the Fields, and in Winter were kept in Houses, with Hay and Oats, where *Yahoo* Servants were employed to rub their Skins smooth, comb their Manes, pick their Feet, serve them with Food, and make their Beds. I understand you well, said my Master; it is now very plain from all you have spoken, that whatever Share of Reason the *Yahoos* pretend to, the *Houyhnhnms* are your Masters; I heartily wish our *Yahoos* would be so tractable. I begged his Honour would please to excuse me from proceeding any farther, because I was very certain that the Account he expected from me would be highly displeasing. But he insisted in commanding me to let him know the best and the worst: I told him he should be obeyed. I owned, that the *Houyhnhnms* among us, whom we called *Horses*, were the most generous and comely Animal we had; that they excelled in Strength and Swiftness; and when they belonged to Persons of Quality, employed in Travelling, Racing, and drawing Chariots, they were treated with much Kindness and Care, till they fell into Diseases, or became foundered in the

Feet; but then they were sold, and used to all kind of Drudgery till they died; after which their Skins were stripped and sold for what they were worth, and their Bodies left to be devoured by Dogs and Birds of Prey. But the common Race of Horses had not so good Fortune, being kept by Farmers and Carriers, and other mean People, who put them to greater Labour, and feed them worse. I described as well as I could, our Way of Riding; the Shape and Use of a Bridle, a Saddle, a Spur, and a Whip; of Harness and Wheels. I added, that we fastened Plates of a certain hard Substance called *Iron* at the Bottom of their Feet, to preserve their Hoofs from being broken by the Stony Ways on which we often travelled.

My Master, after some Expressions of great Indignation, wondered how we dared to venture upon a *Houyhnhnm's* Back; for he was sure, that the weakest Servant in his House would be able to shake off the strongest *Yahoo*; or by lying down, and rouling upon his Back, squeeze the Brute to Death. I answered, That our Horses were trained up from three or four Years old to the several Uses we intended them for; That if any of them proved intolerably vicious, they were employed for Carriages; that they were severely beaten while they were young for any mischievous Tricks: That the Males, designed for the common Use of Riding or Draught, were generally *castrated* about two Years after their Birth, to take down their Spirits, and make them more tame and gentle: That they were indeed sensible of Rewards and Punishments; but his Honour would please to consider, that they had not the least Tincture of Reason any more than the *Yahoos* in this Country.

It put me to the Pains of many Circumlocutions to give my Master a right Idea of what I spoke; for their Language doth not abound in Variety of Words, because their Wants and Passions are fewer than among us. But it is impossible to express his noble Resentment at our savage Treatment of the *Houyhnhnm* Race; particularly after I had explained the Manner and Use of *Castrating* Horses among us, to hinder them from propagating their

Kind, and to render them more servile. He said, if it were possible there could be any Country where *Yahoos* alone were endued with Reason, they certainly must be the governing Animal, because Reason will in Time always prevail against Brutal Strength. But, considering the Frame of our Bodies, and especially of mine, he thought no Creature of equal Bulk was so ill-contrived, for employing that Reason in the common Offices of Life; whereupon he desired to know whether those among whom I lived, resembled me or the *Yahoos* of his Country. I assured him, that I was as well shaped as most of my Age; but the younger and the Females were much more soft and tender, and the Skins of the latter generally as white as Milk. He said, I differed indeed from other *Yahoos*, being much more cleanly, and not altogether so deformed; but in point of real Advantage, he thought I differed for the worse. That my Nails were of no Use either to my fore or hinder Feet: As to my fore Feet, he could not properly call them by that Name, for he never observed me to walk upon them; that they were too soft to bear the Ground; that I generally went with them uncovered, neither was the Covering I sometimes wore on them, of the same Shape, or so strong as that on my Feet behind. That I could not walk with any Security; for if either of my hinder Feet slipped, I must inevitably fall. He then began to find fault with other Parts of my Body; the Flatness of my Face, the Prominence of my Nose, my Eyes placed directly in Front, so that I could not look on either Side without turning my Head: That I was not able to feed my self, without lifting one of my fore Feet to my Mouth: And therefore Nature had placed those Joints to answer that Necessity. He knew not what could be the Use of those several Clefts and Divisions in my Feet behind; that these were too soft to bear the Hardness and Sharpness of Stones without a Covering made from the Skin of some other Brute; that my whole Body wanted a Fence against Heat and Cold, which I was forced to put on and off every Day with Tediousness and Trouble. And lastly, that he observed every Animal in this Country naturally to abhor the *Yahoos*, whom the Weaker avoided, and the Stronger drove from them. So that supposing us to have the Gift of Reason, he could not see how it were possible to cure that natural Antipathy which every Creature discovered against us; nor consequently, how we could tame and render them serviceable. However, he would (as he said) debate the Matter no farther, because he was more desirous to know my own Story, the Country, where I was born, and the several Actions and Events of my Life before I came hither.

I assured him, how extreamly desirous I was that he should be satisfied in every Point; but I doubted much, whether it would be possible for me to explain my self on several Subjects whereof his Honour could have no Conception, because I saw nothing in his Country to which I could resemble them. That however, I would do my best, and strive to express my self by Similitudes, humbly desiring his Assistance when I wanted proper Words; which he was pleased to promise me.

I said, my Birth was of honest Parents, in an Island called *England*, which was remote from this Country, as many Days Journey as the strongest of his Honour's Servants could travel in the Annual Course of the Sun. That I was bred a Surgeon, whose Trade it is to cure Wounds and Hurts in the Body, got by Accident or Violence. That my Country was governed by a Female Man, whom we called a *Queen*. That I left it to get Riches, whereby I might maintain my self and Family when I should return. That in my last Voyage, I was Commander of the Ship and had about fifty *Yahoos* under me, many of which died at Sea, and I was forced to supply them by others picked out from several Nations. That our Ship was twice in Danger of being sunk; the first Time by a great Storm, and the second, by striking against a Rock. Here my Master interposed, by asking me, How I could persuade Strangers out of different Countries to venture with me, after the Losses I had sustained, and the Hazards I had run. I said, they were Fellows of desperate Fortunes, forced to fly from the Places of their Birth, on

Account of their Poverty or their Crimes. Some were undone by Law-suits; others spent all they had in Drinking,
Whoring and Gaming; others fled for Treason; many for
Murder, Theft, Poysoning, Robbery, Perjury, Forgery,
Coining false Money; for committing Rapes or Sodomy;
for flying from their Colours, or deserting to the enemy;
and most of them had broken Prison. None of these durst
return to their native Countries for fear of being hanged, or
of starving in a Jail; and therefore were under a Necessity
of seeking a Livelihood in other Places.

During this Discourse, my Master was pleased often
to interrupt me. I had made Use of many Circumlocutions
in describing to him the Nature of the several Crimes, for
which most of our Crew had been forced to fly their
Country. This Labour took up several Days Conversation
before he was able to comprehend me. He was wholly at
a Loss to know what could be the Use or Necessity of
practising those Vices. To clear up which I endeavoured
to give him some Ideas of the Desire of Power and Riches;
of the terrible Effects of Lust, Intemperance, Malice,
and Envy. All this I was forced to define and describe
by putting of Cases, and making Suppositions. After
which, like one whose Imagination was struck with something never seen or heard of before, he would lift up
his Eyes with Amazement and Indignation. Power, Government, War, Law, Punishment, and a Thousand other
Things had no Terms, wherein that Language could
express them; which made the Difficulty almost insuper-
able to give my Master any Conception of what I meant:
But being of an excellent Understanding, much improved
by Contemplation and Converse, he at last arrived at a
competent Knowledge of what human Nature in our
Parts of the World is capable to perform; and desired
I would give him some particular Account of that Land,
which we call *Europe*, especially, of my own Country.

CHAPTER FIVE

THE AUTHOR AT HIS MASTER'S COMMANDS INFORMS HIM OF
THE STATE OF ENGLAND. THE CAUSES OF WAR AMONG THE
PRINCES OF EUROPE. THE AUTHOR BEGINS TO EXPLAIN THE
ENGLISH CONSTITUTION.

THE Reader may please to observe, that the following
Extract of many Conversations I had with my Master,
contains a Summary of the most material Points, which
were discoursed at several times for above two Years;
his Honour often desiring fuller Satisfaction as I farther
improved in the *Houyhnhnm* Tongue. I laid before him, as
well as I could, the whole State of *Europe*; I discoursed of
Trade and Manufactures, of Arts and Sciences; and the
Answers I gave to all the Questions he made, as they arose
upon several Subjects, were a Fund of Conversation not to
be exhausted. But I shall here only set down the Substance
of what passed between us concerning my own Country,
reducing it into Order as well as I can, without any Regard to Time or other Circumstances, while I strictly
adhere to Truth. My only Concern is, that I shall hardly
be able to do Justice to my Master's Arguments and Expressions; which must needs suffer by my Want of Capacity,
as well as by a Translation into our barbarous *English*.

In Obedience therefore to his Honour's Commands, I
related to him the *Revolution* under the Prince of *Orange*;
the long War with *France* entered into by the said Prince,
and renewed by his Successor the present Queen; wherein
the greatest Powers of *Christendom* were engaged, and which
still continued: I computed at his Request, that about a
Million of *Yahoos* might have been killed in the whole
Progress of it; and perhaps a Hundred or more Cities
taken, and five times as many Ships burnt or sunk.

He asked me what were the usual Causes or Motives
that made one Country go to War with another. I answered, they were innumerable; but I should only mention
a few of the chief. Sometimes the Ambition of Princes, who

never think they have Land or People enough to govern:
Sometimes the Corruption of Ministers, who engage their
Master in a War in order to stifle or divert the Clamour
of the Subjects against their evil Administration. Difference in Opinions hath cost many Millions of Lives: For
Instance, whether *Flesh* be Bread, or *Bread* be *Flesh*:
Whether the Juice of a certain *Berry* be *Blood* or *Wine*:
Whether *Whistling* be a Vice or a Virtue: Whether it be
better to *kiss a Post*, or throw it into the Fire: What is the
best Colour for a *Coat*, whether *Black, White, Red* or *Grey*;
and whether it should be *long* or *short, narrow* or *wide,
dirty* or *clean*; with many more. Neither are any Wars
so furious and bloody, or of so long Continuance, as those
occasioned by Difference in Opinion, especially if it be
in things indifferent.

Sometimes the Quarrel between two Princes is to decide
which of them shall dispossess a Third of his Dominions,
where neither of them pretend to any Right. Sometimes
one Prince quarrelleth with another, for fear the other
should quarrel with him. Sometimes a War is entered
upon, because the Enemy is too *strong*, and sometimes because he is too *weak*. Sometimes our Neighbours *want* the
Things which we *have*, or *have* the *Things* which we want;
and we both fight, till they take ours or give us theirs.
It is a very justifiable Cause of War to invade a Country
after the People have been wasted by Famine, destroyed
by Pestilence, or embroiled by Factions amongst themselves. It is justifiable to enter into a War against our
nearest Ally, when one of his Towns lies convenient for
us, or a Territory of Land, that would render our Dominions round and compact. If a Prince send Forces
into a Nation, where the People are poor and ignorant,
he may lawfully put half of them to Death, and make
Slaves of the rest, in order to civilize and reduce them
from their barbarous Way of Living. It is a very kingly,
honourable, and frequent Practice, when one Prince desires the Assistance of another to secure him against an
Invasion, that the Assistant, when he hath driven out the
Invader, should seize on the Dominions himself, and kill,

imprison or banish the Prince he came to relieve. Ally-
ance by Blood or Marriage, is a sufficient Cause of War
between Princes; and the nearer the Kindred is, the
greater is their Disposition to quarrel: *Poor* Nations are
hungry, and *rich* Nations are *proud*; and Pride and Hunger
will ever be at Variance. For these Reasons, the Trade
of a *Soldier* is held the most honourable of all others: Because a *Soldier* is a *Yahoo* hired to kill in cold Blood as
many of his own Species, who have never offended him,
as possibly he can.

There is likewise a Kind of beggarly Princes in *Europe*,
not able to make War by themselves, who hire out their
Troops to richer Nations for so much a Day to each Man;
of which they keep three Fourths to themselves, and it is
the best Part of their Maintenance; such are those in
many *Northern* Parts of *Europe*.

What you have told me, (said my Master) upon the Subject of War, doth indeed discover most admirably the
Effects of that Reason you pretend to: However, it is happy
that the *Shame* is greater than the *Danger*; and that Nature
hath left you utterly uncapable of doing much Mischief:
For your Mouths lying flat with your Faces, you can hardly
bite each other to any Purpose, unless by Consent. Then,
as to the Claws upon your Feet before and behind, they are
so short and tender, that one of our *Yahoos* would drive
a Dozen of yours before him. And therefore in recounting
the Numbers of those who have been killed in Battle, I
cannot but think that you have *said the Thing which is not*.

I could not forbear shaking my Head and smiling a little
at his Ignorance. And, being no Stranger to the Art of
War, I gave him a Description of Cannons, Culverins,
Muskets, Carabines, Pistols, Bullets, Powder, Swords,
Bayonets, Battles, Sieges, Retreats, Attacks, Undermines,
Countermines, Bombardments, Sea-fights; Ships sunk
with a Thousand Men; twenty Thousand killed on each
Side; dying Groans, Limbs flying in the Air: Smoak,
Noise, Confusion, trampling to Death under Horses Feet:
Flight, Pursuit, Victory; Fields strewed with Carcases left
for Food to Dogs, and Wolves, and Birds of Prey; Plun-

dering, Stripping, Ravishing, Burning and Destroying. And, to set forth the Valour of my own dear Countrymen, I assured him, that I had seen them blow up a Hundred Enemies at once in a Siege, and as many in a Ship; and beheld the dead Bodies drop down in Pieces from the Clouds, to the great Diversion of all the Spectators.

I was going on to more Particulars, when my Master commanded me Silence. He said, whoever understood the Nature of *Yahoos* might easily believe it possible for so vile an Animal, to be capable of every Action I had named, if their Strength and Cunning equalled their Malice. But, as my Discourse had increased his Abhorrence of the whole Species, so he found it gave him a Disturbance in his Mind, to which he was wholly a Stranger before. He thought his Ears being used to such abominable Words, might by Degrees admit them with less Detestation. That, although he hated the *Yahoos* of this Country, yet he no more blamed them for their odious Qualities, than he did a *Gnnayh* (a Bird of Prey) for its Cruelty, or a sharp Stone for cutting his Hoof. But, when a Creature pretending to Reason, could be capable of such Enormities, he dreaded lest the Corruption of that Faculty might be worse than Brutality itself. He seemed therefore confident, that instead of Reason, we were only possessed of some Quality fitted to increase our natural Vices; as the Reflection from a troubled Stream returns the Image of an ill-shapen Body, not only *larger*, but more *distorted*.

He added, That he had heard too much upon the Subject of War, both in this, and some former Discourses. There was another Point which a little perplexed him at present. I had said, that some of our Crew left their Country on Account of being ruined by *Law*: That I had already explained the Meaning of the Word; but he was at a Loss how it should come to pass, that the *Law* which was intended for *every* Man's Preservation, should be any Man's Ruin. Therefore he desired to be farther satisfied what I meant by *Law*, and the Dispensers thereof, according to the present Practice in my own Country: Because he thought, Nature and Reason were sufficient Guides for a reasonable Animal, as we pretended to be, in shewing us what we ought to do, and what to avoid.

I assured his Honour, that *Law* was a Science wherein I had not much conversed, further than by employing Advocates, in vain, upon some Injustices that had been done me. However, I would give him all the Satisfaction I was able.

I said there was a Society of Men among us, bred up from their Youth in the Art of proving by Words multiplied for the Purpose, that *White* is *Black*, and *Black* is *White*, according as they are paid. To this Society all the rest of the People are Slaves.

For Example. If my Neighbour hath a mind to my *Cow*, he hires a Lawyer to prove that he ought to have my *Cow* from me. I must then hire another to defend my Right; it being against all Rules of *Law* that any Man should be allowed to speak for himself. Now in this Case, I who am the true Owner lie under two great Disadvantages. First, my Lawyer being practiced almost from his Cradle in defending Falshood; is quite out of his Element when he would be an Advocate for Justice, which as an Office unnatural, he always attempts with great Awkwardness, if not with Ill-will. The second Disadvantage is, that my Lawyer must proceed with great Caution: Or else he will be reprimanded by the Judges, and abhorred by his Brethren, as one who would lessen the Practice of the Law. And therefore I have but two Methods to preserve my *Cow*. The first is, to gain over my Adversary's Lawyer with a double Fee; who will then betray his Client, by insinuating that he hath Justice on his Side. The second Way is for my Lawyer to make my Cause appear as unjust as he can; by allowing the *Cow* to belong to my Adversary; and this if it be skilfully done, will certainly bespeak the Favour of the Bench.

Now, your Honour is to know, that these Judges are Persons appointed to decide all Controversies of Property, as well as for the Tryal of Criminals; and picked out from the most dextrous Lawyers who are grown old or lazy: And having been byassed all their Lives against Truth and

Equity, lie under such a fatal Necessity of favouring Fraud, Perjury and Oppression; that I have known some of them to have refused a large Bribe from the Side where Justice lay, rather than injure the *Faculty*, by doing any thing unbecoming their Nature or their Office.

It is a Maxim among these Lawyers, that whatever hath been done before, may legally be done again: And therefore they take special Care to record all the Decisions formerly made against common Justice and the general Reason of Mankind. These, under the Name of *Precedents*, they produce as Authorities to justify the most iniquitous Opinions; and the Judges never fail of directing accordingly.

In pleading, they studiously avoid entering into the *Merits* of the Cause; but are loud, violent and tedious in dwelling upon all *Circumstances* which are not to the Purpose. For Instance, in the Case already mentioned: They never desire to know what Claim or Title my Adversary hath to my *Cow*; but whether the said *Cow* were Red or Black; her Horns long or short; whether the Field I graze her in be round or square; whether she were milked at home or abroad; what Diseases she is subject to, and the like. After which they consult *Precedents*, adjourn the Cause, from Time to Time, and in Ten, Twenty, or Thirty Years come to an Issue.

It is likewise to be observed, that this Society hath a peculiar Cant and Jargon of their own, that no other Mortal can understand, and wherein all their Laws are written, which they take special Care to multiply; whereby they have wholly confounded the very Essence of Truth and Falshood, of Right and Wrong; so that it will take Thirty Years to decide whether the Field, left me by my Ancestors for six Generations, belong to me, or to a Stranger three Hundred Miles off.

In the Tryal of Persons accused for Crimes against the State, the Method is much more short and commendable: The Judge first sends to sound the Disposition of those in Power; after which he can easily hang or save the Criminal, strictly preserving all the Forms of Law.

Here my Master interposing, said it was a Pity, that
Creatures endowed with such prodigious Abilities of Mind
as these Lawyers, by the Description I gave of them must
certainly be, were not rather encouraged to be Instructors
of others in Wisdom and Knowledge. In Answer to which,
I assured his Honour, that in all Points out of their own
Trade, they were usually the most ignorant and stupid
Generation among us, the most despicable in common
Conversation, avowed Enemies to all Knowledge and
Learning; and equally disposed to pervert the general
Reason of Mankind, in every other Subject of Discourse,
as in that of their own Profession.

CHAPTER SIX

A CONTINUATION OF THE STATE OF ENGLAND, UNDER QUEEN ANNE. THE CHARACTER OF A FIRST MINISTER IN THE COURTS OF EUROPE.

My Master was yet wholly at a Loss to understand
what Motives could incite this Race of Lawyers to
perplex, disquiet, and weary themselves by engaging in
a Confederacy of Injustice, merely for the Sake of injuring
their Fellow-Animals; neither could he comprehend what
I meant in saying they did it for *Hire*. Whereupon I
was at much Pains to describe to him the Use of *Money*,
the Materials it was made of, and the Value of the Metals:
That when a *Yahoo* had got a great Store of this precious
Substance, he was able to purchase whatever he had a
mind to; the finest Cloathing, the noblest Houses, great
Tracts of Land, the most costly Meats and Drinks; and
have his Choice of the most beautiful Females. Therefore since *Money* alone, was able to perform all these Feats,
our *Yahoos* thought, they could never have enough of it to
spend or to save, as they found themselves inclined from
their natural Bent either to Profusion or Avarice. That,
the rich Man enjoyed the Fruit of the poor Man's Labour,
and the latter were a Thousand to One in Proportion to

the former. That the Bulk of our People was forced to
live miserably, by labouring every Day for small Wages
to make a few live plentifully. I enlarged myself much
on these and many other Particulars to the same Purpose: But his Honour was still to seek: For he went upon
a Supposition that all Animals had a Title to their Share
in the Productions of the Earth; and especially those who
presided over the rest. Therefore he desired I would let
him know, what these costly Meats were, and how any
of us happened to want them. Whereupon I enumerated
as many Sorts as came into my Head, with the various
Methods of dressing them, which could not be done without
sending Vessels by Sea to every Part of the World, as well
for Liquors to drink, as for Sauces, and innumerable other
Conveniencies. I assured him, that this whole Globe of
Earth must be at least three Times gone round, before
one of our better Female *Yahoos* could get her Breakfast,
or a Cup to put it in. He said, That must needs be
a miserable Country which cannot furnish Food for its
own Inhabitants. But what he chiefly wondered at, was
how such vast Tracts of Ground as I described, should be
wholly without *Fresh-water*, and the People put to the
Necessity of sending over the Sea for Drink. I replied, that
England (the dear Place of my Nativity) was computed to
produce three Times the Quantity of Food, more than
its Inhabitants are able to consume, as well as Liquors
extracted from Grain, or pressed out of the Fruit of certain Trees, which made excellent Drink; and the same
Proportion in every other Convenience of Life. But, in
order to feed the Luxury and Intemperance of the Males,
and the Vanity of the Females, we sent away the greatest Part of our necessary Things to other Countries, from
whence in Return we brought the Materials of Diseases,
Folly, and Vice, to spend among ourselves. Hence it
follows of Necessity, that vast Numbers of our People
are compelled to seek their Livelihood by Begging, Rob-
bing, Stealing, Cheating, Pimping, Forswearing, Flattering, Suborning, Forging, Gaming, Lying, Fawning,
Hectoring, Voting, Scribling, Stargazing, Poysoning,

Whoring, Canting, Libelling, Free-thinking, and the like Occupations: Every one of which Terms, I was at much Pains to make him understand.

That, *Wine* was not imported among us from foreign Countries, to supply the Want of Water or other Drinks, but because it was a Sort of Liquid which made us merry, by putting us out of our Senses; diverted all melancholy Thoughts, begat wild extravagant Imaginations in the Brain, raised our Hopes, and banished our Fears; suspended every Office of Reason for a Time, and deprived us of the Use of our Limbs, untill we fell into a profound Sleep; although it must be confessed, that we always awaked sick and dispirited; and that the Use of this Liquor filled us with Diseases, which made our Lives uncomfortable and short.

But beside all this, the Bulk of our People supported themselves by furnishing the Necessities or Conveniencies of Life to the Rich, and to each other. For Instance, when I am at home and dressed as I ought to be, I carry on my Body the Workmanship of an Hundred Tradesmen; the Building and Furniture of my House employ as many more; and Five Times the Number to adorn my Wife.

I was going on to tell him of another Sort of People, who get their Livelihood by attending the Sick; having upon some Occasions informed his Honour that many of my Crew had died of Diseases. But here it was with the utmost Difficulty, that I brought him to apprehend what I meant. He could easily conceive, that a *Houyhnhnm* grew weak and heavy a few Days before his Death; or by some Accident might hurt a Limb. But that Nature, who worketh all things to Perfection, should suffer any Pains to breed in our Bodies, he thought impossible; and desired to know the Reason of so unaccountable an Evil. I told him, we fed on a Thousand Things which operated contrary to each other; that we eat when we were not hungry, and drank without the Provocation of Thirst: That we sat whole Nights drinking strong Liquors without eating a Bit; which disposed us to Sloth, enflamed our Bodies, and precipitated or prevented Digestion. That, prostitute Female *Yahoos* acquired a certain Malady, which bred Rottenness in the Bones of those, who fell into their Embraces: That this and many other Diseases, were propagated from Father to Son; so that great Numbers come into the World with complicated Maladies upon them: That, it would be endless to give him a Catalogue of all Diseases incident to human Bodies; for they could not be fewer than five or six Hundred, spread over every Limb, and Joynt: In short, every Part, external and intestine, having Diseases appropriated to each. To remedy which, there was a Sort of People bred up among us, in the Profession or Pretence of curing the Sick. And because I had some Skill in the Faculty, I would in Gratitude to his Honour, let him know the whole Mystery and Method by which they proceed.

Their Fundamental is, that all Diseases arise from *Repletion*; from whence they conclude, that a great *Evacuation* of the Body is necessary, either through the natural Passage, or upwards at the Mouth. Their next Business is, from Herbs, Minerals, Gums, Oyls, Shells, Salts, Juices, Seaweed, Excrements, Barks of Trees, Serpents, Toads, Frogs, Spiders, dead Mens Flesh and Bones, Birds, Beasts and Fishes, to form a Composition for Smell and Taste the most abominable, nauseous and detestable, that they can possibly contrive, which the Stomach immediately rejects with Loathing: And this they call a *Vomit*. Or else from the same Store-house, with some other poysonous Additions, they command us to take in at the Orifice *above* or *below*, (just as the Physician then happens to be disposed) a Medicine equally annoying and disgustful to the Bowels; which relaxing the Belly, drives down all before it: And this they call a *Purge*, or a *Clyster*. For Nature (as the Physicians alledge) having intended the superior anterior Orifice only for the *Intromission* of Solids and Liquids, and the inferior Posterior for Ejection; these Artists ingeniously considering that in all Diseases Nature is forced out of her Seat; therefore to replace her in it, the Body must be treated in a Manner directly contrary, by interchanging the Use of each Orifice; forcing Solids and Liquids in at the *Anus*, and making Evacuations at the Mouth.

But, besides real Diseases, we are subject to many that are only imaginary, for which the Physicians have invented imaginary Cures; these have their several Names, and so have the Drugs that are proper for them; and with these our Female *Yahoos* are always infested.

One great Excellency in this Tribe is their Skill at *Prognosticks*, wherein they seldom fail; their Predictions in real Diseases, when they rise to any Degree of Malignity, generally portending *Death*, which is always in their Power, when Recovery is not: And therefore, upon any unexpected Signs of Amendment, after they have pronounced their Sentence, rather than be accused as false Prophets, they know how to approve their Sagacity to the World by a seasonable Dose.

They are likewise of special Use to Husbands and Wives, who are grown weary of their Mates; to eldest Sons, to great Ministers of State, and often to Princes.

I had formerly upon Occasion discoursed with my Master upon the Nature of *Government* in general, and particularly of our own *excellent Constitution*, deservedly the Wonder and Envy of the whole World. But having here accidentally mentioned a *Minister of State*; he commanded me some Time after to inform him, what Species of *Yahoo* I particularly meant by that Appellation.

I told him, that a *First* or *Chief Minister of State*, whom I intended to describe, was a Creature wholly exempt from Joy and Grief, Love and Hatred, Pity and Anger; at least makes use of no other Passions but a violent Desire of Wealth, Power, and Titles: That he applies his Words to all Uses, except to the Indication of his Mind; That he never tells a *Truth*, but with an Intent that you should take it for a *Lye*; nor a *Lye*, but with a Design that you should take it for a *Truth*; That those he speaks worst of behind their Backs, are in the surest way to Preferment; and whenever he begins to praise you to others or to your self, you are from that Day forlorn. The worst Mark you can receive is a *Promise*, especially when it is confirmed with an Oath; after which every wise Man retires, and gives over all Hopes.

There are three Methods by which a Man may rise to be Chief Minister: The first is, by knowing how with Prudence to dispose of a Wife, a Daughter, or a Sister: The second, by betraying or undermining his Predecessor: And the third is, by a *furious Zeal* in publick Assemblies against the Corruptions of the Court. But a wise Prince would rather chuse to employ those who practise the last of these Methods; because such Zealots prove always the most obsequious and subservient to the Will and Passions of their Master. That, these *Ministers* having all Employments at their Disposal, preserve themselves in Power by bribing the Majority of a Senate or great Council; and at last by an Expedient called an *Act of Indemnity* (whereof I described the Nature to him) they secure themselves from After-reckonings, and retire from the Publick, laden with the Spoils of the Nation.

The Palace of a *Chief Minister*, is a Seminary to breed up others in his own Trade: The Pages, Lacquies, and Porter, by imitating their Master, become *Ministers of State* in their several Districts, and learn to excel in the three principal *Ingredients*, of *Insolence*, *Lying*, and *Bribery*. Accordingly, they have a *Subaltern* Court paid to them by Persons of the best Rank; and sometimes by the Force of Dexterity and Impudence, arrive through several Gradations to be Successors to their Lord.

He is usually governed by a decayed Wench, or favourite Footman, who are the Tunnels through which all Graces are conveyed, and may properly be called, *in the last Resort*, the Governors of the Kingdom.

One Day, my Master, having heard me mention the *Nobility* of my Country, was pleased to make me a Compliment which I could not pretend to deserve: That, he was sure, I must have been born of some Noble Family, because I far exceeded in Shape, Colour, and Cleanliness, all the *Yahoos* of his Nation, although I seemed to fail in Strength, and Agility, which must be imputed to my different Way of Living from those other Brutes; and besides, I was not only endowed with the Faculty of Speech, but likewise with some Rudiments of Reason, to a Degree, that with all his Acquaintance I passed for a Prodigy.

He made me observe, that among the *Houyhnhnms*, the *White*, the *Sorrel*, and the *Iron-grey*, were not so exactly shaped as the *Bay*, the *Dapple-grey*, and the *Black*; nor born with equal Talents of Mind, or a Capacity to improve them; and therefore continued always in the Condition of Servants, without ever aspiring to match out of their own Race, which in that Country would be reckoned monstrous and unnatural.

I made his Honour my most humble Acknowledgements for the good Opinion he was pleased to conceive of me; but assured him at the same Time, that my Birth was of the lower Sort, having been born of plain, honest Parents, who were just able to give me a tolerable Education: That, *Nobility* among us was altogether a different Thing from the Idea he had of it; That, our young *Noblemen* are bred from their Childhood in Idleness and Luxury; that, as soon as Years will permit, they consume their Vigour, and contract odious Diseases among lewd Females; and when their Fortunes are almost ruined, they marry some Woman of mean Birth, disagreeable Person, and unsound Constitution, merely for the sake of Money, whom they hate and despise. That, the Productions of such Marriages are generally scrophulous, rickety or deformed Children; by which Means the Family seldom continues above three Generations, unless the Wife take Care to provide a healthy Father among her Neighbours, or Domesticks, in order to improve and continue the Breed. That, a weak diseased Body, a meager Countenance, and sallow Complexion, are the true Marks of *noble Blood*; and a healthy robust Appearance is so disgraceful in a Man of Quality, that the World concludes his real Father to have been a Groom or a Coachman. The Imperfections of his Mind run parallel with those of his Body; being a Composition of Spleen, Dulness, Ignorance, Caprice, Sensuality and Pride.

Without the Consent of this illustrious Body, no Law

can be enacted, repealed, or altered: And these Nobles have likewise the Decision of all our Possessions without Appeal.*

CHAPTER SEVEN

THE AUTHOR'S GREAT LOVE OF HIS NATIVE COUNTRY. HIS MASTER'S OBSERVATIONS UPON THE CONSTITUTION AND AD-MINISTRATION OF ENGLAND, AS DESCRIBED BY THE AUTHOR, WITH PARALLEL CASES AND COMPARISONS. HIS MASTER'S OBSERVATIONS UPON HUMAN NATURE.

THE Reader may be disposed to wonder how I could prevail on my self to give so free a Representation of my own Species, among a Race of Mortals who were already too apt to conceive the vilest Opinion of Human Kind, from that entire Congruity betwixt me and their *Yahoos*. But I must freely confess, that the many Virtues of those excellent *Quadrupeds* placed in opposite View to human Corruptions, had so far opened my Eyes, and enlarged my Understanding, that I began to view the Actions and Passions of Man in a very different Light; and to think the Honour of my own kind not worth managing; which, besides, it was impossible for me to do before a Person of so acute a Judgment as my Master, who daily convinced me of a thousand Faults in my self, whereof I had not the least Perception before, and which with us would never be numbered even among human Infirmities. I had likewise learned from his Example an utter Detestation of all Falsehood or Disguise; and *Truth* appeared so amiable to me, that I determined upon sacrificing every thing to it.

Let me deal so candidly with the Reader, as to confess,

* On the evidence of a direction, in a contemporary hand, in a copy of Motte's first edition (for an analysis of which *v. Rev. of Eng. Studies. III.* 12. 1927. pp. 470-3) it has been suggested that these three lines are misplaced and should be inserted after the second paragraph on p. 125 (Part II. ch. 6). There appears to be insufficient evidence to justify the emendation. [J.H.]

that there was yet a much stronger Motive for the Freedom I took in my Representation of Things. I had not been a Year in this Country, before I contracted such a Love and Veneration for the Inhabitants, that I entered on a firm Resolution never to return to human Kind, but to pass the rest of my Life among these admirable *Houyhnhnms* in the Contemplation and Practice of every Virtue; where I could have no Example or Incitement to Vice. But it was decreed by Fortune, my perpetual Enemy, that so great a Felicity should not fall to my Share. However, it is now some Comfort to reflect, that in what I said of my Countrymen, I *extenuated* their Faults as much as I durst before so strict an Examiner; and upon every Article, gave as *favourable* a Turn as the Matter would bear. For, indeed, who is there alive that will not be swayed by his Byass and Partiality to the Place of his Birth?

I have related the Substance of several Conversations I had with my Master, during the greatest Part of the Time I had the Honour to be in his Service; but have indeed for Brevity sake omitted much more than is here set down.

When I had answered all his Questions, and his Curiosity seemed to be fully satisfied; he sent for me one Morning early, and commanding me to sit down at some Distance, (an Honour which he had never before conferred upon me) He said, he had been very seriously considering my whole Story, as far as it related both to my self and my Country: That, he looked upon us as a Sort of Animals to whose Share, by what Accident he could not conjecture, some small Pittance of *Reason* had fallen, whereof we made no other Use than by its Assistance to aggravate our *natural* Corruptions, and to acquire new ones which Nature had not given us. That, we disarmed our selves of the few Abilities she had bestowed; had been very successful in multiplying our original Wants, and seemed to spend our whole Lives in vain Endeavours to supply them by our own Inventions. That, as to my self, it was manifest I had neither the Strength or Agility of a common *Yahoo*; that I walked infirmly on my hinder Feet; had found out a Contrivance to make my Claws of no Use or Defence, and to remove the Hair from my Chin, which was intended as a Shelter from the Sun and the Weather. Lastly, That I could neither run with Speed, nor climb Trees like my *Brethren* (as he called them) the *Yahoos* in this Country.

That, our Institutions of *Government* and *Law* were plainly owing to our gross Defects in *Reason*, and by consequence, in *Virtue*; because *Reason* alone is sufficient to govern a *Rational* Creature; which was therefore a Character we had no Pretence to challenge, even from the Account I had given of my own People; although he manifestly perceived, that in order to favour them, I had concealed many Particulars, and often *said the Thing which was not.*

He was the more confirmed in this Opinion, because he observed, that as I agreed in every Feature of my Body with other *Yahoos*, except where it was to my real Disadvantage in point of Strength, Speed and Activity, the Shortness of my Claws, and some other Particulars where Nature had no Part; so, from the Representation I had given him of our Lives, our Manners, and our Actions, he found as near a Resemblance in the Disposition of our Minds. He said, the *Yahoos* were known to hate one another more than they did any different Species of Animals; and the Reason usually assigned, was, the Odiousness of their own Shapes, which all could see in the rest, but not in themselves. He had therefore begun to think it not unwise in us to *cover* our Bodies, and by that Invention, conceal many of our Deformities from each other, which would else be hardly supportable. But, he now found he had been mistaken; and that the Dissentions of those Brutes in his Country were owing to the same Cause with ours, as I had described them. For, if (said he) you throw among five *Yahoos* as much Food as would be sufficient for fifty, they will, instead of eating peaceably, fall together by the Ears, each single one impatient to *have all to it self*; and therefore a Servant was usually employed to stand by while they were feeding abroad, and those kept at home were tied at a Distance from each other. That, if a Cow died of Age or Accident, before a *Houyhnhnm* could secure it for his own *Yahoos*, those in the Neighbourhood would come in Herds to seize it, and then would ensue such a Battle as I had described, with terrible Wounds made by their Claws on both Sides, although they seldom were able to kill one another, for want of such convenient Instruments of Death as we had invented. At other Times the like Battles have been fought between the *Yahoos* of several Neighbourhoods without any visible Cause: Those of one District watching all Opportunities to surprise the next before they are prepared. But if they find their Project hath miscarried, they return home, and for want of Enemies, engage in what I call a *Civil War* among themselves.

That, in some Fields of his Country, there are certain *shining Stones* of several Colours, whereof the *Yahoos* are violently fond; and when Part of these *Stones* are fixed in the Earth, as it sometimes happeneth, they will dig with their Claws for whole Days to get them out, and carry them away, and hide them by Heaps in their Kennels; but still looking round with great Caution, for fear their Comrades should find out their Treasure. My Master said, he could never discover the Reason of this unnatural Appetite, or how these *Stones* could be of any Use to a *Yahoo*; but now he believed it might proceed from the same Principle of *Avarice*, which I had ascribed to Mankind. That he had once, by way of Experiment, privately removed a Heap of these *Stones* from the Place where one of his *Yahoos* had buried it: Whereupon, the sordid Animal missing his Treasure, by his loud lamenting brought the whole Herd to the Place, there miserably howled, then fell to biting and tearing the rest; began to pine away, would neither eat nor sleep, nor work, till he ordered a Servant privately to convey the *Stones* into the same Hole, and hide them as before; which when his *Yahoo* had found, he presently recovered his Spirits and good Humour; but took Care to remove them to a better hiding Place; and hath ever since been a very serviceable Brute.

My Master farther assured me, which I also observed my self; That in the Fields where these *shining Stones* abound, the fiercest and most frequent Battles are fought, occasioned by perpetual Inroads of the neighbouring *Yahoos*.

He said, it was common when two *Yahoos* discovered such a *Stone* in a Field, and were contending which of them should be the Proprietor, a third would take the Advantage, and carry it away from them both; which my Master would needs contend to have some Resemblance with our *Suits at Law*; wherein I thought it for our Credit not to undeceive him; since the Decision he mentioned was much more equitable than many Decrees among us: Because the Plaintiff and Defendant there lost nothing beside the *Stone* they contended for; whereas our *Courts of Equity*, would never have dimissed the Cause while either of them had any thing left.

My master continuing his Discourse, said, There was nothing that rendered the *Yahoos* more odious, than their undistinguished Appetite to devour every thing that came in their Way, whether Herbs, Roots, Berries, corrupted Flesh of Animals, or all mingled together: And it was peculiar in their Temper, that they were fonder of what they could get by Rapine or Stealth at a greater Distance, than much better Food provided for them at home. If their Prey held out, they would eat till they were ready to burst, after which Nature had pointed out to them a certain *Root* that gave them a general Evacuation.

There was also another Kind of *Root* very *juicy*, but something rare and difficult to be found, which the *Yahoos* fought for with much Eagerness, and would suck it with great Delight: It produced the same Effects that Wine hath upon us. It would make them sometimes hug, and sometimes tear one another; they would howl and grin, and chatter, and roul, and tumble, and then fall asleep in the Mud.

I did indeed observe, that the *Yahoos* were the only Animals in this Country subject to any Diseases; which however, were much fewer than Horses have among us, and contracted not by any ill Treatment they meet with, but by the Nastiness and Greediness of that sordid Brute. Neither has their Language any more than a general Appellation for those Maladies; which is borrowed from the Name of the Beast, and called *Hnea Yahoo,* or the *Yahoo's-Evil*; and the Cure prescribed is a Mixture of *their own Dung* and *Urine,* forcibly put down the *Yahoo's* Throat. This I have since often known to have been taken with Success: And do here freely recommend it to my Countrymen, for the publick Good, as an admirable Specifick against all Diseases produced by Repletion.

As to Learning, Government, Arts, Manufactures, and the like; my Master confessed he could find little or no Resemblance between the *Yahoos* of that Country and those in ours. For, he only meant to observe what Parity there was in our Natures. He had heard indeed some curious *Houyhnhnms* observe, that in most Herds there was a Sort of ruling *Yahoo,* (as among us there is generally some leading or principal Stag in a Park) who was always more *deformed* in Body, and *mischievous in Disposition,* than any of the rest. That, this *Leader* had usually a Favourite as *like himself* as he could get, whose Employment was to *lick his Master's Feet and Posteriors, and drive the Female* Yahoos to *his Kennel*; for which he was now and then rewarded with a Piece of Ass's Flesh. This *Favourite* is hated by the whole Herd; and therefore to protect himself, keeps always *near the Person of his Leader.* He usually continues in Office till a worse can be found; but the very Moment he is discarded, his Successor, at the Head of all the *Yahoos* in that District, Young and Old, Male and Female, come in a Body, and discharge their Excrements upon him from Head to Foot. But how far this might be applicable to our *Courts* and *Favourites,* and *Ministers of State,* my Master said I could best determine.

I durst make no Return to this malicious Insinuation, which debased human Understanding below the Sagacity of a common *Hound,* who hath Judgment enough to distinguish and follow the Cry of the *ablest Dog in the Pack,* without being ever mistaken.

My Master told me, there were some Qualities remarkable in the *Yahoos*, which he had not observed me to mention, or at least very slightly, in the Accounts I had given him of human Kind. He said, those Animals, like other Brutes, had their Females in common; but in this they differed, that the She-*Yahoo* would admit the Male, while she was pregnant; and that the Hees would quarrel and fight with the Females as fiercely as with each other. Both which Practices were such Degrees of infamous Brutality, that no other sensitive Creature ever arrived at.

Another Thing he wondered at in the *Yahoos*, was their strange Disposition to Nastiness and Dirt; whereas there appears to be a natural Love of Cleanliness in all other Animals. As to the two former Accusations, I was glad to let them pass without any Reply, because I had not a Word to offer upon them in Defence of my Species, which otherwise I certainly had done from my own Inclinations. But I could have easily vindicated human Kind from the Imputation of Singularity upon the last Article, if there had been any *Swine* in that Country, (as unluckily for me there were not) which although it may be a *sweeter Quadruped* than a *Yahoo*, cannot I humbly conceive in Justice pretend to more Cleanliness; and so his Honour himself must have owned, if he had seen their filthy Way of feeding, and their Custom of wallowing and sleeping in the Mud.

My Master likewise mentioned another Quality, which his Servants had discovered in several *Yahoos*, and to him was wholly unaccountable. He said, a Fancy would sometimes take a *Yahoo*, to retire into a Corner, to lie down and howl, and groan, and spurn away all that came near him, although he were young and fat, and wanted neither Food nor Water; nor did the Servants imagine what could possibly ail him. And the only Remedy they found was to set him to hard Work, after which he would infallibly come to himself. To this I was silent out of Partiality to my own Kind; yet here I could plainly discover the true Seeds of *Spleen*, which only seizeth on the *Lazy*, the *Luxurious*, and the *Rich*; who, if they were forced to undergo the *same Regimen*, I would undertake for the Cure.

Yahoos choosing a leader

His Honour had farther observed, that a Female-*Yahoo* would often stand behind a Bank or a Bush, to gaze on the young Males passing by, and then appear, and hide, using many antick Gestures and Grimaces; at which time it was observed, that she had a most *offensive Smell*; and when any of the Males advanced, would slowly retire, looking often back, and with a counterfeit Shew of Fear, run off into some convenient Place where she knew the Male would follow her.

At other times, if a Female Stranger came among them, three or four of her own Sex would get about her, and stare and chatter, and grin, and smell her all over; and then turn off with Gestures that seemed to express Contempt and Disdain.

Perhaps my Master might refine a little in these Speculations, which he had drawn from what he observed himself, or had been told by others; However, I could not reflect without some Amazement, and much Sorrow, that the Rudiments of *Lewdness, Coquetry, Censure*, and *Scandal*, should have Place by Instinct in Womankind.

I expected every Moment, that my Master would accuse the *Yahoos* of those unnatural Appetites in both Sexes, so common among us. But Nature it seems hath not been so expert a Schoolmistress; and these politer Pleasures are entirely the Productions of Art and Reason, on our Side of the Globe.

CHAPTER EIGHT

THE AUTHOR RELATETH SEVERAL PARTICULARS OF THE YAHOOS. THE GREAT VIRTUES OF THE HOUYHNHNMS. THE EDUCATION AND EXERCISE OF THEIR YOUTH. THEIR GENERAL ASSEMBLY.

As I ought to have understood human Nature much better than I supposed it possible for my Master to do, so it was easy to apply the Character he gave of the *Yahoos* to myself and my Countrymen; and I believed I could yet make farther Discoveries from my own Observation. I therefore often begged his Honour to let me go among the Herds of *Yahoos* in the Neighbourhood; to which he always very graciously consented, being perfectly convinced that the Hatred I bore those Brutes would never suffer me to be corrupted by them; and his Honour ordered one of his Servants, a strong Sorrel Nag, very honest and good-natured, to be my Guard; without whose Protection I durst not undertake such Adventures. For I have already told the Reader how much I was pestered by those odious Animals upon my first Arrival. I afterwards failed very narrowly three or four times of falling into their Clutches, when I happened to stray at any Distance without my Hanger. And I have Reason to believe, they had some Imagination that I was of their own Species, which I often assisted myself, by stripping up my Sleeves, and shewing my naked Arms and Breast in their Sight, when my Protector was with me: At which times they would approach as near as they durst, and imitate my Actions after the Manner of Monkeys, but ever with great Signs of Hatred; as a tame *Jack Daw* with Cap and Stockings, is always persecuted by the wild ones, when he happens to be got among them.

They are prodigiously nimble from their Infancy; however, I once caught a young Male of three Years old, and endeavoured by all Marks of Tenderness to make it quiet; but the little Imp fell a squalling, and scratching, and biting with such Violence, that I was forced to let it go; and it was high time, for a whole Troop of old ones came about us at the Noise; but finding the Cub was safe, (for away it ran) and my Sorrel Nag being by, they durst not venture near us. I observed the young Animal's Flesh to smell very rank, and the Stink was somewhat between a *Weasel* and a *Fox*, but much more disagreeable. I forgot another Circumstance, (and perhaps I might have the Reader's Pardon, if it were wholly omitted) that while I held the odious Vermin in my Hands, it voided its filthy Excrements of a yellow liquid Substance, all over my Cloaths; but by good Fortune there was a small Brook hard by, where I washed myself as clean as I could;

although I durst not come into my Master's Presence, until I were sufficiently aired.

By what I could discover, the *Yahoos* appear to be the most unteachable of all Animals, their Capacities never reaching higher than to draw or carry Burthens. Yet I am of Opinion, this Defect ariseth chiefly from a perverse, restive Disposition. For they are cunning, malicious, treacherous and revengeful. They are strong and hardy, but of a cowardly Spirit, and by Consequence insolent, abject, and cruel. It is observed, that the *Red-haired* of both Sexes are more libidinous and mischievous than the rest, whom yet they much exceed in Strength and Activity.

The *Houyhnhnms* keep the *Yahoos* for present Use in Huts not far from the House; but the rest are sent abroad to certain Fields, where they dig up Roots, eat several Kinds of Herbs, and search about for Carrion, or sometimes catch *Weasels* and *Luhimuhs* (a Sort of *wild Rat*) which they greedily devour. Nature hath taught them to dig deep Holes with their Nails on the Side of a rising Ground, wherein they lie by themselves; only the Kennels of the Females are larger, sufficient to hold two or three Cubs.

They swim from their Infancy like Frogs, and are able to continue long under Water, where they often take Fish, which the Females carry home to their Young. And upon this Occasion, I hope the Reader will pardon my relating an odd Adventure.

Being one Day abroad with my Protector the Sorrel Nag, and the Weather exceeding hot, I entreated him to let me bathe in a River that was near. He consented, and I immediately stripped myself stark naked, and went down softly into the Stream. It happened that a young Female *Yahoo* standing behind a Bank, saw the whole Proceeding; and inflamed by Desire, as the Nag and I conjectured, came running with all Speed, and leaped into the Water within five Yards of the Place where I bathed. I was never in my Life so terribly frighted; the Nag was grazing at some Distance, not suspecting any Harm: She embraced me after a most fulsome Manner; I roared as loud as I could, and the Nag came galloping towards me, whereupon she quitted her Grasp, with the utmost Reluctancy, and leaped upon the opposite Bank, where she stood gazing and howling all the time I was putting on my Cloaths.

This was Matter of Diversion to my Master and his Family, as well as of Mortification to my self. For now I could no longer deny, that I was a real *Yahoo*, in every Limb and Feature, since the Females had a natural Propensity to me as one of their own Species: Neither was the Hair of this Brute of a Red Colour, (which might have been some Excuse for an Appetite a little irregular) but black as a Sloe, and her Countenance did not make an Appearance altogether so hideous as the rest of the Kind; for, I think, she could not be above Eleven Years old.

Having already lived three Years in this Country, the Reader I suppose will expect, that I should, like other Travellers, give him some Account of the Manners and Customs of its Inhabitants, which it was indeed my principal Study to learn.

As these noble *Houyhnhnms* are endowed by Nature with a general Disposition to all Virtues, and have no Conceptions or Ideas of what is evil in a rational Creature; so their grand Maxim is, to cultivate *Reason*, and to be wholly governed by it. Neither is *Reason* among them a Point problematical as with us, where Men can argue with Plausibility on both Sides of a Question; but strikes you with immediate Conviction; as it must needs do where it is not mingled, obscured, or discoloured by Passion and Interest. I remember it was with extreme Difficulty that I could bring my Master to understand the Meaning of the Word *Opinion*, or how a Point could be disputable; because *Reason* taught us to affirm or deny only where we are certain; and beyond our Knowledge we cannot do either. So that Controversies, Wranglings, Disputes, and Positiveness in false or dubious Propositions, are Evils unknown among the *Houyhnhnms*. In the like Manner when I used to explain to him our several Systems of *Natural Philosophy*, he would laugh that a Creature pretending to *Reason*, should value itself upon the Knowledge of other Peoples Conjectures, and in Things, where that Knowledge, if it were certain, could be of no Use. Wherein he agreed entirely with the Sentiments of *Socrates*, as *Plato* delivers them; which I mention as the highest Honour I can do that Prince of Philosophers. I have often since reflected what Destruction such a Doctrine would make in the Libraries of *Europe*; and how many Paths to Fame would be then shut up in the Learned World.

Friendship and *Benevolence* are the two principal Virtues among the *Houyhnhnms*; and these not confined to particular Objects, but universal to the whole Race. For, a Stranger from the remotest Part, is equally treated with the nearest Neighbour, and where-ever he goes, looks upon himself as at home. They preserve *Decency* and *Civility* in the highest Degrees, but are altogether ignorant of *Ceremony*. They have no Fondness for their Colts or Foles; but the Care they take in educating them proceedeth entirely from the Dictates of *Reason*. And, I observed my Master to shew the same Affection to his Neighbour's Issue that he had for his own. They will have it that *Nature* teaches them to love the whole Species, and it is *Reason* only that maketh a Distinction of Persons, where there is a superior Degree of Virtue.

When the Matron *Houyhnhnms* have produced one of each Sex, they no longer accompany with their Consorts, except they lose one of their Issue by some Casualty, which very seldom happens: But in such a Case they meet again; or when the like Accident befalls a Person, whose Wife is past bearing, some other Couple bestows on him one of their own Colts, and then go together a second Time, until the Mother be pregnant. This Caution is necessary to prevent the Country from being overburthened with Numbers. But the Race of inferior *Houyhnhnms* bred up to be Servants is not so strictly limited upon this Article; these are allowed to produce three of each Sex, to be Domesticks in the Noble Families.

In their Marriages they are exactly careful to chuse such Colours as will not make any disagreeable Mixture in the Breed. *Strength* is chiefly valued in the Male, and *Comeliness* in the Female; not upon the Account of *Love*, but to preserve the Race from degenerating: For, where a Female happens to excel in *Strength*, a Consort is chosen with regard to *Comeliness*. Courtship, Love, Presents, Joyntures, Settlements, have no Place in their Thoughts; or Terms whereby to express them in their Language. The young Couple meet and are joined, merely because it is the Determination of their Parents and Friends: It is what they see done every Day; and they look upon it as one of the necessary Actions in a reasonable Being. But the Violation of Marriage, or any other Unchastity, was never heard of: And the married Pair pass their Lives with the same Friendship, and mutual Benevolence that they bear to all others of the same Species, who come in their Way; without Jealousy, Fondness, Quarrelling, or Discontent.

In educating the Youth of both Sexes, their Method is admirable, and highly deserveth our Imitation. These are not suffered to taste a Grain of *Oats*, except upon certain Days, till Eighteen Years old; nor *Milk*, but very rarely; and in Summer they graze two Hours in the Morning, and as many in the Evening, which their Parents likewise observe; but the Servants are not allowed above half that Time; and a great Part of the Grass is brought home, which they eat at the most convenient Hours, when they can be best spared from Work.

Temperance, *Industry*, *Exercise* and *Cleanliness*, are the Lessons equally enjoyned to the young ones of both Sexes: And my Master thought it monstrous in us to give the Females a different Kind of Education from the Males, except in some Articles of Domestick Management; whereby, as he truly observed, one Half of our Natives were good for nothing but bringing Children into the World: And to trust the Care of their Children to such useless Animals, he said was yet a greater Instance of Brutality.

But the *Houyhnhnms* train up their Youth to Strength, Speed, and Hardiness, by exercising them in running Races up and down steep Hills, or over hard stony Grounds; and when they are all in a Sweat, they are ordered to leap over Head and Ears into a Pond or a River. Four times a Year the Youth of certain Districts meet to shew their Proficiency in Running, and Leaping, and other Feats of Strength or Agility; where the Victor is rewarded with a Song made in his or her Praise. On this Festival the Servants drive a Herd of *Yahoos* into the Field, laden with Hay, and Oats, and Milk for a Repast to the *Houyhnhnms*; after which, these Brutes are immediately driven back again, for fear of being noisome to the Assembly.

Every fourth Year, at the *Vernal Equinox*, there is a Representative Council of the whole Nation, which meets in a Plain about twenty Miles from our House, and continueth about five or six Days. Here they inquire into the State and Condition of the several Districts; whether they abound or be deficient in Hay or Oats, or Cows or *Yahoos*? And where-ever there is any Want (which is but seldom) it is immediately supplied by unanimous Consent and Contribution. Here likewise the Regulation of Children is settled: As for instance, if a *Houyhnhnm* hath two Males, he changeth one of them with another who hath two Females: And when a Child hath been lost by any Casualty, where the Mother is past Breeding, it is determined what Family in the District shall breed another to supply the Loss.

CHAPTER NINE

A GRAND DEBATE AT THE GENERAL ASSEMBLY OF THE HOUYHNHNMS; AND HOW IT WAS DETERMINED. THE LEARNING OF THE HOUYHNHNMS. THEIR BUILDINGS. THEIR MANNER OF BURIALS. THE DEFECTIVENESS OF THEIR LANGUAGE.

ONE of these Grand Assemblies was held in my time, about three Months before my Departure, whither my Master went as the Representative of our District. In this Council was resumed their old Debate, and indeed, the only Debate that ever happened in their Country; whereof my Master after his Return gave me a very particular Account.

The Question to be debated, was, Whether the *Yahoos* should be exterminated from the Face of the Earth. One of the *Members* for the Affirmative offered several Arguments of great Strength and Weight; alledging, That, as the *Yahoos* were the most filthy, noisome, and deformed Animal which Nature ever produced, so they were the most restive and indocible, mischievous and malicious: They would privately suck the Teats of the *Houyhnhnms* Cows; kill and devour their Cats, trample down their Oats and Grass, if they were not continually watched; and commit a Thousand other Extravagancies. He took Notice of a general Tradition, that *Yahoos* had not been always in their Country: But, that many Ages ago, two of these Brutes appeared together upon a Mountain; whether produced by the Heat of the Sun upon corrupted Mud and Slime, or from the Ooze and Froth of the Sea, was never known. That these *Yahoos* engendered, and their Brood in a short time grew so numerous as to overrun and infest the whole Nation. That the *Houyhnhnms* to get rid of this Evil, made a general Hunting, and at last inclosed the whole Herd; and destroying the Older, every *Houyhnhnm* kept two young Ones in a Kennel, and brought them to such a Degree of Tameness, as an Animal so savage by Nature can be capable of acquiring; using them for Draught and Carriage. That, there seemed to be much Truth in this Tradition, and that those Creatures could not be *Ylnhniamshy* (or *Aborigines* of the Land) because of the violent Hatred the *Houyhnhnms* as well as all other Animals, bore them; which although their evil Disposition sufficiently deserved, could never have arrived at so high a Degree, if they had been *Aborigines*, or else they would have long since been rooted out. That, the Inhabitants taking a Fancy to use the Service of the *Yahoos*, had very imprudently neglected to cultivate the Breed of *Asses*, which were a comely Animal, easily kept, more tame and orderly, without any offensive Smell, strong enough for Labour, although they yield to the other in Agility of Body; and if their Braying be no agreeable Sound, it is far preferable to the horrible Howlings of the *Yahoos*.

Several others declared their Sentiments to the same Purpose; when my Master proposed an Expedient to the

Assembly, whereof he had indeed borrowed the Hint
from me. He approved of the Tradition, mentioned by the
Honourable Member, who spoke before; and affirmed, that
the two *Yahoos* said to be first seen among them, had been
driven thither over the Sea; that coming to Land, and
being forsaken by their Companions, they retired to the
Mountains, and degenerating by Degrees, became in Pro-
cess of Time, much more savage than those of their own
Species in the Country from whence these two Originals
came. The Reason of his Assertion was, that he had now in
his Possession, a certain wonderful *Yahoo*, (meaning myself) which most of them had heard of, and many of them
had seen. He then related to them, how he first found me;
that, my Body was all covered with an artificial Com-
posure of the Skins and Hairs of other Animals: That, I
spoke in a Language of my own; and had thoroughly
learned theirs: That, I had related to him the Accidents
which brought me thither: That, when he saw me without
my Covering, I was an exact *Yahoo* in every Part, only
of a whiter Colour, less hairy, and with shorter Claws. He
added, how I had endeavoured to persuade him, that
in my own and other Countries the *Yahoos* acted as the
governing, rational Animal, and held the *Houyhnhnms* in
Servitude: That, he observed in me all the Qualities of
a *Yahoo*, only a little more civilized by some Tincture of
Reason; which however was in a Degree as far inferior to
the *Houyhnhnm* Race, as the *Yahoos* of their Country were to
me: That, among other things, I mentioned a Custom we
had of *castrating Houyhnhnms* when they were young, in
order to render them tame; that the Operation was easy
and safe; that it was no Shame to learn Wisdom from
Brutes, as Industry is taught by the Ant, and Building by
the Swallow. (For so I translate the Word *Lyhannh*, although it be a much larger Fowl) That, this Invention
might be practiced upon the younger *Yahoos* here, which,
besides rendering them tractable and fitter for Use, would
in an Age put an End to the whole Species without destroying Life. That, in the mean time the *Houyhnhnms*
should be *exhorted* to cultivate the Breed of Asses, which,

as they are in all respects more valuable Brutes; so they have this Advantage, to be fit for Service at five Years old, which the others are not till Twelve.

This was all my Master thought fit to tell me at that Time, of what passed in the Grand Council. But he was pleased to conceal one Particular, which related personally to myself, whereof I soon felt the unhappy Effect, as the Reader will know in its proper Place, and from whence I date all the succeeding Misfortunes of my Life.

The *Houyhnhnms* have no Letters, and consequently, their Knowledge is all traditional. But there happening few Events of any Moment among a People so well united, naturally disposed to every Virtue, wholly governed by Reason, and cut off from all Commerce with other Nations; the historical Part is easily preserved without burthening their Memories. I have already observed, that they are subject to no Diseases, and therefore can have no Need of Physicians. However, they have excellent Medicines composed of Herbs, to cure accidental Bruises and Cuts in the Pastern or Frog of the Foot by sharp Stones, as well as other Maims and Hurts in the several Parts of the Body.

They calculate the Year by the Revolution of the Sun and the Moon, but use no Subdivisions into Weeks. They are well enough acquainted with the Motions of those two Luminaries, and understand the Nature of *Eclipses*; and this is the utmost Progress of their *Astronomy*.

In *Poetry* they must be allowed to excel all other Mortals; wherein the Justness of their Similes, and the Minuteness, as well as Exactness of their Descriptions, are indeed inimitable. Their Verses abound very much in both of these; and usually contain either some exalted Notions of Friendship and Benevolence, or the Praises of those who were Victors in Races, and other bodily Exercises. Their Buildings, although very rude and simple, are not inconvenient, but well contrived to defend them from all Injuries of Cold and Heat. They have a Kind of Tree, which at Forty Years old loosens in the Root, and falls with the first Storm; it grows very strait, and being pointed like Stakes with a sharp Stone, (for the *Houyhnhnms* know not the Use of Iron) they stick them erect in the Ground about ten Inches asunder, and then weave in Oat-straw, or sometimes Wattles betwixt them. The Roof is made after the same Manner, and so are the Doors.

The *Houyhnhnms* use the hollow Part between the Pastern and the Hoof of their Fore-feet, as we do our Hands, and this with greater Dexterity, than I could at first imagine. I have seen a white Mare of our Family thread a Needle (which I lent her on Purpose) with that Joynt. They milk their Cows, reap their Oats, and do all the Work which requires Hands, in the same Manner. They have a Kind of hard Flints, which by grinding against other Stones, they form into Instruments, that serve instead of Wedges, Axes, and Hammers. With Tools made of these Flints, they likewise cut their Hay, and reap their Oats, which there groweth naturally in several Fields: The *Yahoos* draw home the Sheaves in Carriages, and the Servants tread them in certain covered Hutts, to get out the Grain, which is kept in Stores. They make a rude Kind of earthen and wooden Vessels, and bake the former in the Sun.

If they can avoid Casualties, they die only of old Age, and are buried in the obscurest Places that can be found, their Friends and Relations expressing neither Joy nor Grief at their Departure; nor does the dying Person discover the least Regret that he is leaving the World, any more than if he were upon returning home from a Visit to one of his Neighbours: I remember, my Master having once made an Appointment with a Friend and his Family to come to his House upon some Affair of Importance; on the Day fixed, the Mistress and her two Children came very late; she made two Excuses, first for her Husband, who, as she said, happened that very Morning to *Lhnuwnh*. The Word is strongly expressive in their Language, but not easily rendered into *English*; it signifies, *to retire to his first Mother*. Her Excuse for not coming sooner, was, that her Husband dying late in the Morning, she was a good while consulting her Servants about a convenient Place where his Body should be laid; and I observed she behaved herself at our House, as chearfully as the rest: She died about three Months after.

They live generally to Seventy or Seventy-five Years, very seldom to Fourscore: Some Weeks before their Death they feel a gradual Decay, but without Pain. During this time they are much visited by their Friends, because they cannot go abroad with their usual Ease and Satisfaction. However, about ten Days before their Death, which they seldom fail in computing, they return the Visits that have been made by those who are nearest in the Neighbour-hood, being carried in a convenient Sledge drawn by *Yahoos*; which Vehicle they use, not only upon this Occasion, but when they grow old, upon long Journeys, or when they are lamed by any Accident. And therefore when the dying *Houyhnhnms* return those Visits, they take a solemn Leave of their Friends, as if they were going to some remote Part of the Country, where they designed to pass the rest of their Lives.

I know not whether it may be worth observing, that the *Houyhnhnms* have no Word in their Language to express any thing that is *evil*, except what they borrow from the Deformities or ill Qualities of the *Yahoos*. Thus they de-note the Folly of a Servant, an Omission of a Child, a Stone that cuts their Feet, a Continuance of foul or unseasonable Weather, and the like, by adding to each the Epithet of *Yahoo*. For Instance, *Hhnm Yahoo*, *Whnaholm Yahoo*, *Ynlhmndwihlma Yahoo*, and an ill contrived House, *Yn-holmhnmrohlnw Yahoo*.

I could with great Pleasure enlarge farther upon the Manners and Virtues of this excellent People; but intend-ing in a short time to publish a Volume by itself expressly upon that Subject, I refer the Reader thither. And in the mean time, proceed to relate my own sad Catastrophe.

CHAPTER TEN

THE AUTHOR'S OECONOMY AND HAPPY LIFE AMONG THE
HOUYHNHNMS. HIS GREAT IMPROVEMENT IN VIRTUE, BY
CONVERSING WITH THEM. THEIR CONVERSATIONS. THE
AUTHOR HATH NOTICE GIVEN HIM BY HIS MASTER THAT HE
MUST DEPART FROM THE COUNTRY. HE FALLS INTO A SWOON
FOR GRIEF, BUT SUBMITS. HE CONTRIVES AND FINISHES A
CANOO, BY THE HELP OF A FELLOW-SERVANT, AND PUTS TO
SEA AT A VENTURE.

I HAD settled my little Oeconomy to my own Heart's
Content. My Master had ordered a Room to be made
for me after their Manner, about six Yards from the
House; the Sides and Floors of which I plaistered with
Clay, and covered with Rush-mats of my own contriving;
I had beaten Hemp, which there grows wild, and made of
it a Sort of Ticking: This I filled with the Feathers of
several Birds I had taken with Springes made of *Yahoos*
Hairs; and were excellent Food. I had worked two Chairs
with my Knife, the Sorrel Nag helping me in the grosser
and more laborious Part. When my Cloaths were worn
to Rags, I made my self others with the Skins of Rabbets,
and of a certain beautiful Animal about the same Size,
called *Nnuhnoh*, the Skin of which is covered with a fine
Down. Of these I likewise made very tolerable Stockings.
I soaled my Shoes with Wood which I cut from a Tree,
and fitted to the upper Leather, and when this was worn
out, I supplied it with the Skins of *Yahoos*, dried in the
Sun. I often got Honey out of hollow Trees, which I mingled with Water, or eat it with my Bread. No Man could
more verify the Truth of these two Maxims, *That, Nature is
very easily satisfied*; and, *That, Necessity is the Mother of Invention*. I enjoyed perfect Health of Body, and Tranquility
of Mind; I did not feel the Treachery or Inconstancy
of a Friend, nor the Injuries of a secret or open Enemy.
I had no Occasion of bribing, flattering or pimping, to
procure the Favour of any great Man, or of his Minion.

I wanted no Fence against Fraud or Oppression: Here was neither Physician to destroy my Body, nor Lawyer to ruin my Fortune: No Informer to watch my Words and Actions, or forge Accusations against me for Hire: Here were no Gibers, Censurers, Backbiters, Pick-pockets, Highwaymen, House-breakers, Attorneys, Bawds, Buffoons, Gamesters, Politicians, Wits, Spleneticks, tedious Talkers, Controvertists, Ravishers, Murderers, Robbers, Virtuoso's; no Leaders or Followers of Party and Faction; no Encouragers to Vice, by Seducement or Examples: No Dungeon, Axes, Gibbets, Whipping posts, or Pillories; No cheating Shop-keepers or Mechanicks: No Pride, Vanity or Affectation: No Fops, Bullies, Drunkards, strolling Whores, or Poxes: No ranting, lewd, expensive Wives: No stupid, proud Pedants: No importunate, over-bearing, quarrelsome, noisy, roaring, empty, conceited, swearing Companions: No Scoundrels raised from the Dust upon the Merit of their Vices; or Nobility thrown into it on account of their Virtues: No Lords, Fidlers, Judges or Dancing-Masters.

I had the Favour of being admitted to several *Houyhnhnms*, who came to visit or dine with my Master; where his Honour graciously suffered me to wait in the Room, and listen to their Discourse. Both he and his Company would often descend to ask me Questions, and receive my Answers. I had also sometimes the Honour of attending my Master in his Visits to others. I never presumed to speak, except in answer to a Question; and then I did it with inward Regret, because it was a Loss of so much Time for improving my self: But I was infinitely delighted with the Station of an humble Auditor in such Conversations, where nothing passed but what was useful, expressed in the fewest and most significant Words: Where (as I have already said) the greatest *Decency* was observed, without the least Degree of Ceremony; where no Person spoke without being pleased himself, and pleasing his Companions: Where there was no Interruption, Tediousness, Heat, or Difference of Sentiments. They have a Notion, That when People are met together, a short

Silence doth much improve Conversation: This I found
to be true; for during those little Intermissions of Talk,
new Ideas would arise in their Minds, which very much
enlivened the Discourse. Their Subjects are generally
on Friendship and Benevolence; on Order and Oeconomy;
sometimes upon the visible Operations of Nature, or ancient Traditions; upon the Bounds and Limits of Virtue;
upon the unerring Rules of Reason; or upon some Determinations, to be taken at the next great Assembly; and
often upon the various Excellencies of *Poetry*. I may add,
without Vanity, that my Presence often gave them sufficient Matter for Discourse, because it afforded my Master
an Occasion of letting his Friends into the History of me
and my Country, upon which they were all pleased to dis-
cant in a Manner not very advantageous to human Kind;
and for that Reason I shall not repeat what they said: Only
I may be allowed to observe, That his Honour, to my great
Admiration, appeared to understand the Nature of *Yahoos*
much better than my self. He went through all our Vices
and Follies, and discovered many which I had never mentioned to him; by only supposing what Qualities a *Yahoo*
of their Country, with a small Proportion of Reason,
might be capable of exerting: And concluded, with too
much Probability, how vile as well as miserable such a
Creature must be.

I freely confess, that all the little Knowledge I have of
any Value, was acquired by the Lectures I received from
my Master, and from hearing the Discourses of him and
his Friends; to which I should be prouder to listen, than
to dictate to the greatest and wisest Assembly in *Europe*. I
admired the Strength, Comeliness and Speed of the Inhabitants; and such a Constellation of Virtues in such
amiable Persons produced in me the highest Veneration.
At first, indeed, I did not feel that natural Awe which the
Yahoos and all other Animals bear towards them; but it
grew upon me by Degress, much sooner than I imagined,
and was mingled with a respectful Love and Gratitude,
that they would condescend to distinguish me from the
rest of my Species.

When I thought of my Family, my Friends, my Country-men, or human Race in general, I considered them as they really were, *Yahoos* in Shape and Disposition, perhaps a little more civilized, and qualified with the Gift of Speech; but making no other Use of Reason, than to improve and multiply those Vices, whereof their Brethren in this Country had only the Share that Nature allotted them. When I happened to behold the Reflection of my own Form in a Lake or Fountain, I turned away my Face in Horror and detestation of my self; and could better endure the Sight of a common *Yahoo*, than of my own Person. By conversing with the *Houyhnhnms*, and looking upon them with Delight, I fell to imitate their Gait and Gesture, which is now grown into a Habit; and my Friends often tell me in a blunt Way, that *I trot like a Horse*; which, however, I take for a great Compliment: Neither shall I disown, that in speaking I am apt to fall into the Voice and manner of the *Houyhnhnms*, and hear my self ridiculed on that Account without the least Mortification.

In the Midst of this Happiness, when I looked upon my self to be fully settled for Life, my Master sent for me one Morning a little earlier than his usual Hour. I observed by his Countenance that he was in some Perplexity, and at a Loss how to begin what he had to speak. After a short Silence, he told me, he did not know how I would take what he was going to say: That, in the last general Assembly, when the Affair of the *Yahoos* was entered upon, the Representatives had taken Offence at his keeping a *Yahoo* (meaning my self) in his Family more like a *Houyhnhnm* than a Brute Animal. That, he was known frequently to converse with me, as if he could receive some Advantage or Pleasure in my Company: That, such a Practice was not agreeable to Reason or Nature, or a thing ever heard of before among them. The Assembly did therefore *exhort* him, either to employ me like the rest of my Species, or command me to swim back to the Place from whence I came. That, the first of these Expedients was utterly rejected by all the *Houyhnhnms*, who had ever seen me at his House or their own: For, they alledged, That because I had some Rudiments of Reason, added to the natural Pravity of those Animals, it was to be feared, I might be able to seduce them into the woody and mountainous Parts of the Country, and bring them in Troops by Night to destroy the *Houyhnhnms* Cattle, as being naturally of the ravenous Kind, and averse from Labour.

My Master added, That he was daily pressed by the *Houyhnhnms* of the Neighbourhood to have the Assembly's *Exhortation* executed, which he could not put off much longer. He doubted, it would be impossible for me to swim to another Country; and therefore wished I would contrive some Sort of Vehicle resembling those I had described to him, that might carry me on the Sea; in which Work I should have the Assistance of his own Servants, as well as those of his Neighbours. He concluded, that for his own Part he could have been content to keep me in his Service as long as I lived; because he found I had cured myself of some bad Habits and Dispositions, by endeavouring, as far as my inferior Nature was capable, to imitate the *Houyhnhnms*.

I should here observe to the Reader, that a Decree of the general Assembly in this Country, is expressed by the Word *Hnhloayn*, which signifies an *Exhortation*; as near as I can render it: For they have no Conception how a rational Creature can be *compelled*, but only advised, or *exhorted*; because no Person can disobey Reason, without giving up his Claim to be a rational Creature.

I was struck with the utmost Grief and Despair at my Master's Discourse; and being unable to support the Agonies I was under, I fell into a Swoon at his Feet: When I came to myself, he told me, that he concluded I had been dead. (For these People are subject to no such Imbecillities of Nature) I answered, in a faint Voice, that Death would have been too great an Happiness; that although I could not blame the Assembly's *Exhortation*, or the Urgency of his Friends; yet in my weak and corrupt Judgment, I thought it might consist with Reason to have been less rigorous. That, I could not swim a League, and probably the nearest Land to theirs might be distant above an Hundred: That, many Materials, necessary for making a small Vessel to carry me off, were wholly wanting in this Country, which however, I would attempt in Obedience and Gratitude to his Honour, although I concluded the thing to be impossible, and therefore looked on myself as already devoted to Destruction. That, the certain Prospect of an unnatural Death, was the least of my Evils: For, supposing I should escape with Life by some strange Adventure, how could I think with Temper, of passing my Days among *Yahoos*, and relapsing into my old Corruptions, for want of Examples to lead and keep me within the Paths of Virtue. That, I knew too well upon what solid Reasons all the Determinations of the wise *Houyhnhnms* were founded, not to be shaken by Arguments of mine, a miserable *Yahoo*; and therefore after presenting him with my humble Thanks for the Offer of his Servants Assistance in making a Vessel, and desiring a reasonable Time for so difficult a Work, I told him, I would endeavour to preserve a wretched Being; and, if ever I returned to *England*, was not without Hopes of being useful to my own Species, by celebrating the Praises of the renowned *Houyhnhnms*, and proposing their Virtues to the Imitation of Mankind.

My Master in a few Words made me a very gracious Reply, allowed me the Space of two *Months* to finish my Boat; and ordered the Sorrel Nag, my Fellow-Servant, (for so at this Distance I may presume to call him) to follow my Instructions, because I told my Master, that his Help would be sufficient, and I knew he had a Tenderness for me.

In his Company my first Business was to go to that Part of the Coast, where my rebellious Crew had ordered me to be set on Shore. I got upon a Height, and looking on every Side into the Sea, fancied I saw a small Island, towards the *North-East*: I took out my Pocket-glass, and could then clearly distinguish it about five Leagues off, as I computed; but it appeared to the Sorrel Nag to be only a blue Cloud: For, as he had no Conception of any Country beside his own, so he could not be as expert in distinguish-

ing remote Objects at Sea, as we who so much converse
in that Element.

After I had discovered this Island, I considered no farther; but resolved, it should, if possible, be the first Place
of my Banishment, leaving the Consequence to Fortune.

I returned home, and consulting with the Sorrel Nag,
we went into a Copse at some Distance, where I with my
Knife, and he with a sharp Flint fastened very artificially,
after their Manner, to a wooden Handle, cut down several
Oak Wattles about the Thickness of a Walking-staff, and
some larger Pieces. But I shall not trouble the Reader with
a particular Description of my own Mechanicks: Let it
suffice to say, that in six Weeks time, with the Help of the
Sorrel Nag, who performed the Parts that required most
Labour, I finished a Sort of *Indian* Canoo; but much
larger, covering it with the Skins of *Yahoos*, well stitched
together, with hempen Threads of my own making. My
Sail was likewise composed of the Skins of the same Animal; but I made use of the youngest I could get; the
older being too tough and thick; and I likewise provided
myself with four Paddles. I laid in a Stock of boiled Flesh,
of Rabbets and Fowls; and took with me two Vessels,
one filled with Milk, and the other with Water.

I tried my Canoo in a large Pond near my Master's
House, and then corrected in it what was amiss; stopping
all the Chinks with *Yahoos* Tallow, till I found it stanch,
and able to bear me, and my Freight. And when it was as
compleat as I could possibly make it, I had it drawn on a
Carriage very gently by *Yahoos*, to the Sea-side, under the
Conduct of the Sorrel Nag, and another Servant.

When all was ready, and the Day came for my Departure, I took Leave of my Master and Lady, and the whole
Family, my Eyes flowing with Tears, and my Heart quite
sunk with Grief. But his Honour, out of Curiosity, and
perhaps (if I may speak it without Vanity) partly out of
Kindness, was determined to see me in my Canoo; and
got several of his neighbouring Friends to accompany him.
I was forced to wait above an Hour for the Tide, and then
observing the Wind very fortunately bearing towards the

Island, to which I intended to steer my Course, I took a second Leave of my Master: But as I was going to prostrate myself to kiss his Hoof, he did me the Honour to raise it gently to my Mouth. I am not ignorant how much I have been censured for mentioning this last Particular. Detractors are pleased to think it improbable, that so illustrious a Person should descend to give so great a Mark of Distinction to a Creature so inferior as I. Neither have I forgot, how apt some Travellers are to boast of extraordinary Favours they have received. But, if these Censurers were better acquainted with the noble and courteous Disposition of the *Houyhnhnms*, they would soon change their Opinion. I paid my Respects to the rest of the *Houyhnhnms* in his Honour's Company; then getting into my Canoo, I pushed off from Shore.

CHAPTER ELEVEN

THE AUTHOR'S DANGEROUS VOYAGE. HE ARRIVES AT NEW-HOLLAND, HOPING TO SETTLE THERE. IS WOUNDED WITH AN ARROW BY ONE OF THE NATIVES. IS SEIZED AND CARRIED BY FORCE INTO A PORTUGUEZE SHIP. THE GREAT CIVILITIES OF THE CAPTAIN. THE AUTHOR ARRIVES AT ENGLAND.

I BEGAN this desperate Voyage on *February* 15, 1714/5, at 9 o'Clock in the Morning. The Wind was very favourable; however, I made use at first only of my Paddles; but considering I should soon be weary, and that the Wind might probably chop about, I ventured to set up my little Sail; and thus, with the Help of the Tide, I went at the Rate of a League and a Half an Hour, as near as I could guess. My Master and his Friends continued on the Shoar, till I was almost out of Sight; and I often heard the Sorrel Nag (who always loved me) crying out, *Hnuy illa nyha maiah Yahoo*, Take Care of thy self, gentle *Yahoo*.

My Design was, if possible, to discover some small Island uninhabited, yet sufficient by my Labour to furnish me with Necessaries of Life, which I would have thought a greater Happiness than to be first Minister in the politest

Court of *Europe*; so horrible was the Idea I conceived of returning to live in the Society and under the Government of *Yahoos*. For in such a Solitude as I desired, I could at least enjoy my own Thoughts, and reflect with Delight on the Virtues of those inimitable *Houyhnhnms*, without any Opportunity of degenerating into the Vices and Corruptions of my own Species.

The Reader may remember what I related when my Crew conspired against me, and confined me to my Cabbin. How I continued there several Weeks, without knowing what Course we took; and when I was put ashore in the Longboat, how the Sailors told me with Oaths, whether true or false, that they knew not in what Part of the World we were. However, I did then believe us to be about ten Degrees *Southward* of the *Cape of Good Hope*, or about 45 Degrees *Southern* Latitude, as I gathered from some general Words I overheard among them, being I supposed to the *South-East* in their intended Voyage to *Madagascar*. And although this were but little better than Conjecture, yet I resolved to steer my Course *Eastward*, hoping to reach the *South-West* Coast of *New-Holland*, and perhaps some such Island as I desired, lying *Westward* of it. The Wind was full West, and by six in the Evening I computed I had gone *Eastward* at least eighteen Leagues; when I spied a very small Island about half a League off, which I soon reached. It was nothing but a Rock with one Creek, naturally arched by the Force of Tempests. Here I put in my Canoo, and climbing a Part of the Rock, I could plainly discover Land to the *East*, extending from *South* to *North*. I lay all Night in my Canoo; and repeating my Voyage early in the Morning, I arrived in seven Hours to the *South-East* Point of *New-Holland*. This confirmed me in the Opinion I have long entertained, that the *Maps* and *Charts* place this Country at least three Degrees more to the *East* than it really is; which Thought I communicated many Years ago to my worthy Friend Mr. *Herman Moll*, and gave him my Reasons for it, although he hath rather chosen to follow other Authors.

I saw no Inhabitants in the Place where I landed; and

being unarmed, I was afraid of venturing far into the Country. I found some Shell-Fish on the Shore, and eat them raw, not daring to kindle a Fire, for fear of being discovered by the Natives. I continued three Days feeding on Oysters and Limpits, to save my own Provisions; and I fortunately found a Brook of excellent Water, which gave me great Relief.

On the fourth Day, venturing out early a little too far, I saw twenty or thirty Natives upon a Height, not above five hundred Yards from me. They were stark naked, Men, Women and Children round a Fire, as I could discover by the Smoke. One of them spied me, and gave Notice to the rest; five of them advanced towards me, leaving the Women and Children at the Fire. I made what haste I could to the Shore, and getting into my Canoo, shoved off: The Savages observing me retreat, ran after me; and before I could get far enough into the Sea, discharged an Arrow, which wounded me deeply on the Inside of my left Knee (I shall carry the Mark to my Grave.) I apprehended the Arrow might be poisoned; and paddling out of the Reach of their Darts (being a calm Day) I made a shift to suck the Wound, and dress it as well as I could.

I was at a Loss what to do, for I durst not return to the same Landing-place, but stood to the *North*, and was forced to paddle; for the Wind, although very gentle, was against me, blowing *North-West*. As I was looking about for a secure Landing-place, I saw a Sail to the *North North-East*, which appearing every Minute more visible, I was in some Doubt, whether I should wait for them or no; but at last my Detestation of the *Yahoo* Race prevailed; and turning my Canoo, I sailed and paddled together to the *South*, and got into the same Creek from whence I set out in the Morning; choosing rather to trust my self among these *Barbarians* than live with *European Yahoos*. I drew up my Canoo as close as I could to the Shore, and hid my self behind a Stone by the little Brook, which, as I have already said, was excellent Water.

The Ship came within half a League of this Creek, and

sent out her Long-Boat with Vessels to take in fresh Water (for the Place it seems was very well known) but I did not observe it until the Boat was almost on Shore; and it was too late to seek another Hiding-Place. The Seamen at their landing observed my Canoo, and rummaging it all over, easily conjectured that the Owner could not be far off. Four of them well armed searched every Cranny and Lurking-hole, till at last they found me flat on my Face behind the Stone. They gazed a while in Admiration at my strange uncouth Dress; my Coat made of Skins, my wooden-soaled Shoes, and my furred Stockings; from whence, however, they concluded I was not a Native of the Place, who all go naked. One of the Seamen in *Portugueze* bid me rise, and asked who I was. I understood that Language very well, and getting upon my Feet, said, I was a poor *Yahoo*, banished from the *Houyhnhnms*, and desired they would please to let me depart. They admired to hear me answer them in their own Tongue, and saw by my Complection I must be an *European*; but were at a Loss to know what I meant by *Yahoos* and *Houyhnhnms*, and at the same Time fell a laughing at my strange Tone in speaking, which resembled the Neighing of a Horse. I trembled all the while betwixt Fear and Hatred: I again desired Leave to depart, and was gently moving to my Canoo; but they laid hold on me, desiring to know what Country I was of? whence I came? with many other Questions. I told them, I was born in *England*, from whence I came about five Years ago, and then their Country and ours was at Peace. I therefore hoped they would not treat me as an Enemy, since I meant them no Harm, but was a poor *Yahoo*, seeking some desolate Place where to pass the Remainder of his unfortunate Life.

When they began to talk, I thought I never heard or saw any thing so unnatural; for it appeared to me as monstrous as if a Dog or a Cow should speak in *England*, or a *Yahoo* in *Houyhnhnm-Land*. The honest *Portugueze* were equally amazed at my strange Dress, and the odd Manner of delivering my Words, which however they understood very well. They spoke to me with great Humanity, and said they were sure their Captain would carry me *gratis* to *Lisbon*, from whence I might return to my own Country; that two of the Seamen would go back to the Ship, to inform the Captain of what they had seen, and receive his Orders; in the mean Time, unless I would give my solemn Oath not to fly, they would secure me by Force. I thought it best to comply with their Proposal. They were very curious to know my Story, but I gave them very little Satisfaction; and they all conjectured, that my Misfortunes had impaired my Reason. In two Hours the Boat, which went loaden with Vessels of Water, returned with the Captain's Commands to fetch me on Board. I fell on my Knees to preserve my Liberty; but all was in vain, and the Men having tied me with Cords, heaved me into the Boat, from whence I was taken into the Ship, and from thence into the Captain's Cabbin.

His Name was *Pedro de Mendez*; he was a very courteous and generous Person; he entreated me to give some Account of my self, and desired to know what I would eat or drink; said, I should be used as well as himself, and spoke so many obliging Things, that I wondered to find such Civilities from a *Yahoo*. However, I remained silent and sullen; I was ready to faint at the very Smell of him and his Men. At last I desired something to eat out of my own Canoo; but he ordered me a Chicken and some excellent Wine, and then directed that I should be put to Bed in a very clean Cabbin. I would not undress my self, but lay on the Bed-cloaths; and in half an Hour stole out, when I thought the Crew was at Dinner; and getting to the Side of the Ship, was going to leap into the Sea, and swim for my Life, rather than continue among *Yahoos*. But one of the Seamen prevented me, and having informed the Captain, I was chained to my Cabbin.

After Dinner *Don Pedro* came to me, and desired to know my Reason for so desperate an Attempt; assured me he only meant to do me all the Service he was able; and spoke so very movingly, that at last I descended to treat him like an Animal which had some little Portion of Reason. I gave him a very short Relation of my Voy-

age; of the Conspiracy against me by my own Men; of
the Country where they set me on Shore, and of my five
Years Residence there. All which he looked upon as if
it were a Dream or a Vision; whereat I took great Offence:
For I had quite forgot the Faculty of Lying, so peculiar
to *Yahoos* in all Countries where they preside, and consequently the Disposition of suspecting Truth in others of
their own Species. I asked him, Whether it were the Custom of his Country to *say the Thing that was not*? I assured
him I had almost forgot what he meant by Falshood; and
if I had lived a thousand Years in *Houyhnhnmland*, I should
never have heard a Lie from the meanest Servant. That
I was altogether indifferent whether he believed me or
no; but however, in return for his Favours, I would give
so much Allowance to the Corruption of his Nature, as
to answer any Objection he would please to make; and
he might easily discover the Truth.

The Captain, a wise Man, after many Endeavours to
catch me tripping in some Part of my Story, at last began
to have a better Opinion of my Veracity. But he added,
that since I professed so inviolable an Attachment to
Truth, I must give him my Word of Honour to bear him
Company in this Voyage without attempting any thing
against my Life; or else he would continue me a Prisoner
till we arrived at *Lisbon*. I gave him the Promise he required; but at the same time protested that I would
suffer the greatest Hardships rather than return to live
among *Yahoos*.

Our Voyage passed without any considerable Accident.
In Gratitude to the Captain I sometimes sate with him at
his earnest Request, and strove to conceal my Antipathy
against human Kind, although it often broke out; which
he suffered to pass without Observation. But the greatest
Part of the Day, I confined myself to my Cabbin, to avoid
seeing any of the Crew. The Captain had often intreated
me to strip myself of my savage Dress, and offered to lend
me the best Suit of Cloaths he had. This I would not be
prevailed on to accept, abhorring to cover myself with any
thing that had been on the Back of a *Yahoo*. I only desired

he would lend me two clean Shirts, which having been washed since he wore them, I believed would not so much defile me. These I changed every second Day, and washed them myself.

We arrived at *Lisbon*, *Nov.* 5, 1715. At our landing, the Captain forced me to cover myself with his Cloak, to prevent the Rabble from crouding about me. I was conveyed to his own House; and at my earnest Request, he led me up to the highest Room backwards. I conjured him to conceal from all Persons what I had told him of the *Houyhnhnms*; because the least Hint of such a Story would not only draw Numbers of People to see me, but probably put me in Danger of being imprisoned, or burnt by the *Inquisition*. The Captain persuaded me to accept a Suit of Cloaths newly made; but I would not suffer the Taylor to take my Measure; however, Don *Pedro* being almost of my Size, they fitted me well enough. He accoutred me with other Necessaries all new, which I aired for Twenty-four Hours before I would use them.

The Captain had no Wife, nor above three Servants, none of which were suffered to attend at Meals; and his whole Deportment was so obliging, added to very good *human* Understanding, that I really began to tolerate his Company. He gained so far upon me, that I ventured to look out of the back Window. By Degrees I was brought into another Room, from whence I peeped into the Street, but drew my Head back in a Fright. In a Week's Time he seduced me down to the Door. I found my Terror gradually lessened, but my Hatred and Contempt seemed to increase. I was at last bold enough to walk the Street in his Company, but kept my Nose well stopped with Rue, or sometimes with Tobacco.

In ten Days, Don *Pedro*, to whom I had given some Account of my domestick Affairs, put it upon me as a Point of Honour and Conscience, that I ought to return to my native Country, and live at home with my Wife and Children. He told me, there was an *English* Ship in the Port just ready to sail, and he would furnish me with all things necessary. It would be tedious to repeat his Arguments, and my Contradictions. He said, it was altogether impossible to find such a solitary Island as I had desired to live in; but I might command in my own House, and pass my time in a Manner as recluse as I pleased.

I complied at last, finding I could not do better. I left *Lisbon* the 24th Day of *November*, in an *English* Merchantman, but who was the Master I never inquired. Don *Pedro* accompanied me to the Ship, and lent me Twenty Pounds. He took kind Leave of me, and embraced me at parting; which I bore as well as I could. During this last Voyage I had no Commerce with the Master, or any of his Men; but pretending I was sick kept close in my Cabbin. On the Fifth of *December*, 1715, we cast Anchor in the *Downs* about Nine in the Morning, and at Three in the Afternoon I got safe to my House at *Redriff*.

My Wife and Family received me with great Surprize and Joy, because they concluded me certainly dead; but I must freely confess, the Sight of them filled me only with Hatred, Disgust and Contempt; and the more, by reflecting on the near Alliance I had to them. For, although since my unfortunate Exile from the *Houyhnhnm* Country, I had compelled myself to tolerate the Sight of *Yahoos*, and to converse with Don *Pedro de Mendez*; yet my Memory and Imaginations were perpetually filled with the Virtues and Ideas of those exalted *Houyhnhnms*. And when I began to consider, that by copulating with one of the *Yahoo*-Species, I had become a Parent of more; it struck me with the utmost Shame, Confusion and Horror.

As soon as I entered the House, my Wife took me in her Arms, and kissed me; at which, having not been used to the Touch of that odious Animal for so many Years, I fell in a Swoon for almost an Hour. At the Time I am writing, it is five Years since my last Return to *England*: During the first Year I could not endure my Wife or Children in my Presence, the very Smell of them was intolerable; much less could I suffer them to eat in the same Room. To this Hour they dare not presume to touch my Bread, or drink out of the same Cup; neither was I ever able to let one of them take me by the Hand. The first Money I laid out

was to buy two young Stone-Horses, which I keep in a
good Stable, and next to them the Groom is my greatest
Favourite; for I feel my Spirits revived by the Smell he
contracts in the Stable. My Horses understand me tolerably well; I converse with them at least four Hours every
Day. They are Strangers to Bridle or Saddle; they live
in great Amity with me, and Friendship to each other.

CHAPTER TWELVE

THE AUTHOR'S VERACITY. HIS DESIGN IN PUBLISHING THIS
WORK. HIS CENSURE OF THOSE TRAVELLERS WHO SWERVE
FROM THE TRUTH. THE AUTHOR CLEARS HIMSELF FROM ANY
SINISTER ENDS IN WRITING. AN OBJECTION ANSWERED. THE
METHOD OF PLANTING COLONIES. HIS NATIVE COUNTRY COM-
MENDED. THE RIGHT OF THE CROWN TO THOSE COUNTRIES
DESCRIBED BY THE AUTHOR, IS JUSTIFIED. THE DIFFICULTY
OF CONQUERING THEM. THE AUTHOR TAKES HIS LAST LEAVE
OF THE READER; PROPOSETH HIS MANNER OF LIVING FOR
THE FUTURE; GIVES GOOD ADVICE, AND CONCLUDETH.

THUS, gentle Reader, I have given thee a faithful History of my Travels for Sixteen Years, and above
Seven Months; wherein I have not been so studious
of Ornament as of Truth. I could perhaps like others
have astonished thee with strange improbable Tales; but
I rather chose to relate plain Matter of Fact in the
simplest Manner and Style; because my principal Design
was to inform, and not to amuse thee.

It is easy for us who travel into remote Countries, which
are seldom visited by *Englishmen* or other *Europeans*, to
form Descriptions of wonderful Animals both at Sea and
Land. Whereas, a Traveller's chief Aim should be to make
Men wiser and better, and to improve their Minds by the
bad, as well as good Example of what they deliver concerning foreign Places.

I could heartily wish a Law were enacted, that every
Traveller, before he were permitted to publish his Voyages,

should be obliged to make Oath before the *Lord High Chancellor*, that all he intended to print was absolutely true to the best of his Knowledge; for then the World would no longer be deceived as it usually is, while some Writers, to make their Works pass the better upon the Publick, impose the grossest Falsities on the unwary Reader. I have perused several Books of Travels with great Delight in my younger Days; but, having since gone over most Parts of the Globe, and been able to contradict many fabulous Accounts from my own Observation; it hath given me a great Disgust against this Part of Reading, and some Indignation to see the Credulity of Mankind so impudently abused. Therefore, since my Acquaintance were pleased to think my poor Endeavours might not be unacceptable to my Country; I imposed on myself as a Maxim, never to be swerved from, that I would *strictly adhere to Truth*; neither indeed can I be ever under the least Temptation to vary from it, while I retain in my Mind the Lectures and Example of my noble Master, and the other illustrious *Houyhnhnms*, of whom I had so long the Honour to be an humble Hearer.

> ——*Nec si miserum Fortuna Sinonem*
> *Finxit, vanum etiam, mendacemque improba finget.*

I know very well, how little Reputation is to be got by Writings which require neither Genius nor Learning, nor indeed any other Talent, except a good Memory, or an exact *Journal*. I know likewise, that Writers of Travels, like *Dictionary*-Makers, are sunk into Oblivion by the Weight and Bulk of those who come last, and therefore lie uppermost. And it is highly probable, that such Travellers who shall hereafter visit the Countries described in this Work of mine, may by detecting my Errors, (if there be any) and adding many new Discoveries of their own, jostle me out of Vogue, and stand in my Place; making the World forget that ever I was an Author. This indeed would be too great a Mortification if I wrote for Fame: But, as my sole Intention was the PUBLICK GOOD, I cannot be altogether disappointed. For, who can read the Virtues I have mentioned in the glorious *Houyhnhnms*, without being ashamed of his own Vices, when he considers himself as the reasoning, governing Animal of his Country? I shall say nothing of those remote Nations where *Yahoos* preside; amongst which the least corrupted are the *Brobdingnagians*, whose wise Maxims in Morality and Government, it would be our Happiness to observe. But I forbear descanting further, and rather leave the judicious Reader to his own Remarks and Applications.

I am not a little pleased that this Work of mine can possibly meet with no Censurers: For what Objections can be made against a Writer who relates only plain Facts that happened in such distant Countries, where we have not the least Interest with respect either to Trade or Negotiations? I have carefully avoided every Fault with which common Writers of Travels are often too justly charged. Besides, I meddle not the least with any *Party*, but write without Passion, Prejudice, or Ill-will against any Man or Number of Men whatsoever. I write for the noblest End, to inform and instruct Mankind, over whom I may, without Breach of Modesty, pretend to some Superiority, from the Advantages I received by conversing so long among the most accomplished *Houyhnhnms*. I write without any View towards Profit or Praise. I never suffer a Word to pass that may look like Reflection, or possibly give the least Offence even to those who are most ready to take it. So that, I hope, I may with Justice pronounce myself an Author perfectly blameless; against whom the Tribes of Answerers, Considerers, Observers, Reflecters, Detecters, Remarkers, will never be able to find Matter for exercising their Talents.

I confess, it was whispered to me, that I was bound in Duty as a Subject of *England*, to have given in a Memorial to a Secretary of State, at my first coming over; because, whatever Lands are discovered by a Subject, belong to the Crown. But I doubt, whether our Conquests in the Countries I treat of, would be as easy as those of *Ferdinando Cortez* over the naked *Americans*. The *Lilliputians* I think, are hardly worth the Charge of a Fleet and Army to reduce them; and I question whether it might be prudent or safe to attempt the *Brobdingnagians*: Or, whether an *English* Army would be much at their Ease with the Flying Island over their Heads. The *Houyhnhnms*, indeed, appear not to be so well prepared for War, a Science to which they are perfect Strangers, and especially against missive Weapons. However, supposing myself to be a Minister of State, I could never give my Advice for invading them. Their Prudence, Unanimity, Unacquaintedness with Fear, and their Love of their Country would amply supply all Defects in the military Art. Imagine twenty Thousand of them breaking into the Midst of an *European* Army, confounding the Ranks, overturning the Carriages, battering the Warriors Faces into Mummy, by terrible Yerks from their hinder Hoofs: For they would well deserve the Character given to *Augustus*; *Recalcitrat undique tutus*. But instead of Proposals for conquering that magnanimous Nation, I rather wish they were in a Capacity or Disposition to send a sufficient Number of their Inhabitants for civilizing *Europe*; by teaching us the first Principles of Honour, Justice, Truth, Temperance, publick Spirit, Fortitude, Chastity, Friendship, Benevolence, and Fidelity. The *Names* of all which Virtues are still retained among us in most Languages, and are to be met with in modern as well as ancient Authors; which I am able to assert from my own small Reading.

But, I had another Reason which made me less forward to enlarge his Majesty's Dominions by my Discoveries: To say the Truth, I had conceived a few Scruples with relation to the distributive Justice of Princes upon those Occasions. For Instance, A Crew of Pyrates are driven by a Storm they know not whither; at length a Boy discovers Land from the Top-mast; they go on Shore to rob and plunder; they see an harmless People, are entertained with Kindness, they give the Country a new Name, they take formal Possession of it for the King, they set up a rotten Plank or a Stone for a Memorial, they murder two or three Dozen of the Natives, bring away a Couple more by Force for a Sample, return home, and get their Pardon. Here commences a new Dominion acquired with a Title by *Divine Right*. Ships are sent with the first Opportunity; the Natives driven out or destroyed, their Princes tortured to discover their Gold; a free Licence given to all Acts of Inhumanity and Lust; the Earth reeking with the Blood of its Inhabitants: And this execrable Crew of Butchers employed in so pious an Expedition, is a *modern Colony* sent to convert and civilize an idolatrous and barbarous People.

But this Description, I confess, doth by no means affect the *British* Nation, who may be an Example to the whole World for their Wisdom, Care, and Justice in planting Colonies; the liberal Endowments for the Advancement of Religion and Learning; their Choice of devout and able Pastors to propagate *Christianity*; their Caution in stocking their Provinces with People of sober Lives and Conversations from this the Mother Kingdom; their strict Regard to the Distribution of Justice, in supplying the Civil Administration through all their Colonies with Officers of the greatest Abilities, utter Strangers to Corruption: And to crown all, by sending the most vigilant and virtuous Governors, who have no other Views than the Happiness of the People over whom they preside, and the Honour of the King their Master.

But, as those Countries which I have described do not appear to have any Desire of being conquered, and enslaved, murdered or driven out by Colonies; nor abound either in Gold, Silver, Sugar or Tobacco; I did humbly conceive they were by no Means proper Objects of our Zeal, our Valour, or our Interest. However, if those whom it may concern, think fit to be of another Opinion, I am ready to depose, when I shall be lawfully called, That no *European* did ever visit these Countries before me. I mean, if the Inhabitants ought to be believed.

But, as to the Formality of taking Possession in my Sovereign's Name, it never came once into my Thoughts; and if it had, yet as my Affairs then stood, I should perhaps in point of Prudence and Self-Preservation, have put it off to a better Opportunity.

Having thus answered the *only* Objection that can be raised against me as a Traveller; I here take a final Leave of my Courteous Readers, and return to enjoy my own Speculations in my little Garden at *Redriff*; to apply those excellent Lessons of Virtue which I learned among the *Houyhnhnms*; to instruct the *Yahoos* of my own Family as far as I shall find them docible Animals; to behold my Figure often in a Glass, and thus if possible habituate my self by Time to tolerate the Sight of a human Creature: To lament the Brutality of *Houyhnhnms* in my own Country, but always treat their Persons with Respect, for the Sake of my noble Master, his Family, his Friends, and the whole *Houyhnhnm* Race, whom these of ours have the Honour to resemble in all their Lineaments, however their Intellectuals came to degenerate.

I began last Week to permit my Wife to sit at Dinner with me, at the farthest End of a long Table; and to answer (but with the utmost Brevity) the few Questions I asked her. Yet the Smell of a *Yahoo* continuing very offensive, I always keep my Nose well stopt with Rue, Lavender, or Tobacco-Leaves. And although it be hard for a Man late in Life to remove old Habits; I am not altogether out of Hopes in some Time to suffer a Neighbour *Yahoo* in my Company, without the Apprehensions I am yet under of his Teeth or his Claws.

My Reconcilement to the *Yahoo*-kind in general might not be so difficult, if they would be content with those Vices and Follies only which Nature hath entitled them to. I am not in the least provoked at the Sight of a Lawyer, a Pickpocket, a Colonel, a Fool, a Lord, a Gamster, a Politician, a Whoremunger, a Physician, an Evidence, a Suborner, an Attorney, a Traytor, or the like: This is all according to the due Course of Things: But, when I behold a Lump of Deformity, and Diseases both in Body and Mind, smitten with *Pride*, it immediately breaks all the Measures of my Patience; neither shall I be ever able to comprehend how such an Animal and such a Vice could tally together. The wise and virtuous *Houyhnhnms*, who abound in all Excellencies that can adorn a rational Creature, have no Name for this Vice in their Language, which hath no Terms to express any thing that is evil, except those whereby they describe the detestable Qualities of their *Yahoos*; among which they were not able to distinguish this of Pride, for want of thoroughly understanding Human Nature, as it sheweth it self in other Countries, where that Animal presides. But I, who had more Experience, could plainly observe some Rudiments of it among the wild *Yahoos*.

But the *Houyhnhnms*, who live under the Government of Reason, are no more proud of the good Qualities they possess, than I should be for not wanting a Leg or an Arm, which no Man in his Wits would boast of, although he must be miserable without them. I dwell the longer upon this Subject from the Desire I have to make the Society of an *English Yahoo* by any Means not insupportable; and therefore I here intreat those who have any Tincture of this absurd Vice, that they will not presume to appear in my Sight.

FINIS

*This book
was set for Wm. Collins Sons & Co. Ltd., Glasgow
in Baskerville type
and printed on wood free paper
and bound by Hazell Watson & Viney Ltd.
Aylesbury, Bucks.
Introductions © Wm. Collins Sons & Co. Ltd., Glasgow
© Heron Books Ltd., London
Illustrations by Herbert Cole from Gulliver's Travels,
Bodley Head 1900*

Printed and bound in England